THE MAGISTRATE

To my wonderful friends
George & Melissa,
who, even though we are
separated by miles and years,
remain dear to me,

Bill Reynolds

May the Lord enrich your
lives together as you
walk in His light

THE MAGISTRATE

Volume Two
The Order of Croesus

William D. Reynolds

iUniverse, Inc.
New York Lincoln Shanghai

The Magistrate
Volume Two The Order of Croesus

iUniverse, Inc.

For information address:
iUniverse, Inc.
2021 Pine Lake Road, Suite 100
Lincoln, NE 68512
www.iuniverse.com

ISBN: 0-595-30908-9 (pbk)
ISBN: 0-595-66221-8 (cloth)

Printed in the United States of America

Cover art by Linda J. Reynolds

Publisher's Cataloging-in-Publication
(Provided by Quality Books, Inc.)

Reynolds, William D.
The magistrate / by William D. Reynolds.
v. cm.
CONTENTS: Lykos reborn—The Order of Croesus

1. Rome—History—Empire, 30 B.C.-284 A.D.—Fiction.
2. Magistrates, Roman—Fiction. I. Title.

PS3618.E598M34 2003 813'.6
QB133-870

To

Bonnie, John, Michael and Andrew

Contents

▼

Preface xiii

PART I: MEETINGS AND REVELATIONS

Chapter 1 3

Chapter 2 13

Chapter 3 25

Chapter 4 33

Chapter 5 40

Chapter 6 49

Chapter 7 55

Chapter 8 68

Chapter 9 81

Chapter 10 97

Chapter 11 106

Chapter 12 112

Chapter 13 125

PART II: FEAR AND TREMBLING

Chapter 14 133

Chapter 15 139

Chapter 16 154

Chapter 17 160

Chapter 18 165

Chapter 19 180

Chapter 20 196

Chapter 21 212

PART III: CAPTURE AND RELEASE

Chapter 22 223

Chapter 23 232

Chapter 24 242

Chapter 25 257

About the Author 265

Acknowledgments

For this second volume, grateful acknowledgment goes out to numerous individuals who were influential in continuing this adventure: to Sally Axelrod once again for her encouragement and consulting expertise; to Connie Brown and Bonnie Reynolds for editing skills; to my wife, Linda, for gracing the cover with yet another powerful image; and to the many friends, family members, and kind readers who form that substantial network of support that is so vital for any practitioner of the creative arts.

I again acknowledge with unbounded love and gratitude my wife and children, and my parents and in-laws, whose undying devotion supply the necessary energy to see this work to its conclusion. Finally, I thank my Creator and Redeemer, who is the Author of all that is good, and who has so graciously stirred my imagination.

Preface

One of the chief responsibilities of a father is to prepare his children for their world and times. In this day and in this culture, an interested father encounters tremendous forces driving him away from that task. I say "interested" because it is rather easy to turn over the process of childrearing to various experts and interested parties, and to simply pay the bills. That relieves some of the conflict—for a time—but it fails to absolve an individual of the God-given mandate to diligently teach the commands of the Lord at all times. This brings me to my primary purpose for writing this book.

The Magistrate is not a children's story, but it is a story for my children. Although I have always tried to teach the wisdom of God (as best I could discern it) along the way of life's twists and turns, I wanted to leave them with something tangible that would teach the virtues that are so necessary to be a man or woman of character. I hope that they will find the book to be more enjoyable than squirming through a series of dinnertime lectures.

This is a fictitious work. One will find no mention of the city of Diakropolis in the annals of Anatolia, nor will ancient archives mention the likes of Marcellus, Linus or the mysterious Order of Croesus. Nevertheless, there is truth to be found within these pages. Sadly, the prejudice that led to the persecution and exploitation of Christians was an undeniable part of life in that day, and the events depicted within these pages are plausible. The letters of the Roman statesman Pliny the Younger serve as a take-off point for the attitudes of the empire and its representatives, although none of the characters in this story are intended to represent him specifically. Other than Diakropolis, a city of my creation whose name plays upon the concept of passing judgment, the major cities are actual places. Other liberties taken may annoy the purist, but these are meant to enhance the message and to provide enjoyable reading.

I greatly enjoyed this first foray into the world of literature. I could not help but feel connected with the great authors of history in the sense of experiencing the power of the pen to create and stir the emotions. However, I make no pretense in assuming that their standards have been reached.

WDR

PART I

▼

MEETINGS AND REVELATIONS

CHAPTER 1

▼

Morning gathered the city of Nicomedia in her arms and brushed the sleep out of its streets and homes. The sun scaled the hills and emerged through the thin fog like a flat disk of gold. Serpentine mists rose and curled among the trees, dissipating among the moisture-laden boughs. Songbirds conversed excitedly, calling out to one another from their various posts. On the governor's estate, workers of various stripes greeted one another as they crisscrossed the grounds, moving vigorously to shake off the early morning chill. Inside the villa, household attendants and official personnel took up their labors with contrived enthusiasm, united in a secret wish that the celestial ruler of the day had overslept his watch.

One inhabitant, however, remained in his room, oblivious to the buzz of activity within and without: Marcellus, Chief Magistrate of Diakropolis and guest of Linus, Governor of Bithynia. He sat by a window, nearly motionless, just as he had done every morning since his arrival in the capital city. One hand cradled his chin, the other silently tapped out some unconscious cadence. Before him, strewn haphazardly across the table, lay the product of scribes long forgotten, the chronicles of the minutiae of an empire. Marcellus pored quickly but methodically over each item, sifting through the trivia in search of some pearl that he could apply in his own jurisdiction. After each document, he would sigh and mechanically roll up the scroll with quick twists of his wrists, and then toss the item either into a basket on his left or a leather satchel on his right. A brief sip of a drink and glance out the window followed, and then it was on to the next item. So absorbing was the routine that he failed to hear the governor enter his room.

"Today, we play!" announced Linus in a jovial tone. "You have been here for nearly a week and most of that with your face buried in the archives!"

Marcellus pushed back from his work and smiled at the governor.

"I know I have been poor company, but access to such material is impossible in Diakropolis. The library there is terribly thin."

"Well, then, what could be more noble a legacy than erecting a fine new library? I would even consent to it being named after me!" The governor held a pensive look for a moment before breaking into a laugh. "I tell you what, Marcellus," continued the legate, "when you return, you can take as many of these records as you can carry."

"Wouldn't you miss them?"

"No. I have read the worthwhile material. The rest is destined for the ash heap."

"I find much of interest in the old annals."

"Wonderful!" said Linus. "Some men are historians, others are visionaries. You are both. A true leader must see the future through the past. However, today you are a tired public servant in desperate need of a respite from the rigors of administration. Close those things up and change into clothing more appropriate for an outing in the country."

"The country?" asked Marcellus.

"Yes, the country. Remember? Trees and lakes, tiny furry animals scurrying along the ground—that sort of place. The weather is unusually fine and the fresh air will do you good."

The magistrate shrugged and began gathering his reading material. Linus was nearly out of the room when he turned back to address Marcellus.

"Oh, by the way, try to look your best today. There is someone I want you to meet." The governor was gone before Marcellus could inquire further.

A small group had gathered outside the governor's residence, awaiting the coaches that would transport them to Linus' favorite recreation spot. Marcellus was greeted warmly as he emerged from the portico. The governor clutched his arm and led him to greet the others invited on the outing. Most were already familiar and Marcellus wondered why Linus was making such a fuss. Finally, they came to the last of the party.

"Marcellus, I would like to introduce you to Arcadia, daughter of Atarix, a prominent merchant and benefactor in Prusa."

Before Marcellus stood a woman of remarkable and exotic beauty, whose dark Mediterranean skin and hair offset her clear, deep green eyes. She nearly was as tall as Marcellus, and of a shapely figure reflecting a woman of luxury, but not of idleness. The magistrate took the woman's hand in ceremonial greeting. Arcadia returned Marcellus' gaze intently for a moment, then diverted her eyes. For all her timid grace, Marcellus suspected this was a woman who rarely looked away from the object of her desire.

Marcellus tried to remain attentive as Linus recounted Arcadia's father's exploits and philanthropic undertakings, but found his eyes trailing away to observe the woman mingling with other guests. It occurred to Marcellus that he had not regarded the appearance of any woman since the death of his wife—until now. Even so, the allure of her beauty was intermingled with foreboding, like the call of the sirens to an ancient mariner. Marcellus could not shake the initial impression that an encounter with this woman was fraught with danger.

"Come, everyone," called Linus, snapping Marcellus out of his thoughts. "Let's be on our way!" The young magistrate contemplated which coach to board, until Linus grasped his arm and escorted him to his private sedan. "I want you to ride with me and Arcadia."

The rest of the party crowded into the other vehicles and the short journey was underway. Arcadia took a place next to Linus, opposite Marcellus, and sat quietly. Linus smiled discreetly at the magistrate and winked.

"As I was saying, Marcellus—now that I seem to have more of your attention—Arcadia's esteemed father has been a highly valued friend of the empire. Much of what makes Prusa so attractive and habitable owes to his most gracious and sacrificial philanthropy. Why, even now, Atarix has bequeathed one of his family estates to the city for the erection of a more suitable bath, and he even has added a number of his household treasures to embellish its beauty. He is truly of stalwart character. Don't you agree, Arcadia, my dear?"

"You are correct in your assessment, Your Excellency. I can only aspire to a portion of my father's unbridled generosity."

"And how has your father amassed such a fortune, may I ask?" inquired Marcellus.

"He is of the lineage of Croesus, the Lydian king of old," interjected Linus. "You recall your childhood education, I suspect, Marcellus?"

"I do, and have need of no further explanation as to the source of your father's wealth." Marcellus said, nodding politely to Arcadia as he turned to face the passing landscape. The referenced monarch was renowned for his fantastic wealth, culled from the gold veins of his Aegean kingdom south of Bithynia.

"I had the privilege of being the guest of noble Atarix and his lovely daughter during my orientation travels throughout the province," continued Linus. "A finer family is not to be found in Bithynia."

"I hope to make his acquaintance in the future and experience firsthand his benevolence," returned Marcellus. Although new in this high-visibility career, Marcellus already had a keen understanding of the need to massage the local aristocracies for their contributions toward civic projects and assistance in keeping the peace in the volatile, multiethnic communities of the province. He mused whether Linus was being fully truthful or simply patronizing the woman. On numerous previous occasions, Marcellus had heard the governor publicly extol the virtues of a prominent local, only to lambaste the same in private.

"Yes, there is a necessary symbiosis between the magistracies and the town elite, my boy. It requires a sensitive leader, one who measures his words and actions carefully."

"Do you enjoy your new position, Your Honor?" asked the woman.

"You may call me Marcellus. Yes, I find Diakropolis to be an attractive city with many fine features. There is much work to accomplish, however. As opposed to the larger cities of the region, the system of administration seems rather loose. I hope to have some assistance in the future," he concluded, nodding toward the governor.

"We'll see about that shortly, my son. Arcadia has ties to your fair city," Linus continued cheerfully, smiling toward the woman. "Don't you, my dear? Tell Marcellus."

"I have an uncle who is in business there. He is one of the tribe leaders."

"Oh, really?" replied Marcellus. "Your uncle is a phylarch?"

"Yes, well, he is not really my uncle. He is a cousin of my father. He always insisted on being called 'uncle' when I was young and the title stayed. His name is Siros."

Marcellus' eyebrows rose at the name and he leaned forward in his seat.

"Siros is your relation? My, my. I have a bone to pick with him. He is doing a poor job tending to the river in his sector, among other things."

"Now, Marcellus. Tread lightly with those phylarchs, especially Siros. Although they are not 'first men' of the town, they wield a fair amount of power with the people."

Marcellus pondered what he knew about Siros. He was wealthy, without a doubt, more so than any other citizen of Diakropolis, but he had not held any significant office, according to official records. All Bithynian cities were organized into tribes, each with a phylarch at the head. As a tribe leader, Siros was not eligible for higher office, but this condition seemed of his own doing. Unlike most men of great wealth, he seemed content to keep mostly out of the public eye, administering his tribe and sector. Siros' tribe apparently was confined to the Old City, although the man himself maintained a palatial residence at the other end of town. To be certain, Siros had great influence among the council members and those charged with controlling the market. In fact, Marcellus was growing increasingly wary that relationships were a bit too cozy. In all, there was a cloud of suspicion about the man.

The party rolled along in silence for a time, with Linus occasionally pointing out a special feature of the passing scenery to Arcadia, who appeared to be intensely interested. Marcellus was lost in thought about the revelation of Arcadia's relationship to Siros, the recollection of the peculiar afternoon investigating the Old City, and Linus' comments about dealing with the elite of the town. Whether the governor simply was making conversation or devising a plan, Marcellus could not tell. He stole glances at the beautiful woman next to the governor and wondered what role she would play in his own future. They passed by a marsh and Arcadia delighted at the flurry of birds that frantically took flight.

"Oh, did I tell you? I have arranged for us to go to the theater tomorrow afternoon," Linus said excitedly. "Seeing the marsh brought to mind the ill-fated theater the Niceans attempted to erect. The simpletons laid the foundation in marshy ground and it is now crumbling. You would think that they would have consulted with appropriate engineers before such an expensive undertaking. Anyway, back to the theater. It is to be a private performance, one of Cassio's latest speculations. I haven't the slightest idea what it is about. He will only let on that the play is a satire about crime and punishment. I think Cassio is using us as a test audience before he puts up bigger money to unleash his play on the public. I keep telling him that those themes rarely play well for the ruder sort. They crave light-weight comedy—just tickle their fancy and don't make them think. The games make stiff competition for the theater. Actually, I think the two are beginning to look the same. Anyway, it should be an interesting outing. Afterward, we are going to have a splendid banquet to honor our lovely Arcadia. Marcellus, she will need an escort."

Marcellus briefly glared at the governor, but then composed himself.

"It would be my honor to remain at your service, madam."

Arcadia smiled in acceptance and turned away. Linus was enthusiastic at the success of his negotiations thus far, and he continued to chatter away.

"We are nearing our destination, Marcellus. I want to show you my latest and biggest project. Aqueducts and stadiums are not to be sniffed at, but consider the thought of redirecting the sea. Now, *that* is a worthy effort!"

"Redirect the sea?"

"Indeed. We are going to picnic along the shores of a vast lake that lies outside of Nicomedia. As you will see, numerous boats transport the produce of the land to the road that leads to the sea. There it is unloaded at great expense and labor, and then transported to the ships that lay in wait. In my journeys, I have found a partially constructed canal that apparently was dug some time past. I am not sure whether its purpose was to drain the surrounding land or an attempt to connect with the lake. I intend to realize the latter possibility. I already have requested Trajan's approval for the project, although feasibility studies must be done. Imagine, Rome's sleek ships cruising deep into the interior of Bithynia to receive her fruits!"

"That is indeed an auspicious project, Governor," said Marcellus.

"And one worthy of your formidable intellect, Excellency," added Arcadia. Linus beamed.

They arrived at a grassy spot overlooking the lake. The weather was unseasonably warm and the skies were mostly cloudy, but with enough breaks to dapple the countryside with sunshine. A cool breeze made cloaks necessary to counter the wind chill, but overall it was a pleasant day for an outing. Linus' servants had packed a pleasing lunch with all sorts of fruits and vegetables, cold meats, pastries and wine.

After the meal, the governor led the company to a vantage point where the entire lake and the surrounding lands could be surveyed. A number of cargo vessels could be seen in transit, some moving slowly, heavily laden with goods, others high in the water and sleek in their passage. A stiff wind swept across the surface of the gray-blue water from the direction of the sea, doubling the labor of the oarsmen. Even from where the party stood, the oarsmen could be heard straining and cursing as they drove forward.

"Those fellows there have their work cut out for them, eh, Linus?" said an older gentleman, pointing toward a vessel that moved slowly not far offshore, its prow dipping and surging, sending showers of spray across its deck and its crew.

"It's probably loaded with some of the marble from the quarry about five miles yonder," replied the governor. "It will make a fine temple." Linus went on for several minutes pointing out the various types of boats and ships and speculating as to what they were transporting. "It remains to be determined, however, if the lake lies above sea level. I am more naturalist than engineer, so I must rely upon the experts in this area."

A chorus of affirmations arose from the company of guests, assuring the governor that his intellectual capacities were well beyond any in the province, and that he simply lacked the time or the proper equipment to address the question properly; otherwise, he would have little trouble solving the problem himself. Linus gave a self-satisfied smile.

"Well, then," Linus announced, "allow me to take you on a most informative botanical tour of our picnic spot. Follow me, please."

Marcellus leaned toward Arcadia, who had taken a position next to him midway through the governor's lecture.

"I think I will pass on the botany lesson. Will you excuse me?" Marcellus turned and walked toward the lake.

Linus extended his arm to Arcadia, who accepted his escort with a polite smile. As she walked alongside the prefect, she repeatedly looked behind at Marcellus.

"What, or should I say, who, has the honor of your attention, my dear?" Linus asked, as he turned to see the young magistrate making his way toward the waterside. The governor smiled and prodded Arcadia to join Marcellus. She overtook him as he meandered down the slope toward a path that followed the shore. The pair casually strolled along its banks with a number of waterfowl in tow, hoping to take advantage of some bread that Marcellus had stuffed in his cloak.

"What is it like to have royal blood flowing through your veins?" asked Marcellus.

"It is only a small amount. Linus makes it out to be more than it is," Arcadia replied.

"Do you come to Nicomedia frequently?"

"Several times a year. I see about my father's business." Marcellus' face showed a hint of surprise. "Somebody has to watch over the family operations," said Arcadia. "I do the best that I can."

"Judging by the governor's comments, you are more than adequate." They strolled in silence. "You are an only child, then?"

"I had two brothers, but they were killed by bandits. The roads are not safe in Bithynia."

"I am sorry," replied Marcellus, recalling his own encounter with such danger. "What specifically does your father trade in?"

"A bit of everything. Import and export business, you know. We have interests in all the major cities of the region, but not in Diakropolis. We work closely with the Roman officials, hence my acquaintance with Linus." She paused. "You are, I assume, aware of the unfortunate demise of Prusa's chief magistrate."

"Yes, I am. Linus filled me in the other day. A tragic accident."

"He was getting along in years. I suppose such falls are a part of growing old and feeble."

"Your father was quite distraught, I suspect, over the loss of such a longtime friend."

"They did not always see eye to eye. Father has been on the city council for many years. The magistrate was a difficult man to approach and somewhat stubborn in his ways."

"It was evident that Linus lost little sleep at the news of the magistrate's passing, as well," said Marcellus.

"I believe the relationship between government and business should be a dynamic one, molded over time by the forces of mutual benefit and compromise, don't you?" asked Arcadia. Marcellus was taken aback at this burst of economic philosophy.

"Well, yes, but not too malleable. There are laws, you know."

"Of course, don't be absurd. But I am referring to the broad gray area where many of life's transactions occur."

"I have yet to discern just how broad or gray that area actually is, but I think that I understand your basic premise."

Arcadia stopped and gazed out over the lake.

"Linus speaks highly of you, as he would a son."

"He truly has been good to me."

"Your qualities are just the sort that father would like to see in a new chief magistrate."

Marcellus stepped back and eyed her suspiciously.

"Were you invited on this little outing just to recruit me?"

"Not *just*."

"Well, I am flattered, but spoken for. As I told the governor, my assignment is Diakropolis."

"For the time being," returned Arcadia.

"If Linus orders me to Prusa I will go, but there is much to be accomplished in Diakropolis."

"You are Linus' star pupil and Prusa is a plum to be picked. Diakropolis is a nice town, but well beneath a leader of your caliber. While you dawdle there, the opportunity could close."

"And what do you know of my caliber besides the obviously biased information Linus has been providing?" Marcellus asked pointedly. Arcadia laughed.

"A reputation has a way of catching the breeze and floating to unexpected destinations. In other words, you are known in Prusa, and we think you would make an exceptional chief magistrate."

"We?"

"Do you find it odd that a family of some influence would desire to establish a capable leader over their city, rather than await whomever is doled out by the governor?"

"Just as I was *doled out* to Diakropolis?" Marcellus quipped, causing Arcadia to scowl.

"Your situation aside, the Romans often are more interested in dispensing political favors than in supplying their cities with qualified leaders."

"I see. You should know that my first act as magistrate of Prusa would be to eliminate any influence on the selection of government officials by well-heeled citizens. How's that for leadership?" Marcellus broke off in a laugh and continued the walk.

"Very funny," said Arcadia, catching up to him. "I hadn't heard that you were so stubborn."

"Only when asked to do something that I don't want to do," said Marcellus. "Otherwise, I am fairly agreeable."

Arcadia walked quietly beside Marcellus and contemplated a different line of conversation.

"You brought your family with you to Diakropolis?"

"I have only one daughter. She is with me, yes."

"Your wife—is she in Rome?"

"My wife passed away."

"Oh, how tragic."

"You are kind. The sting is still there."

A calculated silence followed.

"It must be difficult to raise a child alone when the demands on you are so great."

"I never thought of raising a child as being hard. Claudia is my daughter. I would do anything for her and I do not consider the task too difficult or the time an inconvenience."

"You truly have a heroic sense of duty."

"You define heroism loosely. I find nothing valiant about fulfilling one's obligations."

Arcadia stopped and glowered at him.

"You certainly are a fine one for pleasant conversation. I am going back to join the others. I doubt that they are arguing over plants and trees."

"What did I say?" asked the puzzled magistrate, as Arcadia briskly climbed up the slope to the picnic site. "By the gods, I had forgotten how difficult those creatures were to talk with," Marcellus muttered aloud. He picked up a stone and heaved it far out into the white-capped water, then resumed his walk.

Linus greeted Arcadia as she rejoined the party on its tour.

"How did things go, my dear?" the governor spoke quietly in her ear.

"Marcellus professes no interest in coming to Prusa—unless you order him there." Arcadia looked at the governor in anticipation.

"He is a young man with a keen sense of duty. Let him finish his work in Diakropolis first. With a bit of time—and with your persuasion—he will come to see Prusa as a worthy goal."

"We don't have that kind of time," muttered Arcadia, as the governor spotted a new specimen of plant and announced his discovery to the group.

CHAPTER 2

▼

The pleasant weather of Nicomedia failed to extend its kind hand toward Diak-ropolis. It was a typical winter day, gray and cold, the kind of chill that penetrates to the bones despite layers of clothing. A slight drizzle was falling. It had been two days since Philip harbored the fugitives from the Old City on their flight to freedom, and he had kept a watchful eye out for visitors to the farm or suspicious traffic on the road nearby. Things had been quiet and the young man presumed that the family had safely arrived at their destination.

Pellas was in good spirits. The addition of an able-bodied young farmhand had afforded the luxury of an additional hour's sleep and the benefits were evident in the farmer's disposition. He tolerated Philip's conversation with a bit more congeniality, occasionally engaging in a minute or two of repartee before brusquely cutting him off. For the moment, Philip was content to sow the seed of a relationship, but he stood ready for any opportunity to engage in deeper conversation.

At mid-morning, the young man emerged from a small stand of trees with an armload of freshly cut firewood. Philip staggered under the weight of the wood as he made his way toward the stable. Pellas sat inside the door making repairs to the plow. Upon reaching the stable, Philip unloaded his burden onto the wood-pile with a relieved grunt.

"There! That should last for a month at least."

Pellas looked up briefly and returned to his task.

"A week, at best," he said plainly.

Philip groaned. "How's the plow coming?"

"It needs a part."

"I can go to town for it, if you'd like."

"That would be helpful," said Pellas, after a moment's pause. "There are a few other things, too. I'll make a list of what I need and where to get it."

"Just let me catch my breath," returned the young man as he flopped to the ground next to the farmer. Philip looked up at the featureless gray sky. "Is it always so dreary and wet in the winter?"

"Oh, no. It's that way in the spring and the fall, too."

"When does it dry up?"

"We have some dry spells in the summer," replied Pellas. "Some days you actually hope for rain." He thought of the hot summer day in the arena and became silent.

"Still, it's attractive land here," continued Philip, scraping furrows in the packed dirt with a stick. "Coming from Ephesus, it is quite a contrast to see so many trees. I'm sure that when spring comes the green will be spectacular." Pellas nodded. "Do you ever get lonely out here by yourself?" asked Philip.

"No."

"I would need a strong reason to move to such a secluded place. Maybe if I was running from something." Philip did not catch the quick shift of Pellas' eyes at the young man's statement.

"Some of us like to experience nature in its native habitat, rather than packaged in small gardens and parks," returned the farmer. "Besides, one can't grow crops very well on a street corner."

"You are right," said Philip, chuckling. "We cover everything with stone and then look for small patches to place grass and trees like museum pieces."

"Hold this," Pellas said, as he gave the young man a tool to hold while the farmer turned the plow upside down.

"Of course," Philip went on, "In the country you don't have the amenities of the city."

"Such as?"

"I like the theater."

"A forum for decadence."

"How about a good restaurant?"

"I prefer to know what I am eating."

"Hmm. There's no gymnasium out here."

"I'd rather build my body where the air is not stale."

Philip smiled and stroked his chin.

"You are a tough nut. A library?"

"The few books of worth could fit in a crate."

"The forum?"

"Useless chatter."

"The baths?"

"For the pampered."

"I'll be sure to stay upwind from you," said the young man, grinning.

The farmer looked up and, for a moment, Philip caught an unmistakable change in the man's countenance. It was a smile, ever so brief, but undeniably real. The smile was gone as quickly as it had come, dissolving into the familiar scowl that now was even more intense from Pellas' embarrassment over his having been taken in by the young man's quip.

"Any man who needs his water warmed is hardly worth knowing and he will desert you the moment times get tough," the farmer said in a huff.

"Hmm. I have never taken a man's bathing habits into consideration before making his acquaintance," Philip replied, trying to remain serious.

"You will find that how a man responds in the major tests of life reflects how he has prepared in the little ones. An excess of leisure and comfort is deficient training when calamity comes."

"Spoken like one who has been through some tough times," said Philip in a leading tone.

"Wisdom doesn't necessarily need experience as its teacher."

"True, and I suppose that a child could learn to talk by himself. This is heady stuff from the lips of a simple farmer. It is better suited for the Acropolis. That's in Athens, by the way," jested Philip.

"I know very well where the Acropolis is located, young man," Pellas replied sharply.

"I'm sorry. I didn't know how well versed you were on things beyond these tranquil pastures. Seriously, Pellas, you are hardly a typical farmer. It is plain that your past was an educated one, and one filled with pain."

"And why do you say that?" asked the farmer, trying to sound nonchalant.

"It's obvious to me that this farm is a barricade against something severe in your past. You live like a recluse, unlike the farmers I passed on my travels. And you have treated me as an invader, a barbarian, although I am happy you have warmed of late."

Pellas sighed.

"If I have chosen to barricade myself, as you suggest, from some undesirable occurrence in the past, I fail to see how this affects you. I never have understood why some people find it necessary to prod others to disclose all their ill experiences so that they can be dissected and analyzed."

"But it is healthy to deal with those things rather than to suppress them."

"You call it healthy; I call it nosy. Give me that hammer."

"When the Master said that you needed help, I sensed that he meant more than simply farm work."

Pellas pounded a pin into place on the plow and looked up at the young man.

"You seem bent on finding out my deepest secrets but, tell me, how much do you know of your Master?"

Philip thought for a moment.

"Well, he is a leader of the fellowship of Christians in this province. He has shown great courage in bringing news of the Savior into a land dominated by all sorts of idols. He is a man of impeccable reputation and he is known throughout Anatolia and beyond."

"Reputations are cheap. The Romans buy them from their poets all the time. What do you know of the Master firsthand?"

"I will admit that I don't have much firsthand experience with him but, then again, I don't necessarily expect much. He is a great man and many seek an audience with him. I have come from Ephesus to learn his ways and to follow his example."

"In other words," replied Pellas, smirking, "you are willing to take orders from a man you know only from secondhand reports."

"They are reports from trustworthy people. Beyond that, the Master has walked with those who knew Jesus."

"Another man of suspicious character who demands much of his followers."

Philip frowned and studied the deeply lined, emotionless face of the farmer as he labored with the plow. Philip had assumed that Pellas was a believer, but now it was clear that the young man had been mistaken. Perhaps he assumed that the Master would send him to a fellow Christian in need. Philip's face brightened as he considered the possibility that his purpose with Pellas was to point him to the Way. Obviously, this was going to be a task of epic proportions, judging from the reception thus far, but Philip thrilled at the possibility that the Master had considered him worthy of the appointment.

"You know, Pellas, sometime I would like to share with you some things that you might find interesting about Jesus."

Pellas lifted his head and gave an icy stare.

"We will limit our conversation to subjects that pertain only to this farm and its operation. I have no need or interest in discussing personal matters with you, and that includes religion. Is that clear?"

"Yes," responded Philip quietly. "Yes, it is."

Pellas grimaced as he rose out of a crouched position that he had maintained for several minutes.

"A word of advice: keep clear of your so-called Master. He is nothing but trouble. And while you're at it, I wouldn't go around town babbling away about Jesus. There are those who would like to see your type made sport of, some of whom might come as a surprise. I'll be back with the list for your trip to the city."

Pellas pulled his cloak tightly around his neck and shuffled across to the house. Philip shook his head and watched the farmer's strong but slightly stooped frame disappear through the front door.

"God," Philip said aloud, "Give me an opportunity to tell him about Jesus. Give me the right words to say at the right time. And give me patience as I wait for that opening." Philip rose and gathered his walking stick and heavy cloak. "Oh, and forgive me for what I've thought about him, although I think bull-headed is a pretty accurate description."

Pellas brought lunch into Cecilia's room and laid the meal out on a small table beside her bed. The girl smiled and begged her father to sit beside her. He pulled a small stool over and sat down.

"Tell me, Father, what have you been doing today?"

"You wouldn't really find it interesting, Cecilia. Just farm work."

"Oh, please tell me. I am so bored."

The farmer looked at the fragile form that lay before him. Her face still was thin and somewhat gaunt, even with the improved diet. Her skin was white from poor nutrition and the countless hours spent inside. Pellas reflected on his daughter's past and recalled the passion she had had for life. He could see her running through the fields, collecting wildflowers to bring home. Because of her voracious appetite for knowledge, Cecilia knew all the flowers by name, as well as the names of the animals and birds, and all manner of natural phenomena. His daughter's keen mind had seemed so well matched to her robust figure then. Now, it was imprisoned in a frame that never again would race across the meadows or dance by moonlight.

"Father?"

"Oh, yes!" replied the startled man. "Well, er, let me see. I worked on the plow, which by the way is in very poor repair. I sent Philip to town for parts."

"Philip?"

"Yes, I guess I never mentioned the name of the lad who is helping me, that is, us."

"That is a nice name, Philip," mused the girl. "How old is he?"

"I suppose he is about your age."

"I would like to meet him someday."

"Out of the question. As I told you…"

"I know. You don't have to go through your lecture again." Cecilia took a small portion of bread dipped in olive oil and slowly placed it in her mouth.

"I hope to plant a new field this year," Pellas continued. "We've cleared a nice piece of land near the stream."

Cecilia chewed methodically, her deep brown eyes staring out the high window toward the sky. Pellas helped her with a drink of cold water he had drawn from the stream that morning.

"What does Philip look like?" Cecilia asked.

Pellas momentarily was taken aback by the question.

"Well, he looks like most young men his age, I guess."

"Now, Father, you can do better than that," the girl playfully scolded. "I am stuck inside this room all day. At least give me a picture with which my mind can play."

"He's about my height, but a bit more muscular."

"Is he handsome?"

"Cecilia! That is of no concern."

"If you won't tell me, I'll make him handsome."

"If you must know, he is as ugly as an ogre. Now, eat your lunch."

The girl downed another piece of bread. "What color are his eyes?" she inquired.

"How am I to know?" protested Pellas. "He is a farmhand. I have not studied his face!"

"I'll make them brown."

"I am not going to play this silly game with you," said Pellas. "Now eat up, I have other chores to do."

"Does he have brown hair, too?" asked the smiling girl.

"No! It is green—with purple spots! Cecilia, don't do this to yourself."

The girl frowned.

"I know what you are thinking, Father, but even though I am disfigured and undesirable, I can dream if I want."

"I don't want you to be hurt, Cecilia. Dreams can take on a life of their own. When the inevitable conflict with reality comes, the heartache can be severe."

Cecilia closed her eyes and bit her lip.

"I am not hungry anymore."

"But you hardly ate, dear. You need nourishment."

"What for? So I can be a fat housebound invalid instead of a thin one?"

"Cecilia, don't talk like that."

"What do you want me to say, Father?" replied the girl, her eyes welling with tears. "I lie here day after day, and my only interaction with other living beings is the short time you give me between chores or before you nod off from exhaustion. I have no prospect of ever leading a normal life again, and now I can't even have the simple pleasure of conversing with a boy my age who is working on my father's farm because the young man might be an informant bent on dragging me off before the magistrate. What's more, it is prohibited that I even imagine what it might be like to meet him because of the pain it would cause, as if a little more pain would even be noticed." Cecilia cried softly.

"I am doing the best I can," Pellas responded gruffly. "I am only one man."

"I know you are, Father," said Cecilia, trying to regain her composure. "But the problem is that you insist on being only one man when there are others that could help."

"You don't understand," Pellas said, gathering the lunch utensils.

"You're right. I don't." Cecilia turned her head away as Pellas returned the dishes to the kitchen and placed the stool back in the corner of the room. "Father, I would like to see the Master again."

Pellas sighed. The conversation already was miserable and his response to this new request would only make matters worse.

"Cecilia, I know you do not understand why I feel the way I do about that man. I hope that in time you will. I have strong reason to believe that he betrayed us and that he was instrumental in all the tragedy that has befallen our family."

"No, that is impossible!" cried Cecilia.

"It may seem so now, but I have had much time to think. I believe he turned us in to the authorities."

"But, why?"

"Who knows? We live in a world filled with twisted minds. Nero, Caligula, Domitian. Power does that to people. It makes them think that they are above the laws of nature, the duty of common decency. They see a world constructed according to their scheme and they seek to manipulate people accordingly, controlling those people they can and dispensing with those they can't."

"I still say it is impossible," Cecilia said, her lips quivering. "Why would he care for my wounds and open his home to us while I healed? Certainly, no one as evil as you suggest would do that."

"I believe it was part of his deception."

"Father, I think it is you who are deceived. God forbid you should think these things. All the more reason for us to see the Master."

"I hope never to set eyes on him again, my dear, unless it is his corpse that I see."

"Father! That is awful! How can you say that about a fellow believer?"

"I am sorry for upsetting you, Cecilia, but I am only being honest. We have nothing in common with that beast. He is to be shunned."

"No! I will not believe it. He is a good man."

"I seem to recall something he once said about the devil masquerading as an angel of light. You may want to ponder that."

Pellas left the room drained by the interchange, but still resolved to remove all vestiges of the painful relationship with the mysterious Master and the faith he promoted. The farmer crouched by the fire and stoked the embers, pondering how, since the arrest, his life had veered so radically from its course. To be certain, things never were ideal, but there was order and direction, a destination to reach, a goal to realize. Now there was only scrapping from day to day, hiding out, and living in fear that this day a knock would come and the final chapter would begin.

Pellas had thought of escape, but to where? The remote parts of the empire were attractive to those seeking anonymity, but open to marauding barbarians. Pellas considered disappearing into one of the large cities, even Rome, where indifference created by the mass of humanity would allow a measure of safety, but the unhealthy conditions surely would make Cecilia worse. There were no options. He would have to stay and make the best out of miserable conditions.

Pellas tossed a fresh log on the fire and watched the moldy bark crackle and peel away as it erupted into flames, revealing the solid wood underneath. How he wished that the memories of the past also would burn off. Over and again, Pellas played out the ordeal of the past months, tracing back to a time when the course of his life was straight and true—a time when he was in control of his family, his destiny. Standing at the point of deflection was the Master, armed with tales of the man from Nazareth who demanded one's unwavering devotion. Pellas did not resent Jesus so much. After all, it was He who went to the cross for His followers, not the reverse, as seemed to be the case with the Master. In the end, the message of Jesus was another on a long list of philosophers that promised fulfillment, but which left all but the most ardent followers grasping for more. Pellas gazed out the window toward the stable. Much remained to be done before day's end. He was tired.

Philip found the blacksmith without much difficulty. The shop was located on the fringe of town and appeared identical to Pellas' description. The part the farmer needed was in stock, which meant that Philip would have enough time to pay a visit to the Master.

"I haven't seen your face around here before," said the burly smith in a gravelly voice.

"I am from Ephesus," Philip replied. "I am staying outside town on a farm. The owner's name is Pellas."

"Ah, Pellas! I haven't seen him in months. I thought maybe he had moved on, what with all that has happened."

"He seems fixed," said Philip, his curiosity piqued by the smith's comments. "He didn't mention anything unusual happening recently."

"Then he wants his business to be kept private," said the bulky man, who shuffled away to a back room.

"You didn't say how much this was," called Philip, holding up the piece of iron.

The smith returned holding two other pieces. "How much do you have?"

Philip opened his hand to reveal a small collection of coins. The smith frowned.

"Hmm. Hard times."

"Pellas said this was all that he had but, if you could wait until first harvest, he would make it good."

"He's an honest man. Keep your money and take these other parts, too. If Pellas has an abundance this year, tell him to pay me a visit."

Philip looked with admiration at the man and smiled.

"On behalf of Pellas, I thank you for your unselfish act of generosity."

The man grunted and returned to his furnace. Philip placed the parts in his bag and navigated the narrow streets of Diakropolis until he found the home of the Master. Dacia greeted him warmly and led him to the aged leader, who was sitting in a chair facing the small interior garden. Philip approached him quietly, unsure if he was asleep.

"Philip, my son. How are you faring?"

"Very well, sir," replied the young man, dropping to one knee at the Master's side. "I have had a very interesting experience thus far."

"I figured as much. You are not accustomed to farm life."

"It is not so much the farm as the farmer."

The elderly man laughed quietly but solemnly.

"You never told me, Master, but I must know something if I am to be a true helper to Pellas. I sense that something serious has happened to him in the past. Do you know what it is?"

"Why do you think this so, Philip?"

"In the first place, the reception the farmer gave me was rude beyond words. It was alarming—as if I had stumbled upon the secret lair of a wild beast. Beyond that, he has misled me about his means. Pellas led me to believe that he was well off, but it appears that he is remarkably poor. He strikes me as one who escaped to the farm, not one who chose such a way of life or who grew up on a farm. Then there was the hint dropped by a blacksmith alluding to 'all that has happened.' I couldn't get anymore out of him, though."

"Oh, so you met Argo?"

"Who is Argo?" inquired Philip.

"A trusted friend and brother, and a top-notch blacksmith."

"I had no idea."

"Nor should you have had. He does a lot of work for the military and he prefers to keep his faith under cloak. For now, it is best that he does this. Now, back to your question."

"Yes, please."

The old man slowly shifted his slender frame in the chair and groaned quietly.

"The Lord has seen fit to give me many years, but this old house is showing signs of wear." The Master smiled. "What has Pellas told you about himself?"

"Virtually nothing. I know that he hates cities and any mention of you or the Lord."

"I had hoped that Pellas would soften," responded the aged man, wearily shaking his head. "I purposefully did not brief you regarding Pellas, realizing that you might jump right in and damage any possibility of rehabilitation before it could get started. Even now, I hesitate to betray his confidence in me."

"Let me assure you, sir, anything that you tell me will go no further."

"That is easier said now than in the passion of conflict. Still, it might help you to deal with Pellas' animosity towards the faith if you understood some of his past. Do you like the man?"

"Well, yes. In a strange way, I do. He is difficult, coarse and abusive, but there is something attractive about him. I really wanted to leave the farm a few days ago, but now I am beginning to feel at home, even with sleeping in a stable. Why do you ask?"

"Because we must never want to know the hidden things about a man just to satisfy our curiosity. Our goal is to bring men to Christ, or, in this case, back to Christ."

"What do you mean?"

The Master placed a hand on Philip's shoulder and leaned close.

"Pellas was a member of our fellowship until something very tragic happened—something for which he has not forgiven me, although I had no power to prevent it." The Master closed his eyes as if recalling the events. "Pellas reluctantly came to me one day. His wife and daughter were already part of our body…"

"Pellas had a wife and a daughter?" interrupted Philip in disbelief.

"Yes, and a son, Alexander. Alexander was responsible for our meeting. Much to Pellas' disapproval, the boy had fallen in with the wrong crowd and, when some thugs had beaten the boy, the family brought him to me for medical care. What followed was a glorious reconciliation between father and son. Both of them made professions of faith and joined the Church."

"I find it incredible that Pellas is a believer. You should hear the way he talks about Jesus."

"You will understand why when I tell you the rest of the story. Several months later, the family was apprehended, along with a number of the body, and taken before the magistrate."

"Lykos said that such happens here in Diakropolis."

"Yes, my son. Suffice it to say that in this city there is a strong undercurrent of hostility that seeks to destroy us. No one renounced his or her faith before the authorities that dark day. All were sentenced to death. One by one, they met their demise on the floor of the arena. During a delay in the carnage, the magistrate offered the remaining believers one last chance to recant. Only one man did."

"Pellas?" asked Philip. The elder nodded. "So Pellas' family perished that day, martyred for the cause of Christ, but Pellas walked away unscathed," recounted Philip, shaking his head. "No wonder." His voice trailed off. "No wonder."

"There are other things to relate but I am not at liberty to divulge them to you. They will have to come from Pellas himself. Now that you know his background, I trust that you will use this information with discretion and compassion."

"Oh, yes sir, I will. I am so happy that you shared it with me, although, at the same time, I feel a tremendous burden that was not there before. So much makes sense to me now. I now know why God brought me here."

"You are a goodhearted lad, Philip. The elders at Ephesus said as much in their letter of introduction. You will be an effective evangelist, but don't judge that from your dealings with Pellas. I do not know if he will come around. Remember, some seed was sown along the rocky soil and failed to grow."

"I understand, Master. I must be going now. I'm sure that I will have a lot to think about on the trip home."

The two men embraced and Philip set out for the farm, heavily laden with goods from Dacia's kitchen. To the west, a ribbon of blue emerged through a slash in the blanket of gray winter clouds, portending a break in the gloomy weather. Philip's spirits lifted as he saw the welcome color. Perhaps one day soon he would see the same sign in the countenance of Pellas.

CHAPTER 3

▼

Evening already had fallen as the sedan chair arrived outside the entrance to Siros' home. Septimus emerged from the vehicle and clapped the sturdy shoulder of the closest dark-skinned colossus who had borne him on the trip from the official compound.

"I could get used to this," Septimus quipped. The slave kept his eyes straight ahead and he did not acknowledge the deputy.

"And well you might, Septimus," came a voice from behind.

Septimus turned to see Titus standing on the steps that led to the massive front door.

"Ah, Titus. Lovely night for a party, don't you think?"

"Indeed it is," returned the man, gazing into the crisp, clear sky. Scarcely an hour earlier, the thick cloud curtain had retracted, revealing tens of thousands of shimmering points of light. "Come in, man, and enjoy the warmth of hospitality, Siros-style!"

Septimus began the ascent up the marble steps with two soldiers in tow. He stopped halfway and stood with hands on hips, surveying the massive columns that supported the intricately carved portico where Titus waited. Resembling a temple more than a residence, Siros' resplendent mansion was cut into a hill along the banks of the river above the city. At night, the glow of its torches could be seen from many vantage points in the city, and the view from the estate was equally impressive. There was a regal aura about the residence: It predated many of the other landmarks of Diakropolis, and the mansion stood like a royal palace perched high above its fiefdom.

"I'd hate to see the cleaning bill for this place," said Septimus, out of the side of his mouth to one of the soldiers.

"Come up, come up!" exhorted Titus. "The party awaits you. Father even refused to let the wine flow until you arrived and *that* is highly unusual."

"I'll say," responded Septimus, as he reached the porch and clasped Titus' outstretched hand. "It was only a few days ago that I couldn't have bought my way in as a servant."

"It is time to call things settled, Septimus. We let this little financial matter linger long enough."

"Now don't make me any more suspicious than I already am, Titus."

Titus faced Septimus before pushing open the thick, mahogany door.

"There is no need to be wary, my good man. Tonight we celebrate things to come, not things past. You are our guest, and for good reason."

"And what reason would that be?" inquired the deputy.

"Why, you are the highest-ranking official—excuse me, second-highest—in the city. We have been remiss in extending the hand of congeniality and cooperation toward our leaders. Father regrets that your brother could not be here to join us, yet he feels that the magnitude of this affair is not diminished in the least by his absence."

"Now I *really* am suspicious."

"You'll get over it once the festivities begin. Come inside."

They passed into a large, brightly lit foyer. In the center stood a large bronze statue of a man of apparent eminence. The torchlight danced upon the smooth surface of the metal and filled the room with light.

"Who's the subject?" asked Septimus.

"Croesus. King of Lydia."

"Lydia, is that around here?" Septimus asked as he scanned the statue. The crown and ornaments on the figure appeared to be inlaid with gold and encrusted with jewels. "Expensive piece," he commented.

"Expensive subject," said Titus.

The men crossed the foyer and went through a second set of doors that opened into a large banquet hall, filled with finely dressed people. The faces of the guests turned toward Septimus and he heard the voice of Siros rise above their whispers.

"Ah, our esteemed guest has arrived."

Septimus quickly surveyed the group and spied the portly host settled in a heavily padded chair at the center table. Septimus bowed as respectfully as he could.

"Most gracious Siros, it is both an honor and a pleasure to be so graciously received into your company."

Siros looked over at Dura, who stood nearby.

"Was it you who said the magistrate possessed only a tongue of brass, my friend? Come, come, Your Honor, and take your place at my side. Let the festivities begin!"

A surge of excited conversation rose as the guests took their places. There were no less than thirty, maybe forty, in attendance. Septimus nodded to Dura and Nikris who, together with Titus, formed a nearly inseparable trio. Dura already seemed loose and animated, presumably from pre-dinner libations. Nikris sat with brawny arms folded and the usual scowl fixed upon his face. Siros was decked in lavish robes and heavy gold bracelets and necklaces. That, combined with the fact that he was the only one sitting in a chair and not reclining at the table, made Siros appear even more massive than usual. He patted Septimus forcefully on the back as the latter took his seat, and Siros began introducing the deputy to the other guests. As Siros singled out each guest, he recited an exhaustive list of his or her credentials and pedigree. It was readily apparent to Septimus that he was in the presence of the cream of Diakropolis, and that by evening's end he would have some idea of why he was there.

"Your prompt assistance in releasing warrants the other day was most appreciated, *Magistrate*," said Siros, leaning closely.

"No problem. I trust that you found what, or whom, you were looking for."

"It grieves me to respond in the negative. Runaway slaves are the bane of the wealthy. However, we will track him down and return him to his rightful place. Nevertheless, your support is greatly valued and will not go unrewarded."

Septimus smiled politely and indulged in the delicacies before him, satisfied that his presence at the party was an act of gratitude for signing a few documents. The dinner proceeded from course to course, with each successive dish surpassing the one previous. Septimus enjoyed exotic dishes of which he had only heard descriptions, all served on platters of gold and silver. Rare fowl were roasted and garnished with fruits from distant lands. All varieties of game were brought in, accompanied by a collection of the finest sauces that Septimus ever had tasted. Fine white bread, a delicacy for all but the wealthy, was in abundance, as were numerous shellfish dishes. Of course, all the fare was thoroughly bathed in wine, imported from the finest vineyards in the empire. Several of the guests excused themselves to empty their stomachs to make room for the later dishes, but Septimus' appetite remained vigorous.

"My, my, Siros. I take it that this is not your usual evening meal," said Septimus, adjusting his belt. "I've never had to purge, but this is testing even my limits."

"We only do this when we wish to honor one of great importance, my good man."

"I assume that you mean me but, even with my ego, I fail to see how a few simple search warrants deserve this response."

"It is not so much what you have done but, rather, what you can do."

"I don't understand."

"Patience, Magistrate."

After the main course, Siros rose and led the group in a solemn offering to the family's guardian spirits. He then clapped for the servants to bring in the sweet and salty foods that would drive the dinner party to indulge in more wine.

"Come, retire with me to another room for a moment," said Siros to Septimus. "We can return for the entertainment after we chat."

Siros rose to his feet with the aid of two servants and escorted Septimus, along with Titus, Nikris and Dura, to a side room. It was paneled with mahogany similar to that which was present throughout the house, and fitted with braziers and lamps of solid gold. Two chairs of ebony inlaid with ivory faced each other, with a small gold-plated table between them. On a marble table next to the wall sat several scrolls, whose ends also were of gold. The room, as well as the entire house, reeked of opulence. Siros motioned Septimus to sit opposite him while the others gathered around.

"I have noticed your eyes roving about the house, Magistrate," Siros began. "Do you approve?"

"I have never seen anything quite like it."

"Nor will you. Not in these parts, at least. Are you interested in how I have come by this great wealth?"

"The question has crossed my mind. I've heard rumors."

"And that is just what they are, rumors. Very few beyond those people gathered in this room know the truth."

"And you intend to include me in this circle of intrigue?" asked Septimus, with a hint of sarcasm.

"Perhaps," replied the host. "The circle must inevitably widen from time to time; that is, if the right man can be found."

"So you invited me to this little picnic for examination?"

"You make it sound so negative, my good man. Consider this: this is the company that such a man could expect to keep."

Septimus reached for a gold dish on the table and ran his fingers along the edge.

"Do the accessories come with it?"

"What, this?" asked Siros with a wave of his arm. "This is but a mere trifle compared to the whole."

"Okay, clue me in," said Septimus, leaning forward.

"Ho! Not so fast, my friend. The circle does not expand quite so readily."

"Don't toy with me, Siros."

"I am not toying with you, Magistrate. The man I am looking for must be carefully selected. Each one gathered here has a specific role ideally suited to his talents. Consider Nikris, here. Would you depend on him to be your accountant? Hardly. However, as chief of security, there is none better. Would Dura strike fear in your heart if you met him in a dark alley? No, no. Nonetheless, there is not a more capable manager of the myriad details involved in operating a business. When each unit performs his task to his potential, we all prosper."

"It appears to me that *you* prosper."

"We *all* prosper," said Siros emphatically. "Have you been to the theater?"

"Once or twice," replied Septimus, puzzled at the question.

"Do you know how the funds were procured for that beautiful facility?"

"I assumed that they were provided from the public coffers."

"Ha! The public coffers would not even have cleared the land. I donated the money." Septimus glanced at Titus, who nodded in agreement. "And the library?"

"I am not one for books," responded the deputy.

"But many of the citizenry are. Did Rome provide that fine structure? Once again, that was a gift from our largesse."

"Okay, I get your point. You are a philanthropist extraordinaire."

"My point is that when I prosper, we all prosper, including the least of citizens. As one of the leaders of Diakropolis, that should interest you."

"No offense, but I can't generate much paternal emotion for the citizens of Diakropolis. Don't get me wrong—it is a fine city, and you seem to have made out well here, but I don't plan to linger long. I prefer a sunnier, more exotic setting."

"So you would prefer to use your meager public pension to run up your gambling debts in someplace glamorous, rather than to remain in these squalid surroundings with freedom to buy a villa or two in the location of your dreams?"

Septimus sat in quiet thought for a moment. "Okay. I'm listening."

Siros motioned to Nikris, who poured a thick liquid from a small pitcher into two silver cups and brought them to Siros and Septimus.

"What is this?" asked the official, peering into the cup.

"Honey, from the *azalea pontica*. I find that it clears the mind when discussing business." Siros downed the drink in one swallow. Septimus shrugged his shoulders and followed suit.

The stimulant felt warm as it slid down his throat. Almost immediately, Septimus felt an invigorating wave pass through his body. He smiled and inhaled deeply.

"I like it," the deputy said brightly.

"Another of life's little pleasures that awaits you." The group huddled more closely. Nikris checked the door out of habit, and then rejoined the group. Siros began in a quiet, but serious tone. "My business involves importing and exporting goods to various regions of the empire. What you see here in Diakropolis is but a small portion of the operation, but it is key. In any line of work, one necessarily runs into bureaucratic entanglements. In years past, this was not so much a problem but, with increased Roman presence and the development of the city as a significant municipality, the encumbrances have become considerable. Taxes, tariffs, inspections, licenses, duplicate records, and so forth require a great deal of time and expense, and these things place a significant drag on our efficiency. On most occasions, we labor under great time constraints. Things must move quickly. Clients expect their product, and a delay of even days may put us in arrears."

"So?" said Septimus abruptly, hopping to his feet. "What do you want me to do for you?" He licked his lips nervously and pulled on his toga several times. "It is hot in here. I could stand a visit to the baths."

"Please, sit down, Magistrate. In time, your body will learn to handle that little drink we shared. Let us conclude our chat, then Titus can show you to my private bath if you are still overheated."

"You have your own bath?"

"Well, it wouldn't do very well for men of *our* position to mingle with the common folk, would it?" asked Siros in a condescending tone. "Let us return to the subject. You asked what you could do for me. Let me be candid. There are times when it is necessary for the governing authorities to be a touch myopic."

"Myopic?"

"Yes, you know, excuse a detail or two. Suspend protocol." Siros turned to the others. "Help me out, boys."

"Look the other way, Septimus," said Titus.

"Oh, I see."

"It is all for the good of the community, mind you," stressed the host. "Remember, our prosperity enriches the community and its leaders."

Septimus rose from his chair and began pompously walking about the room.

"Look, gentlemen, I understand you quite well. You want special exemption from trade regulations. You want tax breaks and cursory inspections that never find any violations. You are willing to pay for them both over and under the table. I've seen it all before—it happens throughout the empire. For better or worse, I have no problem with it. As long as you are not smuggling in mercenaries to sack Rome, it makes little difference to me how you carry out your business. I am not your problem."

Siros, Titus and Dura joined in a chorus of hearty approvals, but Septimus cut them off with a wave of the hand.

"Marcellus is your problem," the deputy continued. "I appreciate the invitation to the banquet, but you are wining and dining the wrong man. You can line my purse with as much gold as you care to part with and I'll turn every cheek I can find. Not Marcellus." Septimus shook his head. "Not Marcellus."

Siros cleared his throat and motioned the deputy again to take his seat.

"Your brother's affinity for the letter of the law has caught our attention—and our admiration." The host motioned toward the others, who were nodding in agreement. "We are aware that your brother holds the position of chief magistrate, but we have not erred in inviting you here this evening. A man of Marcellus' stature is destined for greater positions—and soon. You, Septimus, should seek to dissociate yourself from your brother to pursue your own fortunes. In my circle of friends, the view is that your brother will not last long in Diakropolis. Even now, the office of chief magistrate lies vacant in the prominent city of Prusa. The governor will offer Marcellus the position and I doubt that your brother will refuse. This will leave our fair city with a similar vacancy. Linus, acting on the advice of mutual friends, will agree that the best man for the job is you."

"Siros, that is one piece of fanciful thinking," said Septimus, laughing. "So, that's what the honey of the 'pontica whatever' does to you? Linus can't stand me, and Marcellus would never let the governor subject Diakropolis to my judgment."

A stern look came upon Siros' face.

"You may think it fanciful, Magistrate, but I have operated in this arena for a long time. It will be so. Now, are you with us?"

Septimus drew back and studied the faces of the men in the room. Each gazed intently back at him, awaiting his reply.

"I need to know more."

"Very well," sighed Siros. "Tomorrow you will be picked up after breakfast for a tour of our facility. Come alone. Tell no one where you are going."

"Especially that nitpicking assistant of yours," chimed in Titus.

"You've met Jason?" asked Septimus. "He goes with Marcellus, by the way."

"Are we agreed, Septimus?" asked Siros.

"Agreed. Now, can we have the entertainment in the bath?"

"Dura, show the man to the bath—and take a couple of the dancers with you for a private show."

The stone-faced Gaul led Septimus out of the room, leaving Titus alone with his perspiring father.

"This is a gamble," stated Titus, "showing him the operation before getting a pledge."

"What gamble, son? He will sign on. The hooks already are penetrating deep into his skin. And if by some chance he doesn't like what he sees, we'll trouble him no more." Siros closed his eyes and settled into the chair. "Nor will he trouble us." Siros chuckled inaudibly. "Nor will he trouble us."

CHAPTER 4

▼

A thin canopy of fog, pierced only by the strongest starlight, lay over the city of Diakropolis as a new day emerged. A chorus of barks greeted the gaudy sedan chair of Siros as it lumbered through the agora on the shoulders of eight stout servants. The buildings were still cloaked in pre-dawn darkness. Only the flickers of lamps within the homes and shops of early-risers were visible. Siros ordered a halt outside one of the taverns and motioned his retinue of bodyguards to follow him inside. In one motion, Siros lifted the latch of the door and lunged forward with his full weight, but the door failed to give.

"It's locked!" he growled. "What time is it?"

"It is five o'clock," responded Nikris.

"Five o' clock?" repeated the irritated man. "And we're not open for business? I'd say here is a man who has too much idle time. Rouse him, Nikris."

The Gaul stepped forward and banged his large fist on the door, causing the doorframe to shiver and bits of plaster to dislodge from the adjacent walls.

"Coming! Coming!" replied a frantic voice, obviously moving toward the door with haste. Fingers fumbled at the bolt on the other side of the door. A face appeared as the door cracked open. It was Arias.

Nikris pushed open the heavy door, sending Arias teetering backward. Siros entered the darkened room, sniffing at the stale air.

"Innkeeper! Lights and a fire!" The group took seats at a table near a window. "Where is your man, Nikris? I wish to spend as little time as possible in this dump."

"He should be here by now," replied the Gaul.

"We agreed on the time, did we not?" asked Siros. "I assume this fellow knows the value that I place on punctuality."

"Without a doubt, sire," said Dura. There must be a reason for his tardiness."

"Innkeeper!" bellowed Siros. "Where is the cursed light?" Arias raced around the corner with a small lamp and began to light the various lamps situated around the large room. Slowly, a deep, yellow glow filled the room. "I want wine and bread," continued Siros. "Cheese, too. And why is the fire not yet lit? Don't you have help?"

"Yes, sir. My wife will be along shortly."

"Your wife? How nice. Does she waste the morning away in sleep as do you?"

"No, sir. She has been up for some time."

"Oh? Doing what?"

Arias hesitated. All the believers in Diakropolis knew very well of Siros' hatred for Christians. It would not do to explain that Myra had been engaged in morning prayers when Siros arrived at the inn.

"She was preparing for the day, sir."

"Inform her the day is upon us. Now, are you going to stand there talking, or will you service us?" The other men laughed at the already haggard innkeeper.

"I'm sorry, sir," Arias apologized as he rushed to finish lighting the lamps. "Would you prefer that I light the fire before I bring food and drink?"

Siros flushed with anger.

"Come here, little man."

Arias returned to the table sheepishly. Nikris instinctively rose and stood close to the innkeeper in case the Gaul's talents were required. Nikris towered over the balding host, whose head now glistened with beads of sweat.

"I am not accustomed to making a choice between two essentials," continued Siros. "I want heat *and* I want breakfast—both of them—immediately! I'll give you one minute."

Arias' eyes widened, and then he bolted out of sight, calling for Myra as he ran. Nervous chatter echoed from the back rooms of the tavern. The harried host emerged within the allotted time, carrying a load of tinder under one arm and holding a tray of the requested food and drink above his head with the other. The guests chided Arias as he nervously filled the plates and cups.

A cold wind rushed in from the doorway as a dark, cloaked figure stepped inside. His eyes met Dura's, who then nodded for the man to join the party. Meanwhile, Nikris shooed away Arias. The host willingly raced away to join his wife in the kitchen.

"What is *he* doing here?" asked a panic-stricken Myra, once the couple was out of sight and earshot.

"I have no idea," responded Arias, pacing wildly. "Siros never has been here before. I think that he simply chose our tavern for a meeting place by chance. My, but he is in a foul mood. We'd better stay out of his way."

"There is no such thing as chance with our Lord, Arias. You know, all too well, that trouble for our people follows in the wake of that scoundrel and his gang. We have an opportunity to find out something that may be vital to our welfare."

"Myra, don't be foolish. Siros kills anyone whom he suspects of eavesdropping. I say we stay put right here."

"Innkeeper!" thundered Siros. Arias shot out from the kitchen, nearly slipping in the process.

"Yes, sir?" he asked, half-bowing as he hurried.

"Did you not see we added to our party? More food and drink! And bring the stronger wine! It is too late in the morning for colored water!"

Arias scampered back to the kitchen, nearly colliding with his wife.

"He wants—"

"I heard," interrupted Myra. "The whole agora heard, for that matter. You're too edgy. I'll take it to him—calmly and slowly—with ears pert and ready."

"You're out of your head, woman! How do you think you're going to listen in without their knowledge?"

"Just get the wine and leave that to me."

Arias chose his strongest wine from a cool recess in the wall, while Myra gathered more bread and cheese. She placed the elements on a tray and adjusted her garments to give a disheveled appearance.

"How do I look?" she asked, rotating her somewhat overweight frame from side to side.

Arias looked puzzled. Myra did not wait for a reply; she hoisted the tray and ambled toward the party, taking mental notes of the participants gathered in the dim light. As Myra approached, she could make out some of the conversation. The recently arrived stranger was addressing the group.

"I was followed," he said in a gravelly tone. "It took me a few minutes to give 'em the slip."

"What do you know about the fugitives?"

"They made it out of the city, all right." The cloaked man glanced at Nikris, who returned an icy glare. "I followed the trail into the hills as far as I could, but I lost it at the stream. It got dark fast. They could be anywhere."

"I see there are still sympathizers in the hills," said Siros.

"An endless supply of rats, so it would seem," added Dura.

Conversation broke off abruptly as Myra neared with the food. The man impatiently waited for the innkeeper's wife to serve them and leave. She slowly set out each item, smiling stupidly at each of the men as she went.

"Woman," Siros asked, "is it solely your body that moves at a snail's pace, or is it merely responding at the rate your brain instructs?"

Myra had allowed a bit of saliva to form at the corner of her mouth and she noisily sucked it in.

"Oh, nah, sir," she said in a drawn out, nearly unintelligible slur. "I fine. Cheese good. I have pet goat. She pretty. You wanna see her?"

Siros stared at Myra briefly, then at the others. The group simultaneously burst into a raucous laugh, except Nikris, who remained stone-faced.

"The man has an idiot for a wife," roared Siros. "A match made by the gods!" Siros composed himself and dabbed at his eyes and mouth with a silk handkerchief. "I would love to see your, er, goat, some other time, my dear woman. I am sure that it rivals your unparalleled beauty." Another round of laughter was cut short by Siros, who was anxious to continue their business. "Now, be off with you."

Myra stared blankly at him for a moment, then turned slowly and shuffled away, scraping her feet lethargically on the floor as she went. She did not return to the kitchen, but began idly straightening tables and chairs nearby, periodically scratching her head and rump for embellishment. The party leaned forward and returned to their discussion, although Nikris kept a wary eye on the woman.

"Go on," said Siros. "You found no trace of them in the hills?"

"No. The trail was cold," replied the cloaked man.

"Did you search any of the farms?"

"Tried to, but they're too spread out and we didn't have enough men."

"Reminds me of Lykos," intoned Dura. "He's the only one who could pull off such a move."

"It has the imprint of the Wolf, I'll admit, but he was an old man when I last faced him. Surely he is dead by now."

"One can't be too sure," Dura responded excitedly. "There are stories circulated among the townspeople that attest to the Christians being led by an old phantom who still works his magic by night, prowling about like a cunning wolf."

"Enough of such foolishness, Dura. Really, I'm surprised at you, being taken in like that."

"But what if he is alive and opposing us? He is a formidable foe, Siros."

"You mean he *was* a formidable foe. If Lykos or, more likely, an imitator, is attempting to thwart our enterprise, we will deal with him. Furthermore, let's not admire his work too fondly, Dura. You know how disagreeable that makes me." Siros turned to the Gaul, who was following Myra's movements with intense scrutiny. "Come, Nikris, forget the imbecile. We have serious business to discuss with our man here. Pay attention." Siros addressed the messenger, "And what do you know about the escaped man?"

"His name's Rufus. Recently brought in from Anakrakis. Somehow, he smuggled himself out with the shipment. Someone in town expected him. Clever plan. Rufus was supposed to connect with them somewhere in the agora. Don't know where, though. Of course, you know the rest."

Siros nodded grudgingly.

"Do you have anything else?"

"No," the messenger replied, shaking his head. "What do you want me to do now?"

"Thus far, your reputation as a tracker without peer is less than fitting," sniffed Siros. "Nevertheless, my son seems very fond of you. That is a weak endorsement, I should warn you. I'm willing to allow you a chance to redeem yourself, however. I'll defer to Nikris on your next assignment."

"Get some rest," said the Gaul. "I'll need you later."

The man quickly rose from the table and pulled his hood over his head, until his eyes shone with the light of the lamps deep within the shadows.

"Sire. Gentlemen."

He slipped out the door, casting a quick glance at Myra, who momentarily had stopped her work. Her eyes met his for an instant. Startled by this lapse in judgment, she promptly erupted in a feigned sneezing attack that caught the attention of the men at the table. After Myra concluded, she flashed a vacant smile and returned to her chores.

"This kind of success will only encourage more of the same, Siros," Dura commented anxiously. "Apparently, Lykos knows something of our operation and he has a network in place to pull off more of these escapes."

"Settle yourself, Dura. Granted, whoever engineered this escape is as shrewd as a wolf. However, wolves are hungry and are drawn to the scent, sometimes against their better judgment. We will draw him out and put an end to this nonsense."

"How do you propose to do that?" asked Nikris.

"It will take a little thought. It should be amusing."

"Think quickly!" prompted Dura. "We can ill afford to lose too many workers."

Siros stared off at the corner of the room in thought.

"What concerns me," he wondered aloud, "is how they are obtaining their information. Lykos, if indeed it is he, has been quiet for some time, but obviously not dormant. This escape could not have been successful without leaks in strategic places. It appears that there are moles within our camp. Nikris, update a security check on all of my employees. Look into relatives, affiliations, activities—everything."

"It will be done."

"You can't suspect everyone, sire," countered Dura.

"On the contrary, my man. You *must* suspect everyone." Siros peered out the window at the advancing sunlight. "We must go. Septimus will be arriving within the hour. Do nothing to ruffle his feathers. He is unpredictable and insufferably self-absorbed, but we need his alliance. As long as Rome looks the other way, the Order of Croesus will prosper."

The trio rose from the table, Siros making two attempts before succeeding.

"Innkeeper!" he called. Myra smiled and began to shuffle his way. "Not you, half-wit. Innkeeper, come now if you wish to be paid!"

Arias rounded the wall that separated the kitchen from the dining room.

"Yes, kind sir, you called?"

"We are leaving. Your cheese was putrid and the bread moldy, and if that is your quality wine, change your line of work. Nevertheless, I am feeling generous this morning. Here." He handed Arias a shiny bronze coin.

"Th…thank you for your patronage, sir."

Siros surveyed the small man up and down and then looked at Myra standing behind him, her face composed in a vacuous smile.

"The gods help us," he frowned. "Come, gentlemen."

The group exited onto the street and Siros took his place in the sedan chair. The servants heaved the vehicle to their shoulders and began the short trip to the Old City with two Gauls at the front and Dura and Nikris following behind.

Myra heaved a great sigh of relief and mopped the perspiration from her brow as Siros' entourage moved away from the tavern. Arias clapped his hands together.

"You were brilliant, my dear. A better actor is not to be found in all of Bithynia!"

"You are too kind." Myra smiled and bowed.

"It was an act, was it not?" joked the innkeeper.

"You scoundrel," scolded his wife as she raised her hand in mock assault. Arias cowered, and then laughed. "Tell me, what did you overhear?"

"Little that we didn't already know. The strange-looking man apparently was sent to track Rufus and his family, but he was unsuccessful. They know we're in business but they have no leads." She thought for a moment, trying to recall the conversation of a few minutes earlier. "Ah, yes, here's something new. A meeting has been arranged this morning with the chief magistrate's brother, that fellow Septimus. Siros spoke of an alliance with him."

"I thought the brute already was in their camp," grumbled Arias.

"I guess not as much as Siros wishes him to be."

"I wonder why he is dealing with Septimus rather than the chief?"

"Who knows what is cooking in that vile man's head." Myra grabbed her cloak and moved toward the back door of the tavern.

"Where are you going, Myra?"

"Out to tell John. He may want to know of this meeting."

"Take care. The streets are still dark."

Myra gave a smile of gratitude for her husband's concern. She quietly opened the door and poked her head out, checking both ways for unwelcome eyes. Satisfied that all was clear, she disappeared into the narrow back street. As Myra hurried along the alleyways, a figure emerged from the shadows and followed at a distance. It was the cloaked messenger who, minutes earlier, had been dismissed from the tavern.

C H A P T E R 5

▼

The narrow city streets came to life as Myra wound her way toward John's house. Shutters flew open and spilled out the aroma of morning meals and noises of preparation for another day's work. Several people, mostly merchants heading to the agora, had already taken to the streets. The presence of other people relaxed the innkeeper's wife, although she repeatedly looked around at intervals for suspicious bystanders. As she had just witnessed, the threat of exposure was ever-present under the suspicious, restless eye of Siros.

As Myra drew near to her destination, she pulled her shawl tightly around her face, exposing only her eyes and nose. Turning into an alley that ran behind a long row of houses, she made for a door near the far end, which opened into John's house. Her footsteps on the cobbled pavement echoed off the walls. Presently, she became aware of another set of steps farther behind. Myra turned and peered down the dimly lit passage. She could make out the form of a person moving slowly toward her. Myra knew that it was forbidden to enter the house unless the alley was deserted, so she moved past the doorway and exited onto a larger street.

Myra turned the corner and waited for the alley to clear. Suddenly, she saw something that gripped her with terror. Coming her way, not fifty feet away, was the cloaked man she had seen earlier at the tavern. He was looking from side to side as he walked and failed to see her standing there. Myra's heart raced, knowing that his keen eye would immediately recognize her. Panic-stricken, she rushed back to the door and knocked vigorously, breathlessly counting the seconds until the stranger would appear at the entrance to the alley. Meanwhile, the footsteps at the other end of the passage grew closer.

"Come on, open up," she pleaded under her breath.

Myra began to knock with abandon now, her body pressed against the rough-hewn wood. Suddenly the latch lifted, sending her tumbling headlong across the threshold and pushing the inhabitant of the house back against the door.

"Myra, what gives?" asked Thomas, with a confused look.

"Thomas, bolt the door—quickly!" she exclaimed, hardly able to squeeze out the words.

Thomas did as he was instructed, a look of alarm on his face.

"The shutters, too!"

"They're secure," Thomas replied, checking to make certain. "Now what is this—?"

"Quiet!" Myra hissed, gesturing emphatically. "Out there! A man! Dangerous!" Myra's voice quivered.

Against the woman's protests, Thomas carefully opened the shutters to a crack, which afforded a view to the vicinity of the door. He stared intently for a moment and then broke into a relaxed chuckle.

"Since when have you grown afraid of washerwomen?" Myra gazed at him, puzzled. "See for yourself."

Myra stole to the window and peered out just as the person whom she had seen at the other end of the alley passed by. It was an old woman lumbering along, heavily laden with baskets of dirty laundry. Thomas secured the latch and laughed again, but Myra shook her head insistently.

"No. There was another."

"Another what?"

Thomas had no time to hear the answer, for at that moment a slow methodical knock came at the door. Now Thomas' eyes widened with concern.

"Were you followed?" he whispered.

"I'm sorry, Thomas. I had to break the rules. I had news. But now he has found us." She buried her face in her hands and shook her head mournfully.

"He?"

The knock came again, slow but persistent. Thomas motioned Myra to come close.

"Listen carefully. If it is a foe, he may try to break in. I'll position myself behind the door. I have a knife. Pray that I don't have to use it. See if you recognize who it is, but stay down and be quiet."

Myra nodded and slowly cracked open the shutter. The aperture was too small to get a full view, but what she saw made her heart sink. The partial form of a man, wrapped in the same dirty brown cloak as the one she saw earlier at the tavern, shifted in and out of view. Myra could hear him muttering something under his breath. She carefully closed the shutters and eased away from the window.

"It's him," she said somberly.

"Who?" pressed Thomas.

"I don't know who, but he is evil," she responded, nervously wringing her hands. "He followed me. I have brought ruin upon us."

The knocking began again, its cadence unchanged but with more authority. Thomas cocked his head pensively for a moment and then nodded resolutely.

"This visitor is too courteous for an adversary."

Thomas slipped over to the shutter and positioned one eye over the crack. Like Myra, he could only see a portion of the one at the doorstep. Finally, the man stepped away from the door and looked around in obvious frustration. Thomas clearly saw his face now and called out to the solemn woman.

"It's Targus! Let him in. Quickly!"

Myra looked at Thomas, stunned.

"Are you out of your mind? He's…he's one of them!"

"No, no. You don't understand," Thomas replied, brushing beside her to open the door. Myra cowered back against the wall.

The door flew open and in rushed Targus.

"Thank God, Thomas! I was wondering what had happened." Targus threw back the hood of his cloak and saw Myra, stiff against the wall. "Hello, who's this? Aren't you the tavern keeper's wife?" Targus looked at Thomas for an explanation.

"Obviously, you two know something of each other, but I suspect not all," said Thomas. "Targus, meet Myra, the wife of Arias, tavern keeper and sister in Christ." The cloaked man nodded but continued to eye Myra with suspicion.

"Myra, this is Targus, one of our most trusted and secret scouts. The two of you probably never would have met, except by the Lord's will."

The plump woman slowly relaxed, the color visibly returning to her cheeks.

"I'm pleased to make your acquaintance," she said, holding out her sweaty, trembling hand in greeting.

"Now, come away from the door, you two. We can become better acquainted inside. John should be here any minute. He stepped out on business."

Thomas led Myra and Targus to a small room where they sat and talked, laughing as Targus recalled Myra's performance in the tavern. The woman watched Targus as he recounted the story. He was dark-skinned with thick, unkempt brown hair. Deep creases streaked with dirt lined his face. There was an air of gravity about him, even when he laughed.

Thomas briefed the woman regarding the mysterious agent as much as he dared.

"The less you know about Targus, the better, Myra, All you really need to know is that he is one of the Body."

Targus excused himself to wash, leaving Myra and Thomas alone.

"Why didn't you tell us about him?" asked the woman.

"His task is the most dangerous and vital of all, Myra. One slip and he's a dead man. Absolute secrecy is a must, and now it is a burden that you must bear."

"Oh, I will." Thomas looked into Myra's eyes. "Honest, Thomas. I won't tell anyone," Myra insisted.

"Not even Arias."

"Not Arias? But..."

"Not Arias. No one." Thomas' words were low and grave.

"Okay," she responded with resignation in her voice. "No one."

"Good girl." Thomas squeezed Myra's hand.

At that moment, the front door opened and in walked John, accompanied by Argo. John's eyes immediately fell upon Myra.

"Myra, why are you here?" John asked pointedly.

"She came to deliver important news, John, but she didn't know that we had other sources," said Thomas, as Targus entered the room.

John looked at Targus, then at Myra and Thomas; then John held out his hands in frustration.

"I know, John," Thomas continued apologetically, placing an arm around Myra. "It just so happened that Siros met with Targus earlier in Arias' tavern. Myra overheard the conversation—and I must tell you sometime how she did it—and risked detection to come tell you. She had no idea that Targus was one of us. Don't go too hard on her; the morning's already been quite stressful."

"Okay, okay," said John. He addressed Myra in a serious tone.

"You must leave here and forget that you ever saw this man in your life," John said firmly, pointing toward Targus. Myra glanced at the scout, then back at John, nodding vigorously. "You never saw him, right?"

"Right," came the almost inaudible reply.

"I told her not to tell Arias, either," added Thomas.

"Gracious, no!" exclaimed John. "Don't even think of telling Arias!"

"She won't, John," said Thomas, trying to settle him. "She promised."

John moved to within inches of Myra's face and stared hard. Myra returned the look for a moment and then diverted her eyes.

"You may go now," said John, dismissing her.

Thomas escorted the downcast woman to the back door. Argo noticed her distress, nudged John and gestured in her direction. The leader shrugged his shoulders and called to her.

"Myra." The woman turned, her demeanor showing both the strain of the morning and dejection of the harsh reprimand from John. "You were brave to come here. I appreciate your courage." She managed a weak smile.

"Don't hold it against John, Myra," Thomas said at the door.

"I was only trying to help," she responded, holding back tears.

"He knows that. He's exhausted and he feels the burden of making this operation a success."

"He's not at all like the Master, though."

"No one is, Myra. Who knows but that perhaps the Master was exactly like John at his age." Thomas cracked open the shutter and scanned the alley for signs of life. "It's clear." He opened the door. "Take care and remember, not a word about Targus."

"Yes, I know," Myra said quietly.

Thomas quickly shut the door behind her and returned to the room where the briefing was underway. John looked up.

"Is she all right?" John asked.

"She'll be fine, John. Just throw a few hugs her way."

John nodded. "You haven't missed anything. Targus was about to fill us in on what Siros knows."

"Not much, actually," the rugged scout responded, with a chuckle. "He suspects Lykos is in business, and that's got him hot. I had to feed him something about the escape or he'd be on my trail. I figured it was safe to tell him about Rufus, since the man has no relations in the Old City anymore."

"Why was he meeting with the deputy magistrate?" asked John.

"Drawing him into the fold, why else?"

"Why him and not the chief?"

"I don't think this new fellow is warming up to Siros. In fact, he's stepped on their toes pretty good. I'd look for him to be gone soon."

Thomas' face brightened.

"Perhaps he could be approached, John."

"The chief magistrate? You must be kidding. Have you known a Roman official to care one whit about our plight? Anywhere?"

"I don't know of any," said Thomas, frowning. "But he could be the first."

"We'd do better to direct our energy toward things that we can control. What do you think Siros will do now, Targus?"

"He'll tighten up, for sure. May double the guards at the mine, but it will take a few days to recruit them."

"We need to move now before he does," said Argo, as he planted a hairy fist in the center of the table.

"Whoa, my good smith," cautioned Targus. "Might I point out that we lack a means of escape? I can assure you any recommendation on my part for employment as a mine guard will be greeted with suspicion. They know how Rufus got away from the mine. Every cart will be searched inch by inch. Besides, we can't dribble out one worker at a time."

"He's right," said John. "We need a way to liberate the entire lot, but how could that possibly happen?"

"If the Lord wants them out, a way will come to light," said Thomas confidently.

"Ask Him to work quickly," replied John, rubbing his face. A hint of pessimism tinged his words.

"Certainly." Thomas closed his eyes and immediately began to pray silently, his brow and lips moving intently as he did. John rolled his eyes and gazed at the ceiling, while the others looked at each other, uncertain whether to join Thomas or wait for him to conclude.

"There, it is done," announced Thomas presently, a wide grin on his face. "Now it's down to business. Let's have a look at the mine survey."

"This is no time for levity, Thomas."

"I heartily agree. The map, please."

John reluctantly retrieved the survey from a pocket inside his tunic and carefully handed it to Thomas.

"You have safeguarded it well, my friend," said Thomas kindly. "Your father did not perish for naught. Somehow, this document holds the key to our success. The Master senses it, and so do I. It only remains to be seen in what way."

John smiled grimly. He had fervently protected the document since the day he received it from the Master, not only because of its strategic value to the operation of Lykos, but because it was in essence a last will and testament of his father. Many times he had contemplated how the map had come into his father's hands and how he came to die.

Thomas took the map and briskly unfolded it on the table.

"Have a care with that, Thomas. It's all we have."

"Not so," Targus said, laughing. "I've got another right here." The scout flipped a folded vellum onto the outstretched map. The others in the group stared at the small parcel in puzzlement.

"You mean, all this time…" began John pointedly.

"Not *all this time*," responded the scout in defense, "but I've had it for a few weeks."

"How did you come by it?" asked Thomas.

"As I have told you, Titus can be a bit loose with company secrets. I convinced him I needed it to do my job properly." The group shared a relieved laugh, with the exception of John, who felt that his father's contribution was somehow slighted by the second map.

Thomas rubbed his hands eagerly. "Now, let's see what we can conjure up here."

Thomas, Argo and Targus labored over the map for the better part of an hour. Questions shot back and forth in rapid fire. Schemes were posed, bandied about, and eventually rejected. The mood of the group gradually moved from hopeful to dejected. Even Thomas, who was upbeat as a rule, became a bit morose. Throughout the interchange, John said nothing and merely stared into a corner of the sparsely furnished room.

"Well, I'm spent," concluded Thomas.

"I suppose I'll go try to get some work done," added Argo. "The garrison needs new bridles."

"I could use some food, myself," said Targus. "Judging from your stores, John, I think I could do better in the forest."

"I told you three it was a pointless exercise," said John sharply. "I've looked at that map so much that I see it with my eyes closed. We have no hope for a successful rescue given what little we know."

At that moment, a rap came at the back door. The group snapped to attention.

"It's probably Aelius," said Thomas, starting down the narrow hall. "He said he'd be late."

Aelius was a relatively new believer who worked at the agora, assisting with the opening and closing of the market, and making sure the various merchants did not bend the rules to gain an unfair advantage over a competitor. He possessed a quick wit and approached the work of Lykos with a breezy optimism that belied the tension he felt balancing service to God and the emperor. Unlike John and Thomas, Aelius was married and had a small child, which tempered his willingness to engage headlong in the more risky endeavors of the group. Nevertheless, he willingly offered to do what he could for the cause, and his contributions were vital. Aelius greeted the group warmly and tossed his tunic on a chair.

"The agora's humming today, my friends. I've had my hands full already! It's amazing what damage can be wrought by a single goat. One fellow lost a whole load of linen. I am famished!" He scanned the room in vain for evidence of refreshment. "I see this is not a breakfast meeting. So, what have we decided thus far?"

"We're a bit thin on ideas, Aelius," replied Thomas wearily. Aelius clapped his hands together.

"Aha, then! An infusion of creativity is needed. Good thing I'm here." He took a place at the table and glanced over the map. "What is this?" he asked, his eyes coming to rest on the small parcel at the corner of the table.

"It's another survey of the mine. Targus came by it."

"Two maps! Twice as likely to find a solution," responded Aelius brightly, as he undid the cord and unfolded the second map.

John shook his head and groaned, and then returned to his thoughts. Argo mumbled something again about getting back to work, but settled deeper in his chair and began to nod off. Thomas made interesting shapes with his fingers. Targus worked with his knife at a callous on his foot. Meanwhile, Aelius gazed back and forth between the two maps in deep concentration.

"What's this line here, Targus?" he asked after some time.

"Let me see," answered the scout distractedly. Aelius held up the map.

"This one, coming right to the center of the mine."

"That's a shaft," Targus replied, already engaged again in his task.

"Then why is it not on your map?"

Immediately, every eye was fixed on Aelius.

"What did you say?" John asked pointedly.

"If indeed this is a shaft, it only appears on John's map, not Targus'."

In an instant, the group was tightly huddled around the table, scouring the detail of both maps and talking vigorously at once. Undeniably, the two maps were identical, save for one curious detail: a single, thin line approaching the center of the mine from a direction opposite the known entrance. It indeed appeared to mark out the course of another shaft.

"Men, men!" The voice of John rose over the excited chatter of the group. "Before we get ahead of ourselves, we must investigate this further."

"This is it, John. Praise the Lord! I knew He would show us something grand! Right under Siros' nose, too."

"Settle yourself, Thomas. There must be a logical explanation. I recommend we proceed calmly—."

"I go at once to uncover this mystery," interjected Targus, sheathing his knife. "Until then, we can have no certainty what this means. I will meet you here tomorrow morning."

"I'll go with you," volunteered Thomas eagerly.

"No, Thomas, stealth is key here. Speed, as well. I'll go it alone. You men rest. You may need all of your strength very soon."

Targus gathered up his map and tunic and bade the group farewell. Turning to John, he clasped the leader's arm firmly.

"Young Lykos, stay vigilant, but stay hopeful. Answers tomorrow morning, gentlemen!"

"Targus," called John, as the scout rushed toward the back door. Targus turned. "Take this map. It appears to be more accurate."

The scout smiled and made the exchange. A moment later, he was gone.

CHAPTER 6

▼

Siros entered the office in his riverside warehouse to find Titus hunched over a table, deep in concentration.

"It does a father good to see his son hard at work so early in the morning," Siros said in a booming voice.

"Good morning, Father," responded Titus, without looking up.

"What has you so engrossed that you barely acknowledge me?"

"Come and see."

The portly man drew alongside his seated son and strained his eyes at the object of Titus' attention.

"Last night's work?" Titus nodded. "Let me see, let me hold," Siros said eagerly.

Titus placed in his father's palm a bright coin of bronze. Siros repeatedly turned it over in his palm and then ran his index finger over its surface. He lifted the coin to his eyes and squinted at its markings.

"Getting too old for this," he groused as he moved toward the window where he could inspect the piece in the morning light. "Excellent likeness of Trajan. Is this Jaco's work?"

"His son's."

"Ah, the torch is passed." Siros continued his analysis, holding the coin at all angles against the light. "Uniform thickness. I see we have solved the problem of concavity. Countermarks look good." He held the coin in his palm. "Weight feels correct. Excellent work, my son. The chief magistrate of Tium will be quite pleased."

"Thank you, sir."

Siros returned the coin to Titus and walked over to the small eye-level door, where he could monitor the activity inside.

"Is everything prepared?" Siros asked, as he opened the door and peeked through. "What's this?" he demanded. "Why are they still here?"

"It was my idea," Titus replied, nervously.

"*Your* idea? I explicitly left instructions to shut down and clear out the workers, you thickheaded boy. This is a crucial meeting. Now get them out!"

"Wait, Father. Hear me out. I purposely have kept our operations running for Septimus' visit. Listen, he does not possess your remarkable visionary ability. He must have things laid out for him to see and handle, just as you did a moment ago with the coin. You saw him last night at the house. It was what he could see and touch that excited him. Words hold little sway with a man of his paltry intellect."

"Go on," said Siros, calming a bit.

"I want him to see what we produce and how it is done, to run his fingers through the harvest and smell its potential. Then we will have him, I guarantee it."

Siros pursed his lips in thought for a minute.

"It may work—very astute. Was this your thought, alone?"

"Yes, it was," Titus proudly responded.

A low sound, like the purr of a satisfied lion, emanated from Siros' throat, and he nodded in approval.

"The deputy should be here within the half-hour. I am going to freshen up."

The rumble of chariot wheels and stamping hooves announced the arrival of Septimus and his detachment of soldiers. The burly deputy swung down from the chariot and walked with a swagger toward the greeting party of Siros, Nikris and Dura.

"It is an unparalleled privilege for you to pay our humble business this visit, Your Honor," said Siros, loud enough for the soldiers to hear. "We trust that your stay with us will be rewarding."

"Rome thanks you for your cooperation in this survey of businesses we deem vital to its commerce," returned Septimus. "If you can show my men where they might take their ease, we will begin this tour promptly."

"Most assuredly, noble Septimus. Nikris, show the magistrate's detail to comfortable quarters and see that they have ample libations."

The Gaul escorted the men away. The ranking officer, a centurion, expressed a desire to stay with Septimus for protection, but the latter waved him off with an assurance that all would be well. Siros escorted Septimus into the office, where they joined Titus.

"Dura, please be so kind as to fetch our guest some refreshment. Wine, Septimus?"

"That'll do. And none of that weird honey. My head has yet to fully recover."

"Oh, no, no, no. We need you to be clear-thinking this morning, my friend."

Septimus downed the cup of wine with one pass and wiped his mouth with the back of his arm.

"Let's get to it, gentlemen."

Siros looked at Titus and frowned. He motioned to Dura, who then bolted the entrance door to the office and closed the window shutters. The room glowed with the light from the lamps on the wall. Nikris took his place behind Siros. The sound of guards could be heard assembling outside. Septimus watched these movements with curiosity. Satisfied that preparations were in order, Siros began.

"Over the course of several centuries, few people have had the privilege to view the scene you are about to experience. I exhort you to listen well and to watch carefully. You are entering a temple, so to speak. It is my temple, but I am only the trustee of an Order that dates back to a time that few people remember."

"I thought I was here to see a business operation?" interrupted Septimus. Siros silenced him with a finger.

"My boy, don't let your foolishness precede better judgment. The time for your crass behavior is over. Respect what I reveal to you, and the opportunity to partake of its fruit will be yours."

Septimus glanced around the room at the solemn expressions, then nodded and remained silent.

"Over six hundred years ago, Croesus, King of Lydia, mined the riverbeds of his kingdom for its gold and silver. In order to put this newfound wealth to practical use, he initiated the minting of coins, a creation that would change forever the world of commerce."

Septimus considered a curt remark, but thought better of it and held his tongue.

"I am of the lineage of those original artisans who served that august and clever monarch," Siros continued, "as is, of course, my son, Titus. Indeed, I trace my ancestry to the very house of Croesus. Linked by blood and spirit, we have been endowed by the gods with the same passion to acquire, to mold, even to manipulate the riches of the earth we trod." Siros' voice rose in a crescendo of self-aggrandizing fervor.

"And yet, just as Croesus seized the raw resources at his disposal and shrewdly transformed them into the opulence for which he is legendary, his progeny have, likewise, grasped the opportunity set before them, and they have assembled an engine of perpetual wealth, of which I am now both steward and beneficiary."

Septimus exhaled loudly.

"Look, Siros, I am not a man of words. If I may ask—and let me try to phrase this eloquently—what in the name of Zeus are you talking about?"

Siros grumbled something about dimwitted Romans, but it was inaudible to the rest of the group.

"Let me continue and you will understand. As conquerors came and went, the need and appreciation for our skills diminished. Our methods were appropriated, but not our talent. The wealth of the great house of Croesus was transferred to undeserving hands. Faced with prospects of poverty and servitude, my people decided to use their skill to restore themselves to prominence, and thus commenced the Order of Croesus."

"The Order of Croesus," repeated Septimus. "That name sounds vaguely familiar."

"Soon, you will be intimately acquainted. The Order is a sacred trust, a close-knit family, known only to a few. For centuries, the members of the Order have handed down to successive generations the intricacies of precise coin making, and the benefits have been considerable. The building in which you now sit is the nucleus of our operation."

"Okay, I understand now," said Septimus. "You fellows make coins. I think that's great, I really do. I knew a man in Rome who did the same thing. It's honest work and a great skill. So tell me, why all the secrecy?"

Siros smiled at the deputy and shuddered with laughter. Septimus, confused, looked at the other men.

"What did I say?" the deputy asked.

"It was just something that tickled me," said Siros, "the part about honest work."

"Right. It's honest work. So what?"

Titus joined the conversation.

"Septimus, where are the imperial mints?"

The deputy thought for a moment.

"Well, Rome, of course. Around here, I guess Nicomedia, and maybe Pergamum."

"And Diakropolis?"

"I wouldn't think so."

"You are correct," Titus replied. "There is no *imperial* mint in Diakropolis."

"Then for whom are you making coins?"

As soon as the question left the deputy's lips, an unmistakable expression of comprehension came over Septimus' face, as if he had just witnessed an illicit act. First, his eyes flashed wide as the revelation hit him, then, they narrowed in moral judgment on the perpetrators and, finally, they came to rest, half-closed, as Septimus contemplated the potential benefits of such knowledge.

"I can read on your face that you understand the nature of our enterprise," said Siros. "Yes, the Order of Croesus learned long ago how to use its expertise for personal gain. It has taken diligence, cunning, and a strong measure of cooperation from strategically placed authorities, such as you. Over the years, we have amassed power and wealth that are not to be trifled with. Throughout Bithynia, and even beyond, we are the rulers of those who rule, the creditors of those who lend."

Septimus laughed uncomfortably.

"Dare I ask my role in all this?"

"It is ironic," continued Siros, "that in the hub of our enterprise, the seemingly insignificant town of Diakropolis, we find the one chink in our armor, the Achilles' heel that threatens our immortality."

"What might that be?"

"We are without an ally."

"I thought you implied that you controlled those in power."

"We did, until your brother came."

"Marcellus?" Septimus tightened his lip and nodded. "Yes, I see. He wouldn't go for this at all. What did he say when you asked him?"

"Come now, Septimus, we're not that careless. He knows nothing of the Order or of this operation. However, he is drawing close."

"In what way?"

"His obsession with cleaning up the river. He actually paid us a visit not too long ago—in a boat."

"A boat? Marcellus? When?"

"The day before he left for Nicomedia. He saw nothing, but he is on the scent."

"That could be fatal to your little outfit here."

"It will not cause a *ripple* of disturbance," hissed Siros. "We will see to that."

"Sorry, sorry," Septimus vigorously apologized. "I didn't mean to unsettle you. Let's go back to my role."

"As I told you last night, the governor will offer your brother the office of chief magistrate in Prusa. We will make it difficult to decline. You then will be installed as chief over Diakropolis, despite your assertions that Linus would never do such a thing. At that point, we will have our ally, and the threat will pass. You will have the thing you crave—wealth beyond measure, and absolute license to do with it what you will."

"And if I refuse?"

"Septimus…" interjected Titus.

"Hold your tongue, Titus. Let the man speak," said Siros.

"This is all well and good, your clandestine mint and so forth," Septimus continued, "but what if I decide to adhere to my principles and decline your offer? I may not wish to affiliate with counterfeiters."

"That is your prerogative, my friend. However, choices carry consequences. If you do decide to exercise so foolish an option—and let me apologize in advance for being so graphic—Nikris and his men will relieve you of your miserable, principled existence. Take your time to decide."

Septimus stared at the merchant, sitting smugly with arms folded, and marveled at how trivially the man spoke of such acts of violence. The deputy weighed his options. *It really won't hurt anybody. Marcellus and Claudia will be on to bigger and better things. Marcellus doesn't need the distraction of having to drag me along and keep me out of trouble. This way, I can get my independence and some esteem in my own right. But, is it wrong? This game has been going on for a long time and I can't say that people are miserable over it. The empire loses a little bit, but it's a drop in the sea.* Septimus studied the expressionless face of Nikris, with its set jaw and tense muscles. The deputy knew that he stared into the eyes of a cool, dispassionate assassin.

"All right, gentlemen. I'm in."

Siros smiled broadly as Titus rushed to shake Septimus' hand. Dura looked at Nikris with raised eyebrow. The Gaul remained stone-faced.

"Excellent choice, Magistrate. Now we must have a toast and then some fun—a tour of our little enterprise."

CHAPTER 7

▼

"Come, gentlemen," Siros said merrily, with arms outstretched. "Let us escort our guest on a tour of our humble enterprise."

Siros led the group from the office to a small corridor that ended in a large, wooden door. Nikris stayed close to the deputy to discourage any notion of escape. The door opened into a large storehouse filled with carts and amphorae. Septimus labored to catch his breath in the stale, dusty atmosphere. A number of workers were seen moving briskly as they transferred containers from one end to the other.

"I'll let you do the honors, Titus," said Siros.

"This is our grain warehouse," began the son, talking loudly over the noise of the activity.

"Grain?" asked a puzzled Septimus.

"Yes, grain. We are legitimate businessmen, as well. The grain comes in by oxcart in those large amphorae you see stacked against the wall. Those large doors at the far end of the room open to the street." Septimus peered across the storeroom in the direction that Titus pointed, trying to look interested. "The grain is sifted and transferred to the hold of barges that lie in waiting at the wharf just beyond those doors there." Septimus dutifully shifted his gaze to the opposite end of the room and nodded. "Then the barges are floated down the river to the sea, where our merchant ships distribute the produce throughout the empire."

"This is all incredibly interesting, Titus, but what does it have to do with what we were talking about inside?" Titus led the deputy to a collection of large jars set apart from the others that were still full of grain. "Pick one of these up."

Septimus shrugged his shoulders and obliged. He casually stooped down, took hold of the amphora handles, and gave a jerk. The jar did not give. He smiled at the others who watched without expression. Again, Septimus attempted to lift the jar, grunting as he heaved, but he managed only to raise it an inch.

"What gives?" asked the deputy.

"As you have experienced, those jars obviously are laden with more than grain," continued Titus. "The caravans make a key stop along the way to our facility. There, the bottoms of the jars are filled with raw copper before being covered with the grain."

"I see," nodded Septimus. "Where is this key stop, may I ask?"

Titus looked at Siros.

"He may as well know all, my boy," said the patriarch. "He *is* one of us now."

"There is a mine southwest of here, about a half-day's ride. No one knows of it. It is ours."

"A copper mine—near Diakropolis?" asked Septimus. "And Rome is not aware of it?"

"It is not very accessible," intoned Siros. "And it is heavily guarded."

"How did you come by this, Siros?" inquired the deputy.

"I inherited the property. Centuries ago, the Order needed a base of operations. The gold and silver mines of Lydia had been tapped out, and new sources of raw material were vital. Copper was most desirable. It attracted much less attention than the more precious metals. Usually, those sources were immediately confiscated by the current ruler. Besides, the Order had discovered that there was greater safety in counterfeiting bronze coinage. This was distributed among the common folk, who were ignorant and easily deceived."

"So, you just happened upon this little mine while on an outing?" asked Septimus.

"It was not quite that easy. Our sources informed us of a hidden vein in the hills above the tiny, fortified colony where the Old City now stands. Our reconnaissance showed that, indeed, a relatively untapped source of copper was located there, but that the rights belonged to the colony's chief."

"Let me guess what happened next. An unexplained disease ran rampant through the colony, killing all inhabitants?"

"Septimus, please," protested the obese leader. "What do you take us for, common criminals?"

"Oh, no. You are definitely uncommon," chuckled the deputy. "But, go on."

"The colony was inhabited by a tribe of Celts—Gauls, as we call them. They displaced the Greeks who had founded the city—rather violently, as Gauls are wont to do." Siros looked over at Nikris and winked. "Being no match for the Gauls in battle, a hostile takeover was ruled out. The Order decided that a mutually beneficial partnership would be most practical. The colonists were, of course, fond of their bronze farm implements and tools of war, but they were not especially skilled at the extracting and smelting of the ore. The Gauls were not easily persuaded, being by nature a suspicious, barbaric race." Siros again glanced at Nikris, but failed to get any response. "In the end, however, a treaty was struck. Possession of the mine was ours. In time, so was the city, as the lust for war and new territory moved the tribe on. Since that time, some four hundred years ago, the Order has been based here in Diakropolis."

"Are you saying that the Old City is entirely in your possession?" asked Septimus, with eyes wide.

"Entirely. It may not appear that way in the public records, but follow all paths backward and you will see that it is so."

"We give our employees food and shelter—all subsidized at a fraction of the normal expense," added Dura. "In return, they work hard without grumbling. It's idyllic."

"Amazing," responded the deputy, as he ran his fingers through his hair. "This is good. I'm beginning to like this town."

"Excellent, Magistrate. We want you to be happy here. Go on with the tour, Titus. We digress."

"The ore is taken to another part of the warehouse where it is purified and cast. We'll go there next."

The party moved through the large storeroom. Workers stole brief glances at the men as they passed, but dared not stop or gawk. Septimus watched as the workers silently went about their duties. The stronger ones emptied the contents of the jars into sifters, where the grain was separated from the ore. Other workers collected the metal in small crates that were placed inside a small waist-level door, located across the room. Still other workers transferred the sifted grain back into jars and transported them to the loading area. A few swept the residue, both vegetable and mineral, into a large grate in the center of the floor. Septimus strained to see what was beyond the grate. He could hear the sound of running water.

"Where does that lead?" he asked.

"It's an underground channel leading from the river. It supplies the Old City fountains with water and provides drainage on its way back—an aqueduct and sewer all in one, you might say. It was constructed with the old fortification to ensure water in the event of siege."

"You said it leads *from* the river to the fountains? So the people draw their water from…"

"Yes. It's not ideal, but it's what we have to deal with. The people don't complain."

"I'm sure they are regularly given a chance to voice their opinion," mused Septimus.

Septimus noted that the workers mostly were women, with some older children and a few, somewhat feeble, older men. The only able-bodied men that the deputy saw were posted at various intervals, obviously as guards. They were similar in appearance to Nikris.

"Where are all the male workers?" asked the deputy. "I would think that you'd need some brawn."

"Primarily, they labor at the mines," explained Titus.

"Those fellows over there, the guards," said Septimus. "They are Gauls, too?"

"A few of them. Most are just dressed that way. It keeps the employees in the proper frame of mind."

"What about the big fellow here?" Septimus asked, poking an elbow into the belly of Nikris, who remained close at his side. Siros chuckled.

"Nikris is one hundred percent Gaul, I assure you, both in physique and attitude. He will dismember you in a moment's time, if I give the word."

Septimus looked up at the menacing face of the giant, then turned to his host and smiled.

"Please, don't give it."

Titus showed Septimus the wharf, where several barges lay at harbor, awaiting their cargo. The deputy peered out over the slowly moving river.

"So this is what has Marcellus' dander up. I've seen worse."

"Oh my, yes," responded Siros. "I do wish that your brother would set his mind on other things."

"He has a thing about dirty water. It's personal." Septimus clapped his hands and briskly rubbed them together. "Nice front you have here, gentlemen. Now, when am I going to tour the *real* operation?"

"Not so loud, Magistrate," scolded Siros. "We make no reference of such things outside closed quarters. Besides, sound travels well over water. Titus, let's grant Septimus his wish."

The group moved to the wall with the small door, inside which the ore was placed. Titus rapped on a heavy wooden door and waited. After a moment, he heard the sound of a bolt being worked and then the thick door opened. Septimus was led into a stuffy, hot, windowless room, where at least a dozen men could be seen intensely occupied in some yet unknown activity.

"Behold!" announced Siros, his glistening, reddened face beaming as he swept his arm across the scene. "The creation of wealth lies before you!" Septimus stood motionless and observed, his tongue unconsciously traveling across his lips. "Don't speak, Magistrate. Simply drink in the view."

Septimus' eyes passed slowly from point-to-point. Several of the men were hunched over workbenches, their work brightly illuminated by multiple lamps. They made no sound as they cocked their heads in unison to examine the visitor who interrupted their concentration. Other men, drenched with sweat, stood near a furnace, their leather aprons charred from splashes of molten metal. There was a strong smell of copper in the room. The deputy looked over at Siros, who stood with his eyes closed and nostrils flared as he drank deeply of the smell.

"Let me introduce you," said Titus, breaking the silence. He led Septimus to the furnace. "Gentlemen, we have an official visitor. He is the deputy magistrate..."

"Soon-to-be chief magistrate," interrupted Siros.

"Indeed, future chief magistrate of Diakropolis. He will be our liaison as we work with the Romans to ensure that all remains orderly in our region." The men nodded politely. "Let's begin over at the furnace."

As they drew near the blazing oven, Septimus shuddered at the intensity of the heat and he marveled at the stamina of the men who could labor for so long in that environment.

"Halix, brief the magistrate on your function."

"Certainly, sir," said the oldest of the apron-clad men. His skin was dark and leathery and his face was etched with deep lines, highlighted with copper dust. "We are responsible for melting down the raw ore into a usable form. We wash away the impurities and add other metals to create the proper alloy, depending on the product needed."

"Other metals?" asked Septimus.

"We import tin from Britain and Spain; zinc and lead come from more nearby sources," explained Titus. "Go on, Halix."

"The molten metal is then cast into blanks, or flans, which then go over to Jaco and his team for stamping."

"We have pioneered the use of multiple molds," added Dura. "This has increased our production many times over."

"Is it hard to achieve the purity of official coins?" asked Septimus.

"My dear Magistrate," interjected Siros. "Remember, we are the craftsmen who created this art. The question is, does the purity of the official coinage meet our standards? It is typical to hear of those falsely accused of distributing illegal tender because they had in their possession both our coins and the official currency. Ours was judged authentic."

"My apologies," offered the deputy.

"No offense intended, I'm sure. Let us continue."

"Laertes is in charge of seeing that the image is stamped on the blank. Laertes, explain how this is done for the magistrate."

A muscular man rose from his bench and addressed the party.

"We use dies of hardened bronze with a high tin content. The lower die is set into an anvil, like that on my bench. The upper die is set into this iron punch. See here?" Laertes held up the die for Septimus to inspect. "From there, it's easy. Just place the blank on the lower die, and wallop the end of the punch with a mallet a couple of times." Laertes demonstrated as he spoke, striking the end of the upper die twice in rapid succession. "There you go," he said, holding up the coin. He flipped it to the deputy. "Go buy yourself a drink."

Siros frowned at the man and snatched the coin out of Septimus' fingers.

"Please, Laertes, not until it's properly recorded in the ledger." Siros handed the freshly minted coin to Dura, and then addressed Septimus.

"You'll have plenty of these in time."

"Laertes makes a difficult process seem easy," continued Titus, "but the exact centration, angle, and force necessary to create this coin are skills that have taken years to learn. I daresay you could make a thousand attempts and not produce a single acceptable coin, Septimus."

Laertes nodded proudly and returned to his bench.

"One final station to inspect, Magistrate. Begging the pardon of the other craftsmen in this room, but this is the key to our enterprise."

Titus ushered the deputy to a pair of benches where two men stood. One was a short, balding man with deep-set eyes and a thin beard. The other appeared as his double, only younger and clean-shaven. On their benches were dozens of small tools: punches, chisels, and drill-bits tipped with abrasives.

"Allow me to introduce Jaco and his son, Antaris. You will not find more skilled engravers in the entire empire, I assure you." The pair bowed. "Theirs is a skill that has been passed down from generation to generation within the Order. Feast your eyes on their handsome work."

Septimus drew close to Antaris' bench and inspected a die currently in progress. On it was a partial image of the emperor.

"His nose is a little larger," said the deputy.

"I was not responsible for the original," responded the young engraver, who then pointed at the template coin lying on his table.

Septimus held the coin next to the die and nodded his head.

"I retract my statement, young Antaris. You are an artist, indeed." Antaris nodded confidently. "I trust that you pay them as handsomely as their work, Siros."

"You will not find any of these men residing in the Old City, I assure you," responded the leader.

Septimus bade farewell to the workers as he was led back into the office. The heat of the minting room had produced a powerful thirst, and Septimus drained two goblets of wine in little time. Siros addressed the deputy after he was through with his refreshment.

"There it is, Septimus—the Order of Croesus. Of course, this is only the hub of a vast wheel. Throughout the land, you will become acquainted with men and women of distinction who are part of our ranks. Some figure prominently in the day-to-day affairs of government, others control the lanes of commerce—all are fantastically wealthy. This is what you have bought into, my son. As you can see, it is not a dream. You have handled the product yourself. Each of those coins represents a key that can unlock true happiness. All that is required of you now is your unquenchable devotion, your utmost secrecy, your—oh, I may as well say it—your life. Yes, your life is no longer your own. It must be united with that of the Order. No longer do you operate independently of the Order. It is as if you have died to yourself, and you are reborn with a completely new identity."

Septimus swallowed hard.

"Now, don't be fearful, Magistrate. We all have taken this vow of absolute obedience to the Order. In time, you no longer become conscious that your will must be subject to that of Croesus. Do you think about breathing? No, it is natural. And so it will be with this."

"What now?" asked Septimus. "Are there initiation rites? Do I sign some pledge or cut my wrist in some secret ceremony?"

"No, no, my good man. You have executed the contract with your eyes."

"What do you mean?"

Siros leaned forward and smiled.

"No one sees what you have seen and walks away, my friend," he said calmly with a smile. "You have accepted the terms already. Unless, of course..." Siros nodded toward Nikris.

Septimus understood Siros' intent.

"No, I said I was in, so I'm in. Now, when do I get rich?"

"You already are, Septimus, you already are." The deputy held out his hands in puzzlement and looked at the others. "Oh, bother with these concrete Romans. Dura, give him some spending money."

The Syrian handed the excited official a small purse containing a number of coins. Septimus promptly emptied the bag into his hand and fingered the money. "Is this...?"

"It is real, Magistrate. As fond as we are of our product, we of the Order only partake of official currency. What you see being made here travels throughout the province and beyond, and returns to us in the form of other goods."

"Which you then sell for legal tender. Very nice." A satisfied Septimus replaced the money in the purse and tucked it under his belt. Siros announced that the meeting was over and asked if the deputy had any more questions.

"Just one," replied the deputy as they exited the office. "Your workers—are they all slaves?"

"Technically, no," responded Siros.

"What do you mean, *technically?*"

"Slaves are purchased and are the property of the owner."

"So these people willingly do this work?"

"Again, technically, no." Septimus looked confused. "They have no choice."

"So, they are not slaves, but have no choice whether they work for you or not. Confound it, Siros! Must every simple question have a cryptic answer?"

"Maybe the question wasn't as simple as you thought. Here, I'll give you a ride home and I will reveal the final piece of the puzzle to you. It is most delightful." The men came upon the sedan chair with its waiting transporters. Septimus looked at the chair, which was just barely big enough for the rotund merchant.

"Both of us—in there?"

"No, I will send for my coach. I do not prefer the smell of horses as a rule, but, with your company, it should go unnoticed on this trip."

Septimus did not know how to take that remark, but he accepted the offer. The soldiers spilled out of a nearby building, richer from games of chance, but less sober. The deputy waved for the centurion to go on ahead with the men. Siros' coach followed with his personal bodyguard. He waited to speak until the noise of the procession hid their conversation.

"The Order has not always been as productive as you observed this morning," Siros began. "Obviously, over hundreds of years, conditions fluctuate. New monarchies bring new challenges, and we have had to adjust with the times. Initially, a small circle of individuals managed the operation but as demand for our services increased, more laborers were required. However, we especially have flourished under the Romans. Their insatiable lust for money and recklessness in pursuing it has created a fertile climate for expansion."

Septimus opened his mouth to protest but could not think of anything to say in defense.

"We went the way of the slave market at first, but eventually found it to be costly and unreliable," Siros continued. "Slaves are unscrupulous and require too much oversight. Periodically, a handful of the more astute slaves would comprehend what we were about, and then they would try to usurp control of the operation, as if they could manage it for even half a day. This went on for a number of years. The final straw came about twenty years ago when a full-scale uprising was attempted. The slaves were no match for our Gauls, of course."

"What became of the slaves?" asked Septimus.

"We couldn't have a contingent of hostile slaves on our hands, could we? We put them all in an abandoned shaft in the mine and buried them."

"Case closed."

"Case closed. As a result, however, we were poorly outfitted with workers. We tried to avoid slaves, but we were at a loss as to a suitable replacement. The answer lay in the great fire of Rome."

"I presume that you mean Nero's fire."

"Yes. What devastation. Especially intriguing was the way he handled the issue of fault in the matter. As you may recall, to deflect suspicion that he had engineered the conflagration to rebuild the city to his tastes, Nero accused the small but insubordinate religious cult called Christians."

"I remember. He made good sport of them."

"Yes, quite a show," Siros said wistfully. "Only Nero could have been so creative with his abominations. Imagine—human torches for his gardens. How delightfully vile."

"So, what did that have to do with the Order?"

"Amazingly, the Christians did not protest Nero's persecution. In fact, the miscreants seemed to embrace the whole thing as a point of honor—something about being worthy of their god, the promise of paradise, or some such nonsense. Someone—I forget whom, maybe it was my uncle—suggested that if these Christians were so keen on mistreatment, we should round some up and put them to work. The problem was that there were so few in the region, unlike in the southern cities. However, we were able to procure a handful."

"Procure?" asked Septimus. "How?"

"We offered them prosperity and freedom in the fertile farmlands of Bithynia. It seems that even Christians are not above the enticements of a better life in the here and now. They are quite gullible. I mean, look at the superstition they hold to."

"Didn't they find out it was all a trick?"

Siros laughed. "Most definitely."

"How did you keep them from revolting?"

"Quite simple. The able-bodied men were sent to the mine, while their families were housed in the Old City, where they worked on the wharf. The men were threatened with the safety of their wives and children, and vice versa."

"And those who bucked the plan?"

"The stiff-necked were subjected to your law—prosecuted as enemies of the empire. Even then, we realized some return on the effort. You'd be surprised to see how much a troop of Christians will fetch from the promoters of the games."

Siros reached for a basket of figs and placed several into his mouth. Septimus stared for a moment at the grinning man, smacking his lips as he chewed.

"So some of those workers I saw are Christians?"

"All of them. In time, the religion exploded in the area, primarily due to the efforts of one man called Lykos. He presented quite a conundrum for us. We needed him to increase the supply of workers, but his meddling in our affairs was annoying."

"He knew of the mine?"

"I doubt that he did. He mostly sought to undermine the games. He didn't think that it was very sporting for those of his religion, and he devised a way to steal them from us and send them off to safety. He was quite resourceful. We could have used his skills. Recently, however, I have come to suspect that he has learned of the mine and has reactivated his operation."

"Why not eliminate him? You seem well stocked with men and weapons."

Siros contorted his face as he recalled the failed past attempts at carrying out Septimus' suggestion. "He did not come by his name for naught. Many times he slipped through my grasp. Indeed, I am not certain he even exists today. He would be uncommonly old. Yet," he mused, "another may have taken his name and mission." Siros' thoughts drifted away and there was a momentary silence.

"Back to these Christians," said Septimus. "As plentiful as they are now, how are you enticing them away from their homes and farms?"

"Simple. We abduct them."

Septimus suspiciously eyed the merchant. "You kidnap them?"

"That is correct."

"And all of this with the approval of the local rulers?"

"Most definitely. They prosper, as well. The chief magistrates of Diakropolis have been our strongest supporters; that is, until…"

"I know, I know," apologized Septimus, thinking of Marcellus. "But, there are others who might protest."

"Although I hold no formal office and to the outsider I am only a tribe leader, I control all the elected positions."

"Are you serious?"

"I don't jest about such things, my friend. Marcellus was allowed to install you as his deputy, but all of the lower magistracies are my appointments. The town secretary, the market controller, the treasurers of the oil and grain fund—these are my men." Siros raised his brow and sniffed. "I even own the gymnasiarchs, for that matter."

Septimus began to realize that he was dealing with a truly powerful man. He was curious how such an operation could remain unexposed for so many years, and now he had his answer. The leadership of Diakropolis was no different from the larger cities of Bithynia, just on a smaller scale. The chief magistrate, or *protos archon,* presided over the lesser magistrates, or *archontes,* who formed a type of city council. These leaders ostensibly were elected by the people, as were the various other positions of authority: the secretary and the overseers of the market, public treasuries, census, gymnasiums and sporting events. Officially, Siros was a tribe leader, or phylarch, a middle-class position not considered worthy of the so-called first men of the town. Theoretically, Siros was not qualified to hold office. As was becoming abundantly clear to Septimus, however, the entire power structure of Diakropolis was in Siros' grasp.

"I apologize, Siros, I really do."

"For what?" mumbled the portly merchant.

"I always made you out to be an ordinary thug, but you're not. You are one exceptionally nasty piece of work."

Siros licked his fingers and nodded.

"I take that as a compliment."

Septimus leaned his head back and reflected on all that he had seen and heard that morning; he shook his head. One day earlier, he lived in the most tiresome, lackluster city in the empire but, now, even Rome itself ran a distant second to Diakropolis for opportunity. The deputy ran his finger along the gilded frame of the coach. Such opulence soon would be his to command. Then an unwelcome thought slipped into his grandiose thoughts. *Marcellus would not approve of this.* Septimus tensed his jaw. *Who cares what Marcellus thinks? Must I always play by his rules? He would sooner have me live out my life licking the boots of some bureau-crat and counting heads of grain. This kind of opportunity presents itself once, if at all. Only a fool would say no.* Septimus resolved that nothing his brother could say would persuade him otherwise. Nevertheless, a heated debate with the chief magistrate commenced within his mind:

Septimus, you are uniting with a thief who robs from your own people.

This is not robbery, Marcellus. No one is taking anything from the people. The money is passed freely without knowledge, disrupting no transactions.

But Septimus, the man is a kidnapper—he accosts and holds people against their will.

Marcellus, you know that these Christians are great nuisances and technically should die. Why not put them to use, rather than clog the judicial system and drain the public coffers?

The silent argument raged in the deputy's head, Marcellus prosecuting, Septimus deftly countering each point. Still, he did not feel victorious.

The coach turned onto the road that led to the official quarters. Siros broke the silence.

"You have seen and heard a great deal this morning, Septimus. Yet, we have not specifically discussed your role."

"I thought you needed me to keep the local government out of your business. You know, divert the eyes of Rome to other things."

"Well put, my son, and we do need you to be attentive to those matters."

The coach slowed as it neared its destination. Siros leaned close to Septimus' ear and spoke in a hushed tone.

"However, there are other duties that are equally important. From time-to-time, our labor force becomes depleted, what with unfortunate accidents, illness, transfers…"

"Transfers?" Septimus interrupted.

"Yes. We have other enterprises that don't concern you at this time. As I was saying, when we become too thin with workers, it becomes necessary to replenish the ranks. I won't burden you with details of our methods for apprehending fresh recruits but, suffice it to say, we need prompt execution of justice at those critical junctures."

"And prompt it will be," assured the deputy. "There is no love lost between me and the Christians."

"Ah, yes, I seem to recall that it was an altercation with one of them that landed you in arrears with me. What was his name?"

"Alexander."

"Yes, that's it, Alexander. Fine handicapper before he lost his senses."

"Fine? Goaded me into ten-to-one odds on a long shot with money I didn't have. Then he sneaks off to join the Christians. All the gods in the Pantheon couldn't save him from my wrath. You remember. I helped you nab a whole group of them that night."

"I recall very well how instrumental you were in the success of our incursion, my dear man. That is just the sort of thing we will need to do from time to time. Of course, as chief magistrate, we don't expect you to do the hands-on work. Just pass sentence in a timely fashion and all will be well."

"By the way, when will I know whether the office is to be mine?"

"I expect a messenger with the good news at any time. We will offer to transport your niece and Marcellus' belongings immediately upon his acceptance of Prusa, so your installation could be very soon. Until then, keep all that you know well-hidden in your demeanor."

The driver brought the coach to a halt outside the magistrate's office.

"Here we are," said Siros, patting his thighs. "It has been an eventful day. And look, your aide awaits you."

Siros pointed toward Jason, who had emerged from the door armed with a disapproving expression and an armload of documents. Septimus groaned at the sight of the pesky assistant.

"That is one piece of Marcellus' baggage that I personally will pack."

The deputy thanked Siros for the ride and disembarked, ignoring Jason as he strode into the building. Siros chuckled quietly to himself, watching the aide gesturing wildly as he chased behind the deputy. The steady cadence of Siros' silent, breathy laughter was replaced by the slow rhythm of heavy breathing. He was asleep.

CHAPTER 8

▼

Pellas rolled out of his cot in the predawn darkness and shivered. He had not slept well and he felt irritable and stiff. He splashed his face with chilly water from a nearby basin and wiped it with a ragged towel. The farmer quietly went about his morning duties, taking care to not wake Cecilia. He stoked the embers in the small fireplace that served as an oven and watched as the fire came to life. Before long, the small house was filled with the aroma of roasted rabbit. Cecilia stirred in her small bedroom and coughed.

With frugality, Pellas meted out the provisions brought from Diakropolis by Philip. Pellas gave Cecilia double portions of the more nutritious stores to speed her recovery. The early morning light began to filter into the smoke-filled room from the small opening above the hearth, creating a shaft of gray that slowly stole across the room as the light intensified. Pellas sat and chewed a piece of bread and thought about building a new house, perhaps next to the stream as Philip suggested, one with a proper room for the girl and proper ventilation. Pellas took Cecilia her breakfast and cleaned her room while she ate.

"Sit down, Father, and visit."

"No, dear, I have a lot of chores to do and the morning already is old."

"What are you going to do today?"

"I am trying to make the plow serviceable. Planting season will come sooner than we expect. I am hoping to get two plantings in this year to try to catch up on last year's loss."

"Is Philip going to be staying on with us to help?"

"Oh, I don't know. I wouldn't count on it. He just showed up one day. He could just as easily move on unexpectedly. A boy like him probably has wild dreams that don't include farm work."

"Have you asked him?"

"Cecilia, I don't have anything with which to pay the young man."

"What is keeping him here now, then?"

"Hard to say, but that's why I'm trying to get as much as I can out of him while I can."

"Don't run him off, Father."

"I'm not running him off," protested Pellas, adding in a quiet voice, "at least I'm trying not to do so."

"Where has Philip been sleeping?"

Pellas peered out the window at the hills drenched in the morning mists.

"I fixed him a place in the stable."

"That certainly should keep him from leaving," said Cecilia, sarcastically. "Don't you think he would be more comfortable in the house?"

"Out of the question!" Pellas said in a huff. "He knows nothing of you, remember? And it is to stay that way!" Pellas firmly kissed his daughter on the forehead. "Now, I'm off. I will check on you later."

After tidying up from breakfast, Pellas headed outside to the stable. It already was shaping up to be a fine day, as patches of blue began to show through the thinning fog. The farmer opened the door of the stable and listened for sounds of activity. All was quiet except for the shifting feet of the animals and the noisy breathing of Philip, who still was fast asleep, wrapped in a blanket on a pile of straw. Pellas walked heavily over to his worktable, trying to create as much noise as possible to rouse the young man. The farmer already had retired by the time Philip returned from town the previous evening, and he searched the contents of two sacks for the part he had ordered. The first sack was full of foodstuffs; the sight brought a slight smile of relief to the farmer. He rummaged through the second sack and pulled out several pieces of hardware. He took an iron pin over to his plow and fit it in position.

"Thunder!" he bellowed, startling the animals and Philip.

"What...what happened?" asked the young man, frantically looking from side-to-side.

"This piece is too small! I thought I sent the broken part with you. Didn't you give it to the smith?"

"I did, I did," protested Philip, wiping a piece of straw from his mouth. "Just as you told me."

"Then Argo has not been spending enough time tending his craft! A whole day lost!" Pellas spat on the ground and kicked at the dust. Philip stretched.

"I suppose I could go back today."

"You don't know enough to tell if you've got the wrong part or not."

"Oh, I don't know. I think I could recognize the difference."

Pellas did not reply but studied the iron piece in his hand.

"Why don't you go for it, Pellas?" asked Philip.

"What, me?" replied the farmer, surprised and immediately uncomfortable with the suggestion.

"Yes, you. It's going to be a beautiful day. The walk is nice and Argo said that you haven't been around for a while."

"And what else did that old goat tell you of me?" demanded Pellas.

"Nothing." Philip saw a look of suspicion in Pellas' eyes. "Honestly, nothing. Look, the change of pace would do you good. I could even go with you, if you'd like."

"I don't need advice from you, young man," Pellas said coldly.

"If you are concerned I can show you the way."

"I know the way, boy. I was walking it before you were born!"

"Oh, sorry," Philip said contritely. "I guess you're right about that." Philip thought for a moment. "If you're worried about leaving the farm, I'll keep a good eye on things."

"Just keep quiet and let me think," Pellas said gruffly.

He looked down at the pin in the palm of his hand and considered his choices. *The boy probably could get the right part. Argo just handed him the wrong piece. Unless the smith knew it was wrong, and he's just trying to draw me into town. But what does he care about me? He knows where I live. If he wanted me, he'd just come here. It would be nice to walk to town, though. The boy is right. I could use a change of pace. Make sure that Argo is not spreading reports. Maybe visit the graves. But what about Cecilia? I can't risk leaving him here with her. Pellas sighed. I could give the boy a job to do that would be sure to keep him away from the house. I know, I'll send him off on that harebrained idea of running water down to the house. That will occupy him for a day.*

Pellas turned to Philip.

"I think I *will* take that trip to town."

"Excellent! Do you want company?"

"No, but I have a job for you. I've been thinking about that idea of yours to run water to the house. I'd like to begin."

"Begin? Now?" asked Philip, somewhat nervously.

"Yes, now. What I'd like for you to do today is to find a suitable takeoff point upstream and construct a dam."

"A dam?"

"Yes. You know, like beavers make."

"Why a dam?"

Pellas quickly rummaged for a reasonable answer.

"Well," he began uncertainly, "We need a reservoir of some sort from which to draw the water."

"Why not just divert the stream and make the reservoir down here at the house? I could begin digging that now and we could explore the stream together another day."

"No, that won't do at all," responded the farmer abruptly. "Do it my way," Pellas said pointedly, then added, "Please."

Philip considered another attempt at changing the farmer's mind, but he figured that it would only anger the man.

"All right. Your way."

"You'll want to eat up at the stream so that you can keep working. I'll fetch some provisions for you. Gather your tools. It's a difficult walk back so you don't want to forget anything." Pellas wanted to be more explicit in his instructions to make sure that Philip avoided the house, but he feared arousing the young man's suspicions. "You should still be hard at work up there when I return."

"I don't think it will take that long, Pellas."

"I'm sure it will, that is, if you are planning on doing a quality job."

Pellas went into the house and informed Cecilia that he was going to be working the land far from the house. He left extra food for lunch at her bedside table and said that he would be back to give her supper at the proper time. Satisfied that everything she might need was at hand, Pellas then returned with food and drink for Philip, and the farmer sent the young man on his way up the hill to the stream. Pellas knew that Philip's idea to construct a reservoir near the house was best, but Pellas could deal with that later. He did not set out for town until Philip had disappeared into the woods above the farm. As the farmer quickly moved down the path toward the road to Diakropolis, he cast a watchful eye over his shoulder one last time to ensure that all was in order. Pellas drew a deep breath as he turned off the lane onto the road.

Cecilia lay in her bed, staring at the ceiling, her prayers and devotions completed. Now came the period of oppressive boredom that she despised so greatly. It was during this time that she did daily battle with the dark forces of self-pity and despair. Some days, her spirits were light and the gloom easily could be dispelled. Today was not one of those days. She looked about her cramped room and sighed. There was little furniture and the drab walls and small window did little to cheer her. An urn sat empty on a table next to the wall, yearning to be filled with something colorful and cheering. Her recovery had progressed to the point where she could move herself from bed to chair and back again, but there was no strength in her legs.

Realizing that he would need to spend more time tending the fields, Pellas had constructed special furniture that would allow Cecilia to do more for herself. He sawed the wooden bed frame in two and hinged the two parts. Using a rope and pulley secured to a rafter, Cecilia could elevate her head at will. A makeshift bedside latrine was essential, although it was the most poignant reminder of lost ability. Hanging on the wall within arm's reach was the bell that once called Pellas in from the fields for dinner. In case of emergency, the girl could summon help from even the farthest point on the property. She was surrounded by functionality and it strained the limits of her vast optimism.

Cecilia wondered if the Master had forgotten her. There had been no visitors or messages. Was it true, as her father had said, that the Master and his followers were simply exploiting others? Cecilia vigorously shook her head at that thought and she reminded herself of her father's vehement anger toward the Christians. Certainly, it was Pellas who was preventing any communication with her fellow believers. Indeed, she was unaware of how fervently the Master sought to send someone to check on her health. The aged leader anguished over telling Philip about the girl, in the end presuming that it would do more harm than good. As long as Pellas was adamant about keeping Philip away from the farmhouse and the food supplies seemed to be disappearing faster than anticipated, the Master assumed that Cecilia was alive and well.

Cecilia spied her tablet and stylus lying on the table against the wall. She scolded herself for not reminding her father to place it next to her bed when he left. *I wonder if I could get to it?* She studied the problem carefully. The tablet was just out of arm's reach if she was sitting on the chair adjacent to the bed. *From the chair, I can probably lean over and just make the table. Of course, if I fall, I'll be taking my nap on the floor. Well, here I go.*

The girl pulled herself up in the bed and scooted into the adjacent chair. *So far, so good. Perhaps if I rock the chair I can slide closer.* She swayed back and forth, but nearly tipped over, and she decided that this was not a wise approach. Cecilia decided to return to her initial plan and she sat as straight as possible. With outstretched arms she leaned slowly to her left, watching carefully to make sure that her hands grasped the edge of the table. Soon she passed the point where she could no longer right herself. Her hand landed firmly on the tabletop, stopping her progress. *Now if I can just tip my chair a little bit more I can reach the tablet. Closer...closer.*

Everything happened in the blink of an eye. How the chair slipped out from under her and the table lurched forward, Cecilia never knew. As the table flipped, the urn was launched into the air and found its mark square on the top of her head. An involuntary nap had begun.

Philip trudged up the slope that rose from the stable, counting the steps until he intercepted the stream. Shortly after entering the thin woods that trimmed the edges of the farm, he came upon the noisy, crystal waters rushing over the slippery rocks. A few yards upstream, he found a spot where the ground leveled out.

"This looks good enough," he said aloud, and laid down his tools.

There were a large number of boulders of various sizes within the stream and on its banks. Philip had come with axe to cut timber for the dam but, instead, he decided to create one out of boulders. The smaller ones he lifted or rolled, grunting as he strained. At times, he lost his footing and slipped into the frigid mud, whooping from the chill. To dislodge the larger boulders, he cut a long, sturdy pole of four-inch diameter from a small tree. Buried halfway in the silt, Philip found a stone of ideal size for the final portion of the dam's foundation. He thrust the pole deep under the rock and twisted to drive it deeper. His initial efforts to move the boulder were unsuccessful. Grasping it near the end with both hands, Philip vaulted himself up to waist-high on the pole. Forcing down with all his weight on his locked arms, he bounced vigorously, growling for effect. Suddenly, the trunk snapped at his left hand, and Philip tumbled face down onto the bank. He laughed to himself and reached to wipe away the dirt from his face, when he noticed a heavy flow of blood coming from a gash on his hand.

Philip whistled as he looked down at the blood-soaked hand. He wiggled his fingers and he was relieved to see that all of them were working, but he felt pain as he did so. He emptied the contents of a sack that Pellas had used for his day's provisions and wrapped the hand tightly. Before long, the makeshift bandage was soaked with blood.

"Pellas, old boy," Philip said aloud to his invisible taskmaster, "like it or not, I'm going to need a break."

Philip left his tools and made the descent to the farmhouse. He could feel his pulse throbbing in his hand. He retrieved a cloth from inside the stable and sat down at the entrance. He carefully pulled off the matted bandage, wincing as it separated from the lacerated skin. Using his free hand and his teeth, Philip tore the cloth into strips for a new bandage, but he felt that he should clean the wound first. He walked over to the rainwater cistern that Pellas had built between the house and the stable, and filled a bucket. The young man drew a deep breath, closed his eyes, and plunged his hand into the cold water. His cry of pain split the silence and startled the animals in their pens.

Inside the house, Cecilia stirred on the floor. She opened her eyes and struggled to focus as the room swam around her. She closed them again, hoping the motion would stop, but now *she* felt like the one moving. Slowly, the events that led to her current situation began to come together, although the headache puzzled her until she saw the toppled urn nearby. Cecilia tried to raise her body, but the vertigo intensified and she flopped to the floor. *I need to call Father but I can't get to the bell.* She had no idea that he now was well beyond earshot of the warning anyway. *Maybe he is nearby.* Cecilia cleared her throat.

"Father," she said weakly. There was no response. "That won't do at all." Cecilia took a deep breath and called out with more force. "Father!" All was silent.

Philip carefully wiped the gash on his hand and inspected it closely. It was deep, but not dangerously so. A good bandage was all it needed. He could hear Pellas scolding him now. Not that he had done anything wrong—this was Pellas' means of communicating anything, whether sympathy or displeasure.

Suddenly, a sound caught his attention. Philip stopped and cocked his head to one side. *What was that?* He listened intently but the sound did not recur. He slowly wrapped the lacerated hand with strips of clean cloth. Again, the young man heard the sound and straightened with a start. *That was a voice! It sounded like it said, "Father."* Still unable to localize the sound, Philip sat motionless, ready to fly in the sound's direction when it came again.

Inside, Cecilia decided to summon all her strength for one more cry. In a strange way, she was not upset about her plight. At least it was not boring. *Okay, here goes.* "Father!" she roared in a half call, half scream.

Philip bolted to his feet and stood still and tense. *That was a girl's voice! Calling for her father!* A look of complete perplexity came over his face. It came from the house! Philip frantically finished wrapping his hand and moved slowly toward the house. *The voice came from the back,* he thought as he approached. He carefully walked the perimeter of the small home but he did not see anyone. There were no other calls. *Maybe I'm hearing things. Maybe I lost too much blood.* Philip checked his pulse and recited a few lines of poetry to test his faculties. Lacking evidence of impaired judgment, he resolved to settle the matter.

Philip returned to the back of the house and inspected the grounds closely. There were no footsteps other than his own. He looked at the small window located about six feet up the wall. It was just large enough for a person—a thin person—to squeeze through.

"Hello," he called.

Cecilia's eyes widened at the sound of the voice outside.

"Hello. Is there anyone in there?"

She bit her lip as she frantically tried to decide whether to respond. After a minute of tense silence, Cecilia relaxed as she heard footsteps moving away from the house. *That must be Philip.* She still was lying on the floor, but she was feeling much more clear-headed. She rolled onto her back and stared at the ceiling. Cecilia wished that she could meet the young man, but she knew that, if she did, her father probably would send Philip away. The result would be catastrophic come planting season.

Presently, Cecilia heard a low rumble approaching the house, growing louder as it neared. The sound was followed by a soft thud, then a few seconds of silence. As she listened hard for what might come next, Cecilia became aware that the light from the window had dimmed. Slowly, she turned her head until she saw the reason for the change. Partially obscuring the opening was the head of a young man she had never seen before.

"Hello. Who are you?" Philip asked.

Cecilia was speechless.

"I heard someone calling," Philip continued apologetically, "so I thought I'd better check it out."

The stunned girl stared wide-eyed at the talking head.

"That is an unusual place to relax," Philip said and smiled, waiting for some sort of reply. "Unless, of course, you are hurt." A look of surprise flashed over his face. "Oh, my! Are you hurt? Is that why you were calling?"

"Yes," Cecilia managed to respond.

"I'll be right there!" exclaimed the young man, and he disappeared from view.

"No, don't," called Cecilia, but it was too late.

Philip raced to the front door and pulled on the latch but it was locked.

"Thunder! What did Pellas think I was going to do? Rob him?"

Philip returned to the rear of the house and climbed on top of the large log he had rolled over to help reach the window. Wincing in pain from his hurt hand, he grabbed the ledge, hoisted himself into the opening and wriggled through, tumbling to the floor with a grunt.

"Tell me what's hurt," said Philip.

"Nothing. Just help me to my bed."

"If nothing's hurt, why are you lying here on the floor?"

"My legs are hurt," volunteered Cecilia, reluctantly.

"Let's have a look at them," Philip said as he examined her legs. Cecilia looked away, self-consciously. "They look okay to me. Sort of spindly, but no cuts or bruises. They should work fine."

"But they don't," responded the girl quietly, still looking away.

"What do you mean, they don't?"

"I'm paralyzed."

A wave of embarrassment came over Philip.

"Oh, I'm so sorry. I mean, I didn't…Look, if only I'd…Here, let me help you to your bed." Philip gently gathered the girl in his arms and easily hoisted her frail frame into bed. Cecilia immediately covered herself with her blanket and pulled it tight around her chin.

"Thank you. You may go now."

"Go?" asked Philip in astonishment. "Hardly. I have a thousand questions." He pulled a chair next to the bedside and looked closely at the girl. "You were calling for your father and you look curiously like Pellas." Philip waited for a reply.

"Yes, he is my father."

"But I thought that his entire family had been killed. Are you another daughter that no one knew about?"

"No, I am his only daughter. Most people are unaware that I am alive."

Philip gave a long whistle and scratched his head.

"Amazing. So this is the secret your father has been guarding."

"He has been quite protective of me," she agreed. Philip laughed and shook his head, recalling his volatile interactions with Pellas. "And just what do you find so funny, sir?" scolded the girl.

"Oh, lots of things," he responded, smiling. Philip grew serious, remembering what the Master had told him about the farmer. "And many more that aren't funny. So, what is your name?"

"Cecilia."

Philip silently and repeatedly mouthed the name.

"What are you doing?" asked the girl.

"Nothing. I'm just getting used to the name. It has a nice feel to it. Rolls off the tongue."

The girl flushed. "Thank you. Yours is Philip, I believe?"

"That it is."

She mimicked his silent recitation of her name by doing the same with his.

"It's a fair name, but it gets hung up behind the front teeth."

Philip did a double take and was about to protest when the girl broke into a giggle.

"Okay. I see what I'm up against here," he said sternly, and then smiled. "How old are you?"

"I am eighteen. You?"

"Twenty."

"Where are you from?"

"Ephesus."

"How long have you been in Bithynia?"

"Less than two months."

"Have you worked a farm before?"

Philip folded his arms and scowled.

"Now hold on. You are the mystery person, not me. Let me interrogate you."

"That's not true. You are a mystery to me," responded Cecilia.

"Yes, but no one thinks that I'm dead."

"Fair enough. But you will be if Father catches you in my room."

"I would think that he'd be grateful that I found you."

"He doesn't always react the way I'd hope," said Cecilia sadly.

Philip nodded in agreement and looked around the room.

"So you have been staying in this room all this time? Doesn't it get boring?"

"You wouldn't even begin to comprehend. You are the first person I've spoken to in months besides Father."

Philip rose, righted the table, and set the urn in place.

"You haven't asked me how I came to be paralyzed," continued the girl.

"To be honest, I really don't care to hear the details."

"Details? You know?"

Philip sighed and returned to his chair.

"I know that Pellas had a wife, a son and a daughter, and that all had perished at the hands of the authorities—that is, all but you—on the floor of the arena. They were martyred for their faith."

Cecilia hung her head, a tear forming at the corner of her eye. "Did Father tell you?"

"Oh, no. He hasn't said a word. Someone else told me."

"Who?"

"I'm not sure I should say. He told me to keep this knowledge in confidence."

"How did you come to us?" asked Cecilia, looking hard at Philip.

"I was sent."

"By the 'someone else?'"

"Yes."

"The Master," whispered Cecilia.

"What did you say?"

Cecilia turned to Philip.

"Only the Master would be kind enough to see to our need in this way."

Philip's face brightened.

"Yes, it was the Master, except I became aware of your father's story only a few days ago."

"Why do you now stay? Out of pity?"

"No, not pity. I stay out of duty. At first, I was sent here, but now I see I was called. I belong here, and never have I felt that so much as now."

Cecilia looked out the window and they both sat quietly for a time. Finally, she broke the silence.

"Day and night, Father has drilled into me the grave danger that now shrouds our lives. He believes that we should barricade ourselves on this little farm. That every contact with the outside world carries the threat of arrest and execution."

"He fears for your well-being. He just doesn't know how best to protect you."

Cecilia began to cry quietly.

"If life means staying in this cell and watching my days slip across that tiny window, then give me the arena."

Philip sat uncomfortably, not knowing how to console her. After a minute, he gently spoke to the girl.

"You speak boldly, yet you haven't asked me whether I share your faith."

"I don't need to ask. I know."

Philip leaned forward and took her thin hand.

"Cecilia, there are things you may not know about your father. It is not my place to tell you of them, but you need to be patient with him. In time, God's perfect result will be seen."

The two spent several hours in conversation. Some of it was serious, but a good deal of laughter was shared between them, so great was the burden of secrecy that had been lifted. Philip shared the story of his conversion, a second-generation fruit of the great Apostle John, who served in Ephesus and, under whose teaching, the young man's family trusted Christ. He related the circumstances surrounding his coming to the farm and his experiences with Pellas, up to the injury that brought him within earshot of the fallen girl. Philip then sat engrossed as Cecilia told of her family's salvation and of the events of their last days together. Philip marveled at her composure as she related the details of their arrest and trial. He paced the floor nervously through the account of her presumed death and recovery from the corpses. At times, he begged for a respite, only to request that she continue once he was more collected. When Cecilia concluded, Philip closed his eyes in silent meditation for several minutes.

When he opened them again, the girl was fast asleep, exhausted from the excitement and stress of the day's events. Philip nibbled on the provisions left by Pellas for his daughter's lunch, and the young man studied the sleeping girl's features with admiration. He pondered how God had placed such courage and passionate commitment in such a frail package. Some time later, Cecilia awoke and gasped as she saw Philip sitting next to her.

"Hello, again," he said, smiling. She caught her breath.

"What are you still doing here? Father will be home soon. You need to leave now. In fact, I'm surprised that he hasn't come calling your name."

"Didn't you know he went to town?"

Cecilia looked puzzled.

"No, he said nothing about it."

"It is the first time that he has left since I've been here. I'm not a very good errand boy, at least not for farm equipment."

"Will he be back tonight?"

Philip looked out the window and gauged the hour.

"Yes. In fact, he should be back soon. Had I your courage, I would confront him when he returns. I think the wild beasts would go easier on me, though."

"You didn't seem so concerned earlier," said the girl, with a smile.

"He wasn't due back earlier," laughed Philip. "Your lunch is on the table next to your bed. I only sampled it. We will talk again soon, Cecilia." He moved toward the window.

"Why don't you use the door, Philip?"

"Because I wouldn't be able to lock it once outside. The way I entered is safest. Not easiest, but safest." Philip pulled himself up into the window and slid out. A second later, his face popped up in the opening. "Wasn't that graceful?"

"You had better keep that under wraps, or Caesar will send for you to perform in the Circus Maximus."

"You are too kind."

"Philip? What did you do while I slept?" asked the girl.

The young man thought for a moment. "I talked to God."

"About what?"

"Maybe I'll tell you someday. The grace of our Lord be with you."

"And with you."

CHAPTER 9

▼

The announcement that Linus and his guests would be leaving for the theater in a half-hour stirred Marcellus out of his contemplation. It was mid-morning and he already had been up for several hours, roused out of sleep in the early-morning darkness by an urge to review the report that Jason had prepared on the Old City of Diakropolis.

"Thank you, I will be ready," Marcellus responded to the attendant, who turned quickly and left the doorway.

Marcellus yawned and shook his head to drive away the drowsiness. He had been bothered by the report since first reading it days earlier. It struck him as odd that such little information was available about the history and legal proceedings of the original, walled city. As Diakropolis spread well beyond those first walls, official interest in the primitive fortress had diminished. Marcellus knew that, as tribe leader of the precinct, Siros played a prominent role in the oversight of the sector's public works and civic affairs. Moreover, Marcellus knew from his unofficial tour of the wharf that the enigmatic chieftain maintained a business there, as well. At that point, knowledge ended and speculation began.

It was characteristic of cities in the empire to maintain poor archives. Additionally, the damp climate of Bithynia made preservation of papyri and parchments even more difficult. Beyond that, Marcellus suspected that there was purpose behind the dearth of public records. He had met Siros only twice in his short tenure as chief magistrate. The first encounter was at a lavish reception held in Marcellus' honor, shortly after his arrival in Diakropolis. The profuse flattery of the portly Siros surprised even Marcellus, who had grown accustomed to such flowery, insincere pronouncements while in the company of Linus. Although introduced with the other phylarchs and, supposedly, not one of the *first citizens* of the city, Marcellus recalled watching with keen interest the obsequious behavior toward Siros of those who were of higher rank.

The second encounter came on the day of the contests in the arena. Marcellus recalled gazing around the assembly as, one by one, the unarmed Christians met their demise. None that day had a more eager expression than did the grinning merchant.

The Christians, thought Marcellus. *I have been meaning to ask Linus about them. Perhaps today.* It had been several weeks since Marcellus had thought about how to administer justice toward the sect. As usual, when faced with difficult situations, he coveted the governor's thoughts on the matter. Marcellus knew that his visit to Nicomedia was drawing to a close, so he hoped to speak privately with Linus once more.

Marcellus closed up his documents and placed them into his leather satchel. His thoughts turned to his return trip home in two days, and how delightful it would be to see Claudia again. He hated to be apart from her for so long, but he reasoned that it would be far worse had he left his daughter in Italy. Most ambitious rulers would have not encumbered their progress with a teenaged child, but Marcellus felt otherwise. He wanted to witness her passage into womanhood and have some influence, if possible, on its navigation.

As he dressed, Marcellus wondered how things were faring in Diakropolis. He had left Septimus with strict instructions about what to handle in his absence. The list was short. The magistrate presumed that the deputy would not repeat the same mistake as the last time he was left in charge, but then Septimus was not the average second-in-command. Little did Marcellus know but, at that very hour, his older brother was touring the wharf and becoming inextricably entangled in Siros' web of illicit pursuits.

The coaches arrived at the small theater at approximately eleven o'clock. Marcellus recognized several of the patrons from the outing a day earlier. Linus, a master of official etiquette, was careful to see that Marcellus was properly introduced to all in attendance.

"Come, Marcellus, and meet an old friend just in from Antioch," said the governor, as he vigorously pulled the magistrate toward a balding but trim man about Linus' age. "This is Flavius Antonius—General Flavius Antonius, I should properly say—now retired from the Syrian legions. The two of us were tribunes together many seasons ago, eh, Flavius?" The general patted his bald head and laughed.

"As you can see, the leaves have long since fled the tree, Linus."

"Obviously, the general's appointment was legitimate and not political," continued Linus, referring to the officer's long and distinguished career. "Marcellus is the newly installed chief magistrate of a town called Diakropolis, Flavius."

The soldier offered a strong muscular arm in greeting.

"Diakropolis? I haven't been there, but I think I know about where it is. Off the road from Claudiopolis, isn't it?"

"Yes, sir, you are correct," Marcellus answered respectfully.

The general looked him over.

"You are quite a youth for such a position of leadership. Your skills must be notable."

"It may simply be that I have a well-placed patron, sir," Marcellus smiled and nodded toward Linus.

"Nonsense!" exclaimed the governor. "There isn't a more capable, industrious student of the law in the entire empire, Flavius. Don't let him fool you; Marcellus just needs a dash of good old Roman arrogance and he'll be a complete package."

"I can think of no one better qualified to supply this deficiency than you, you old windbag," chuckled the general, jabbing Linus in the ribs. "Young Marcellus, your mentor could charm the elephants from under Hannibal. How else do you think he managed so well under Domitian and escaped the purge with his head intact?"

"I could only hope to attain a portion of the governor's political prowess, General. The staggering diversity of our empire demands leaders who can sway with words where weapons have ceased to impact."

The general looked at Linus with raised brow, obviously impressed with the young magistrate.

"Well said, young man. Linus, your skills may not be strongly in demand with this one."

"He's a fine boy. Just like a son to me. We will talk later, Flavius. I want Marcellus to meet someone else." The governor took Marcellus' arm and led him toward a small group gathered nearby. "Men like Flavius are the timber with which Rome is built, Marcellus," Linus said in a low tone near Marcellus' ear. "Courageous, tireless—easy to like. There are others equally important, but not so endearing. You're going to meet one now."

They came upon a gathering of men and women who encircled a slender, bearded man. The group was obviously engrossed in what the man was saying. The small circle opened to receive Linus and Marcellus.

"Governor, how delightful to see you this pleasant afternoon," said the man, bowing low.

"Dio Chrystomas, it is an honor to have you join us today. I trust that you will be lunching with us after the play?"

"It would be my highest honor, Your Excellency."

"Dio is, to put it frankly, the leading citizen of Nicomedia. Philosopher, philanthropist, with penetrating insight into the plight of man. Without his contributions, Nicomedia would be merely a frontier outpost."

"No, no, Your Excellency, you are too kind," the man responded, bowing low again.

"Let me add that he is also humble to a fault, Marcellus. Dio, allow me to present a young man who has humored a doting old man by letting him offer a few words of advice as he climbs the ladder of influence. Marcellus, this is Dio Chrystomas, benefactor of Nicomedia."

"Ah, a protégé, Linus? The pleasure of your acquaintance is mine, sir."

"Marcellus is chief magistrate of Diakropolis, Dio."

"I know the town well, Your Honor. In fact, I had heard there was a new magistrate of boundless principle there. A finer city is not to be found in Bithynia, Marcellus."

"Yes, well don't sell him too hard, Dio," interjected Linus. "I'm trying to convince him to go to Prusa."

"You could do no wrong with either choice, Your Honor, although Prusa offers much to an ambitious ruler."

"Thank you for your kind comments, sir," returned Marcellus.

"Dio, we'll look forward to your conversation at lunch. Right now the attendants seem anxious to usher us in to the theater."

Linus directed Marcellus toward the theater entrance and smiled at those who parted to let them through.

"Dio's really nothing more than a filthy-rich blowhard who likes to hear his name," said a smiling Linus through clenched teeth. "But we'll have to let history tag that on to his legacy, won't we, Marcellus?"

The group filed into the theater and took their seats near the stage. As was true throughout the empire, the number of theaters and baths increased with the prominence of the city. The playwright and director, Cassio, had selected a smaller venue for his premiere. It was no small coincidence that this theater had been erected through the generosity of Dio Chrystomas himself. Marcellus looked around at the ornate surroundings. The tiered seating area, or cavea, was constructed out of marble from nearby quarries, he was informed. The stage building occupied three floors and presented an intricate façade of columns, arches and statues. The patrons whispered among themselves as they awaited the start of the play. Marcellus knew nothing of the presentation they were to see, or of its author. From the comments earlier made by Linus, he sensed that their attendance was more out of obligation than of desire.

Cassio came out on stage and profusely thanked the audience for attending, and gave special recognition to Linus and Dio. As the director was about to signal the performance to begin, some late arrivals created a small interruption. Marcellus had been absent-mindedly studying the relief on the façade when Linus nudged him and motioned toward the newly arrived guests. It was Arcadia and an older man. Marcellus drew a breath as he watched Arcadia gracefully take her place farther down the row. He had been somewhat distracted since they left Linus' villa, and now he knew why. Their eyes met and she flashed a confident but gracious smile. Marcellus nodded and turned back to the stage as quickly as possible, swallowing hard as he did so.

Linus leaned close.

"Beautiful, isn't she?" Marcellus faced straight ahead, acknowledging the governor's comment with only a movement of the eyes. "That's her father with her, by the way. I had no idea that he was coming up from Prusa."

Marcellus' eyes opened wider and he held his breath. Now why am I so tense? I have nothing to be nervous about. She is a woman. There are many women about. He is her father. Many women have fathers. Marcellus slowly exhaled so as not to be heard. But she is the daughter of the richest man in Prusa, and Linus wants me there. I know an arrangement when I see one.

The play, a mime, rambled on, and Marcellus attended little to it. The gist of the plot he collected between thoughts of Arcadia. As best he could tell, it was a fable about a gullible foreign peasant and a cunning traveling Roman merchant. The merchant had convinced the naive farmer to turn over all his meager life's possessions to purchase a magic pheasant, one that would produce eggs of gold each clear night with a full moon. The farmer dutifully waited for such a night, while the merchant moved on to another territory. Sometime later, a hungry soldier passing by saw the prized bird in a window and stole it from the farmer. The latter confronted the thief and, in the squabble, the soldier killed the farmer.

The soldier was taken before a judge, who heard testimony from the defendant and other parties who agreed that the soldier had committed the murder. The judge declared the defendant not guilty, however, on grounds that the farmer's stupidity warranted his fate and greater good came from his elimination. Of course, as was true of contemporary Roman theater, the story was laced with bawdy and lewd behavior, which drew gasps and guffaws from the audience.

Marcellus, however, was too preoccupied to be amused by the antics. Before long, his fellow patrons were rising from their seats and moving toward the exit.

"Come, Marcellus," said Linus. "The play is over, mercifully. Ah, here comes Cassio now. We'll see if he can shed any light on the meaning of what we just saw."

The impresario approached the governor and bowed.

"Your Excellency, I trust that you enjoyed the play."

"Quite intriguing, Cassio," replied Linus, searching for words. "I know you were making a statement, but I'm not sure exactly what it was."

"I make no statements, sir. It is purely art. I allow my patrons to interpret as they wish."

"Come now, my good man. You can't tell me that your little production was devoid of all social commentary. If I didn't know better, I'd say you were taking a jab at our system of law."

"Perish the thought, sir. I would never offend the sensibilities of those charged with keeping the law."

"Good. After all, it was our law that secured your freedom. Anyway, I wish you success on the larger stage. It was a stimulating performance."

The playwright bowed again and hurried off to mix with other dignitaries. Linus turned to Marcellus and snickered.

"He's a bald-faced liar and no friend of Rome. He uses the stage to stir up unrest, although I must admit that this play was tame compared to his usual work. These theater gadflies really get my goat. 'Purely art,' he says. At least it will provide for excellent dinner conversation."

"Excuse me, sir, but why did you say that the law secured his freedom?"

"An acquaintance of mine gave Cassio his certificate of manumission shortly before he died, of epilepsy, it is presumed. I was never certain that my friend was in his right mind when he did it. I suspect that Cassio engineered it somehow, but we'll never know. He has used his freedman status to achieve some degree of prominence, if one can call the perpetration of such art forms redeeming. Give me the old tragedies and comedies. This mime and pantomime is vulgar, at best. What did you think of it?"

"Honestly, sir, I was distracted through most of it. But I heard enough to be conversant at lunch."

"Distracted, eh? Now who, I mean, what could have distracted you?"

At that moment, they reached the exit, where a few of the guests stood talking to Arcadia and her father. The narrow portal forced Marcellus to walk close to the woman.

"So, we meet again," Marcellus said politely.

"Yes, we seem to be running in the same circles," Arcadia responded with a smile.

"I see that your father has come from Prusa," continued Marcellus after a brief, uncomfortable pause. "I wasn't expecting to meet him."

"I was taken by surprise, as well. It turned out that my father had business here. He arrived late last night and the governor was kind enough to invite us to the play."

"How thoughtful," Marcellus mused, "how thoughtful. So, will you be lunching with us?"

"I believe so, yes."

"Excellent, then. I'll look forward to another opportunity to chat with you." Marcellus turned to move away, when Linus grabbed his arm and pulled him back.

"Marcellus, you have heard me speak highly of Arcadia's noble father, Atarix, but little did I know that we would bear the honor of a personal visit. Atarix, allow me to introduce Marcellus, chief magistrate of Diakropolis."

Marcellus snapped to attention and bowed his head in a dignified way.

"Sir, it is my honor to make your acquaintance."

The nobleman silently eyed the young judge, scanning his form with dark green eyes that shone from under wild, bushy eyebrows.

"Hmph," came a guttural reply. Linus blinked at the unexpected response and glanced at Arcadia, who was struggling to suppress a giggle.

"As I said, Marcellus," continued Linus, "I had no earthly idea that he was coming, but when I heard that he had arrived in Nicomedia, I knew at once that we must introduce you. You two can get more acquainted over lunch, which, by the way, is waiting for us. To the coaches, everyone."

Linus escorted Atarix toward the vehicles while Marcellus fell in behind, next to Arcadia.

"Was that an approving grunt, or should I be concerned?" he quipped.

Lunch was another adventure in the culinary treasures of the empire. Exotic meats and fruits from every land were represented on the table. The beauty of the day prompted Linus to move the party into the garden. It was sunny with a slight chill in the air, but delightful weather for early winter. Linus sat Marcellus between the two Prusans, which did not assist the magistrate's appetite. He was uncomfortable with both of them, albeit for different reasons. The wine apparently loosened Atarix' tongue a bit, so that now he was conversing with Marcellus in complete sentences. Marcellus wondered how such a seemingly unsociable aristocrat could have as gracious and engaging a daughter as Arcadia. Finally, Linus directed the guests to come inside for more drinks and dessert. The party entered the dining room and took their places around the triclinium.

"I, for one," began Linus, "found that bit of theater to be of little amusement, but let's keep that within these circles."

A light chorus of agreement arose from the reclining guests. Present were Flavius, Dio Chrystomas, Atarix, Arcadia, Marcellus, and a couple of prominent Nicomedian aristocrats with their wives.

"As I told Marcellus, I much prefer true theater, the noble works of Livy or a provocative satire of Juvenal. Give me a Greek tragedy, even."

"Hear, hear," roared Flavius, growing a bit boisterous from the wine. "That fellow, what's his name…?"

"Cassio," replied Linus.

"Yes, Cassio. Get him a real job. Send him to Germany and let him learn something useful, like constructing a siege works. Pah! What a waste! Hand me some of the pastry, Marcellus."

"Come now, General," said Dio. "We must mix the more gentle elements with the rough to have a fruitful society. Look at how we eat. The feast is not complete without these sweet delicacies."

"If you call what we saw a delicacy, I question your mental stability, sir."

Dio bristled.

"Now, let's have a civil debate, gentlemen," said Linus. "Dio, Flavius apologizes. He is so accustomed to the abrasive that he is apt to exaggerate."

"I'm not…" started the general, but stopped short as he caught the stare of Linus, "…accustomed to the theater," Flavius continued benignly. He turned to Dio and smiled. "My apologies, noble sir." The benefactor nodded in acceptance.

"The play bears review, however," said Linus. "I've known Cassio to spice up his works with a barb or two directed toward Rome. What, or who do you think he was shooting at this time?"

"It's apparent that he was commenting on the deplorable lack of protection from the criminal element, especially in the rural areas," said Dio.

"Marcellus can speak firsthand to that, can't you, son?"

The young magistrate nodded. Arcadia leaned close.

"What happened?"

"Long story. I'll tell you later," he whispered.

"We need to empower our soldiers to keep the peace," pronounced the general. "There are few campaigns to occupy their attention anymore. We should make use of them in these villages."

"From what I hear, general, the soldiers often are the perpetrators," countered Dio.

"Those are baseless claims. The men are easy marks for that kind of nonsense."

"Careful, Flavius," interjected Linus. "Not all soldiers are as honorable as you. We have had numerous reports of protection money extorted from the citizenry."

"I don't believe them," huffed the officer, as he put a goblet to his lips.

Marcellus looked at Arcadia and rolled his eyes in quiet amusement at the repartee.

"Marcellus, you're quiet on the subject. I know you said that you halfway paid attention during the play," Linus said, pausing to wink at Arcadia. "What do you think of all this?"

Marcellus quickly swallowed a piece of pastry and cleared his throat.

"Well, sir, I don't feel qualified to offer any comment in the presence of such esteemed minds, but I'm not sure that Cassio's intent was to suggest an insufficiency of justice but, rather, a misappropriation."

The eyes of the group collectively fixed on the magistrate, who fidgeted with a date.

"Go on, son," said Linus.

Marcellus continued in a quiet voice.

"It seems to me that…"

"What's that? Speak up, young man," interrupted one of the other men, straining forward to hear Marcellus' words. Marcellus cleared his throat again.

"Sorry, sir," he responded to the protesting gentleman. He addressed the group.

"To me, the message of the play was that if we use the law to control how people think, we will end up abusing justice. Whether or not the farmer was foolish enough to believe the bird could produce gold does not change the fact that his life was taken by another. To exonerate a killer solely on the basis of the victim's beliefs sends a confusing message to the citizens and sets a harmful precedent."

Linus stroked his chin.

"Intriguing analysis, my son. You think Cassio is suggesting such occurs now?"

"Possibly. We have been known to be intolerant of people of other stripes."

"It all goes with the territory, son," said the general. "We've annexed all sorts of kingdoms through our conquests. Rome looks like a zoo now. We can't embrace everybody and everything, nor do we want to do so. There needs to be a weeding out."

"But general, we can't use the law for that. Eventually, half the people will be needed to police the expressions of the other half. The empire will collapse."

"The young magistrate is right," said Dio. "Any society that sets out to control the thoughts of its people will not last long. Where would we great thinkers be? I, myself, have said numerous things that could be considered disturbing or threatening as I have pondered the machinations of our rulers, but it has been in the name of enlightenment."

"Thinking didn't win this land for Rome, my friend," responded Flavius.

"You underestimate the power of a concept, General."

"Ha! My javelin and your concept—in the Colosseum! Which place at the table would be empty, good people?" Flavius guffawed and looked around the room with eyes that were beginning to redden from the spirits.

Linus jumped into the debate.

"Now, Flavius. You are a man of war and, to be fair, everything to you is a bully to be bludgeoned. Dio is correct."

The general scowled at the governor.

"Well then, let's allow that he's equally correct," continued Linus. "But, going back to what Marcellus said, it is true that the empire has to be a bit more savvy about administering this menagerie that we now oversee; we no longer can simply exact submission by the force of law. In the long run, that will serve only to stimulate insurrection. We need to unify around an ideal. That is why, in my opinion, we need to strongly promote the imperial cult in our territories."

"Come now, Linus. You don't really believe the emperors are gods, do you? To me, they are a band of madmen, paranoiacs who polish the walls to see their assassins sneak up on them."

"Careful with your tongue, Dio," warned the governor, looking around the room.

"Yes, I object to that portrayal," the general said indignantly. "Trajan is a level-headed leader, a fighting man."

"That he is, Flavius," continued Linus. "I have nothing but the utmost respect for him. However, you miss the point, gentlemen. Whether the office is occupied by a noble warrior or by a buffoon, we must bolster the public's perception of the emperor as supreme deity so that we can bring all under one roof, so to speak."

"We have temples, Linus," said one of the men.

"So do all the other gods and goddesses. Our hills are full of them. We must do more. I suggest that we increase the grain and corn doles—and the oil allotments, too. Not that our people can grow their own grain, or take in the baths without oil, but we want them to see those things as necessities that come from the benevolent hand of their supreme prince."

"Those are radical ideas, Linus," said Dio. "You sound like one of those Christians preaching in the agora."

"Those are just some ideas that I've been tossing around, whose time is probably yet to come."

"Too thick for me," yawned Flavius, as he stretched out his full frame on the pillows.

"What about you, Atarix? You've been silent the entire meal."

"Never mind me, Excellency. I am a simple merchant basking in the conversation of great minds and feasting on these delicacies. I like your idea of increased public doles, though. That is, as long as you purchase from me."

A chorus of laughter filled the room, a welcome respite from the serious discussion, and the group commenced with another round of food and drink. After a minute or two, Marcellus interrupted the light chatter.

"I was going to speak to the governor in private about this matter but, since there is such a wealth of wisdom gathered in this room, let me pose this issue to all of you. Dio jogged my memory of a problem that I find particularly difficult as I begin my career as judge, namely that of the Christians."

"The Christians," Dio said pointedly. "They're reproducing like rabbits."

"Let Marcellus speak, Dio," scolded Linus. "Go on, son."

"I'm having some difficulty figuring out what to do with them. I'm sure that my problem is not unique." The magistrate struggled to find words.

"Marcellus, you're not addressing the senate," Linus said kindly. "Just speak your mind. My stars, Dio could be thrown into the Tiber for what he just said."

"I couldn't help but think of them as I watched the play. I'm no sympathizer, mind you, but I find it odd that we label their beliefs as hateful and a threat to the empire, especially in light of all the absurdities we tolerate. Then we send the ones who hold steadfast to their creeds to a most inhumane death, all in the name of patriotism. It seems to me that the punishment doesn't fit the crime."

Flavius had raised himself on one elbow, carefully following Marcellus' words.

"Maybe you don't understand the nature of their crime, son. I've seen campaigns lost when the ranks marched to different drummers. These Christians offer the common folk a seductive thought, this notion that their Christ was God in man's form and will conquer the world. They see themselves as his soldiers, and talk about a day when they will rule with him over all the earth. That's subversive talk, not some harmless belief."

"You seem to know a lot about them," responded Marcellus.

"Sure I do, and about the Jews, too. I've logged a number of years in Palestine and Syria. I know all the tales."

"They seem like a placid sort of people."

"So they do, some of them. Remember, though, that they're a breed of Jew. I don't think anyone would use the word 'placid' to describe *them*."

"Marcellus brings up a real problem for those of us who administer the law in these parts," stated Linus. "I'll confess that I, myself, have been perplexed as to what to do about them."

"I see the parallel with the play, Marcellus," Dio intoned. "The Christian is the stupid farmer who trades his soul for a silly dream of other-worldly riches. The merchant is one of their huckster preachers who disrupt communities, hawking the deception."

"Yes," continued Marcellus, "but is Rome both thief who tries to steal the dream and judge who condemns them unjustly? That is my problem."

"You're taking this all too seriously, my son," said Linus. "Remember, you are here to uphold the law, and the law is clear on this issue. I know the mind of Trajan on the matter. When I arrived here, I found pockets of Christians everywhere I turned. They were being dragged before the court with regularity. It is not pleasurable to pass judgment on them, but it is our duty. As to the method of execution, my view is that it is far better to die a noble death on the arena floor than to waste away in some dungeon. I believe it ennobles the citizenry to witness the heroic demise of these people."

"I think you are both being too gracious with those troublemakers," thundered Flavius. "Since day one, they have been perpetrating a hoax. If anyone represented them in that play, it was the crook who sold the bird. I have it on good authority that the man Jesus they worship was nothing more than a magician. I believe it, too, having spent some time on campaign in Egypt. Those conjurers down in Alexandria are full of tricks. That's where Jesus was from, by the way. He brought his art to Palestine where the folks weren't wise to it."

"They say he came back to life," interjected one of the women.

"Sure he did—after a good flogging and crucifixion," chuckled the general. "A lot of them do, you know," he added sarcastically. "No, the whole operation was planned from the start—a colossal hoax."

"It's a hoax that apparently has stuck," commented Marcellus.

"As a philosophy it does have some appeal," said Dio. "The rigors of stoicism joined with eternal epicurean delights. Not a bad combination."

"You dignify the cult with the label 'philosophy,' my friend," said Flavius. "Rome has no use for these people. You can't get them in the military and they're too distracted by thoughts of heaven to be useful in civic affairs. I have no problem moving them on to the destination for which they long."

"Marcellus, I'll discuss the matter further with you after our guests are gone," said Linus. He rose from the table. "Ladies and gentlemen, I have reached my capacity. Anyone care to join me for a walk?"

"With your pardon, Governor, I beg to be excused from your gracious hospitality," replied Dio. "I am giving a lecture later this afternoon and I need to gather my thoughts. You all are invited, by the way."

Regrets were offered by the each of the guests, although Flavius had to be physically prodded by Linus to do so. Dio bowed to the assembly and strutted from the room.

Flavius slowly brought himself to his feet, working out a cramp in his lower back in the process.

"Linus, old boy, the only walk I'm taking is to my quarters for a nap. All this rich food has made me groggy."

"Arcadia? Atarix?" asked Linus.

"I'd be honored," replied the woman.

"My regrets, Governor, but the two of us must be on our way," corrected Atarix, which drew a puzzled response from the woman. "I have not seen my daughter for several days and I would like to visit with her."

"That is understandable, although I will miss your beautiful company, my dear." The remainder of the group also offered their apologies. "Well, I can see that I am losing my constituency. Marcellus, you have no choice. Come, let us take a walk. The rest of you have a pleasant afternoon."

"Father, why didn't you let me stay?" Arcadia asked pointedly as the pair left the residence.

"Siros was right. Marcellus is a serious threat to us if he stays in Diakropolis. We need to move him out now."

"That's what I'm trying to do."

"Arcadia, we don't have time for your antics to work. He obviously hasn't responded to Linus' request and your charms are working too slowly, if at all." The daughter stiffened.

"My strategy will work. You need to be patient."

"We can ill afford a mistake, my dear."

"Give me one more day. If I have to move the earth, Marcellus will come to Prusa."

Linus and Marcellus strolled leisurely through the grounds of the official residence, the mentor gesturing and chatting away, and the pupil walking with hands clasped behind his back and nodding his head.

"Don't take this Christian thing too seriously, Marcellus. I know that the situation isn't as ideal as you'd like, but for now it has to be this way. I, too, felt a bit sorry for them when I arrived here. Most Christians don't cause trouble, but it seems that some people want them completely eradicated. For heaven's sake, in one town they produced lists of the believers—the docket was clogged hearing their cases."

"What did you do?"

"I followed the law. Those who renounced and took the sacrifices, I let off. Those who didn't were executed for capital offense."

"You see, that's where I am uncomfortable."

"I know you are. I was, too. I had never participated in these trials. I didn't know what to investigate or punish. Should I make a distinction based on gender or age? Was it unlawful to simply bear the name Christian? All these things perplexed me, so I sought the counsel of the emperor, much as you have done with me."

"Did he concur?"

"Yes, he agreed wholeheartedly with my approach, although he stressed that they are not to be sought out or prosecuted anonymously."

"I guess that adds a measure of justice to the act," said Marcellus with resignation. "But why are Christians so vilified?"

"Good question. The best I can tell, their customs include meeting on a certain day, singing a hymn to this Christ as their god, binding themselves to some oath, then taking food together—common food, nothing bizarre—then agreeing to meet again some other day."

"Their oath—is it something heretical?"

"Oh, no. They merely vow not to commit theft or fraud, or adultery."

"That hardly seems subversive, as Flavius suggested."

"Never mind him. He's a good fellow, but he took too many volleys on the helmet. Seriously, I was told all sorts of nefarious tales about these people, but I am convinced that there is no truth to them. I even tortured two of their female slaves—deaconesses, I believe they are called—but found nothing more than excessive superstition."

"Then why…?"

"Marcellus, you need to drop this matter. Trajan has explicitly stated how we are to conduct proceedings. Remember what I told you about his refusal to allow the formation of a company of firefighters?"

"Yes, you told me on our tour of the city."

"He views the Christians in the same light. In his eyes, they are a breeding ground for political unrest. Be they firemen, bakers or Christians—he is against all of these societies. Now, let us change the subject to something more redeeming."

The two men continued on, with Linus pointing out various species of plant and tree as they went. Marcellus listened with interest to the detailed descriptions given by the governor, Linus' vast knowledge being the legacy of his scientist uncle. Finally, mentor and student returned to the house.

"Marcellus, I know that you are scheduled to leave for Diakropolis in two days. I want you to reconsider moving on to Prusa, instead." The magistrate sighed. "I watched you at lunch," continued Linus. "You held your own quite well. Those were not lightweights, you know. It is unusual for anyone to have a reasonable debate with Dio; he is rarely bested. I think that you are more than ready to move on to a more prominent position."

"Sir, I just don't think that I am. I have done nothing in Diakropolis to commend myself for a promotion. I have plans, though, that would make me a more fit candidate in about a year."

"You are stubborn," said Linus, shaking his head. "I can't think of a person alive who would refuse such an opportunity, but, in a strange way, I understand you. Now I just have to explain to Atarix why you're not coming."

"Atarix? He wants me there?"

"Sure. Why do you think he came all the way up here?"

"He didn't speak to me all afternoon."

"Most of his words are foul, so count your blessings."

"But you extolled him yesterday in front of Arcadia."

"You must understand by now that I extol everybody. How else do you think I got where I am today?"

The magistrate acknowledged with a sly smile.

"Why would Atarix want me in Prusa? He hardly knows me."

"As I said, your reputation has preceded you. Also, I think his interest is more than political."

Marcellus stared back blankly, and then his mouth opened slowly in comprehension.

"You mean, me…Arcadia?"

"Yes, you…and Arcadia. Go relax now, and think about your future. I'll be heading to the baths in an hour or so. You're welcome to join me."

CHAPTER 10

▼

Targus positioned himself across from the location indicated by the map for the old shaft. He crouched in a ring of boulders and carefully scanned the hillock some fifty yards away for any irregularity that might indicate the original opening. Upon taking leave of John and the others, he stopped briefly at the Master's house, where, after jogging the elderly man's memory a bit, he confirmed that an entrance to the mine existed on the side opposite the city. The Master could remember no other landmarks that would help the search, however. After taking a few meager stores of food, water, and a small lamp, Targus struck out for the mine site. Unhindered by companions or unwanted delays, he soon reached his destination.

The mine was located in a desolate area about ten miles southwest of the city, situated in a craggy outcropping of rocks. Some trees dotted the site but it remained mostly exposed to view, which presented challenges for escape. A small, natural tunnel opened on the side opposite the city. This led to the original shaft cut centuries ago. Over the years, other shafts had been added, but these were sunk on the other side, several hundred yards away and well out of sight of the initial entry. The newer tunnels opened onto a depressed, level area that created a very manageable and concealed loading site. The original shaft had fallen into disuse and eventually was sealed at both ends when the revolt of slave workers was quelled.

Targus sat for a good hour in a secluded position opposite the location indicated by the map, studying the environs and watching to see if any sentries might make a pass. He took cover for one tense moment when a single guard strolled by, scanning the neighboring trees and rocks nonchalantly as he passed. The scout searched in vain for some evidence of the original entry, but all that he surveyed appeared undisturbed by the enterprise of man. Finally, Targus stepped into the open and dashed across the short distance to the tumbled boulders that rimmed the hillock.

Mindful that he could be discovered at any moment, Targus scampered back and forth, over and under the rocks, searching for any clues that some access to the mine had formerly existed. It seemed as though the years had thoroughly erased all trace of the opening. Suddenly, Targus heard a sharp sound nearby and instinctively jumped into a small clearing within the boulders. The noise, made by a small forest animal and magnified by the silence of the desolation, proved providential, for Targus found that his safe haven opened into a small cave. Targus sat tensely for several minutes, straining to hear evidence that watchmen might be nearby. Finally, he breathed a sigh of relief and turned his concentration to the entrance of the cave. It was more of a triangular crevasse in the rock, with cracked edges that suggested the collapse of a larger opening. *This is could be it,* thought Targus. He knew that he did not have the luxury of time and must promptly search out every lead. Taking a flint from his pack, he soon had the small lamp lit. He then took a long drink of water and a portion of food in preparation for an uncertain journey.

Entrance into the cave required the scout to crouch on all fours. Even then, it was a tight squeeze, and Targus felt his clothing catch on the rough edges of the opening. Soon, he popped through into a more spacious room and was able to rise to full height. The light from the outside failed quickly and soon the walls of the cave were illuminated only by the flicker of the small lamp. The air was damp and musty. Targus prayed as he moved slowly forward. *Lord, you know I'm a man of the earth. But I prefer to be on it, not in it. If this is what it takes to get these people free, I'm willing. I just hope this cave is deserted, my lamp stays lit, and that there are no surprises.*

After about twenty paces, Targus had crossed the room and reached a wall. He ran his fingers over its cool wet surface and looked from side to side. A dark opening appeared a few yards away. The opening led to a sloping tunnel that Targus now began to cautiously descend. The roof was high enough to provide several inches clearance, except at intervals where large horizontal braces hung down. Because of this, Targus walked with his right hand extended above his head, holding the lamp with his left. He made mental notes of the passage and the number of paces to each landmark, reciting the details over and over in his mind as he walked. He knew such details would be essential for those who would follow.

Presently, the passage opened up into another large open space as evidence by the quick drop in light intensity. Targus paused for a moment to allow his vision to acclimate. Gradually, the opposite side of the room came into dim view and he stepped forward. Immediately, however, he felt his footing give way and he lunged backward to his original position. Looking down, he saw that only a small ledge continued into the room before the floor plunged away into utter darkness. He was in the old shaft.

His heart raced as he pondered his near demise, then he reviewed his situation with more characteristic composure. As he did, his other senses awakened to the setting. The air on his face was cooler and wetter than before. His hearing, now acute from minutes of absolute silence, detected a hollowness to the atmosphere. The incessant dripping of water sounded far off. An oppressive metallic smell filled his nostrils and soured his taste. The ledge was actually a landing that dropped away to his left in a narrow spiral staircase cut out of the rock. Had he the benefit of full light, he would have seen that it descended a few hundred feet below.

Targus tightened his cloak around him and began the treacherous descent. Grasping the lamp firmly in his right hand, his left remained in constant contact with the wall of the shaft, now wet with cold, subterranean sweat. *One, two, three.* He counted each step carefully, noting what details he could for future reference. *Sixteen, seventeen.* Targus detected a slight shiver in the steps. Pebbles rattled free and plunged into the void below. The scout took each step more cautiously now, still counting as he went. *Thirty-five, thirty-six.* His left hand met iron rings at intervals, sunk into the rock to secure some kind of safety cord for the mineworkers of old. Targus wondered how many souls had made an unfortunate misstep and plummeted to their demise. *Forty-two, forty-three...*

Without warning, his musing became reality as the step, weakened by years of water expansion within hairline cracks, began to give way beneath his right foot. As his weight shifted toward the blackness of the shaft's core, Targus clawed the wall to his left, groping for a hold. Miraculously, his searching fingers found a ring and clutched it, even as the step completely crumbled beneath him.

The terrified scout now hung by a hand. Precious oil spilled from the lamp held in his other. The rough metal dug into Targus' fingers and compressed them into a painful knot. He knew his strength would give way within seconds. Slowly, he worked his feet up the wall, desperately stretching to touch the last intact step. He managed to catch the edge with the toe of his shoe, but this too crumbled and left him dangling once again. Summoning all of his strength, Targus made the climb again, bearing left to come closer to the step. Finally, his left foot found secure footing and he heaved his thin but muscular torso up to safety.

A decision was now required. Should he return the way he came and leave the mystery of the unexplored shaft to others? His lamp would not hold much longer, he reasoned, and a dead scout is a poor guide. The plight of the captives came to mind, however, and without delay he lunged forward to the shadowy steps beyond. After catching his balance, he stood motionless for several moments in hopes that the step was secure. Sensing no infirmity, Targus pressed his body against the wall and exhaled deeply. The sigh soon became a laugh as he recalled his prayer back at the entrance. *Lord, You either weren't listening or You have an unusual sense of humor,* he thought.

Targus refreshed his memory as to the number of steps he had taken down the staircase, making special note of the damaged area, and moved on with a renewed sense of urgency. He hugged the wall more closely now and greedily took whatever finger holds he could manage. Clutching, stepping, waiting—the descent continued with painstaking monotony until his count reached one hundred twenty-four. At that point, the wall opened up into a new passage. The scout was both relieved and frustrated at the change. He welcomed a release from the tension of the stairway, but wondered where this next leg might lead. He eyed his faltering lamp with concern and entered.

The new passage descended less acutely, but that advantage was offset by its size and difficulty. Originally cut to join the original shaft with the newer ones, one could only pass through the tunnel in a crouched position. After several yards, the discomfort of such a position became quite evident and, before long, Targus yearned desperately for an opportunity to stretch.

Small boulders were strewn about the floor of the tunnel, making the going tough for Targus. Numerous times the scout dashed his shin against a rock or stubbed his toe. It was harder to judge distance, as well, because of the inability to step it off. Soon the floor became littered with debris. The pieces were brittle and irregular, and crunched loudly as he compressed them beneath his feet and hands. Targus had to move much more slowly, fearing that the sound, amplified by the deathly silence of the shaft, might alert someone at the end of the tunnel of his coming. He also thought better of bringing along the lamp and left it on a boulder as a beacon for his return. Although it cast only a dim glow on the tunnel ahead, the scout's eyes were now perceptive to the faintest of illumination. Soon, however, Targus was out of breath and he gulped the stale air. *Better rest for a moment.*

The fatigued scout crouched with his back against the wall, and tried to stretch his back and neck. He then cleared the ground to sit and picked up an item from the floor. It was a small log, about a foot long. Its ends flared into smooth knobs. Targus ran his hand along its smooth surface. *Strange wood.* His other hand touched a more rounded object. He picked it up and weighed it. It seemed hollow, not like a stone. As he passed his hand over the object, the smooth round contour changed to one of sharp irregularity. He puzzled over the object for a moment, his left hand cradling the smooth roundness and the right pressing what felt like bony prominences. Suddenly, a sick feeling came over the scout. He ran two fingers of his right hand up the side of the object and gasped as they slid into two depressions. It was a human skull!

Targus abruptly discarded the skull and recoiled as it dashed against the opposite wall. He scrambled to his knees, then to the balls of his feet, conscious that he was surrounded by the decaying skeletons of an untold number of people. His heart pounded in his head and his starvation for air became acute.

Had he known the full tale of the mine, Targus would have anticipated the presence of the skeletons, although his emotions likely would have been no different. The bones, of course, belonged to the renegade slaves who dared cross the Order of Croesus in past years. Entombed forever in the bowels of the mine, the bones served as a sobering reminder that any who dared to cross the Order understand that their sentence for rebellion would be severe.

Little did Targus know, however, how beneficial those skeletons would be to the men of Lykos. The guards feared the dark recesses of the mine, and no place presented greater terror than that subterranean graveyard. The tales grew tall among them that the sealed shaft harbored an evil of Herculean proportions. A particularly harsh punishment was to assign a delinquent guard to the post for a day, while the others taunted from a safe distance. Usually, however, none dared linger in the vicinity for long. Consequently, it afforded a convenient gathering place for the miners to commiserate beyond the watchful eye of the slave masters.

Targus regained his composure and now breathed evenly. He resolved to go on, although his emotions begged for a return to sunlight. He groped along for a few minutes more, and then came to a place where the height of the tunnel increased to about eight feet. A short distance further he came to a large wall of boulders that marked the terminus of the passage. The light from the distant lamp was only a faint beacon now. He considered returning for it, but desired to pass through the bones only once more.

The scout conducted a blind inspection of the barricade, running his hands over the entire surface. It was evident that this was a solid seal of rocks and that great effort would be required to break through. Tools would be required and he had none—none except the bony implements to his back. Swallowing hard, Targus fetched a good-sized femur from the pile and returned to the wall. Reasoning that the highest stones would be the easiest to dislodge, he wedged the bone into a crevasse and began to pry. Cold sweat began to stream down his face and neck. Soon his lamp would grow dark.

After several minutes and bones, Targus succeeded in removing the first stone, a small boulder about a foot in diameter. Another tumbled down shortly after and soon an opening large enough to admit a man of his size was created. He poked his head through but to his great disappointment saw nothing. The air was heavy with the stale, musty odor of a blind passage.

Targus reached through and touched another wall about two feet away. He pulled through the opening and lowered himself to the ground, sequestered now in a narrow space between the two walls. Beginning at one end of the enclosure, he worked his hands quickly along the boulders to get an idea of their arrangement. As he neared the far end, he dislodged some loose pebbles and was startled to see a tiny shaft of light enter the chamber. Crouching to eye level as best he could, he peered through the slit between the boulders and indeed saw the glow of some sort of fire beyond. The light was painful to his dark-adapted eyes and he quickly turned away to recover. As he did so, however, his ear caught the unmistakable sound of voices. They were muffled beyond recognition, but advanced toward his position and then stopped.

The scout held his breath. Movement on his part might reveal his presence, so he had little choice but to press his ear to the crack and wait. He detected a fair amount of motion and the rattling of chains. A gruff voice grunted something and then there was silence. After several minutes, two of them took up a low conversation. To Targus' satisfaction, they had situated themselves immediately opposite his position.

"They're gone," said one, puzzled. "Why have they left us alone?"

"Fools," said the other. "For all of their fierceness, they run like little children."

"Do you think there's something to be afraid of here?" asked the one with reservation.

"They say there are phantoms nearby, but I've been in the mine as long as any and I've not seen or heard a thing. I actually prefer it here. It's the one place a man can get some peace in this hole."

"Well, I don't like it one bit. I wish I knew what was on the other side of this wall."

"God only knows."

"I'm thinking that God can't see this deep."

"Hush, you're sounding like one of those pagans with their ghost stories. God knows we're here."

"Yes, you *have* been down here the longest," the other laughed. "How long before they return?"

"Long enough to develop a powerful appetite. It's not easy to tell time, you know. Now, quiet down, I want some sleep."

A quiet settled on the other side and Targus contemplated his next move. He had been listening to the conversation with mounting enthusiasm and was now certain that a pair of brothers were on the other side of the wall. The difficulty lay in communicating with them without causing a commotion. After racking his brain, he pressed his mouth to the crack.

"The Lord God be praised!" he called in a hoarse whisper, reasoning that phantoms would hardly express such a sentiment. The salutation did not go unheeded. Targus heard a sudden rustling of chains as the pair stirred in alarm. "May our Lord Jesus Christ be exalted forever," he called again.

"Who goes there?" asked the veteran mineworker.

"A friend—and brother in the faith," answered Targus.

"Good prank, but how did you get on the other side of the wall?" the miner replied, thinking it was another of the captives.

"This is no prank," replied Targus tersely. "I have come by another way. It exits on the opposite side of the mine."

"Another way? Are you certain?" said the second man.

"Of course I am, my skeptical friend. I stood in the sunlight just an hour or so ago."

"How did you slip by the guards?"

"There are none. It is a deserted shaft."

"I say it is a trick," said the second man. "He's a spy. All right, you've had your fun. Come out and show yourself."

"Listen to me," said Targus in frustration. "I have come from Diakropolis to explore this shaft, to see if it could serve as a way of escape. The Master sent me. I was with him this very morning."

"The Master," replied the first man thoughtfully. "Then you really are telling the truth."

"Yes, yes," said Targus. "And this tunnel may be the means to your deliverance!"

"Well what are we waiting for," said the second enthusiastically. He dropped to his knees and began to claw at the stones.

"Not so fast," said the first, pulling his companion away. "There's bound to be more to the story. You there, what is your name?"

"It'd be better for us all if you did not know. I am also in the employ of your slave master."

"Aha! I knew there was a catch!"

"No, you don't understand. I am a scout by trade and have been hired by Siros to do some surveying in the hills. But, I am a true believer and work with the Master and his company searching for a way to free you and your families. You have not been forgotten."

"So, you *are* a spy," said the second.

"That sums it up," replied Targus with a laugh.

The pair mulled over the strange news and the unseen messenger.

"All right, then, you've earned our trust," said the first man, "but considering that we're pretty hopeless, that's no great feat. Be quick about your intentions before the guards come back."

Targus scratched his head. "I've been so preoccupied with making it to this point that I haven't given a thought about what to do when I arrived, much less if I contacted anyone."

"Think quickly then."

"I only came to gather information. I'll have to consult with my leaders. Can you be here tomorrow at the same time?"

"It was our punishment to be here now. I suppose we could do the same tomorrow, but I don't enjoy the flogging that comes with it."

"Perhaps a few more stripes will be worthwhile exchange for freedom, my friend," replied Targus.

"To leave this place, I would give the flesh off my entire back."

"How long have you been here?" asked the scout gravely.

"Who can say," came the downcast reply, "who can say."

"I've been here six months," said the second man. "His beard was already long when I arrived."

"Courage, my brothers. Liberation is at the door. I must go now. Until the guard returns, do your best to dislodge one of these stones. Conceal your work, though."

The men exchanged parting words and Targus began the arduous trek back to fresh air. Meanwhile, the two miners began to work feverishly on their end. The light from the lamp was only a glimmer in the distance, but that was more than enough to guide Targus back. The skeletons were less intimidating on the return trip, so buoyed were his spirits from the providential meeting. The stairs still presented a hazard, however. He carefully recounted their number, shuddering at the spot where he slipped. Soon came the final squeeze through to the alcove and the welcome bath of light from the outside world.

Targus flopped onto the small plot of ground within the boulders, overcome with the weariness of his journey. The sky overheard was already growing dark with the coming evening. He glanced at the small lamp just as the flame consumed the last of its fuel and went out. *So you were listening, Lord* he thought and drifted into a deep sleep.

CHAPTER 11

▼

Philip made his way back to the stream and gathered his tools, just as Pellas came into view on the lane leading to the farm. The light was beginning to diminish and, with it, the temperature. Hindered by his injured hand and distracted by thoughts of Cecilia, Philip figured little more could be done on the dam. He returned to the stable until Pellas called him for dinner.

Philip settled into his place at Pellas' table and quietly began to eat. Neither man was feeling talkative. Pellas was not in a pleasant mood. Although he had enjoyed the walk to town, his spirits gradually dampened as the day wore on. Argo, the blacksmith, had apologized for giving Philip the wrong part, and he promised his assistance should anything be needed on the farm. Pellas then had stopped by the market and found that grain prices were depressed, owing to a surplus, making it vital that the farm operated at peak production in the coming year. Next, the farmer had paid a visit to the gravesites of Phaedra and Alexander, bringing to recall a host of bitter memories. Pellas was happy to return to the farm and to Cecilia. There was no evidence of the girl's unexpected visit from Philip.

"How did it go today?" asked the farmer, breaking the silence.

"Fine," responded Philip, still looking at his food. "I found a suitable place for a dam and began working on it."

"Began? It is unfinished?"

"I hurt my hand about an hour after I started. Cut it when a pole I was using snapped in two." Philip brought up the bandaged hand from his lap for Pellas to see. "It bled a fair amount. I bandaged it but it still prevented me from doing as much as I normally could have done."

"I suppose so," replied Pellas. He returned to his food and mulled the possibilities should Philip become useless to him from the injury. "Did you clean it well?"

"The best I could. I apologize, but I had to return to the stable for proper bandages." Pellas tensed.

"I see. Well, that is understandable."

The two men were silent again.

"How was your trip to town?" Philip inquired.

"Productive. Argo had given you the wrong part."

"I'm sorry that it cost a day's work."

"No problem. Argo was so apologetic, I'm sure that the oversight will more then pay for itself."

Their conversation continued intermittently for the rest of the meal. Neither revealed much of significance. Philip was curious as to what else had occupied Pellas' time in Diakropolis, but he did not dare reveal what he knew. Pellas, on the other hand, was puzzled as to why the normally exuberant young man was so reserved. This was not because of an interest in Philip's personal affairs but, rather, a preoccupation with his own personal security. Pellas struggled to think of a way to secure an answer without appearing concerned. Finally, he decided to directly ask the young man.

"You are more quiet than usual this evening—not, of course, that that is a problem. I was content taking my meals in solitude before you came."

Philip made no reply but looked up at the farmer.

"It's just that this is out of character for you," Pellas continued. "I am wondering whether something is ailing you. Your hand, perhaps?"

Philip pondered the irony of his feelings. Was it not but a couple of weeks ago that he stood in a violent storm, pleading for shelter from this rude man? Now, Philip not only felt obligated to stay, but he feared being sent away—away from a place where he was sorely needed, away from a man who was at once repulsive, yet strangely attractive, and away from a newfound kindred spirit, in whose fragile constitution Philip had sensed virtue in its purest form. He could not leave, but Philip knew that he could not do that of which Pellas was so capable; that is, to live a lie.

Pellas interpreted the boy's silence as indifference and he began to clear the table.

"Pellas," said Philip, quietly.

The farmer stopped with his back to the young man.

"Yes?" Pellas responded cautiously.

"I know."

The farmer proceeded to take the bowls over to a small pantry.

"You know what?" Pellas asked nonchalantly, still facing away.

"I know your story."

Pellas sighed and returned to the table. He looked at Philip with a wry smile.

"You held your knowledge well, longer than I expected."

"I found out only two days ago."

"Your Master?"

"Yes. He reluctantly told me. Argo said something that made me suspicious and I prevailed on the Master to tell me about you."

"Once a traitor…"

"I needed to know so that I could better help you."

Pellas rubbed his face.

"I see. Is it vital to pry into my private affairs in order to milk my goats, mend my fences, till my soil?"

"I want to do more than that."

"I don't recall your asking if I desired more than that."

Philip threw his napkin on the table.

"Why must you be so stubborn? You can't wall yourself off from everyone else. It only brings pain in the end."

"Pain? The last time that wall was breached, fools swept in and destroyed all that I had. If I can erect a fortress ten times higher and stronger, then I aim to do so." The two men stared past each other in silence for a moment. Pellas glanced over at the closed door to Cecilia's room. He hoped that she was still asleep, as she was before he had invited Philip inside. "What did your Master tell you?"

"Just enough to help me understand. How he came to know you, your profession of faith, the tragic loss of your family…"

"Yes, they *all* died because of him," Pellas interrupted sternly, not so much to accuse the Master again, but to counter any suspicion that there might be a member of Pellas' family yet alive.

"Yes…all," repeated Philip, looking hard into the eyes of the farmer. "The Master also told me of your encounter with the magistrate."

"That?" said Pellas, chuckling. "That was a mere formality to clear my name. You Christians take such statements to be so solemn, so crucial. Mere words. That is all they are, just words."

"The Savior taught us that the things that proceed out of the mouth of a man come from the heart," Philip countered. "There is no such thing as mere words."

Pellas rose and returned to the small kitchen area.

"So, now you know all about me. My façade has been pulled down; the act is over. I have nothing to fear from you. I have a clean slate with the authorities and I have no interest in associating with the Master or his people ever again. We now can continue our relationship out from under the cloud of intrigue. My proposition is simple: Help me with the farm for a season so that I can get back on my feet, and I will see to it that you are properly compensated."

"I said that I would stay and help. This news has not changed that decision."

"Good. Now it is time for you to return to the stable."

Philip rose and slowly walked to the door. He hesitated before lifting the latch, and then turned to the farmer, who was cleaning off the bowls and utensils.

"There is one other thing."

"Ah, I knew that things would not be so simple. You wish to complain about your accommodations. Tomorrow, I will see that you..."

"No, it's really not about that," Philip interrupted.

Pellas looked at the young man through narrowed lids, his suspicion beginning to mount.

"What is it, then?"

"I have learned something else. I did not intend to find out, mind you." A nervous quiver entered Philip's speech as he struggled to find appropriate words to use. Pellas drew closer. "Please, you must know that no one had a hand in this...except God, of course."

"Say what you know," Pellas replied gruffly.

"I...I told you that I hurt my hand today, working at the stream. It was hurt quite badly, or so I thought. My hand was bleeding heavily and I knew that I needed proper dressing, so I came back to the stable for bandages and ointment. While I was at the cistern, I heard a call, a voice calling 'Father.' It was so faint at first that I thought it was a trick of the wind, or an animal in this distance. However, the call came twice more, and it was unmistakable: A young woman in this house seemed to be in distress and she was calling for her father."

Pellas' chest tightened at both the coming revelation and the thought that Cecilia had been upset, but he remained cool. Pellas encouraged Philip to hasten on with his account.

"I circled the house, calling out, but saw no sign of anyone and I did not hear the voice again. Finally, out of concern for the young woman's well-being, whomever she was, I climbed up and looked through the window in the back of the house." Pellas' nostrils flared in mounting anger. "On the floor, I saw a girl obviously dazed and injured. I had no choice, Pellas, but to come to her aid. You had bolted the door, so I climbed in through the window and helped her. She revealed to me that she was your daughter, Cecilia, and she told me of her terrible ordeal and of your concern for her safety. I'm sorry. I know this is not what you wanted to happen."

Pellas breathing now was regular and heavy as he glared at the perspiring young man.

"Sit down," Pellas said sternly.

Philip obeyed and, as he took his seat, Pellas slipped to the door and bolted it. He then went to the door of the bedroom and peeked in at Cecilia, who still was sleeping peacefully. Pellas carefully closed the door and took a seat opposite Philip.

"You must be quite satisfied. It has been a fulfilling day for you, having satiated your curiosity regarding my affairs."

"No, that was not my intent at all," objected the helper.

"So you say." Pellas pointed at the bedroom door. "In that room lies the only thing that is dear to me. The man who comes between my daughter and me will plead that he be given an easier fate, like facing a pack of ravenous wolves in the woods at night. I'm not naïve. I didn't think that I could keep her presence here a secret forever. Frankly, I expected her whereabouts to be betrayed by your Master, not by this unfortunate turn of events."

"The Master has never mentioned her, I assure you."

"Let's hope he keeps it that way."

"Pellas, I will help you protect her."

"You?" Pellas asked incredulously.

"Yes. We only talked for a short time, but already I feel a bond with Cecilia. I will work with you to restore her to health and to keep her safe. I anguished over whether or not to tell you these things. I knew that I couldn't hold it in, yet I feared that you would send me away."

"Stop!" growled the farmer. "Stop all this nonsense. You speak like a silly boy. You haven't lived enough years to comprehend the torture, the torment of my soul that is embodied in that sleeping child. For you, this is a giddy new adventure but, for me, I will spend every ounce of my being to see that no harm comes to her. Let God Himself come for her, if He dares. He will have to deal with me first!" Philip's mouth opened in astonishment at Pellas' words. "You fear that I will send you away? Oh, no, young man. You will stay right here with me. The Master and I have a gentlemen's agreement. We know too much about each other. You, on the other hand, are untested. I will keep you close."

"What are you going to do, put me on a leash?" Philip laughed nervously.

"That might do. You will now sleep in the house, where I can better monitor your activity. However, you are to have no interaction with Cecilia."

"But that is folly," protested Philip. "I know about her now. Why can't I see her?"

"Those are my terms, and they are unilateral. Since, as you say, God arranged for this chance meeting today, perhaps you should plead your case with Him. Now, let's go get your things."

Philip hesitated as he pondered his options, a scowl fixed on his face.

"Fine," he huffed. "I'm sick of that stable anyway."

As they moved to the doorway, Pellas grabbed a coil of cord.

"What is that for?" asked Philip.

"You suggested it," replied the farmer, as he began to loop one end around Philip's waist.

"Now, see here!" exclaimed the helper, yanking away the rope. "I'm not one of your beasts. You need to learn that people are not lurking behind every rock bent on causing you misery. If my aim was to turn you in, do you think for a moment that I would have put up with the abuse you have heaped upon me? I would have done my job and happily returned to more comfortable accommodations, rather than spend these weeks freezing in a rat-infested, manure-filled stable, sleeping on hay! I pity you for the terrible things that have happened and, no, I have never experienced even a fraction of your grief. But, as God is my witness, I commit myself to helping you—voluntarily, not out of compulsion or fear. You, sir, will again learn to trust another human being. Your first lesson begins now. Unlatch the door."

Philip stomped out into the chilly night to retrieve his belongings. When he returned, Pellas was not in the room. Philip heard muffled voices coming from Cecilia's bedroom, but he could not make out the conversation. He unrolled his blanket on the floor and lay down. After several minutes, the farmer emerged from the bedroom and went to his cot, which sat in a small alcove, separated by a curtain. Philip listened to the creaking of the wood frame as the man settled himself for the night.

"Is she all right?" Philip asked, once the noise stopped.

"Who?"

"Cecilia, of course," responded Philip, annoyed.

"As far as you are concerned, there is no one here by that name. Go to sleep."

Philip sighed and closed his eyes. Sleep overtook him as he prayed for Cecilia.

CHAPTER 12

▼

John awoke early. His small apartment was still bathed in darkness. He lay on his cot for a few moments, his mind becoming alert to the events of the previous day. His thoughts had frequently drifted to the unexpected discovery on the map but he tempered his excitement, conjuring up various explanations for the discrepancy lest he become too disappointed should the existence of a long-forgotten shaft prove false. Soon, John became vaguely aware of a presence in the darkness. His mind raced. *Siros has found us. Targus was captured and told all.* The leader of Lykos quickly contemplated what to do. Whoever was in his room certainly held the advantage; a quick escape would doubtless fail. John let his breathing become more rhythmic, hoping to deceive the intruder into thinking he was asleep again.

"There'll be no return to sleep for you, young Lykos," said a voice.

"Targus?" returned John, propping up on an elbow.

"Your ruse wouldn't fool a novice tracker," the other replied with a laugh.

"How did you get in, and why are you here so early?"

"As to the first question, call it a trade secret. The answer to the second, however, cannot wait for idle men to stir." John pulled a chair close to the man, whose features he could just make out.

"Go on."

"We have an opportunity—a very real one, at that. When are the others due?"

"You said same time as yesterday, so I would imagine not for a few hours yet."

"Too long. Go rouse them. I'll borrow a corner of your room for a short nap."

Even in the darkness, John sensed that fatigue etched itself deeply in the face of the scout. Targus had undoubtedly been on the move since they parted the day before. John quickly donned his cloak and left to retrieve the companions of Lykos, eager to learn more about the opportunity that lay before them.

John returned a half hour later with Thomas and Argo. Moments later, the light from a small lamp cast a dim glow on the form of Targus, curled in his cloak and sleeping soundly.

"I'm back, Targus," John said, nudging the scout slightly.

At once, Targus opened his eyes and sat bolt upright, alert to the setting.

"You could have used my cot, you know."

"Such niceties only make it harder to wake up," returned the scout, showing no sign of fatigue. He quickly scanned the group. "Where is the other?"

"Aelius has duties at the agora this morning. I'll fill him in later."

Targus nodded, but did not seem pleased.

"It is the will of God." The scout motioned the men to come close. "It is also God's will to bring to light a possible means to free our brothers from the mine. Aelius' observation was no error. There is indeed another shaft, although apparently it has fallen into disuse for some time through the twisted courtesy of Siros."

Immediately the room came alive with excited comments and questions. John silenced the men with a hand.

"Please, let Targus continue his story. We will search out this matter thoroughly, I assure you."

"When I left you yesterday, I thought it best to probe the Master's memory regarding the discrepancy in the maps."

"Why didn't we think of that, John?" interjected Thomas, prodding his friend in the shoulder. John's cheeks flushed.

"The old man has a keen mind. He remembered that the entrance to the mine faced south but could recall no other clues as to its precise location. I staked out the area for about an hour, studying the lay of the land. Other than a single passing sentry, who was obviously making a scheduled circuit of the mine, all was quiet. Eventually, I had to do some climbing in the open. Time and cleverness had hidden the old opening well, but in the end I found it. It is accessible, but barely so."

"Just how barely?" asked John.

"It will take someone with certain special skills," Targus winked. "But we'll speak of that in a moment." The scout then went on to hastily recount the story of his eventful descent into the mine, interrupted at intervals by comments, questions and expressions of amazement. Whether intentionally or in the interest of time, Targus failed to mention some of the physical features of the passage, as well as the shocking discovery of the skeletons.

"You're a better man than I, Targus," said Argo after the scout concluded his tale. "All that burrowing and scraping in the dirt is for moles, not bears like me."

"Think of what our brothers in the mine go through every day," added Thomas solemnly. "All the more reason to do everything in our power to break them out of that place. What do we do now, John?"

"I'll tell you we do," interrupted the blacksmith. "A window of opportunity has opened. I say we go for the whole lot—today!"

"And do what with them?" John replied. "Our network is much too thin to handle a large contingent of escapees. It was a miracle that we got Rufus and his family out."

"That place you hid them the first night was prime," said Targus. "Close enough to reach quickly, but off the beaten path."

"It's not secure," responded John. Argo looked at him, puzzled. "Pellas' place," the leader clarified.

"Pellas? Is he back in?" asked the burly smith.

"Not voluntarily. His farmhand Philip helped us out. He hid the family in the stable and moved them along before Pellas ever knew."

"I met the kid yesterday. Pellas sent him to the shop. Spirited young man."

"He has plenty of energy, all right, but I don't think that Pellas will be amenable to a mob of escaping Christians spending the night on his property."

"Still hostile to us?"

"He'd turn the entire lot of us in just for spite, I fear," responded John.

"We could redouble our efforts to locate allies in the hill country," suggested Thomas.

"How? Go knock on doors?" laughed Targus.

"It's hard, Targus," said John. "Our ranks have been decimated by Siros. We hardly have group gatherings anymore. I don't know who's left."

"I still say we need to strike while the iron's hot," stated Argo forcefully.

"Spoken like a true smith," said Targus.

Argo smiled at the observation, but then turned serious again. "So, what does our leader say?"

John thought for a moment. "We need a test run. Targus, can you arrange for half dozen or so miners to make a break mid-afternoon today? They must have no family in the Old City. We can't put others at risk yet. Then you can lay low—we can't afford to raise Siros' suspicions toward you."

"They are already raised, my friend. I crossed paths with Nikris late last evening on the way back from the mine. He asked many questions. He wants me to report to his man in Anakrakis by sunset."

"Can't you tell him no?" asked Thomas. "You are free to come and go as you please, aren't you?"

"So I thought," replied the scout, shaking his head. "It would be unwise for me not to comply."

"And for us," added John. "Targus is too valuable to our mission to compromise his standing with Siros. How soon then before you think we can move?"

"I see no need for delay on my account."

"But you know the way," said Argo.

"No fear, gentlemen. Realizing I would potentially be out of commission, I recruited my replacement for the job. I will have him meet up with you at the mine."

"Who is this man?" asked John suspiciously. "We may not approve of him."

"Little choice you have, John," laughed the scout. "You'll know him when you see him. He is not a believer but has a soft heart—and a mutual dislike for our nemesis. He also possesses those 'special skills,' as you will see."

"This is not good," grumbled Argo. Thomas placated the smith with a gesture.

"I'll confess to more than a little reservation about this," said John after a moment of thought, "but we've trusted our good scout so far, and I am not going to stop now. We'll head southwest after the break to the one friendly house of which we're sure. It's out of the way, but at least we're certain that Belarius will not turn us away."

"How many will be coming?" asked Thomas.

"You. Me. Are you up for it, Argo?"

"Aye," said the blacksmith grimly. "But no caves or tunnels for me."

"What kind of bear are you?" laughed Targus.

"And Aelius makes four," continued John. "Now, if there are–." Thomas cleared his throat.

"Perhaps we might leave Aelius to tend his young family. The risks are uncertain. Besides, we need eyes and ears in the agora."

"Thomas is right," said Argo. "We shouldn't be too hasty to make widows."

"Weren't you for storming the fortress a moment ago?" said John, scowling. "All right, it is dawn now. In an hour the city will be stirring. We'll make our move then. I know of a southbound caravan we can travel among for cover."

"Three of us will be no match if we are discovered by the guards," complained Argo. "If we're opening up this mission to all willing participants Thomas and I can have a small army in no time. You'd be surprised how many folks would like to see Siros taken down."

"Not this time. This is still a test."

"As you wish," the smith reluctantly agreed, "but I think you are putting the whole operation at risk by pulling your punches. We need to strike while…"

"While the iron's hot, I know," John interjected, his ears flushing with impatience. "I hear what you're saying, Argo, but it's a risk I'm prepared to take. I can't put so many lives in jeopardy."

"I agree with John," Thomas said emphatically. "We can only have one leader, Argo, and John wears that mantle. Remember, Siros is one wily fox."

Argo pushed back from the table.

"I, for one, am sick of hearing how clever Siros is. I say we march right down his throat and snatch what is ours!"

Targus leaned close to the others and spoke in a serious tone.

"Hear me now. In the past months, I've had a window into the man's mind and it's not pretty. There's none more bent on doing us harm. At night, while you fellows sleep, he sits in a chair with eyes half opened, glazed over like a reptile. You know what he's doing? Planning our doom. He has a net spread over the city such, as you can't imagine. Oh, there's a hole or two still in it, but he's running the net, boys, running the net."

The group fell silent and solemnly contemplated Targus' words. Unexpectedly, the scout slapped the table and gave a laugh, startling the company.

"But, remember, 'Greater is He who is in me!'" Targus exclaimed, clapping Argo on the back. The group joined him in a relieved but wary chuckle.

John eyed each man and waited for further questions.

"It's settled, then. We will meet at the south end of the agora in an hour ready to move."

The room emptied quickly. Thomas and John lingered at the threshold.

"I appreciate your show of support, Thomas," John said candidly.

Thomas smiled and clasped John's shoulder.

"Any plan is fraught with peril, my friend."

"They like you better, you know," John continued, gazing through the partially open door into the awakening street beyond. "Perhaps…"

"*You* are the leader," interrupted Thomas.

"Come, Thomas. Only because a very aged man declared me so."

"The Master's mind is sound, and you know it. He has the faculties to discern such things, John."

"Does he? It was *your* vigilance that saved us at the way station. It was *your* diversion that saw Rufus and his family to safety. How long must you follow my steps and correct my oversights? Just say the word and the mantle is yours."

"It is not required that a leader plan for every contingency. Your so-called oversights are opportunities for me to assist. Ask the Master; he'll tell you the same. Perhaps that is why he made the choice he did. Now, I'm off. Clear your head and I'll see you shortly."

John remained in the doorway as Thomas left, pondering his friend's counsel. He ran his fingers through the tight waves of his hair and looked around the apartment. He had been gone so long the room was an inhospitable mess. He scrounged around the meagerly stocked pantry and found a hunk of stale bread. After scraping the mold off with a fingernail, he took an unsavory bite, only to pitch it with disgust into a corner. *Clear the mind, eh? Maybe a walk will do me good,* he thought.

Pulling on his cloak and drawing the hood close, John stepped into the narrow stone street that passed before his home and entered the mundane workday of Diakropolis. Two men exchanged words in a doorway, stopping briefly to take account of him, then returned to their conversation. A woman drew water from a small cistern while her young child strained on her tiptoes to splash a hand in the pool. A dog sniffed through some freshly tossed refuse at the curb. A shopper quibbled with a grocer over the price of quail hanging ominously from the low-hanging eaves of his store. To the casual observer, it was a day like any other in the city.

John meandered through the avenues of the city, his mind preoccupied with the words of Targus, and the disquieting fact that he stood in the path of the evil devices of Siros. An overturned vegetable cart jarred John to awareness of his surroundings and he realized he had unconsciously arrived on the Master's block. *Must I always run to him when I have questions?* John smirked. He recalled his last meeting with the Master and how the answer to his need for a safe venue for Rufus' family had been met in the coincidental visit by Philip. *I suppose I must if I want answers.* John found the front door unlocked and let himself in.

John found the Master in his interior garden, tending a vine that wrapped thickly around a trellis. The early morning sunlight filtered into the garden and illuminated the Master's snow-white hair. Lingering mists curled lazily along the ground and gave a dream-like quality to the scene. John paused to watch the dignified old man move slowly from branch to branch, carefully examining the growth before selecting the proper branches for pruning.

"How do you know what to prune?" John asked from the shadows.

The old man turned and squinted.

"Who's there?" he asked calmly.

"It's John. May I disturb you?"

"John! Why, of course, you may 'disturb' me. Come, join me." John entered the garden and hugged the Master. "To what do I owe the honor of this visit from the leader of Lykos?" John sheepishly looked down at his feet. "Are there problems, John?"

"You may have heard that Rufus and his family are safe at the caves."

"I hadn't heard, but I felt confident that was the case. They'll be safe there. The caves have been a reliable refuge for many a year."

"Our task is far from complete."

"It seems never-ending, doesn't it?"

"We know that Siros is boiling and will not sleep until he sniffs us out. Although we have an opportunity now with the abandoned shaft to free those in the mines, we don't have enough safe houses to handle them. We've lost so many to the Order that those believers who haven't been captured or killed are too scared to come out of hiding. It would be foolhardy to liberate our people only to see them slaughtered in the hills. Surely you've seen how few believers gather to meet anymore." The Master sighed but said nothing as John continued. "Even now, the remnant that is Lykos goes possibly to its demise." John's voice trailed off.

"What do you want from me, John?" Fatigue and resignation were evident in the elder's tone.

"Take your rightful place as our leader. You are Lykos, not me."

The aged man slowly walked to a bench and carefully sat down.

"I am old, soon to go the way of the earth. You are the leader, now, my son."

"I am the leader only by your decision."

"Nevertheless, you *are* the leader."

"You picked the wrong man. Thomas is far better with people than I."

"And a valuable companion and encourager for a leader. No one goes it alone, John."

"I can see that you are going to resist me on this matter."

The Master smiled and placed a hand on John's shoulder. "I'm not resisting you, John. It's time for *you* to lead. As long as I draw breath, however, I will uphold all that you undertake in fervent prayer. That I *do* pledge." John hung his head. "Don't be downcast. Our ability to tap into the eternal power of heaven should bring hope and gladness."

"In my heart, I know that prayer is the most effective weapon we have, but I am fearful."

"What do you fear, my son?"

John ran his fingers along the coarse bark of the vine and sighed.

"I've asked myself that question many times. I fear leading my brothers…sisters…to deprivation…torture…even to death. I fear being responsible for tragedy and heartache among families. I fear mistaking my emotions for God's voice. And I fear my own appointment with death."

"These fears are all natural. I had them, too. For reasons known only to Him, God has chosen to prolong my days on this earth. Perhaps it was to have this conversation. Remember, don't underestimate your value to God as His child; but don't overestimate your necessity to His program on earth. The Lord raises up leaders for the times. My time is nearly past. Your time is just beginning. God will carry you through your days and grant you the results He ordains." John smiled grimly and nodded.

"Now, what was your original question?" asked the Master. John looked at him with a puzzled expression. "Ah, yes. How do you know which branches to prune and which to leave? Now, that is a difficult question." The elderly man thought for a moment.

"It requires observation to see which branches have been productive. That, of course, means patience—a very difficult attribute to develop. Finally, it takes a willingness to wound the plant for its eventual good. That is the hardest part, John—for both the gardener and the plant. The process is a picture of how God deals with us. He wants us to draw our sustenance from Him alone, just as the branch must do with the vine. As He examines our lives, He will often prune away those things that give us false security, for He knows they will wither under the tests of life. A man of prayer will stay firmly affixed to the vine."

"I said that I know prayer is our most effective weapon," replied John, slightly distressed.

"Do you? That may be soon put to the test."

John looked intently into the graying eyes of the Master, who returned the gaze with unblinking intensity that seemed to hearken back to the remote past. The two remained locked in the stare for nearly a minute.

"Who are you?" asked John presently. The Master stirred.

"Who am I? I don't understand."

"Master, you teach well from the world around us and have a remarkable ability to look inside a man, but you've never told anyone about you—your life, how you came to Christ, your struggles. Perhaps I would be a more fit leader if I better knew my mentor."

A look of pain crossed the face of the elder.

"You ask for something that I have never given. Somehow, though, it seems right that now you should know these things. Come to my room."

John took a seat in the Master's private chamber. The dull gray sunlight streamed in through a high window, bathing the cluttered room in a pale, somber glow. The elder paced slowly across John's view, contemplating how to begin. He picked up the military helmet from a table and gently stroked the faded plume. Finally, the Master spoke.

"In the history of man, I don't think there ever was a more unlikely candidate for redemption than I. I was born in Caesarea, on the shores of the Great Sea in Palestine. I am a Roman." The elder caught the look of surprise on John's face. "Yes, a Roman. You will hear more astounding things than that, my son. My father was a military man; I followed in his footsteps. Suffice it to say, I was sold out to the empire—body, soul and spirit. I served in Palestine and beyond, ever ready to put life and limb on the line for the emperor. I hated two things passionately: the enemies of Rome and the Christians."

"Why the Christians?"

"Because they represented the consummate stupidity and feebleness of the human mind. Imagine, following a dead Jew who claimed to be God. Beyond that, their Messiah, this Jesus, was not content to join the Pantheon of our gods; no, He aimed to supersede our gods, to displace and conquer them. This was folly, and only an enemy of the empire would ally himself with such thought.

"Then, one day I met a man who shared my disposition, yet he was in a position to bring about action, our leadership being weak-willed about such things at the time. The man's name was Saul."

"Not the same Saul…"

"The very one. You know his story well, and his miraculous conversion. We worked together to destroy this renegade new religion. He devised, while I, in my capacity as centurion, looked the other way. However, I moved on and lost touch with him, until one day many years later. I was in Rome on business that will pierce my soul for the rest of my days. I had never softened in my hatred of the Christians. A valiant fellow officer by the name of Marcus was one of them. For years, he had stood in the way of my advancement. If there was a promotion to be had, it went to Marcus, not me. Somehow, his faith escaped the notice of the emperor. I know now that it was God's providence. Soon, the climate was right to bring Marcus down, so I exposed him. He was brought to trial in Rome, where

I made my accusations before the emperor. Marcus made no defense, at least none that sought to sway the emperor from the inevitable sentence. I still remember Marcus' testimony before the court that day. Rest assured that all who gathered came under the hearing of the gospel, and they will be judged accordingly.

"After Marcus' trial, I happened across Saul, now called Paul, some years later, this time as he was being held prisoner in a dungeon and marked for death. We talked of his life and conversion, and how his hate had been transformed to love by Jesus. He knew me well, that Paul, for we were kindred spirits at one time. In that repulsive, dark dungeon, which so aptly exemplified my soul, Paul shed light on the source of my hatred toward God. Like all men, pride was food and drink to me, and I feasted well upon it. For once, however, that which had sustained me for so many years had turned bitter to my taste and sour to my stomach. Paul spoke to me of Jesus and, although I had heard the story from Marcus many times, for the first time I comprehended its truth. I had been like the Pharisees listening to one of Jesus' simple parables, blank to its meaning.

"I received the commission that I had anticipated. I was made the second-highest ranking officer in the Syrian legion, second only to the general. But for all my glory, the picture of Marcus' lifeless body tumbling down the steps to the Tiber—judged rightfully, so I thought—would not leave my mind. While on the ship to Palestine to assume my command, I placed my trust in Christ.

"Now, I found myself in the difficult position of serving two masters. Shortly after, we were ordered to Jerusalem to lay siege to the great city. There, I experienced cruelties of unspeakable proportion on the part of both sides. The tension within my life mounted daily as we campaigned. Finally, I could tolerate the duplicity no longer and I did the unthinkable: in the dead of night, I deserted."

John made no comment; he sat transfixed on the old man's face.

"The next months were ones of tremendous fear and danger. I traveled always at night, certain I would be apprehended at any moment and suffer the same fate as Marcus, but for far less noble reasons. I moved north, staying clear of cities, surviving off the land. As I moved further away, I felt liberated and I actually reveled in my circumstances. Soon, however, winter came, and the elements dealt harshly with me. Mind you, I had not long been a Christian. I understood only a fraction of what you or I do today. In my heart, I felt that I had justly deserted an evil slave master but, similarly, that I had been deserted by the One I sought to follow. In my distress, I came upon a village and pleaded for food and shelter.

"The people there gave abundantly to me out of the little that they had, and it was not long before I learned why. The entire village had been brought to Jesus through the efforts of Paul some years before. We rejoiced together as we shared stories of the Apostle. They encouraged me in the faith and taught me what it meant to follow Jesus by their actions.

"After winter had passed, I sought to move further from my past. The villagers aided my flight by sending a guide with me. We moved from village to village, from one tribe of believers to another. Everywhere, I saw the fruit of the tireless ministry of Paul and his disciples. I moved through the region of Lycia, still only by night. There, I chose a new name—Lykos, the Wolf, because, like the wolf, I moved by stealth under the cover of darkness. The name also gave life to the ravenous spirit growing within me, which was desperately hungry for more of Jesus. Finally, the name resembled my true name, Lucius, and it daily reminded me of my past, even as I would imagine Paul continually was reminded of his past, through the similarity to Saul.

"The first city that I dared to enter was Ephesus. I spent considerable time there secreted away within the church, learning at the feet of John and Timothy. Eventually, I deemed it safe to embark on a ministry of my own. Bithynia was attractive to me. I learned that Paul had wanted to carry the gospel here himself. Additionally, it was remote enough that I could feasibly maintain some anonymity. I wandered through the region and found the people of the villages receptive to the gospel. It was as if the land was fully seeded, just waiting for the quickening rain of knowledge. However, it was not quite so simple in the cities; there, I found tremendous corruption and hostility to the message of Christ, even as you see now.

"In the providence of God, I settled here in Diakropolis and began a church, periodically venturing back into the countryside to tend to those fellowships. The evil grew great, however, and I found my children of faith persecuted, dragged before the authorities and killed. My anger grew hot and I formed a network by which I could snatch my children away to a place of safety. I gave the network my name: Lykos. To those around me, I simply became known as the Master, although I preferred being known as the Servant. With the aid of others, I established a series of safe houses leading across the province to a haven deep within the forested mountains of Pontus, a series of caves known only to a few.

"Along the way, I became the enemy of those who practiced lawlessness and persecution, of whom Siros was chief. I must sadly tell you that there are many like Siros in the cities of the province, men who shake their fists at the living God and refuse to acknowledge Him. We did battle, Siros and I. With the able help of courageous men such as your father, those intended for the gladiators or wild beasts would slip through his fingers to safety. Even now, I marvel that I wasn't executed or assassinated. It just wasn't my time. But, I was no fool, either. As a seasoned warrior, I knew how to best him at his game. I felt I had God on my side and became obsessed with undoing all the wrongs that had been committed with my approval.

"Soon, I discovered that Siros operated a mine and manned it with slave labor working in the harshest of conditions. I labored night and day to reach those poor slaves with the good news that their physical captivity need not extend to their souls. The gospel spread among them like wildfire and my passion to see them free raged even greater. I pled their cause before the magistrate and the city council, only to watch their tolerance change to open hostility and threats. With the emperor Domitian in power, a new hatred of those of the faith was kindled. My boldness brought exposure to all of us. The church was scattered, tortured, and, like your father, killed. The slaves, meanwhile, many of whom now were believers, followed my lead and took matters into their own hands, lashing out in rebellion. The outcome was tragic. All but one perished, buried somewhere deep in the bowels of the earth. That one was flung at my doorstep, a message of warning affixed by knife into his back.

"At once, I retreated in fear and confusion. What whirlwind had I reaped? My words, which once had been the vehicle of life, charted also a course unto death. Where was my God? Had He left me in the heat of battle—when I needed Him most? I died that day, or so I thought. You see, what I had yet to learn was that the clash between God and Satan, or Paul and Saul, or even Lykos and Lucius for that matter, was not a game of war as I had understood it, pitting strength against strength, strategy against strategy, with the loser the weaker opponent. Somewhere in the war plan of God was His permission for the enemy to strike victoriously—that somehow in the tragedy of suffering in the body for Christ's sake, the strategy of our enemy would be exposed for the ineptitude that it is. This was the essence of Christ's teaching—that we should not fear the one who can kill our bodies, but rather He who holds power over our souls.

"It took years to understand this truth, just as it did to rebuild the church. In time, we were growing and healthy again, yet much more cautious. Siros forgot about me, Domitian was gone, and Trajan ascended the throne. Things seemed quiet—until recently. When I learned that Siros had not only strengthened his diabolical enterprise, but had done so on the backs of our brethren, those same wrenching indignations erupted.

"Do I grieve over the persecution of my children? Daily. Do I wish to see an end to this accursed engine of hell? As God is my witness, I would draw my last breath this very moment if it would bring about such. There is within me a quest for justice here and now, and that is Lykos, not Lucius. The fear is gone. Ha, what does a relic like me have to fear anyway? But, I am feeble—I cannot lead."

There now was an extended time of quiet and stillness. The Master had strolled around the room as he related the tale, periodically handling an object as he spoke, but now he occupied his seat behind the cluttered desk. John sat motionless, struggling to grasp all that he had heard in the previous minutes.

"There it is, John," sighed the old man, now looking far older than when he had begun. "Learn from my story what you will. You alone now know the tale, and I ask that it remain that way. In the telling of my past, I realized that there was still more to prune from this old vine. I'm glad that you asked when you did."

John rose from the chair and clasped the trembling hands of the Master. He was speechless. The hour was late and he knew he must join the others without delay.

"Go now, son," said the Master kindly. "Lead, but remember the battle is the Lord's."

CHAPTER 13

▼

The darkness of late evening engulfed the governor's villa and, with it, came the quiet of inactivity. Linus' residence was a center of perpetual activity, with the receiving of dignitaries, conducting of official business, and the endless program of banquets and state dinners. All of this excited Marcellus, but he relished the opportunity to think in solitude. He walked along a terrace overlooking the city and ran his finger through a layer of frost that already had accumulated on the balustrade. The cold wind that swept across the city made him shiver uncontrollably, but he had resolved not to seek the warmth of his chamber until his decision had been made.

Linus had approached him after dinner once more about taking the chief magistracy of Prusa, evidently prodded to do so by Atarix. Again, Marcellus had refused, but he worried that he was placing the governor in a difficult situation. Marcellus had only one day left in Nicomedia before returning home, and he desired to spend that day certain of his destination.

A chill wind blew in from the northwest, carrying a faint smell of the sea. As Marcellus breathed deeply, he became aware of a new fragrance, sweet and aromatic. He puzzled over the smell for a moment. It was winter and the flowers were gone. Presently, he became aware that he was not alone and turned to find Arcadia standing a few feet away.

"Arcadia, I didn't know that you were there."

"I saw someone walking on the terrace and I came to see who would be out in this cold. I thought that you had retired early."

"I just needed to be alone. This house is a busy place."

"You'll grow accustomed to a constant audience as you rise in position, Marcellus."

"That's not necessarily something I look forward to."

Arcadia looked around.

"So, what are you doing out here—besides freezing?"

"I was just looking over the city lights for the last time—and thinking."

"What? You're leaving tomorrow?" the woman asked anxiously. "I thought that you had another day here."

"Yes, but tomorrow will be spent in final meetings and preparations to leave. I doubt that I'll have these moments again."

"It's a beautiful scene, isn't it?" asked Arcadia, as she gazed out at the points of light that dotted the blackness.

"Yes, it is." Marcellus nodded.

"However…" Arcadia paused.

"Not so beautiful as Prusa," Marcellus continued with a sly smile, anticipating her thought.

"As a matter of fact, it's not," replied Arcadia, defensively. "The view from my house is much more spectacular."

"Yes, well, I've heard about your house, if that's what it can be called."

"Oh, it's not only *my* house. There are many elegant homes in Prusa. It's a very beautiful city, and a very desirable place to live."

"I have no doubt, but I have made the decision to return to Diakropolis," said Marcellus, emphatically. "I'll have to do my best to endure its squalor."

"Oh, come, Marcellus. Let's not squabble. I didn't come outside to goad you into coming to Prusa."

"You mean the campaign to entice Marcellus out of Diakropolis has been defeated?" the magistrate asked jokingly. "Somehow, I don't believe that."

"That's hardly a polite thing to say. You shouldn't turn on your supporters. We're simply looking out for you and trying to promote your career."

"I'll handle my career, thank you."

"Don't be so smug, Magistrate. There are many other capable leaders for Prusa. And now that I see how ungrateful you are, I'm glad you're not coming."

Marcellus softened.

"Look, I'm sorry. I guess I've gotten a bit testy after hearing from Linus, then you, then your father, and Linus again. It's a hard enough decision without your collective input."

"Maybe we are trying to tell you something that you're too thick-headed to understand on your own."

"Thick-headed? Now who's being impolite?"

"It's just that I've never met someone with so much ambition who can't recognize when the door is flung wide open for him."

"Maybe I don't like where the door leads," countered the magistrate. "Maybe I don't want to be your father's personal public servant, always running interference for his pet projects."

"Well, I never!" Arcadia huffed indignantly.

"I wouldn't act so put out, Arcadia. I've been in this province long enough to know how the system operates. At least in Diakropolis, I have the chance to be my own man."

"So that's all that's important to you—being your own man. And I thought you were more selfless than that."

"Rome has enough lapdogs—civil servants who sell out to the rich under the guise of helping the common man."

"Let me see," said Arcadia, frowning. "You have insulted my intelligence, my family's ethics, and lectured me on politics—all in the last five minutes."

"It has been a busy conversation, hasn't it?" replied Marcellus.

Arcadia turned her face from the magistrate and looked off in the distance.

"I'm sorry, Arcadia," sighed Marcellus. "We do set about to arguing, don't we?" He put an arm on her shoulder; her muscles tensed. "Everything tells me that I should go to Prusa. Everything except my heart. Or my conscience. Or instinct. Or fate. Or…whatever it is. All I know is that I am compelled to return to Diakropolis."

Arcadia continued to gaze off in the distance.

"If that's the case, I guess we have little else to talk about."

"And why is that?" bristled Marcellus. "Are you only interested in me as long as there is a chance that I might come to Prusa? Are you ready to give up the trail now that you have lost the scent? As I recall, I was the selfish one just a minute ago."

"It's not like that at all," protested Arcadia.

"Then how is it?" demanded Marcellus, gesturing emphatically. "Instruct me, that I may be wise in discerning hidden meanings. I've been in Nicomedia for a week and a half. I came to study, to learn how to govern my city. Yet, instead of discovering what I might do to better Diakropolis, I am besieged by advice to go to Prusa, where, for some reason, they are in desperate need of a novice magistrate. Here in Nicomedia, I am everyone's friend. Noble Marcellus, beneficent and wise beyond his years. A star on the horizon! Governor Marcellus? Certainly! Emperor Marcellus? Even better! Let's beseech him to come to Prusa. What's this? He declines? Bad Marcellus. Ignorant and selfish! Let's try him again tomorrow. Still obstinate? Let's try him again the next day, and the next. Oh, his mind is made up? In that case, we have no further need of him. He's just a fool."

Arcadia wheeled around.

"Oh, be quiet, you silly oaf!" Marcellus ceased his tirade and looked around self-consciously. "You'd be the last to know that there might be another reason," she continued.

"Like what?" he asked impassively.

Arcadia lowered her head and gazed at the terrace floor.

"Perhaps the reason I want you to come to Prusa is…entirely personal."

Marcellus swallowed hard and pulled at the collar of his garments. He could think of no response to that sentiment. He faced the city and firmly grasped the balustrade with both hands. Arcadia turned away from him and drew a deep breath.

"I had hoped," she continued quietly, "that you would come to my city on the merits of the position alone to spare me this. Linus told me how much you loved your wife and I found it too awkward to express how fond of you I was becoming. But, since you have made your decision, I guess that doesn't matter anymore."

Marcellus clenched his teeth and shivered. The cold was heightened by his insecurity over this revelation. Since his wife's death, he had not been the recipient of any other woman's affection. Marcellus felt strangely exhilarated, despite his uneasiness.

He cleared his throat to speak, but the words did not come. He cleared it again.

"I'm sorry…I didn't know."

Marcellus turned to face Arcadia, who stood with her back to him. In the dim light, it appeared that she was quietly crying. He reached out his hand to touch her, but withdrew it. A flood of emotions came over him at once. He recalled his first meeting with Arcadia, and his slight suspicion at her manner of speech and the way she carried herself. There was an air of meekness and deference in her comportment, but he sensed that it was manufactured to mask her true self—shrewd and manipulative. Even now, Marcellus could not help but question her professed disappointment over his decision to return to Diakropolis.

All his doubt was offset, however, by an embryonic hope that maybe she was being honest in her expression of affection. Up until this time, the thought of another woman was disagreeable to Marcellus but now, standing out in the cold with the warmth of a beautiful woman so close, the idea had a certain acceptability, even a practicality, to it. An older woman would be beneficial to Claudia, he reasoned. Moreover, there was the question of male progeny. Septimus was always after Marcellus about this.

Marcellus' face contorted as he tried to sort out the conflicting thoughts swirling in his head. Arcadia continued to quietly cry. Finally, Marcellus moved close and gathered her in his cloak. Arcadia nestled comfortably in his arms and pressed her cheek to his chest. He gently stroked her long, brown hair and breathed in her perfume.

"I have an idea, Arcadia," he said softly. "What if you returned to Diakropolis with me?"

"I can't leave my father," she replied, without looking up.

"Why? Is he ill?"

"No, but I am the only family he has. It would be too hard on him, and on me."

"You could visit him frequently. He could come to Diakropolis."

Arcadia pulled back slightly and gazed at Marcellus.

"Linus told me that you brought your daughter to Bithynia because you couldn't bear to be apart from her. Would you suggest otherwise for another man?"

"No, I suppose not," Marcellus responded, returning Arcadia's gaze with kind eyes.

The couple stood motionless for several moments, Arcadia wrapped in the cloaked arms of Marcellus, each looking deeply into the other's eyes. Slowly, the space between their faces began to close and Arcadia closed her eyes in anticipation. Marcellus held his breath. As he felt the warmth of her lips nearing his, he abruptly brought his hands around and rested them on the woman's shoulders, stopping any further progress. Arcadia opened her eyes and stepped back, puzzled.

"Arcadia," he said kindly, but with a hint of caution. "I…I…"

"Yes, what is it?" she responded softly.

"I will reconsider my decision." A smile spread over the face of the woman and her wide eyes sparkled with the light of nearby torches. "But I am fatigued now," Marcellus continued, "and I wish to do nothing that might cloud my judgment."

Arcadia nodded and gave a brief, quiet laugh.

"I understand, Your Honor. I guess we stand adjourned."

"I guess so," replied the magistrate, as he gave her shoulders a gentle squeeze before releasing her. "Good night."

"Good night." Arcadia moved away toward the house. "If the cold gets to you, you can—oh, never mind."

"I can what?" inquired Marcellus, his head cocked in suspicion.

"Linus said that there are extra blankets in the pantry." Arcadia laughed and disappeared into the house.

Arcadia smiled as she strode down the hall. She passed a room where a candle still burned and poked her head inside the door. In a chair sat Atarix, half snoozing. He opened one eye at the sound of his daughter's voice.

"Well?" came the one-word question, brief, but pregnant with meaning.

The daughter merely smiled.

"Go to sleep, Father."

PART II

▼

FEAR AND TREMBLING

CHAPTER 14

▼

Early the next morning found Marcellus already busy at preparing for his departure. By the time the rest of the house stirred, he had already met with the captain of the guard to review the proposed route back to Diakropolis and to shore up any needed provisions. Marcellus had awakened clear-headed about matters of the previous evening. The wavering that he had felt in the presence of Arcadia was gone, and he was more resolved than ever to return to his current assignment. However, more than once that morning, he had reflected on their meeting. Marcellus could not shake his doubts over the genuineness of Arcadia's sentiments toward him, and daylight brought more suspicion than trust.

Marcellus met with the chief magistrate of Nicomedia over breakfast to discuss common concerns, including the difficulties of managing city finances. He finished out the morning rummaging once more through the city archives for any profitable material, and then returned to the governor's villa for lunch. Marcellus found Linus dining alone under a canopy adjacent to the gardens. The sky was heavy and overcast, threatening rain.

"Marcellus, where have you been all morning?" inquired the governor. "Arcadia has been looking for you."

"I had a few appointments and was preparing for the trip home," responded the magistrate, popping a handful of nuts into his mouth.

"I trust that everything is in order." Marcellus nodded and chewed. "Is your destination set?" Marcellus eyed Linus suspiciously.

"I thought it was clear that I intended to return to Diakropolis," said Marcellus.

"Hmm. Arcadia seemed to suggest otherwise."

"I did not intend to leave her with that impression. I've decided to return to my post."

"Very well. If that is your final decision, I'm with you all the way." Linus leaned toward the young judge. "That *is* your final decision?"

"Yes, sir."

"Splendid. We'll hear no more on the subject."

"Thank you, sir."

The governor took a bite of fish and washed it down with wine.

"No, Marcellus, we'll anticipate great things coming out of Diakropolis with you at the helm. Prusa is no longer an issue. You'll hear no more of it from me."

"I appreciate that, Your Excellency," Marcellus said cautiously, suspecting that the official had not yet had his final say.

"How rude of me! Care for wine?"

"No, thank you, sir."

Linus rose from his table and belched. He placed a hand on Marcellus' shoulder.

"You are a wise young man. Always have been. If you are convinced that this is the proper course to take, I trust your judgment. Henceforth, I will be silent on the subject."

Marcellus looked at the governor and winced.

"Sir, you've mentioned not mentioning my decision any further three times now."

"Oh, have I?" asked Linus, nervously brushing the crumbs from his garments. "Your choice has me in sort of a bind, Marcellus. I'll be straight with you. I don't intend to be in Bithynia for a long time, but I do aim to leave the place better off than I found it. Atarix and his allies control the merchant lanes, no matter how enamored you are of Roman sovereignty. What's more, Trajan's desire to eliminate the trade unions places more power squarely in their hands. I was hoping for an opportunity to bring Atarix in check in a friendly way…"

"An opportunity you saw in a liaison between Arcadia and me?"

Linus gave a subtle smile and nodded.

"I'll admit that there was secondary gain for me in the enterprise," said Linus, "but, mind you, your best interest is always paramount."

"I believe you, sir."

"But tell me, son. Didn't you find anything the least attractive in her?"

"Certainly. There is much to which I'm attracted. But something—I can't put my finger on it—makes me cautious."

"Oh, I know the thought of marrying another woman can be a bit uncomfortable, but it's not that uncommon. Look around. I'm quite an oddity, married for so long to the same woman."

"I'm not intimidated by the idea of remarrying, sir."

"Then what is it? You won't find a more attractive, wealthy, and eligible woman in the entire empire."

"That may be true, although the empire is vast. I don't know the reason for my hesitation. A look in her eyes, an inflection in her speech—a vague feeling that she wants to possess, not to share a relationship."

"Oh, Marcellus. Always analyzing. There's no law that says you have to love her."

"No, but love would help," laughed the magistrate. "I invited her to come to Diakropolis with me to become better acquainted, but she did not want to leave her father."

"That sounds reasonable. It's rumored that he's been infirm."

"Ha! It's amazing how much vitality returns at the sound of jingling coins. You watch—Atarix, Siros, and the whole lot will outlive me."

"I assure you that I won't be around to see the outcome, Marcellus," said the governor. "All the more reason to see you on the right path—a path of strategic alliance and calculated advancement. With the right moves, you'll become so powerful that you can order up whatever you want. Let's forget Prusa. Under your leadership, I have no doubt that Diakropolis will be the epicenter of a tremor that shakes Anatolia and the entire empire! Besides, I have enough influence to see that a certain woman pays a visit to your jewel of a city." Linus raised his goblet in a toast.

"To Marcellus! Singular, resourceful, indomitable—in every way like his mentor!" Marcellus joined in the toast and shared a laugh with his devoted patron. "Now, how about one more visit to our splendid baths before you go?"

"Thank you, but I have a few last-minute things to prepare. I'll join you at the evening meal."

Marcellus returned to his quarters and gathered his personal effects. He gladly accepted the governor's offer to borrow whatever documents he wished, and Marcellus' satchel bulged with scrolls and parchments. Among them, he had selected a copy of *Lex Pompeii,* the principal legislative code of Bithynia, and a comprehensive military history. Linus also insisted that Marcellus take several volumes of his uncle's works on natural history. These Marcellus wrapped and packed with care.

The gloom created by the thick bank of deep, gray clouds that covered the city filled Marcellus' room. He rarely slept in the afternoon, but this day he felt unusually drowsy and lethargic. He closed the curtain and stretched out on the bed, figuring a short nap would make him a livelier dinner guest. As Marcellus lay with his hands behind his head, staring at the ceiling, he wondered again what mischief Septimus had gotten into and the problems that he would have to sort through when he arrived home. He then pondered what Claudia would think of Arcadia. Would she find the idea of her father remarrying to be repugnant? Marcellus thought of the girl's mother, recalling the ease of his late wife's company and of her gentle ways, then drifted off to sleep.

Marcellus slept far beyond the brief nap that he had intended, awakening briefly on several occasions, only to lapse back to sleep after a glance around the dusky chamber. His sleep was shallow and dreamless for the most part but, as time progressed, unsettling images began to appear, causing him to shift uncomfortably on the bed. The images seemed human in form but they were indistinct. Gradually, the images became more recognizable, and Marcellus realized that he was in Rome, in the great Colosseum, which was filled to capacity. At first, he seemed to be observing the scene from high above, as if he were a bird, but then found himself standing on the floor of the giant arena itself, facing the emperor's box.

The faces of the audience were indistinguishable, but the image of the chief prince was clear. The potentate motioned to two figures standing nearby. Marcellus turned to observe two innocent-looking young girls dressed in flowing white gowns move solemnly toward him. As they approached, he could see that they bore several articles in their outstretched hands. The first girl placed on his head a dull, gray helmet, its metal beaten and irregular from numerous encounters in the ring. The second girl fitted an armored sleeve on his left arm. Her companion then placed a clean, shiny sword in his right hand. In an instant, the two girls vanished.

Marcellus looked at the sword and armor and realized that he was outfitted for combat. A sense of apprehension came over him as he examined the battle gear. The noise of the crowd swelled. Marcellus looked up and saw the face of the emperor turned toward the end of the arena. The magistrate gazed toward a tunnel enveloped in fog. From it emerged a sturdy figure, thoroughly armored and striding toward him. A visor covered the man's face. Marcellus gripped his sword tightly and unconsciously assumed a battle pose, his left forearm raised to fend off a blow. The man—an opponent, Marcellus assumed—drew closer. The sound of the crowd surged and ebbed, reverberating like the crashing surf against a rocky shore. The foe now was within striking range, but to Marcellus' amazement, he strode past without as much a glance in his direction. The warrior took up position a short distance away with his back turned to Marcellus and stood poised as if to strike in battle.

A whoop arose from the crowd. Marcellus strained to see whether another opponent approached from beyond the gladiator. A small being emerged from the fog. It moved slowly, but steadily, toward the armored combatant. As the figure came into clear view, Marcellus saw that it was a lamb. Without hesitation, the animal padded directly up to the gladiator and stood still. With astounding speed, the warrior fell upon the lamb with his sword, hewing off the creature's head with one swipe of his blade. The uproar of the crowd was deafening. Marcellus looked at the scene in astonishment. The gladiator had once again assumed a fighting pose. The dead lamb lay at his feet in a pool of blood, still twitching. Marcellus looked at the emperor, who sat calmly with a faint smile.

A second lamb approached and the horrible scene was reenacted—then a third, and a fourth. With nauseating repetition, a steady stream of the harmless creatures marched to their doom, never turning to the right or to the left. The ground was thick and matted with their blood, and the carcasses were piling high. A large, cloaked man lumbered back and forth, tossing the bodies into an old, wooden cart, stained dark red from use in this terrible trade. He laughed derisively as he went about his gruesome task.

Marcellus instinctively tightened his grip on his sword. He inched toward the armored man. As he came closer, a horrifying sight made him gasp. The faces of the lambs were human—men, women and children. Filled with revulsion, Marcellus quickly drew alongside the gladiator and opened his mouth to protest, but no words came forth. Anxiously, Marcellus turned to appeal to the emperor's sense of decency but, to his further dismay, the staid countenance of Trajan was warped into that of a grotesque, leering despot. The faces of the vast assembly now were clear, as well, but this, too, presented a revolting scene—all were masked with the mocking grin of the comedian. Gradually, the crowd enjoined the chilling laugh of the cloaked undertaker. A shrill, pulsating sound echoed in the arena as the spectators roared with amusement at the carnage.

Unable to contain his indignation, Marcellus stepped between the assassin and his next prey. The gladiator stopped and held his sword aloft. Marcellus struggled to speak but remained mute. The foe reached out with his other arm and began to push Marcellus to one side. Marcellus dug his heels in and resisted. The combatant pushed harder but Marcellus resisted yet more. For what seemed like minutes, the two strained at each other, neither giving way. Marcellus slowly brought back his sword to striking position and, for a time, the two mirrored each other in pose. Marcellus sensed pain streaking down his arms as he held his sword ready with the right and pushed with the left. His whole body ached, but he dared not to relax. Finally, spent and exhausted, Marcellus' arms fell to his sides.

To his amazement, the figure before him stayed utterly motionless. Marcellus moved closer. He could detect no sign of breathing or quiver of muscle, yet the man did not change his position. Slowly, Marcellus grasped the hinged visor and lifted it. He gasped. The face was that of Septimus, but there was no flesh, only stone. Still, the taunting laughter rocked the stadium. The large, cloaked man came over to the stony figure and took the sword from its hand. He then moved to the line of lamb-people and vigorously crashed down on them, grunting loudly as he went. Marcellus wheeled in a frenzy and fell upon the shrouded figure with the flat of his sword, driving him to the ground. Marcellus repeatedly struck him until there was no movement. Straddling the man, Marcellus lifted away the hood that hid his face. Before him was the unmistakable visage of Siros, his face marred and ashen from the apparently fatal assault by Marcellus.

Marcellus stared at the face for several moments, aghast but unable to move. Slowly, the eyelids opened and the being became animated once again. Marcellus dropped his sword and began to recoil from the figure. He wanted to run, but he struggled even to lift his feet. Slowly, Marcellus moved away, but the floor of the arena had turned to a crimson-colored mud that bogged him down and rose ever higher on his legs. He glanced over his shoulder and saw that Siros had not returned to the slaughter of the lambs but was bearing down on him, closing the distance between them with shocking speed. The sound of the crowd shook the stadium. The muddy, bloody arena floor began to swell with waves that violently rocked Marcellus as he tried to escape. Still, Siros advanced. Marcellus turned to face the man, now violent with rage. Marcellus lifted his armored arm and drew back his sword, all the while straining to keep his footing. Everything around him was in motion, swaying and spinning. Before him, the image of Siros now swelled to gargantuan height, its massive arm outstretched to deliver the telling blow, but the strike never came.

CHAPTER 15

▼

As it turned out, Marcellus need not have worried what mischief Septimus had instigated in his absence. The deputy had spent the hours after his liaison with Siros awash in wine and wayward women. While Marcellus busied himself with last-minute preparations for departure from Nicomedia, the reprobate brother groped through Diakropolis nursing a horrendous headache. Meanwhile, Marcellus' secretary, Jason, stayed clear of the dyspeptic deputy and transacted official business in the magistrate's name.

All was quiet in the Old City, as well. Siros and his security force had occupied the day performing background checks on all those under his control, both captive and free. No detail was too insignificant to escape the scrutiny of Nikris and his agents. Nothing of importance was uncovered that would affect John and the company of Lykos, although several lower-level guards were severely flogged for operating a loan-sharking ring using pilfered coins.

The lull in business as usual afforded an excellent opportunity for success in the latest attack on the stronghold of Croesus. John, Thomas and Argo sat crouched within a tight ring of boulders near the mine. A heavy bank of clouds hid the noon sun. Soon, a steady rain began to fall. John pulled his cloak tight around his neck, exposing the scabbard of a short sword that hung at his waist. The blacksmith looked up at the sky and grimaced as raindrops pelted his face.

"This is all we need," he growled. "The paths will be boggy, for sure."

"Don't be so gloomy," said Thomas. "This could be as much to our advantage as not."

"Thomas is right," added John. "God is in control of the elements. This rain will keep the guards inside." Argo grunted and pulled his cloak over his head.

"It also seems to have deterred our guide," he stated sourly. "I knew we should have waited until Targus was with us."

"What about that 'hot iron', Argo?" replied John sharply.

"My friends, we'll get nowhere with this kind of talk. Besides, we should keep silent. We may be overheard."

The group fell to silence at Thomas' urging. All that was heard was the steady thud of the pelting raindrops on their cloaks. Presently, the sound of a forest bird came from above. The attention of the three was immediately drawn to the noise.

"Good day," came a voice hidden by the branches of a nearby tree. A moment later, an odd-looking man dropped into their midst and sized up the startled group. "So you are the great liberators Targus mentioned. I heard you coming from a great distance. You stand little chance if you don't curb your tongues."

"And who is this scrawny eavesdropper?" commanded Argo, who stood indignantly, his hand on the hilt of his sword.

"Steady, Argo," said John, restraining the smith with a hand. "Let's not spoil the welcome. Friend, I take it you are the guide our good scout promised. I am John."

"Ah, yes," smiled the man, squinting warily at John. "The leader of Lykos. The dauntless wolf has come to snatch his own from under the distracted nose of Siros. Pleasure to meet you." He extended a hand. "I trust you are prepared."

"As much as our limited knowledge of the situation allows. This is Thomas, a leader of equal measure." Thomas thrust his hand out and grasped the hand of the man, still extended toward John in greeting, and shook it vigorously.

"Our gratitude in advance for your selfless act, my friend."

The man forced a smile and withdrew a step.

"Let us not race ahead of ourselves, gentlemen. Terms first."

"Agreed," said John.

"Let's start with a name," said Argo bluntly.

"Fair enough. The name's Sebastian. And you, my burly, hotheaded friend, must be Argo the blacksmith. 'Get on his good side and it will go well with you,' warned Targus. The trick is finding one, I can see."

"Alright, Sebastian," interjected John before Argo's ire could boil over, "you know us fairly well. Tell us something about yourself. What is your motivation to help us?"

"Of course," laughed Sebastian. "I should expect you would want to know what ilk is addled enough to lead you into the jaws of the beast." Sebastian grinned and wiggled his brow, which was generously furnished with coarse, wiry hair. He then began to move stiffly to and fro, his gaze directed towards the trees in contemplation, as if preparing for a dramatic recitation. The others settled on the ground, anticipating some tale.

Sebastian was a strange man, both in appearance and mannerisms. His thin, tawny face was deeply creased and covered with several weeks' worth of ungroomed whiskers. His restless eyes, set deep in their sockets, shone with a wildness that suggested a troubled past and a present barely contained. Ill-fitting clothing hung awkwardly on his sinewy frame and shifted inelegantly from side to side as he moved about the enclosure. His motion was jerky and somewhat writhing, and his frame alternately straightened and bent. With each change in posture, a look of discomfort passed across his face followed by a sigh. Despite evidence of some physical handicap, however, there was a coordinated grace about the man that hinted of the reason Targus recruited him. He stopped abruptly at intervals, seemingly poised to speak, only to continue with his restless maneuvering. Finally, the odd ballet ceased and Sebastian spoke.

"Here are my credentials," he said abruptly, thrusting out a bare arm from under his cloak. "And here is my pledge."

The men gazed intently at Sebastian's arm, which was markedly disfigured by deep, contracted, purplish scars along its length.

"There are more, if you care to investigate. My legs are quite lovely. My neck is drawn so tight to my belly my flesh burns with pain each time I stand erect. Mere eating and drinking is a dreaded effort. How did I come by these marks? Ask the one who owns this mine, for in a moment of twisted recreation, he administered each one with a red hot brand—rightful punishment, so he claimed, for a job ill-performed. With every laborious breath I draw, I curse the crazed animal that scours this earth for plunder. I have waited for an opportunity to avenge my wounds, but what can a cripple like me do? When Targus spoke of your plan, I saw my opportunity to steal from the thief himself. Thus I offer myself to you a willing accomplice to your enterprise."

The trio of men watched the animated account with varied expressions. Argo, partly biased by Sebastian's initial greeting to him, maintained an air of disdain. Thomas leaned forward in sympathy as the man spoke, his brow knit in compassion. John studied Sebastian cautiously, trying to detect any hint of deception in the man's words.

"We're not going to steal any copper, if that is why you're here," John said as Sebastian concluded.

"No, no. You are after something more valuable to Siros, by far, Lykos. I know about you Christians, and I know something of his hatred for you. I know how he longs to possess your kind for his sordid pleasure and how he quakes with rage when one slips through his fingers. I know what you seek, my friends, and it would give me delight to help you find it, for in that quest, I may find a moment's ease from my travail."

"Are you one of us, then?" asked Thomas eagerly. "Are you a believer?"

"Consider me sympathetic to your cause," replied Sebastian.

"We'd much rather have you joined to our cause," said Thomas. "Perhaps you would like to hear more about Jesus."

Argo nudged John and motioned toward the mine. John nodded and said, "As much as I'd like to continue this conversation, we must remember our task. Time is of the essence."

"Yes, let's set about the business at hand," said Sebastian, immediately drawing to the edge of the enclosure and setting his eye on the rocky hillock a short distance away. "The guards are not likely to be about, not in the rain. Are we ready?"

The others nodded and were soon quickly away, scampering across the clearing to the nearest boulders. Sebastian looked briskly both ways and then scurried up and over the rock at their backs. The others followed suit, Argo bringing up the tail, puffing as he tumbled over into an alcove within the boulders. None of the men of Lykos spoke, but all were amazed at the agility of their guide.

"Here we are," whispered Sebastian. "Exactly as Targus described. That opening leads to the old shaft."

"That?" said Argo, incredulously. "A snake would lose half its skin going through there."

"It's bigger than it looks," chuckled Sebastian.

"And so am I," huffed Argo. "I'll stay here."

"That was my intention anyway, Argo," said John. "You and Thomas keep watch while Sebastian and I go in."

"I would prefer the smiley one come with me," said Sebastian.

"Thomas? Why?" asked John, a bit offended.

"I like him—and he seems more adaptable. A very important trait."

John reluctantly yielded to Thomas, who shrugged and smiled sheepishly. After a brief round of well-wishing, Sebastian dropped to all fours and slipped effortlessly through the crevasse into the darkness of the shaft. Thomas squeezed in with some difficulty but joined him in the space beyond.

"I am beginning to understand why Targus recruited you for the job," said Thomas quietly.

"One makes the most of one's handicaps. Now be quiet and watchful. This is no child's play."

Sebastian took a small lamp and a flask of oil out of a pack at his side. Soon the small chamber was illuminated with the dim light. "Here we are at Siros' doorstep," said the man with a greedy smile. "Time for a little thievery."

"What did you do to earn those scars?" asked Thomas.

"I'm a gravedigger—or was," replied Sebastian. "We do lots of business with Siros, as you might expect. I botched a job. It was one of his competitors."

"Botched?"

"Competitors go in the river, chained to a block. I mistakenly buried him and registered the name with the authorities. Siros had to do some fancy maneuvering on that one."

"All those scars just for that?"

"You don't understand, my innocent friend. Many have perished at the hand of Siros for much smaller mistakes. He took particular delight at my pain that day—slow and easy he took it. Left me for dead."

"That's horrible. How did you survive?"

"Search me. Sometimes one is convinced Hades has come calling, but you can't will to die."

"God sustained your life to help us," Thomas said after a brief pause.

"It's as reasonable a guess as any others."

"It's no guess, Sebastian. Things happen for a purpose. God ordained your association with us. He is calling you to be His child."

"Child? Now that's a dandy notion. I haven't had a father since I was a wee thing."

"I can show you how right now."

"No time now. We've got to get moving."

"There might not be another opportunity, Sebastian. Best to square with God first."

"I'll make you a deal. If we pull this off, I'll square with God. Until then, this rogue orphan has a score to settle with someone no one would want for a child."

Sebastian led Thomas along the path previously taken by Targus. The scout's careful mental notes were invaluable as the pair managed the obstacles that presented along the way. Sebastian negotiated the crumbled stairway with the nimbleness of a cat. He passed a length of rope through the rings on either side of the defect to help the return journey. Thomas was more awkward with his turn, but successfully crossed the hazard. Leaving the lamp as a beacon at the mouth of the tunnel, they began the final descent toward the miners, quite pleased with their quick progress.

"I can't imagine doing this without a companion," whispered Thomas presently. "Targus must have been glad to get out of here."

"Death takes some getting used to."

"Death? What do you mean?"

"It's all around us. You're walking on it now." Thomas froze. "Steady now, my friend. They can't hurt you."

"Th-they?"

Sebastian took Thomas by the hand and drew him forward through the bones that littered the floor of the tunnel. Thomas became aware of the debris strewn about and, although he had no direct knowledge of the skeletons, surmised the worse from Sebastian's hints.

"Are these...?"

"Indeed. Apparently, there is a good reason this shaft is sealed. It seems that scoundrel Targus left an important detail out of his account. No matter. It's all the same to me."

Thomas, who was unaccustomed to such casual encounters with human remains, gripped Sebastian's arm tightly and tried to train his mind on other things, although with each crunch and rattle he found his attention pulled back to the gruesome surroundings. Finally, the sounds died away and the ground became smooth. A short distance further and the two were at the wall of rocks.

"Here's where we do business with Siros," whispered Sebastian. "Let's hope our luck holds and your friends are waiting."

"Our success depends on the will of the Lord, not luck," replied Thomas. "They'll be there."

Sebastian carefully scaled the rock wall and found the small opening to the other side. He slipped into the narrow crawlspace between the two partitions, wincing in pain as he straightened his frame. A thin shaft of light from the adjacent mine shaft outlined what would be the portal to freedom for several fortunate souls. Sebastian positioned himself as comfortably as possible and began to scratch the rock lightly. There was no answer. He continued his signal for many minutes, pausing momentarily to listen for movement. Sebastian was just about to return to Thomas when muffled voices became audible. He could not tell whether they belonged to guards or miners, but after a time decided that he must make contact. A few taps were answered with the same and Sebastian sighed with satisfaction.

A flood of light burst into the crawlspace and dazzled Sebastian's eyes to the point of pain as the boulder was pried free from the wall. A face appeared and squinted into the dark recess.

"Greetings," said Sebastian quietly, startling the man.

"So, you are not a phantom. I have passed some anxious hours wondering if you would come back."

"I am not the man who spoke to you yesterday, but he sends his regards. We must make the most of our time, however. I have been instructed to lead six of you to safety, but none can have family in the Old City."

"Why such a restriction?" replied the man suspiciously.

"Siros might vent his wrath on them should we fail."

The man spat on the ground, his dirty face taut with disgust. "Siros belongs here, among things that crawl in the earth."

"Patience, friend. No one knows that better than I. We must respect his might, however. How quickly can you round up a party?"

"That depends on the guards. I will go as quickly as possible."

The man repositioned the stone and departed. Sebastian returned to Thomas with the news and then took up his position once again in the cramped recess. It was difficult to measure time in that setting, but after what seemed a good while by Sebastian's reckoning the stone was removed once more.

"Here we are, six souls eager to smell fresh air," said the miner who had first greeted Sebastian. "Once word got out, it wasn't hard to recruit. Move them through quickly. We may not have much time."

One by one, the men filed through the small opening and snaked their way to Thomas. Sebastian's concern that some might be too large was allayed by the somber realization that most were emaciated to the point of skin and bones. Finally, the sixth began to push through when the first miner stopped his progress.

"You don't look familiar. Are you new?"

"I came two weeks ago."

"Two weeks," sniffed the first. "I've been here two years. You have family?"

"No, well, yes, in a way."

"What way?"

The other grew anxious. "Look, I've got to get to my wife and children. I can't stay here. My skin is crawling. I can't sleep."

"Quiet, son, you bring trouble. We're all a little beside ourselves down here. Is your family in the Old City?"

The man hesitated. "Yes."

"You'll have to stay, then."

"No, I can't," the man called in a dangerously loud voice. He began to struggle through the opening, the first miner restraining him and Sebastian blocking his forward movement. "Let me go!"

"The guards will be on us soon," said the first, dragging his distraught companion from the opening. "May God grant us success," he said to Sebastian as he heaved the stone and shoved it into place.

The disqualified miner clawed frantically at the stone. The first man wrestled him to the ground in an effort to settle him, but the contact broke into a full scuffle. This proved to be fortuitous, for as the guards arrived, they assumed it was common scrap and ignored the partially dislodged stone in the wall. After a thorough whipping, the two miners were dragged away and danger passed.

The journey back was difficult but uneventful. The bones did not unsettle the escapees as much as Sebastian had expected. Steeled by their hard labor in the bowels of the earth and the prospects of breathing once again the sweet fresh air of the open land, the men shuffled through the bones without so much as a grunt. Nor did the treacherous climb up the staircase slow the team. Emotions soared as the group wound their way ever higher, each man in his own way expressing the elation that was welling up within. One by one, the former miners emerged into the tight alcove where John and Argo waited. Each covered his face as he came into the shadowy light of the space. It was the first light the men had seen in some time.

John greeted each man with a blessing and a vigorous hug. Thomas' face beamed brightly as he emerged through the crevasse, his fists clenched in a silent cheer. Finally, Sebastian presented himself, his countenance one of smug satisfaction mixed with the impish delight of a successful prankster.

"Well done, well done," said John, as loud as he dared, brushing the dirt and pebbles off the wiry man.

"Yes, good job," added Argo, chagrined at his earlier assessment of the guide.

John surveyed the party cramped in the small recess.

"Only five, Sebastian?"

"The sixth had family. It hurt to leave him behind, but there's wisdom in the plan."

"We'll return soon. All went well, though?"

"Here we stand," replied Sebastian, triumphantly.

"Excellent. Now, the next task is to leave the premises without a trace of our having been here. How are your legs, men?"

One of the miners chuckled.

"How are yours? What do you think we do down there, play dice?"

The group shared a laugh, and then John motioned them to leave. The men scampered across the short distance to the ring of boulders where they had begun. Sebastian lagged behind and smoothed the tracks as they went. The rain had let up a bit by now and it was possible that some of Siros' men might make a circuit of the area. John addressed the entire group in a hushed tone.

"Gentlemen, we are far from safety yet. The first leg has gone according to plan, but we are not yet home. Our route will be difficult, but we must stay off any traveled paths. We will head southwest, directly away from the mine. I hope to put many miles between this place and us before nightfall."

"That's good," said Sebastian. "The most direct path away from here is best. There may be guards in the area."

"Bring them on," said Argo. "I'll give them a taste of the finest steel in Bithynia."

"Pray it doesn't come to that, Argo. You don't know whom you are dealing with. Now listen, we will be climbing a lot. I apologize for your feet, my brothers."

"Forget our feet," said one of the miners.

"If mine are raw to the bone but we're safely gone, that's all right with me," added another.

"There's the spirit," said John, smiling at the determination of the small company. The escapees looked haggard, but all had eyes ablaze with hope. "Physically, you men are a sight, but something tells me a fire burns inside."

"We have been in hell, no doubt," said one grimly, "but even in that desolate place, there was a spirit among us that Siros' worst threats couldn't quench. Count us in when you return for our brothers."

"Your aid will be sought, I assure you." Turning to Sebastian, John said, "My friend, your task is finished. I don't know how to begin to thank you."

Sebastian scuffed the ground with his feet and looked at Thomas, who returned his gaze briefly and lowered his head.

"Look," began their guide haltingly, "you fellows may find yourselves in a spot, and I've really no need to get back right away, and I know a good deal of this country, and…"

"Why don't you come with us?" suggested Thomas with a knowing smile.

"I suppose that would be fine," responded Sebastian, with an awkward grin.

The company wasted no time evacuating the ring of boulders. They scampered away in a straight line, clambering over boulders, through trees and down gullies. Their pace was surprisingly swift for their number, but incentives ran high. The ultimate destination was the highly secret haven simply called "the caves." Its location was known only to a select few, including the Master, John and Thomas. Rumors of its existence abounded among the people of the town and, to date, Siros had failed to discover the site, but not for his lack of trying.

At one time, Siros had launched an exhaustive search of the region around Diakropolis under the assumption that the caves were nearby. His failure to discover the site led him to conclude that the caves were only figurative. In reality, the caves were some distance away in the mountainous region of Pontus, requiring several days' journey, depending on speed of travel. Because of this distance, the Master had developed a network of safe houses to provide food and shelter for those in flight, but these had been decimated by persecution. This night the party hoped to reach the farm of Belarius, well out of their way, but a certain sanctuary.

The team had traveled at an unabated pace for twenty minutes and signs of fatigue were showing. John called for a halt behind a rock formation near a small thicket of trees. The group sunk to the ground, panting. Skins of water were passed around and drained gratefully. A few minutes more and they would be on the move again. John carefully surveyed the landscape. Argo listened intently to one of the miners while the others caught a brief rest. Thomas, meanwhile, sidled next to Sebastian, who was rubbing his sore feet.

"Well, Sebastian, it appears that we were successful."

"That we were, fellow thief, and sweet is the thought of it, too."

"Sweeter still if more was achieved than simply inconveniencing Siros."

"Meaning...?"

"Before we went down the shaft I believe you said you'd square with God if He brought us out safely."

"So I did."

"He's waiting to hear from you. Listen, let God deal vengeance to Siros—and let Him deal mercy to you. Trust me, you'll never find satisfaction in repaying that man for the evil he did to you, even if you pulled down the pillars of his house on top of him."

"I wouldn't mind giving it a try," Sebastian responded, his jaw set defiantly.

"See, even now your appetite for revenge grows again, and repeatedly will until you are consumed by it."

"How do you know?" came a brusque reply.

"Look at Siros. Revenge is his stock in trade."

Sebastian shuddered briefly at the thought of bearing any resemblance to Siros, and then studied the ragged band of escapees.

"These men here look like common sort. This God of yours cares for such people?"

"God doesn't separate people into groups like we do. He only has two sorts: those who are His children and those who aren't."

"It would seem that His children often fare worse."

"So it would seem, but there is a purpose even in suffering. It makes us more like His Son."

"God has a Son?"

"Yes. His name is Jesus. He is the Christ—God's chosen One to save us from our sins and give us eternal life."

"Whoa, my friend. You are talking way over the head of a gravedigger."

"You are more clever than you credit yourself, Sebastian. Tell me, what do you think happens to all those folks you bury."

Sebastian contemplated the question for a moment and then responded, "Time was, I would have said nothing. They just ceased to be. Then, one night there was this girl; she was as dead as I've ever seen anyone be. Mauled from head to toe. I was about my business there at the gravesite while one of her family, her father, I think, was tending to her body. All of a sudden, she comes alive! I ran so hard I thought my side would burst. Later, I started thinking: Where was she all that time she was dead? And where am I when I'm asleep? My body's on the bed, but where am I?"

"Those are deep thoughts from a common gravedigger. Yes, there is a part of you that lives forever. It's the real you and one day it is going to leave that troubled body of yours. When it does, it is going to one of two places—either to the presence of God or to a place apart from Him, forever. All of us must decide in this life which place we will go."

"Tell me about where God lives."

"It's called heaven. Only a few have gotten a glimpse, but they say it is a place of unspeakable joy and beauty. We are made whole there."

"And the other place?"

"Unspeakable grief and darkness. Unending pain and death."

"A continuation of this life," mused Sebastian as he stroked his scarred, misshapen arm. Thomas placed a hand on the crippled man's shoulder.

"God has the power to heal you—your wretched body with all its scars, but more importantly, your soul. You are marred on the outside, Sebastian, but all of us are marred on the inside. That's what God calls sin. Sin will lead us to that place apart from God, but God offers you a way to His home. You can't do anything about your body, but you do have a choice about your soul. But you have to make a decision before you leave this body—a decision made by faith in God's Son, Jesus."

"What does Jesus have to do with my decision?" asked Sebastian, growing a bit perplexed. "And who is Jesus for that matter? You speak of him as if he could walk right up at any moment."

Thomas then realized that he had falsely assumed that the poor gravedigger knew something of the background of those he had come to aid. He begged Sebastian's forgiveness for his oversight and for the remainder of their respite talked enthusiastically about the life of the Savior. Sebastian's interest was piqued with the account of Jesus' torture and death at the hands of his unscrupulous accusers.

"There's more to squaring with God than meets the ear," said Sebastian once Thomas concluded.

"It's both simple and hard. Simple because nothing is required except a choice. Hard because you have to mean it."

Suddenly, the men heard a snap coming from the trees.

"Down," whispered John as he motioned them all to be silent.

Several more cracking sounds were heard, and then the unmistakable sound of conversation. At least two people were advancing toward the refugees out of the thicket. John settled himself into a position where he could spy the trees. What he saw made his heart sink. A small company of Gauls, arrayed in full battle out-fit, was fast closing in on the Christians. There were five Gauls, maybe six. From the looks of it, they had been hunting, for each carried a string of rabbits slung over his shoulder. There was not much time to prepare the group.

"Gauls…upon us," John whispered urgently. "Remember what I said before."

John again turned to face the Gauls, now only fifty paces away. If they maintained their present course, they would pass immediately by the rocks. Only a miracle would prevent the refugees' discovery. John unsheathed his sword. Thomas and Argo did likewise, while Sebastian and the miners armed themselves with large rocks. The coarse talk of the Gauls now was clearly audible. The refugees stayed motionless against the rocks. One by one, they heard each of the hunters pass by, the Gauls' conversation unbroken. After a few moments, all was quiet. The company let out a collective sigh of relief. Slowly, John raised his head and peeked over the top of the boulder, while his men eyed him hopefully. A satisfied smile spread over John's face as he confirmed that the Gauls were gone.

"Hallelujah," Thomas said quietly.

"Hallelujah," echoed the other men.

John rose to his full height and stepped into the open.

"What have we here?" a voice growled.

John wheeled around and stood face-to-face with a fearsome warrior, a sixth guard who apparently had emerged later from the forest. John pulled his sword from its scabbard and poised for battle. The other men scrambled to their feet and did the same.

"Got fight in 'em!" the guard called. It seemed to John that the Gaul was addressing someone else, and it was not long before John understood why. The other five guards emerged nearby from hiding. It was a trap.

The first Gaul laughed viciously.

"Saw you from the forest. Looks like you have something of ours. Now put your little dagger away, boy."

John had only a fleeting moment to decide his course of action. Without hesitation, he lunged at the Gaul, toppling him backward.

"Run!" John shouted to his men.

They did not heed his order but, instead, turned to face the advancing five guards. John smote his sword against that of the Gaul, again knocking him to the ground.

"Sebastian! Go! Now!"

Sebastian hesitated for a moment, and then heaved his stone at the guards, striking one in the head. The Gaul fell to the ground, dazed.

"Won't leave you!" Sebastian called.

There now were four guards to deal with. John still had the upper hand over the first Gaul, driving him down with another clash of the sword.

"In the name of God, run!" John screamed.

Thomas and Argo had engaged two of the Gauls in individual combat while the others pelted as many as they could with large rocks. This put the guards at a great disadvantage because they could not protect both fronts. Another Gaul went down, dazed from a rock to the forehead. The blacksmith's foe struggled to see through a stream of blood that flowed from a cut above his eye. Argo shoved the handicapped guard to the ground with a powerful thrust of his leg and prepared to drive his blade through the opponent's chest. John caught the intended act out of the corner of his eye.

"Argo, stay your hand!" John commanded. It was too late. The fatal blow had been delivered. "Sebastian! To the trees! Fly!"

Sebastian complied with the order this time, sensing that the battle was in hand. Two guards lay dazed, another dead, and the other three nearly dispatched. Sebastian called the liberated miners to his side and bolted away toward the small forest.

The three pair of opponents fought on. The advantage held by the men of Lykos appeared to be slipping away as the Gauls fought with almost inhuman rage. Metal crashed against metal as the swords of the warriors rained down on their lesser-trained rivals. John's hopes wavered as he saw one of the stunned Gauls staggering to his feet to join the conflict.

Just as the tide seemed destined to turn decidedly against the men of Lykos, a rain of large stones came upon the Gauls once again, sending them backward. Sebastian had returned with the company of miners. In that brief respite from battle, John gave the order for all to make for the trees. In an instant, they took flight, bounding over obstacles in their way. John held the rear and glanced over his shoulder. The four Gauls had been joined by the fifth, now recovered from his stupor, and they were in determined pursuit.

The two parties raced through the forest, dodging trees and fallen limbs. The men of Lykos were less encumbered than their pursuers and kept an even distance from them. They exploded out of the forest onto a rugged terrain of deeply rutted, rocky ground. Large boulders lay strewn about, creating a labyrinth of passages. It was difficult to keep the band of nine men together through the twists and turns and their progress slowed. The panting of the guards could be heard close behind. Thomas led the company down into a deep furrow, the walls of which initially came to eye level, but extended to well above their heads as they went further. The trench, carved by the ravages of numerous earthquakes over the years, extended for over a hundred feet. As the nine men reached the midpoint, the enemy entered behind them. John tried to count the pursuers, but the narrow passage prevented a full tally. If he had been able, John would have seen that only three came from behind, for the other two had entered ahead of the men of Lykos.

Thomas halted the company, which compressed to a tight knot because of their forward movement.

"Why are you stopping?" yelled John.

"We are hemmed in," came the discouraging reply.

Indeed, there was no way forward, backward, up or down—a classic trap. Fish pulled up in a net, a lion caught in a snare—any representation would do, but none gave a solution. The two contingents of Gauls slowed to a walk, laughing between their deep breaths as they witnessed the look of despair on their prey. The only conundrum for the Gauls was whether to dispatch of them slowly, one by one, or to collect and drive the refugees back to the mine.

John swallowed hard. He wanted to weep. He did not care whether he lost his life, but he anguished over those whom he had led to this point. *God! Did you bring us here to die at the hands of these demons? Please, Lord, help us!*

CHAPTER 16

▼

"Today, I want you to show me the place where you were working."

With those words, Pellas greeted a groggy Philip as the young man opened his eyes for the first time. It was the day after Philip's discovery of Cecilia, the first day of a new relationship between the farmer and the farmhand. Philip hoped that today would be less turbulent, but he realized that this was unlikely. Now that he knew of the girl's plight, it would take more than Pellas' rage to drive him away. In time, perhaps, Philip could assuage the man's paranoia and earn his trust.

The door to Cecilia's room remained closed while the two men breakfasted. Several times, the farmer tended to the girl, and Philip could hear the vague sound of their conversation. The young man suspected that Cecilia desired his company, as well, judging from the swells in Pellas' voice and the flush of his face when he exited the room.

"We need to tend to the chores first," said the farmer. "After lunch, you will take me to the site that you chose for this water trough of yours."

The pair moved quickly through their tasks, speaking little. The preoccupation of both their minds was the frail young woman incarcerated in her little room, but the men shared no common ground on the subject. A tense silence prevailed, interrupted only by an occasional directive from the farmer or a light-hearted remark by Philip to break the tension. Thick clouds gathered overhead and chilly gusts at times heralded advancing storms.

"We should grab some provisions and quickly head to the stream," said Pellas, after evaluating the weather.

"We can go there tomorrow," suggested Philip.

"No, I want to see it today."

"As you wish."

The young man knew that Pellas wanted to keep him away from the farm as much as possible, but this was folly. It would be impossible to concoct a fresh excuse each day. Nevertheless, Philip understood that Pellas was living day-to-day, and he complied with the request.

Pellas collected some bread and cheese while Philip filled two skins with water. The young man also grabbed an axe in case a little work was needed. After the farmer checked on Cecilia, the men began the climb up the steep slope to the stream. Pellas carefully inspected the work done by Philip the previous day. Philip suspected that the farmer was trying to determine how much time he had spent on the project. His suspicions were confirmed when the farmer opened his mouth.

"How long did this take you, half an hour?"

"Hardly," chuckled Philip. "It took that long just to move one of those rocks there."

"Is this where you cut your hand?" Pellas asked, studying the bloodstained end of a broken pole.

"Yes, sir."

The farmer surveyed the proposed course down to the house.

"It might work. At least it will keep you occupied for some time."

"Sir, I want to talk to you about that," began Philip, hoping to open a dialogue about Cecilia.

Pellas held his flat palm toward the young man, indicating that there would be no discussion on the matter.

At that moment, the wind picked up and, with it, a solid rain shower began.

Pellas grumbled over the change in weather and suggested that they take shelter under a large rock until the storm passed. The two unlikely partners huddled in silence for several minutes waiting for a break, but it only rained harder. Minutes turned to hours as the rain continued without abating. They ate their lunch and watched the stream swell with its new contents.

"Can't stay here much longer," Pellas said. "We may have to get soaked."

"I'm ready when you are."

They prepared to make their move into the downpour. Pellas crouched, ready to spring out of the shelter, a silly move, considering that the men would be soaked long before they covered the distance to the house. At that moment, however, the rain began to let up. They paused a minute more as the rain slowed to a steady drizzle.

"How about that?" said the farmer, smiling. It was the first pleasant expression that Philip had seen all day.

The men gathered their belongings and crawled out from under the large boulder. The trees dripped steadily on them as they negotiated the banks of the rushing stream. Abruptly, however, another downpour came from the canopy above them. The rain lasted only a few seconds, long enough for the two to consider a return to shelter. The rain stopped, but something strange happened that froze the men in their steps. Imperceptibly at first, but undeniable within moments, they detected motion beneath their feet.

"Tremor," Pellas said coolly.

The vibrations beneath them did not excite the men. Both had lived long enough in the region to experience numerous earthquakes, including some of significant magnitude. It was to them as the variability of the sea to the sailor. Pellas took a step onto a small rock adjacent to the stream. Another tremor, stronger than the first, shook him from his footing. Philip leaped forward to steady the farmer.

"Let's get across," Pellas said, with a hint of apprehension.

They scarcely had crossed the stream when a third shock commenced. It was significantly stronger than the first two, causing the trees to rock overhead. Pellas and Philip braced themselves against a boulder, waiting for the tremor to subside. The trees now swayed erratically, and the stream splashed wildly as its bed shook. The boulder to which they held tight shifted uneasily and the ground shook with increasing intensity. The two men looked at each other in wide-eyed fear, realizing that this was no minor tremor.

The next forty-five seconds were a cacophony of noise and violent shaking. Huge rocks dislodged from the ridge above the men's position and came careening down the slope to smash into the small cluster of trees surrounding them. Trunks crashed around them as massive trees were uprooted and toppled by the force. Branches rained down like arrows. The men dared not to crawl under anything for fear of being crushed by the shifting weight.

"Got...to...make...a...break!" yelled Pellas over the din. He pointed to a breach in the devastation through which the slope down to the house could be seen.

"There!"

Before the men could move, a loud crash thundered around them. Philip turned to see a large tree, felled by the quake, come slicing down from above, like a missile shot from a catapult. He dove to one side, but Pellas was not as quick. Philip heard the farmer scream in pain as the massive trunk toppled onto him.

Branches, rocks and mud pummeled Philip as the impact exploded both tree and ground into projectiles.

The young man scrambled to his feet, scraping mud and debris from his face.

"Oh, God, no!" he screamed aloud, as he crawled frantically to the place where Pellas lay. Diving through branches Philip found the farmer, alive but grimacing in pain.

"Pellas! I'll get you out!"

"No!" bellowed the man in agony. "Leave me! Cecilia!"

"Stay calm!" came the stern reply. "I need to see how you're pinned!"

Philip was not aware of it at the time, but the tremors had ceased, as had the noise. Now all was deathly silent, except for the agonized cries of the immobilized farmer.

"Leave me, you fool!" Pellas demanded, half in tears. "Go...to...Cecilia!"

Philip did not reply, rather, he anxiously inspected the farmer's situation. Pellas was pinned at the thigh beneath a portion of the trunk about a foot in diameter. Most of its branches had been sheared off by the other trees. Fortunately, the ground beneath was soft, or Pellas' legs would have been crushed beyond hope.

"I can get this off. Where's the axe?" Philip plunged beneath the rubble where he last recalled leaving the tool. Pellas moaned loudly.

"Leave me, I say," he said between sobs. His face was ashen and the vitality in his voice was departing. "Go to Cecilia."

"Here it is!" Philip shouted triumphantly. "Praise the Lord!" Philip returned to the farmer and set to work.

"Cover your face, Pellas."

Philip vigorously hacked at the trunk, sending shards of wood everywhere. Periodically, the young man checked Pellas for signs of life. The farmer looked bad, but he still breathed. In between axe strokes, Philip panted words of encouragement.

Philip's limbs ached as he slowly advanced through the wood. After a particularly forceful blow, Pellas would gasp in pain. Philip was halfway through the trunk when the axe slipped from his numb hands, toppling him backwards. He grabbed the axe and staggered back to the task, his chest heaving from the effort.

"Why won't you leave me?" asked the swooning farmer, haltingly.

"I...can't...leave...you...to...die," grunted Philip between blows.

"Curse you, boy!" the pinned man violently erupted. "If you care for my daughter, see to her safety!"

Philip stopped and looked hard at Pellas.

"I don't know what plight Cecilia is in at this moment, but I do know yours. I commit her to God's care. You, I am determined to save. Now, quiet, man, and conserve your strength!"

The farmer said no more. He held onto consciousness by the slimmest of margins. The pain in his legs was gone now and this concerned Philip. A few more blows and he would be through. Finally, the trunk split in two. Philip wrapped his arms tightly around the portion that lay across Pellas. Summoning his remaining strength, Philip heaved the trunk to one side in one great effort.

"There! You're free!"

Pellas was unconscious. Philip clasped his fingers to the fallen man's neck and was relieved to feel a pulse. He climbed over the fallen timber and dislodged boulders to find the stream. Philip soaked his cloak in the cold, silty water and wiped Pellas, reviving him somewhat.

"Pellas, can you hear me?" The farmer responded with a lethargic moan. "Can you move your legs?" Slowly, Pellas' extremities began to move. "You're going to be all right!" Philip said joyfully.

How Philip managed to carry the farmer down the hill to the house and to place him on his cot still is a mystery, but one last surge of energy enabled the young man to hoist Pellas to his back and negotiate the irregular terrain. The house was still standing, though some of the roof had been damaged by the shock. As they passed the stable, Philip noticed that one wall had caved in, leaving the structure in precarious shape.

"I guess that means I'll be in the house for good," said the young man with a smile to Pellas.

To Philip's greater relief, Cecilia was completely unharmed by the tumult. The girl squealed with delight when he burst into the house, breathlessly calling out her name. Her joy was cut short by the news that her father was injured, but she maintained her composure.

Philip gathered Cecilia into a chair and set her next to Pellas with a cloth and a bowl of water. Meanwhile, the young man stoked the embers and brought up a hearty fire that bathed the room in warmth and light. There were no closed doors now. Cecilia and Philip tended to Pellas' wounds and chattered away about their separate experiences during the tremor, memories of past quakes, the mercy of God to spare Pellas, and numerous other topics.

"You can't be serious?" responded Cecilia in disbelief, when Philip asked if she had been afraid during the tremor. "If God can deliver me from the jaws of hungry beasts, He can also protect me from the finicky appetite of the ground!"

Pellas held silent throughout their conversation. The earthquake had done more than merely to shake his physical being. Deep within his heart, the after-shocks reverberated as Pellas pondered the heroic effort of Philip to save him, when everything he had done to the boy deserved otherwise. What manner of God motivated this young man and his soul mate, Cecilia? In name, it was the same God that Pellas had once professed. In power, however, it was an altogether different One.

CHAPTER 17

▼

The Gauls halted their advance on the trapped men in the trench and conferred among each other. The higher-ranking guard appeared to be listening to advice from the two in his company, no doubt to decide whether to dispatch the nine or capture them for return to Siros and certain torture. The other two guards on the opposite side taunted the men of Lykos while waiting for orders.

John anxiously assessed their predicament. His men were in the deepest portion of the gully, so a quick climb out was impossible. Their only real choice was to charge the pair of Gauls to their rear and take whatever losses came.

"Our choices are simple," said John, then he briefly laid out the options. "Either way we face peril—possibly loss of life."

"I'm not going back!" affirmed one of the freed miners. A chorus of agreement followed.

"John, there is another possibility," said Thomas.

"Say it, then."

"God has done miraculous things when people call upon His name in times of crisis."

"You're right, Thomas, but I hardly see how that applies here."

"And why not? Are we any less important to the Lord than others?"

"Well, no," the leader responded impatiently, checking the foes, who were still in conference. "But what do you suggest? They'll be on us in seconds."

"I say we get on our knees and pray," Thomas replied emphatically.

"Pray? Now?" John was incredulous.

"Why is that so outrageous, John? The Master did nothing without prayer."

"Look, I'm all for prayer, but we can plan on a swift exit from this life if we drop our guard."

"John," Thomas pleaded earnestly. "Prayer *is* our guard."

John was silent. He looked at the faces of the men around him. Their lives were held in the balance of his decision.

"I'd rather die praying, I think," Sebastian said humbly.

"What about our mission, Thomas?" asked John. "Do we put it in peril?"

"The Lord will carry on the mission as He sees fit. The only peril is that we forget we can only move as far as God permits."

The guards began to stir; a decision had been reached. The chief of the group called to the others to take as many alive as possible, but not to be overly careful should there be resistance. The Gauls slowly advanced.

"What'll it be, John? You're the leader."

John drew his mouth tight and stared beyond his small band, beyond even the vicious Gauls who were not more than fifty feet away from them on both sides. John dropped to his knees.

"Sovereign God and Father of our Lord, Jesus Christ!" he began, in a thunderous voice.

The others of the company simultaneously dropped to their knees and joined their leader in fervent prayer. The Gauls momentarily halted and listened.

"In our distress, we call upon You for deliverance!"

The guards laughed derisively.

"We know that Your arm is not too short to save us from the forces of evil that oppose us now!"

The laughter and taunts grew more intense. John continued in an even louder voice.

"For Your glory we ask that You now stretch out Your mighty hand and destroy those who would oppose and mock Your holy name."

"Enough of this!" shouted the leader of the guard. "Take them!"

The men of Lykos and their charges rose to their feet and tightened their ranks, five facing the three, four against the two. Contact was only seconds away. What happened next was the subject of many a conversation for years to come. As the Gauls rushed the company of Christians, ranting and whooping in their horrific fashion, two things happened in immediate succession. The first was John's final cry before blows commenced.

"In the name of Jesus, deliver us, Lord!" John's voice soared above the tumultuous calls of the attackers.

The second was nothing short of a miracle. The floor of the trench vibrated lightly, and then began to shake. Cracks then appeared in the sides of the trough. The Gauls froze, looking around in dismay.

"Down, everyone!" called John.

The company dropped to the ground in a heap and the men covered their heads. The shaking now was violent. Cracks became fissures and a thick slab of rock, over fifteen feet long and several feet high, dislodged from the side of the trench to their right and collapsed against the opposite wall, sealing the men in a tight enclosure. They saw nothing more for the remaining half-minute of shaking, but the sound of the upheaval occurring around them was both horrific and awesome. They heard the crash of boulders tossed around like breadcrumbs, the deep roar of massive plates of rock grinding against each other, and the muffled cries of the guards as the yawning earth swallowed them up. Then, as quickly as it had started, the chaos was over.

The company waited in darkness and silence for about a minute. The only sound was that of settling sand and an occasional shift of a rock. The air within the divinely constructed cocoon was thick with dust. Then John began to cry. Or was it a laugh? The two sounds were indistinguishable at first. However it began, soon the entire group was joined in uproarious laughter, expressing their unmitigated joy at seeing the hand of the Lord come to their defense.

"An earthquake, Thomas!" exclaimed John. "He sent an earthquake!"

"I know, John, I know!" was all that Thomas could reply.

The laughter continued for a few moments more, and then began the slow process of extricating themselves from the rubble. The men were piled on top of one another in two layers. The stone roof eliminated any hope of exit from above. John, having occupied the lead position in the company prior to the tremor, was closest to what might be an exit, but all was dark. Then a small boulder shifted and a faint shaft of light poured in through a crack ahead of him. John slid forward toward the light and began pushing away the debris. As he did so, more light poured in, and with it, the sweet air of freedom. Soon, an opening large enough for a man was created and John slithered out of the enclosure. One by one, the nine exited the space to the outside.

The company looked around in awestruck silence, for the trench had been filled from end-to-end with rock and sand, with the exception of the small triangular space that they had occupied. The guards had met certain death, buried alive by the hand of the Lord.

"This was our ark, John," Thomas said.

An inspection of the company revealed nothing more than scrapes and bruises from the tremor. Quite a few mouths and eyes required rinsing from the limited supply of water they carried with them, but the other inconveniences were burdens gladly borne in light of the situation. The group offered prayers of thanksgiving for their deliverance before leaving. The daylight was growing dim, from both the hour of day and the clouds of dust that filled the sky. Though exhausted, there was still some distance to cover before the company could rest. As the men proceeded, John walked alongside Thomas, ahead of the others.

"I'm not worthy of all this, Thomas," he said in a hushed tone.

"What are you talking about, John?"

"Be honest. You know very well. Back there, I was ready to fight the Gauls and take whatever came, even death."

"You were brave."

"Brave? Stupid. Foolish." John tapped the side of his head in frustration. "Limited to my own meager capacities."

"Come on, man. Who can face such a foe?"

"Apparently, you can."

"What did I—?"

"Thomas, you saw beyond our predicament to the power of heaven. You had the presence of mind to call upon God. All I could think to do was to pit my body against that of our foes' and see who came up victorious."

"You're being too hard on yourself, John. All leaders are."

"Leader. Ha! The forces we are up against are beyond my capabilities. Lykos needs a leader who is as good as Croesus is evil, one who sees into the unseen world and formulates strategy accordingly. A man so fully infused with the power of God that the forces of darkness flee from his presence."

"John," laughed Thomas. "Who would you suggest, Elijah? Peter?"

"No, my friend. You."

"Me?" the surprised man asked loudly. The others stopped their conversations to listen.

"Shh. Yes, you. Why are you so shocked?"

"I'm not a leader, John."

"Am I? Who reminded us back there that God can deliver His children from any danger? Who always sees that our efforts are bathed in prayer? Who understands better than you that we are engaged in a spiritual battle? Who?"

"Come on, John, stop this line of talk."

"No, I'm serious. You embody all that the Master teaches and lives before us. You are the true leader of this enterprise. You are Lykos—a spiritual wolf, hungry for the things of God."

"No, John. You are the one tapped by the Master to carry us forward. I stand by you as your helper, your counselor—if I should be so presumptuous—and your friend. I will hear no more of this talk. As a leader, your mind is filled with every sort of detail that must be managed. You heard my counsel and *you* acted on it. God heard *your* words and acted on our behalf. If anything, you are unsure of yourself—not an undesirable place for a leader, if that uncertainty calls him regularly to the foot of the Lord. Now, pay attention where we are going and rest your mind."

The group continued, even as darkness settled on the land. The going was difficult, especially with the altered terrain brought about by the tremor. Finally, John picked up a familiar path and led the exhausted men along its way. After traveling another mile, the flicker of light could be seen coming from a remote farmhouse. As the men approached the light, they were greeted by an exuberant couple that burst out of the house with open arms and cries of joyful greeting. The men of Lykos were safe.

CHAPTER 18

▼

The terrifying phantasm in the image of Siros that threatened Marcellus was, of course, only an inhabitant of his nightmare, but the rocking he experienced was real. He awoke to a chamber in violent motion. Disoriented, Marcellus first tried to move to the door, but he immediately tumbled to the floor. Plaster crashed around him, shaken loose by the force of the tremor. Cries came from within the building as both master and slave sought shelter from the destructive and disrespectful force.

Marcellus knew that his greatest risk was the potential collapse of the villa. In the dusty gloom, he located the window and crawled toward it. He threw open the curtains and gazed at the turbulent scene below. His room overlooked a terrace some fifteen feet below. Huge fissures opened up as the pavement buckled under the strain. A loud cracking sound came from behind. Marcellus wheeled in time to see a portion of the ceiling begin to give way. Without hesitation, he leapt from the room to the terrace below, a thick plume of plaster dust chasing him as he cleared the window.

Marcellus hit hard on the stone below and felt pain in his right ankle as it turned inward. The quake was in full force as he staggered to his feet and limped away from the building. He managed to reach the balustrade and wrapped his arms around the marble railing, but a sudden upward thrust of the pavement crumbled the rail and sent him tumbling headfirst into a garden several feet below.

As Marcellus lay on his back, dazed and gasping for air, he felt the tremor subside and soon all was calm. He climbed to his feet and winced from the pain in his ankle. Dust and smoke filled the air, making it difficult to get his bearings.

Presently, Marcellus heard the confused cries of the villa's inhabitants coming from behind. It was difficult to reach the villa because of injury and obstacle but, eventually, he gained the garden entry. There Marcellus found utter chaos. Several men rushed to quench a fire that had begun when a brazier toppled to the floor and ignited a large curtain. Two slave women hovered around another who wailed inconsolably, presumably over the loss of a loved one. The floor was littered with debris and several servants combed the rubble for valuable items. Deeper into the house, Marcellus could see that a major support had cracked and that the roof sagged dangerously. A group of men had assembled cautiously to inspect the damage. Marcellus limped toward them, winding his way through the debris.

"Marcellus!" came the familiar voice of the governor out of the group. "I feared for your safety when I didn't see you." Linus hurried over to the magistrate. "What's this? Are you injured?"

"Sprained my ankle jumping from the room."

"Good thing. Ceiling collapsed." Linus called to someone deeper inside the structure. "Tell them to call off the search. Marcellus is here." Linus clasped Marcellus' shoulders. "You were the first I searched for, my boy. I am so glad that you're safe."

"What about Arcadia?"

"She's fine. Atarix, too. I guess the opposite side of the house is sturdier."

"Is the house badly damaged?"

"It's too early to tell. These men have all matters in hand. Come, there's serious work to be done."

Linus led Marcellus and a small contingent of soldiers from the house and down a lane that led to the nearby military garrison. Once they gained a more public thoroughfare, numerous people approached, all in various states of distress and wanting something from the governor. To those in official capacity, whether soldiers or public servants, Linus gave directives, while to the citizens he offered encouragement, consolation or advice. The governor was calm and collected in the whirlwind of demands and Marcellus watched in awe.

"Now is the time a leader shows his mettle," Linus said to Marcellus, as they moved along. "Give me an able general in battle, but a crisis like this requires men of our ken."

The headquarters appeared to be in good condition. A door lay splintered to one side of the entry and serious cracks were noted in one of the columns but, otherwise, little external damage could be seen. Inside, there was a good deal of debris lying about. Linus greeted the ranking officer and ordered that a large table be cleared.

"Here we will direct relief operations. We need maps. Tribune, what do we know of damage within the city?"

"I just sent out scouts, sir. They should return shortly."

"Excellent. We need to ascertain the location of the epicenter. It may well be that we experienced only the fringe of the quake, and that other areas are worse off. Send your fastest messengers along the main roads. Have them gather as much information as they can in an hour. We'll compare reports and determine the direction of the greatest damage."

"Yes, sir."

"And send soldiers to the temples and the agora. We'll have no looting. I authorize deadly force, if necessary, but have them show restraint."

The tribune saluted and left to his task. Linus impatiently looked around the room.

"Where are the magistrates?" he asked loudly. "Probably tending to their own interests," he muttered under his breath.

"Marcellus, I'm putting you in charge of fires and water supply until the other magistrates arrive. You're on your own. You men do whatever he says," the governor called to those gathered in the room.

The next two hours were the fastest that Marcellus could recall. The scene was one of constant motion and talk as information arrived, tallies were updated, maps were consulted, and orders were given. The young magistrate felt a pang of guilt over the invigoration that he derived from the tragedy, but he could not help but to enjoy the opportunity to fully use his skills. In short order, Marcellus had every significant fire located and either controlled or put out. The water supply was in fair shape. Some cracks in the aqueduct created a decrease in flow, but there was ample supply to the fountains. Dealing with the anxieties of the citizenry was a more difficult task, but Marcellus transferred this responsibility to the true magistrates of Nicomedia, who had trickled in over the course of a half-hour, armed with a variety of excuses as to their delay.

Linus was in and out of the headquarters, overseeing various stations, nodding and amending as he went. He was present when the scouts began to return with their reports from the outlying regions. The governor collated the information and quickly studied it.

"It appears that the hardest hit area is to our south. We've confirmed this even in our own city. Little damage to the north and toward Byzantium. To the east, conditions are no worse. We just need to hear from the direction of Nicea and Prusa to know for sure. Where is that messenger? I said one hour!"

Dusk was advancing when an exhausted scout on a spent horse raced up to the outside of the garrison. The man was escorted to Linus and given a moment to recover his breath.

"It looks bad to the south, sir. I met a scout from Nicea who said it's quite a mess. He thinks Prusa may be worse, though."

"That's what I feared," said the governor, shaking his head in sad contemplation, but then snapping to attention. "Right! Here's the plan. Tribune, I will set out for Nicea at daybreak. The magistrates there are reasonably capable and they should have things well in hand. I'll need a detachment to accompany me and to refresh the soldiers there. I'm sure that they'll be beyond fatigue when we arrive. Marcellus, you will accompany me and go beyond to Prusa." There was a barely perceptible change in the young magistrate's countenance. "This is an emergency, son. The city likely will be in disarray. I need your skills to bring order. Now, finish here and get some rest. It may be the last you get for some time."

When all matters appeared to be in hand, Marcellus transferred his luggage to the garrison, where he attempted to catch a few hours of sleep. The villa was deemed too dangerous for habitation until the engineers could properly assess the extent of damage. He passed a relatively sleepless night in the garrison; the clamor of nearby activity and the continual recapitulation of the day's events made sleep fleeting. Marcellus' foremost concern was for Claudia's welfare. With his new assignment, it would be days before any news would arrive of her condition and how Diakropolis had weathered the earthquake. The hour before dawn was a busy one as the large company assembled for departure. Marcellus managed only a few words with Linus.

"Sir, how long do you wish me to stay in Prusa?"

"Actually, I don't wish you to leave at all, but we've been over that, haven't we? Just stay until the city is stable, and then you can return to Diakropolis. I know you're anxious to get home. Trust me, if there was any indication that the tremor was more severe in that direction, I wouldn't do this." Marcellus offered his appreciation and the governor moved on to attend to other matters.

"How would you like a travel companion?" came a female voice from behind. Marcellus turned to see Arcadia dressed in travel clothes.

"I'd like that very much. I was wondering how you fared, but Linus assured me that you were well."

"How is your ankle?"

"I almost forgot about it." Marcellus bobbed up and down on the injured leg. "Only a little pain. I'm sure that you are concerned about your city."

"We've survived earthquakes before, but you never know when one will level you."

"It was fortunate that your father was here, don't you think?"

"Yes. The gods showed us favor. And you, as well."

"How so?"

Arcadia looked at Marcellus with bafflement.

"Don't you know about your room in the villa?"

"No, what of it? I sent some soldiers for my luggage."

"The roof totally collapsed after you jumped out the window. It seems that we have both been spared a cruel fate." Arcadia inched closer.

Marcellus ran his fingers through his hair.

"Yes," he responded distantly, "I suppose we have."

Travel was slow to Nicea. The entourage was heavily laden with supply carts and the roads were disrupted in many areas. By evening, the group arrived in the city, which, as expected, showed more damage than Nicomedia. By now, reports from Prusa had arrived, verifying even greater devastation there. Already, a stream of refugees had begun to pour into the city, bearing tales of fire, lack of water, and lawlessness. Linus added to the troops that would accompany the magistrate to his temporary post.

The company set out early the next morning, although Marcellus joined with a contingent on horseback that sped rapidly toward the city, in advance of the train of supply carts and carriages. Arcadia, who had remarkable skill with a horse, insisted on accompanying Marcellus, stating that he would need her familiarity with the city to become properly oriented. Atarix stayed with the slower entourage in his lush private carriage. Along the way, they paused to confer with fleeing citizens, each bearing the sad news of widespread destruction.

Another day of exhausting travel brought Marcellus and company to a ridge overlooking the city, as the last hour of daylight streaked through the clouds. Plumes of smoke still ascended from numerous locations throughout the town, bathing the town in an ashen haze. They passed the aqueduct, ruptured and only dribbling, evidence of damage further up the line. The group rode slowly through the main street, silently absorbing the scenes of devastation before them. Collapsed buildings stood adjacent to ones that appeared to be relatively unscathed. The remains of a temple formed a heap of crumbled marble, with a lone column standing to mark the site of the once-proud edifice. Marcellus looked over at Arcadia, who appeared staid and unmoved.

"Where are the people?" Marcellus wondered aloud.

"We saw many on the road," Arcadia replied without emotion. "Perhaps they have all fled."

As the group approached the agora, Marcellus' question was answered. On the cracked pavement ahead, groups of citizens, displaced from their homes, huddled around watch fires. The colonnade that surrounded the shops of the market was toppled like a collection of child's blocks. The city council building that bordered the square also had collapsed.

"Centurion, go see that the shops are secure and be on guard for looters," said Marcellus to the officer at his side. The soldier peeled off with a small company of men and raced away. Marcellus drew up to the scared and shivering groups and dismounted.

"Are there any officials of the city present?" the magistrate called. There was no response. "Who is in charge here?" Again, no one spoke.

Finally, one older man, his face caked with dried blood and his arm bandaged, rose from one cluster and addressed Marcellus.

"And who are you? Another public servant come to strip what's left of our possessions off our backs?" A chorus of jeers erupted from the people.

Marcellus was taken aback at the man's pointed words.

"I have been appointed temporary chief magistrate by His Excellency, Linus, governor of Bithynia and Pontus."

The old man cackled and soon several others joined him.

"Welcome to Prusa, fine sir. Rule it well!" The old man turned and hobbled back to his place, then sat down, cursing loudly.

"I can't help you if you don't cooperate," said Marcellus.

"Oh, we've already been helped, Mr. Magistrate," the old man continued, without looking up. "Helped out of our homes, our money..." The man sobbed.

"I don't understand what you are talking about, but I want to help," Marcellus said in frustration.

At that moment, the centurion pulled up.

"The shops have been picked clean, sir."

"Picked clean? You mean, looted?"

"Yes, sir. Very little structural damage, but ransacked inside."

Marcellus turned to the old man who sat with his head buried in his tattered cloak.

"Who did this?" The man did not move. "You there! Tell me, who did this?"

The man raised his head and looked at the magistrate.

"Come now, don't you know?" asked the old man, incredulously. Marcellus' cheeks flushed.

"I have ridden two days straight from Nicomedia on orders from the governor. I am not in a mood to play games. Either answer the question straight or you will be arrested."

One of the women in the group leaned toward the old man and spoke softly.

"I don't think he knows, Archaelus. You'd better talk."

The man stood and faced Marcellus.

"Forgive me, sir," Archaelus said contritely. "These have been awful days."

Marcellus softened.

"I understand. Go on."

"When the quake was over, we knew that it was a big one. Many of our homes were ruined, as you can see. Those of us here are merchants or craftsmen who depend on the agora for our livelihood. Naturally, in the confusion we looked to the officials for aid. We were told that all structures were unsafe and we were herded to the theater, which remained intact. We were told that the soldiers would look after our things. They didn't want looters, they said. We were promised food and water."

"How is it that you are here, then?"

"By the next morning, we had nothing."

"Nothing?"

"That's right. No food, no water. We had no clothing, nothing with which to dress wounds. People were falling ill left and right, exposed to the cold, you name it. Some of us tired of these conditions and tried to leave the theater, but we were driven back, that is, those people who would be driven."

"What do you mean, 'driven back?' How, and by whom?"

"Soldiers, sir. Soldiers."

Marcellus stared at the man in disbelief, then at his guard. The centurion could only shrug his shoulders.

"Where were your city officials?"

"With the soldiers. The secretary of the agora addressed us, himself."

"What happened to the others, those who refused to return to the theater?" Marcellus asked, fearing the answer.

"You tell me. We never saw them again. Just when we organized a breakout, they left."

"Left?"

"They were gone. Fled the city, I guess. By the time we made it to our homes and shops, everything of value had been taken."

Marcellus turned back to his party.

"This is outrageous! Citizens plundered by those entrusted to safeguard them? This can't be true!"

"It may well be, sir," responded the magistrate's guard captain, the same man who valiantly stood with Marcellus earlier during the ambush. "You know, most of these provincial troops are recruited from the region. They don't share the same call of duty as those soldiers of Roman stock."

Marcellus knew his captain was correct in his assessment. He also had heard of the corruption that was rampant throughout the leadership of the cities of Bithynia. Seeing it in real life turned the magistrate's stomach. He would address that matter at the proper time. Now, however, the more pressing needs were basic.

"Centurion, have your men fetch wood and stoke these fires hot. See what water can be found and tend to the most seriously ill. The supply carts should be here sometime tomorrow. We will have to make do until then."

The magistrate's party quickly dissolved, the men going about their tasks. Arcadia remained motionless, deep in thought.

"Care to join us?" Marcellus called to the pensive woman. "There's plenty to do here."

"Oh, I'm sorry," Arcadia responded, snapping out of her thoughts. "Marcellus, if it is not too much trouble, I'd like to check on my home."

"Sure, that's understandable. How insensitive of me. Take a couple of soldiers with you, but don't be gone long."

"That won't be necessary. I'll just take my attendant with me. I'll be back shortly."

Marcellus watched Arcadia leave. She had said little since leaving Nicomedia. He assumed that it was due to shock over the devastation in her home city, magnified further by the revelation that her own leaders had behaved so atrociously. Arcadia remained an enigma to him, embraceable, yet, one to be approached with caution. Marcellus returned to his assessment of the agora.

Arcadia and her aide quickly stole along the darkened streets of Prusa, avoiding the flicker of lamps and watch fires that marked those who refused to leave the devastation. She made her way to a large villa situated on a small hill that overlooked the town proper. The house appeared to be uninhabited. Arcadia strained to assess the integrity of the building and she ran her hands along the columns to check for obvious fractures. Satisfied that there seemed to be little damage, she pushed open the door and stepped inside. The interior was completely dark, except for the glow of a lamp emanating from a room in the rear. Warning the aide to keep silent, the pair slipped quietly through the halls and took up a position outside the lit room. Arcadia pressed her ear to the door, listened to the muffled conversation for a moment, and then entered.

"What are you doing here, and where did these things come from?" Arcadia asked abruptly.

Arcadia's sudden entrance startled a group of men slumped in all forms of repose. They jumped to their feet.

"Ma'am!" said the man closest to the door. "We didn't expect you so soon! Welcome, and feast your eyes on a treasure trove courtesy of the gods!" The man gestured toward a roomful of goods, piled to the ceiling. Arcadia quickly scanned the collection, which included textiles, household goods, statues and foodstuffs.

"You mean to say that you've looted your own people? You vicious pirates!"

"Come now, ma'am. We wouldn't call it looting. We merely were cleaning up the trash. 'Quakes is so messy, you know."

"Never mind that, now. Are any of the archons here?"

"Demetrus is in the back with the market secretary."

"All right, get these things out of here, and be quick about it!"

"Out?" asked the man, incredulously. "Where to?"

"I don't care where, just remove these things from the premises, now! And don't go through the city."

The men looked at each other, confused, but they did not dare cross Arcadia. She heard them grumbling about the effort as she left. The archon, one of the lesser-ranking city officials, was huddled with the secretary of the agora in a private study beyond the interior garden. They, too, shot to attention as Arcadia burst into the room.

"Was this your idea, plundering the city?"

"Arcadia," replied the archon. "So nice to have you back. How was Nicomedia?"

"Answer my question, Demetrus."

"Yes, rather, should I say, it was your father's vicarious decision. I'm sure that he will approve. He's not one to overlook an advantage."

"You know, Demetrus, sometimes your evil shocks me."

"I'm just a pupil eager to please his master. Besides, since when have you become so altruistic?"

"There are complications," replied Arcadia, eyeing the man with disdain. The archon straightened in his chair.

"What complications?" he asked, tentatively.

"Linus has sent the chief magistrate of Diakropolis to administrate the city until order can be restored."

"That's good. Then you were successful in your recruiting?"

"No. Trust me; he's not the one you want here right now. That is why I have the men removing your booty from my house."

"We brought it here for safekeeping," protested the official. "Where can we take it now?"

"That's your problem. I have to go. If I don't return, the magistrate will send soldiers looking for me."

"Where is he now?" asked the secretary.

"He is at the agora. The people there told him that they had been looted and the magistrate is very displeased."

The archon shook his head and laughed.

"Ah, bring him here. I've never met a magistrate who couldn't see the logic in our market economics."

"You may have met your first, then. Mind what I say, Demetrus. He has both the ear and the arm of the governor on his side. Don't be foolish. Now, I want all of you out of here within the hour. The magistrate may want to pay a visit this evening."

In the meantime, Marcellus made the rounds of the groups of people gathered throughout the agora. All shared the same woeful tale of destroyed homes and missing friends and relatives. Many of the citizens, he learned, had indeed fled to nearby cities because of their plight. Marcellus did his best to encourage the assembly, but he had little to offer since the supply wagons were not due until sometime the following day. He directed the soldiers to construct makeshift shelters to protect the townspeople against exposure. There was little threat of looting since little remained to steal. Some shop owners chose to stay near their businesses to protect what was left behind. A minor disturbance arose over who was to inhabit the shelters and several able-bodied men had to be evicted in favor of the injured and the children.

"Tell me, did anyone come to assist you prior to our arrival?" Marcellus asked one woman.

"No sir. No one, that is, except those of that strange religion."

"What religion?" Marcellus asked intently.

"They're called Christians, I believe."

"Tell me more. What did they do?"

"Several of them came looking for the wounded. Those who would go, the Christians carted off somewhere. Personally, I wouldn't go with them. It's rumored that they do strange things to people."

"What kind of strange things, woman?" Marcellus' curiosity now was piqued.

"From what I've heard, they may eat them."

Marcellus chuckled. "That's quite a tale."

"That's not the half of it. There are things I wouldn't mention in mixed company."

"Where can I find one of these savages?" Marcellus asked, with a hint of a smile.

The woman gazed around the agora, shading her eyes from the light of the fire.

"There's a couple over there, I believe. Standing over that man by the fountain."

Marcellus looked and saw two men bent over an injured man, apparently trying to persuade him to come with them. Waving off his guard, the magistrate walked over and stood nearby, where he could overhear the conversation. The wounded man lay on a pallet, one leg badly maimed and his hair caked with blood.

"Come on, friend, you're badly hurt," said one of the men. "We can help you."

"Another night in the cold and you could be in serious trouble," the other man said earnestly.

"Where will you take me?" asked the injured man, his voice shaking from exposure and the loss of blood.

"We have a place—it was spared by the tremor. We'll see that you get food and water, and proper bandages."

The injured man consulted his wife, who declined the aid and sent the men away. As the two reluctantly left, Marcellus caught up with them.

"You there, hold!" he called. The two men turned, startled.

"You mean us, sir?"

"That's right. My name is Marcellus. I recently have arrived in Prusa at the request of the governor." The men looked at each other in fear at the mention of the governor. "I couldn't help but overhear your conversation a moment ago. I've been told that you, or those with whom you are affiliated, have been tending to the wounded."

The two men remained silent, each waiting for the other to speak.

"Come now. I'm not going to bite. I need information, and, as acting chief magistrate, I have the power to get it, so you might as well tell all."

"It's true, what you said," said one of the men, not volunteering any additional details.

"You mentioned a place where you were taking the injured. An infirmary?"

"No, sir. It's a house."

"Have you been instructed to do this? By the magistrate, perhaps?"

"No, sir."

"Are you for hire?"

"No, that's not it, either."

"What is your motivation, then?"

The spokesman puffed his cheeks and nervously blew out the air, while his companion scratched at the broken pavement with his foot.

"Come now, speak up."

"We are…following the example…of our Master," the one man said, haltingly.

"Your Master?" confirmed Marcellus. "Is he some philanthropic individual?"

The two men looked at each other.

"You might say that, sir."

"Does he reside in Prusa?"

"No, sir."

Marcellus impatiently tapped his foot.

"My good men, I have much more to do than to spend time extracting information from the two of you. Speak all that you know, and do it quickly. I have the power to arrest you for contempt."

The spokesman cleared his voice and apologized.

"Forgive us for not being forthright, sir. We are followers of the one called Jesus Christ; many call us Christians. He is our Master, and we follow His example. If He were here, He would be tending to the weak and sick, so that is why we are here."

Marcellus stroked his chin.

"I see. I've had some interaction with your sect."

The spokesman stiffened, his jaw tense, while the other man slumped and uneasily wagged his head.

"You have nothing to fear from me at this time. There are far more serious concerns before us than legal conundrums. Your makeshift hospital, is it nearby? I want to pay a visit."

"A visit, sir?" The man swallowed hard.

"Yes. I need to see if you are properly rendering aid. That is one of my first responsibilities here." Marcellus called over the centurion.

"I am going with these men. Give me two soldiers. The fountain here is not completely dry. Have someone take out what water is usable. Also, if Arcadia returns, have her wait for my return."

Marcellus followed the men to a portion of town where the buildings appeared to be spared the brunt of the earthquake's damage. Turning down a small street, they followed a long, unbroken wall until they stopped at a single darkened door. The sign on the door indicated a leatherworker's shop, but, upon entering, Marcellus saw that it opened into a large open courtyard, bordered on three sides by a large two-story home. Torches and lamps blazed in the courtyard and windows, and a number of people had congregated in the open area. One by one, each person ceased his activity as the presence of the magistrate and soldiers was acknowledged. A robust, bearded man came forward and greeted Marcellus' two escorts.

"This is the new chief magistrate, sent by Linus," one volunteered. "He arrived only hours ago."

The bearded man acknowledged Marcellus briefly but respectfully, and then he turned to the men with a look of apprehension.

"We met him—or he met us—in the agora, and he ordered us to bring him here."

The bearded man nodded in resignation, then turned to the magistrate.

"Grace and peace to you, Your Honor. I am Hermas and this is my home." He sent the escorts away to bring refreshments for their guest.

Marcellus looked around at the home. Numerous windows and doors opened onto the courtyard. A wooden staircase led to a balcony, where a line of rooms could be detected. A large cistern occupied the center of the yard, and women busily filled vessels while taking peeks his way. Everywhere, there seemed to be activity.

"Your home seems to be solid, Hermas."

"Our Lord was gracious to us."

"I see," hemmed the magistrate. "He was not so kind to the rest of the city. I approached your men at the agora, trying to persuade one of the injured to come with them. I assume that they would have brought him here?"

"Yes, sir. We have been attending to the wounded here."

"That's admirable. Your men tell me that you do this neither under compulsion nor for profit."

"The only compulsion is to honor our Master. There is ample profit in that, alone."

"You, then, are some sort of priest?"

"No, we have no priests," said the bearded man, smiling. "Officially, I am called a deacon."

"A deacon? I've a vague recollection of that title. What does it mean?"

"Simply put, I am a servant."

"You, the owner of this home, a servant?" Marcellus laughed. "You deprecate yourself, sir."

"No, no. It is a high privilege. Our Lord said that he who would be greatest would be servant of all."

"I'll admit that it is a strange teaching," pondered the magistrate. "But, I'm not here for a lesson," he briskly continued. "I need to see that the injured are being properly cared for."

"By all means, sir. Come inside."

Hermas guided Marcellus through the various rooms of the house. Each was filled with cots on which lay men, women, and children in various states of trauma. The magistrate learned that the wounded were primarily poor, working-class citizens and slaves. The more well-to-do Prusans, if injured at all, either had left the city or had received medical attention at the formal hospitals.

"Why do you not avail yourself of the hospitals' services?" asked the magistrate.

"We tried one, but we were refused entry. The hospital already was full. The other hospital was said to be unsafe."

"Are there no surgeons available?"

"None who cared to make themselves so."

"Some of these wounded are going to need a surgeon's expertise. I'll see that surgeons become available."

The kitchen area was a smoky hub of activity, as women vigorously labored over pots of soup and loaves of bread. Each momentarily paused to study the officials, and then returned to her work and conversation. Marcellus was impressed with the cheerful industry of the attendants as they darted throughout the house, engaged in their various tasks. Finally, the magistrate found himself back in the courtyard near the entrance.

"I must say, Hermas, you are performing a noble task."

"My only grief is that many refuse care."

"Yes, well, that is another issue. I must return now to the agora. I will try to encourage others to avail themselves of your aid."

"Thank you, sir. I hope to speak with you again—on deeper matters."

Marcellus studied the earnest face of the deacon, and he recalled the discussion with Linus regarding Christians.

"I hope that won't be necessary."

The magistrate took one last look at the makeshift hospital, and then exited into the advancing night.

CHAPTER 19

▼

Marcellus returned to the agora and searched for Arcadia. The only light in the public square came from the scattered watch fires. The temperature had dropped significantly and both citizens and soldiers were gathered in tight circles around the fires.

"Centurion, have you seen Arcadia?"

"Over there, sir," he replied, and pointed to a shadowy spot near the entrance of the felled council house. Marcellus strode over to Arcadia.

"Why are you shivering here in the dark? There's plenty of warmth to go around."

"I prefer my own company at this moment."

"Did your home fare well?"

"Yes, it did. Parts of the city were spared much damage; our home was one of the fortunate ones."

"I've seen firsthand how some people fared better than others," Marcellus replied coolly. "I'm glad you were one of them. Can you show me to the garrison? I'd like to set up a command center."

"I can, but I don't think the building is usable. It was hard hit."

"Hmm. The council building here is a wreck. How about the former chief magistrate's home?"

"It is near the garrison. That entire block was wiped out."

"I could set up camp here, I suppose."

"Here? Nonsense. Your life is in danger with this element."

"Is it? I've found these folks to be quite gracious."

"Trust me, they'll turn on you. Look at how they've looted their own kind."

Marcellus carefully eyed Arcadia.

"It is interesting how catastrophes bring out the best and the worst in people."

Arcadia returned Marcellus' gaze briefly, then she looked away.

"I know what you mean."

"How about putting me and my officers up for the night? In the morning, we can find a more suitable headquarters."

"That possibly would work," the woman uneasily replied. She knew that more time was needed to empty the house of the plundered goods. "Let me go on ahead and arrange things, then my assistant can bring you along later."

"There's no need for any fuss. I was more than willing to sleep on the pavement here. We'll come with you now."

Arcadia knew that any further excuses would arouse suspicion, so she consented as graciously as possible.

"On the way, Marcellus, I'd like for you to inspect the rest of the city. There are some very valuable artifacts in the temples and libraries that need checking."

Arcadia managed to gain another hour before reaching her home. Marcellus was impressed at the grandeur of the home and he compared it to the grand estates that overlooked Diakropolis.

"I'm sure that your Uncle Siros—or whatever relation he is—would be envious of your situation," said Marcellus, as he looked over the city from the terrace. He could see the fires burning brightly at the agora.

"The view is especially magnificent during the day," said Arcadia, bringing Marcellus a goblet of wine.

"Tell me, have you seen any of the city officials since we arrived?"

"As a matter of fact, it slipped my mind to tell you. I did see one of the archons and the secretary of the agora, but only briefly. They were in a hurry. So much going on, you know."

Marcellus nodded and sipped.

"I'm surprised the secretary was not at the agora."

"He has other duties, too, especially now that there is no chief magistrate. All the officials do. I'm sure that you will meet them tomorrow."

The remainder of the conversation was equally bland, with Marcellus subtly fishing for information without trying to appear obvious, and Arcadia keeping her replies purposely vague. After a while, the magistrate excused himself and met with his officers to develop a strategy for the town.

The next morning, a mountain of needs confronted the magistrate, but he placed water supply, public health and safety at the top of the list. He made an exhaustive tour of the city by daylight, cataloguing all damage and casualties.

Marcellus ordered the hospital to expand its capacity and he transferred the more seriously wounded from Hermas' house. A corps of engineers was dispatched to assess damage to the aqueduct. Structures that posed a threat to the populace were cordoned off and condemned.

Marcellus managed to gain an audience with those officials who remained in Prusa. He interrogated them about their affairs since the tremor and he upbraided them for allowing such confusion at the agora, but he did not relate what the townspeople had said about the officials' behavior. In their defense, the officials itemized an impressive list of heroic activities—or alibis, Marcellus could not say which—that had occupied every minute of their time. By late afternoon, when the supply train arrived, Marcellus was exhausted and famished. He saw little of Arcadia that day. When they did meet, she would say only that she had been engaged in humanitarian efforts.

Marcellus found a suitable headquarters at one of the gymnasiums. It was centrally located, spacious enough to handle the traffic, and moved him away from the home of Arcadia and Atarix. The magistrate knew enough of Bithynian practices to connect the principal citizen, Atarix, to the suspicious actions of the officials. Until facts were clear, Marcellus preferred to act independently of their advice. However, this landed him in hot water with Arcadia, who accused the magistrate of avoiding her company, which partly was true. To settle things between them, Marcellus accepted an invitation to dinner the third night after his arrival.

One hardly would have suspected that a major earthquake had rocked Prusa, judging from the banquet that Atarix had prepared. Although Septimus may have turned his nose at the fare, having experienced one of Siros' renowned fêtes, to Marcellus, this was a feast beyond compare.

"Welcome, welcome," greeted the host, in a display of congeniality that took Marcellus by surprise.

Atarix wore a clean white toga with gold stripes descending from the shoulders, which stood in stark contrast to his dark, Mediterranean complexion.

"My regrets that we were not in a position to properly receive you upon your arrival."

"Given the circumstances, noble Sir, I can hardly fault you," replied Marcellus. "I apologize for my appearance, but I traveled light, and I failed to bring more suitable clothing."

"Nonsense, my son. We'll see to that later." Atarix ushered Marcellus from the entry to a large atrium, adorned with fine mosaics and sculpture.

"My daughter," Atarix pronounced with a dignified gesture, heralding the arrival of Arcadia.

She was clothed in a purple tunic of the finest fabric, over which was draped an equally elegant mantle of white wool. Her hair was elaborately braided and put up, revealing gold earrings that gleamed with the fire from the lamps. She smiled and curtsied slightly, and then joined her father at his side.

"You have been busy, Magistrate," Arcadia said, with benign sarcasm. "So much so that we had to arrange a feast to enjoy your company."

Marcellus blushed, partly at Arcadia's beauty but, also, knowing that he had purposely avoided her.

"I am your servant," was all that Marcellus could think to say.

Marcellus had expected a much larger party, and he was surprised when he was led into a small triclinium off the atrium. Already present were three other dinner guests. The party rose as the magistrate entered the room.

"Allow me to introduce my good friend, Midas," Atarix said gaily, gesturing toward a man his age. "He's a fellow businessman from our rival city of Myrlea. Actually, his name is Euclideus, but he doesn't care for the name and neither do I." Atarix laughed vigorously.

The man bowed low in greeting. In appearance, he was similar to the other wealthy merchants Marcellus had seen throughout Bithynia—an overweight frame, hidden under layers of expensive fabric and jewelry, and a face that evidenced a diet far too rich and voluminous.

"And this is Midas' mistress—current mistress, that is," Atarix added with a wink. "What's your name, my dear?"

"Daphne," squeaked a high-pitched voice from behind Midas.

Midas stepped aside at this point to reveal a thin young woman, less than half his age, dressed in an ill-fitting toga. Her heavily applied makeup cracked as she flashed a vacant smile. In Rome, her attire would have confirmed Marcellus' suspicions that she formerly had been employed in a brothel. The magistrate politely acknowledged the woman, and then glanced at Arcadia, who was struggling to suppress a smile.

The third figure was an athletic-looking man, a few years younger than Marcellus and a few inches taller.

"And this," continued Atarix, placing a hand on the young man's shoulder, "is Apollos. He also has come from Myrlea, where he serves as secretary of the gymnasia. He is a longtime family friend." Atarix leaned close to Marcellus. "He's also a prospective suitor for my daughter. You might say that he is to me as you are to the governor." The young man stepped forward and vigorously grasped Marcellus' arm in greeting.

Atarix sat Marcellus next to him at the head table, with the odd couple of Midas and Daphne flanked to his right. Arcadia was seated between the two younger men to the left of Atarix. The fare was as elegant and exotic as anything the magistrate had tasted in the governor's house, but Marcellus found the meal to be a bit unsettling. He could not help thinking of the homeless citizens of Prusa, scraping for anything edible, as Marcellus picked through the pheasant dish before him.

"How are the relief efforts proceeding, Marcellus?" asked the host.

"Very well. I anticipate that the aqueduct will be serviceable within two or three days. The damage was not as severe as I had feared. I've noticed, however, that you have no problem with water here."

"Natural springs," replied Atarix, in between chewing. "Being the oldest family in Prusa has its advantages as to the choice of home sites."

"What about the agora?" asked Midas. "I've heard that it is a ruin."

Atarix shrugged and licked his fingers.

"It is, indeed. But an agora is easy to establish—a flat surface and you're up and running, if you're not picky."

"I am so glad," replied the relieved merchant. "I have creditors calling on me for payment."

The group continued in discussion about the effects of the earthquake on the economy. Marcellus took advantage of a brief lull in the conversation.

"No one has asked about the people."

"The people?" asked Atarix. "How do you mean, my boy?"

Marcellus smiled and shook his head as he looked around the table.

"The citizens. Fellow Prusans, remember?"

"Of course! How are they?"

"There are many displaced from their homes. We've had to construct makeshift barracks and ask for food donations."

"Yes, you know, Father," intoned Arcadia. "You directed that a cartload of food be sent."

"I did?" Atarix scratched his head. "Oh, yes! I did!" he quickly added, seeing the look on his daughter's face.

"Your kindness is not to be outdone, Atarix," said Marcellus, trying to sound sincere.

The remainder of the conversation was cordial, but tedious. Apollos gladly shared of his exploits at the athletic contests and his brief stint as a charioteer. He had shed his toga, and the lamplight highlighted the definition of his muscles as he recreated his endeavors in pantomime. As Marcellus watched, he took mental inventory of his own stature, which was reasonably toned, but all too typical for one who administrated more than he exercised. Atarix sat in rapt attention to the young man's tales, smiling and clapping at various points. Arcadia seemed to relish the stories, as well, and she leaned toward the strapping man as he spoke. Marcellus could not shake the pangs of jealousy that began to surface. Meanwhile, on the other side of the table, Midas continued to eat, while Daphne toyed with her companion's oily hair. It was an altogether unpleasant experience, and Marcellus was happy to leave.

The next day, however, the magistrate again was invited to dinner at the home of Atarix, and the next, and the next. The odd couple of Midas and Daphne now was gone, but Apollos was present at each meal. With each evening, the feelings of jealousy mounted, and Marcellus felt his resolve to return to Diakropolis waning. Finally, on the fifth evening he was to dine at the estate, Marcellus was determined to talk with Arcadia. He had not been able to manage time alone with her on any of the previous nights and, to his concern, Arcadia had not sought time with him. Marcellus' desire to be with her had steadily mounted, no doubt from observing the competition's effectiveness with the woman. That morning, the magistrate sent for proper clothing and a barber. He also paid a visit to the gymnasium and baths, now fully operational. As Marcellus reviewed the progress of the relief efforts, the captain of his guard from Diakropolis visited him.

"Sir, the men and I were wondering what your thoughts were on returning to Diakropolis, seeing as how recovery is going well in the city."

"Our assignment is to place the city on sure footing, Captain. It is up to me to decide when that point had been reached."

"May I ask what criteria is to be used, so that we can gain some idea as to our progress?"

"It is difficult to establish criteria, Captain," returned the magistrate, vaguely. "We are uncovering new things daily. Our goals must remain somewhat flexible." The captain shifted on his feet.

"I'm sorry for the intrusion, sir, it's just that you placed public safety and health and water supply foremost, and these concerns all have been dealt with."

"Captain," replied Marcellus, growing testy, "I know what I have said and I will decide when it is time to depart. Is that clear?"

"Yes, sir. Sorry, sir. I'll tell the men." The captain turned to leave.

"By the way, I'd like to tour the city once more this afternoon."

"Yes, sir, I'll send for horses."

"Not horses. I'd like to go by chariot. See if there is one available. Perhaps," Marcellus paused for a moment as if in casual thought, then continued, "the prior chief magistrate's chariot?"

The captain stood silent. He and the magistrate had conversed frequently during their time in Nicomedia and on the way to Prusa, knit together by their common experience in the skirmish with the Gauls. The captain repeatedly had heard the resolve with which the magistrate spoke of returning to Diakropolis. Now, there seemed to be a hint of doubt.

"Captain?" The magistrate's voice called him out of his thoughts.

"Yes, sir! A chariot will be ready within the hour, sir!"

Marcellus moved methodically through the city, dictating his observations to a scribe at his side, much as he often did with Jason in Diakropolis. *Jason. Now there's someone I haven't thought about for a while. I wonder how the young man is faring with Septimus?* Marcellus traveled up and down the streets of Prusa, examining the progress of repairs and periodically stopping to inquire of supervisors. The captain of the guard announced the magistrate as he passed through crowded streets, and moved the people to one side. Marcellus gave a dignified nod to the citizens as he went.

"Seems as though you're now well recognized as the chief magistrate," observed the captain, as he pulled alongside the chariot.

"News travels fast."

"You've done an excellent job pulling the city to its feet. It's proper that they should honor you."

The small entourage turned down a narrow street of homes and shops. The walls of the homes were only occasionally interrupted by the appearance of a door or a high, narrow window.

"This road looks familiar," commented Marcellus.

"They all look the same to me," responded the captain. "In fact, I don't care for this neighborhood at all."

"I know where we are now." Marcellus pointed to a walled house ahead on his left. "This is where that fellow lives who was taking in the wounded the first night of our arrival. What was his name?"

"I can't help you there, sir."

Marcellus struggled to recall the name.

"Hermas! That's it, Hermas. He impressed me. I wonder how he is doing? Let's stop for a moment."

"Sir, let me remind you that there are some areas of Prusa we have been warned about," the scribe said quietly. "This is one of those areas. Besides, you have a dinner engagement this evening."

"I've wandered alone through worse areas than this back home. We'll only stay a minute."

The captain went to the door and knocked loudly. A young servant girl opened the door and stood wide-eyed before him.

"Tell the master of the house that the acting chief magistrate of Prusa desires an audience with him."

The girl ran off, leaving the soldier at the open door and, moments later, she returned with Hermas.

"A thousand apologizes for the rudeness of my servant," said Hermas. He scooted the girl on her way with a gentle swat to her backside. He saw the magistrate standing in his chariot in the street. "Please, come inside from the street, Your Honor. You grace my home with this visit."

"No need for that. I'm just touring the city and decided to check on you."

"Thank you for your kindness, sir, but can't you spare even a minute to come inside?"

Marcellus checked the daylight in the sky.

"Perhaps, just a minute."

He stepped down and entered the courtyard, which was much tidier and less crowded than several nights previous. He nodded to the captain to remain outside with the small detachment of soldiers.

"May I get you something to eat or drink?" asked Hermas.

"That won't be necessary. I have another engagement this evening."

"Then allow me to provide an appetizer!" Hermas clapped his hands and another servant appeared, carrying a tray with wine, cheese and a loaf of bread. "Come, sit for a minute."

"Tell me, Hermas," began Marcellus, taking a small portion of cheese. "How did things go here after I left? Did the wounded receive proper care?"

"Yes, sir. On your orders, the hospital opened its doors to those who would go. They all are doing well now, except for one who was too badly hurt to be helped."

"What do you mean, 'those who would go?'"

"Some refused to leave the safety of my home."

"Refused proper medical attention? Why?"

"They felt they were at greater risk in the city hospital," Hermas replied vaguely.

"They have little respect for Roman medicine?"

"Oh, no, sir. It's not that at all." Hermas leaned close. "I was straightforward with you that night, and I will be so now. Some of those people are my closest friends—brothers and sisters who share my faith. They fear the Romans because of what they have done to others of our faith. That night, many were concerned that, by going to the hospital, they would be placed on a list, to be healed only to face future persecution."

"I don't understand what you're talking about," Marcellus said indignantly. "We do no such thing."

"Perhaps, you, sir, are unaware of the practices of your fellow magistrates and governors. Some of my own household have perished at the hands of our leaders."

Marcellus reflected again on the conversation with Linus, including the governor's statement that lists of names of Christians were produced in one town.

"I don't expect you to understand the complexities of government, Hermas," replied Marcellus, with a hint of pomp. "I assure you that the judgments rendered were appropriate."

"If that is your assessment, then I misjudged you, sir."

Marcellus carefully eyed the man. Hermas did not flinch.

"Go on."

"I am not an ignorant man," continued the host. "I understand the perceived threat that people of my faith present to those people who wish to maintain flexible standards, if such can be called standards at all, whether they are Roman officials, wealthy merchants, or peasants. We merely are ambassadors of the One True God, and we are bound to proclaim His message throughout the empire. We desire to live at peace with the government and its people, and we strive to be productive subjects, but our calling is higher and greater even than that of the emperor."

Marcellus smiled slyly and sat back.

"I know I tell you this at great peril to my life, but, with all due respect—and I sincerely respect you for your humanity—nothing can happen to me except that it be ordained by God."

"You speak of God as if He lives in one of your rooms here."

"He is even nearer than that, Your Honor. He is present before you."

Marcellus sat up straight and looked uneasily at Hermas.

"I thought you were a sane man, Hermas. Do you expect me to believe that you are God?" Hermas chuckled.

"No, I am not God, but He lives within me."

Marcellus eyelids narrowed in contemplation of the man's statement.

"Within you? So these are the *deeper* things of which you spoke earlier?"

"Yes, sir." Hermas excitedly leaned forward. "If I could have but an hour of your time, what wonderful things I could show you."

Marcellus abruptly stood.

"Hermas, I applaud your efforts in serving your fellow man. If there is any way I can be of service, let my office know. I must leave for my other engagement now." The magistrate thanked his host for the refreshment and promptly rejoined his men.

"That was more than a brief hello," said the captain, when Marcellus returned to the chariot. "Everything all right, sir?"

"Yes, Captain," replied Marcellus, looking down the street, his jaw set. "Let's move on."

Atarix paced the floor of the foyer awaiting the arrival of Marcellus for dinner, while Arcadia preened herself in a mirror.

"I expect we will hear tonight that our young magistrate has chosen to stay with us in Prusa, my dear. Then we can return to business as usual, and I can quit getting letters from that tiresome Siros. I am not accustomed to being rebuffed for so long."

"I think my method, in all likelihood, would have been as successful as yours, Father," replied Arcadia, as she applied eyeliner with a small spatula.

"Your method would have you living in Diakropolis by now. No, no. My plan seems to be the way to Marcellus' heart. No man can resist power and privilege for long. Women make some men do silly things, but the intelligent man knows that women will come by the cartload, once he has taken the mantle of authority."

"Father!" scolded Arcadia.

"Not so in my case, mind you," Atarix quickly added. "Your mother was my only interest." He concealed a brief smile. "Back to Marcellus, I believe that he is responding well to the accolades I've ordered."

"You are such a rascal. One day, you are going to meet your match. Then what will you do?"

"Then it will be your turn. Mind your tongue, young lady. I am not only trying to ensure the security of our livelihood, but to procure a husband for you, as well. I must admit, however, that I'm not certain about this one. He's a little soft-hearted."

"You prefer soft-headed, like Apollos?"

"I can't help it if Apollos has spent too much time in the exercise of his body at the expense of his mind. Besides, the oaf has played his part—and well, I might add. Your Marcellus is ripe to become a Prusan."

"I still say he's going back to Diakropolis."

"I disagree. I've carefully observed him. I can sense the jealousy he has for you, and his growing appreciation for the niceties of position. By the way, where is he? He's late!" Atarix boomed.

The pair waited several minutes more before Marcellus' coach drew to a halt before the massive entry to the house.

"Greetings, Magistrate. I was wondering if you would be able to make it tonight."

"My apologies for being tardy, sir. I was on an extensive tour of the city in order to answer your anticipated questions more precisely, but I got delayed."

"That is most considerate. I see that you have obtained garments more appropriate for your position," Atarix observed.

"Yes, I found this in storage."

Marcellus adjusted the front of the toga. He felt awkward in the clothes and he was certain that he appeared that way, as well. Arcadia emerged from inside the house and smiled with approval. She rushed to Marcellus' side and took his arm in hers to usher the magistrate inside.

Marcellus looked around with anticipation as he walked toward the dining area. Thus far, each successive dinner had produced a variety of dinner guests with one constant, Apollos.

"Apollos is not coming tonight," said Arcadia. Whether this was merely coincidence or she had read his mind, Marcellus was not sure.

"Oh, I'm sorry," Marcellus responded disingenuously.

"No, I thought it would just be the three of us," interjected Atarix from behind. "I've come to appreciate your company, my son, and I don't wish to share your attention this evening."

The trio reclined to another feast, which helped Marcellus to understand why the wealthy tended to increase in girth. He marveled at how Arcadia kept her figure with such sumptuous fare.

The conversation was more serious this dinner, and dealt with philosophies of regulation of business by the empire, methods of maintaining safe lanes of commerce, and other topics of interest to Atarix. Toward the end of the meal, the host excused his daughter and servants, leaving the two men alone.

"You're pleased with your efforts to establish order after the earthquake?" asked the host, as he filled Marcellus' goblet with wine.

"I truly am. I had no experience at this, but it has gone better than I expected."

"Have the people responded well to you?"

"Yes. I'm surprised that they have, given the short time I've been here. Why, even the Christians have accepted me."

"Christians? What business do you have with them?" Atarix asked pointedly, his countenance visibly changed. Marcellus hesitated.

"A group of them were at the agora the night of my arrival, tending to the wounded. I saw to it that space was made at the hospital for their patients."

"Keep away from the Christians. They are dangerous. You should know that as a magistrate."

Marcellus chuckled but remained serious.

"The only thing I have observed as a magistrate is that Christians make very powerful people nervous for some odd reason."

The two men looked at each other for a moment, and then Atarix softened.

"Come, my son. Let's talk of greater things." Atarix filled his goblet with more wine, but Marcellus shook off his host. Atarix continued talking.

"The whole business of leadership is quite complicated, you know. Take you and me, for instance. As a well-off merchant and benefactor, I need the civic leadership to assist me in reaching my goals. Therefore, I look for like-minded individuals to support those goals. I must be careful not to support those officials too vigorously, lest they achieve a measure of power beyond what is conducive to my desires, and quash my influence. Yet if I fail to undergird them in their pursuits, the officials' allegiance may be diffused, thus rendering them ineffective for my services."

Marcellus opened his mouth to speak, but he was silenced with a finger by Atarix.

"I am not intimating anything illicit. This relationship between merchant and politician is symbiotic, mutually beneficial. You, the ambitious ruler, desire great things for your city. Where do you get the funds? Taxes, you say? Unpopular. Philanthropic gifts are the answer. You coddle the wealthy, procure funds, honor the donor with a proclamation or, better yet, procure more of his funds to allow him to produce a festival. Your city rises in stature, as do you. However, if you become indebted too heavily to this benefactor, he controls you. Not enough, and you fall short, and become a laughingstock ruler with a half-built theater or bath. Do you see the delicate balance?"

Atarix silenced Marcellus once more.

"These are conundrums over which leaders continually wrestle. Great is the man who achieves balance. But, these things do not concern you yet. In the town of Diakropolis, such conflicts are not at issue."

"What do you mean?" asked the magistrate.

"Take a writing tablet and list the great men who have come from Diakropolis. Write down the prominent leaders of the empire who have done a stint at the helm of that city. I'll save you the trouble. There are none, nor will there be. Diakropolis is not a great city. Its leading citizens are provincial, and its leaders are destined to be mediocre because of a fatal inability to lead those citizens out of that mindset. You will be the same. Enjoy the fruitful years of your life there—in the rain." Atarix took a long draft of his wine, and then wiped his face with his sleeve.

Marcellus ran his finger along the rim of his goblet and thought. Life was easier when he simply followed Linus' script for him, but now he had broken off the path and there were distinct forks in the road—divergences that must be negotiated well, lest he find himself detoured and unable to progress. Marcellus wanted time to think, but he knew that time brought only more confusion. To compound matters, Atarix was not finished.

"Tell me something, Marcellus. You are a better judge of your generation than I am. Do you think Apollos has the mettle to assume the chief magistracy upon your departure?"

Marcellus looked up at Atarix to detect any hint of levity in his host's countenance, but there was none.

"Truly, sir, I think you could do better. Unless you feel Prusa would be best administered by a narcissistic imbecile."

"Ooh," smiled the merchant. "I like that. Narcissistic imbecile." Atarix softly repeated the phrase.

"I'm sorry, it's not like me to insult. It's just that I've found Apollos to be shallow and self-absorbed. Not the makings of a leader, in my estimation."

"Your estimation counts for little in this city, but that is by your own choice."

"You speak as if my mind is made up," countered Marcellus.

"Isn't it?" the host asked pointedly.

"Maybe not. I'm my own man. It may please me to accept the offer."

"It had better please you to make up your mind—tonight, even—or the offer may be rescinded.

"The governor would not be so fickle."

"The governor, fox that he is, will respond to the desires of his influential constituents—that is lesson number one for effective rule, my boy. Now be sensible.

When you leave tonight, spend some time in thought as to your future. The weight of sage advice is on the side of taking this appointment but, rest assured, there will be little lost sleep over a man who is too stubborn to see the wisdom of such a move."

Atarix moved to within inches of Marcellus' face.

"If you so choose, you can seize the lead role or disappear from the stage. Your fate is as you wish it to be."

Atarix stood and yawned.

"The wine was uncommonly strong tonight. I am afraid my clear thinking is coming to an end. Feel free to visit with my daughter. If you choose to return to Diakropolis, you won't have many hours left."

Atarix left Marcellus alone in the *triclinium* and approached Arcadia, who was waiting outside.

"The fruit is ready for the picking, my dear, but bear in mind one thing. Do not misconstrue my earlier statement regarding a husband as implying that I would, in any way, compromise our first priority—namely, securing a stable future for our way of life. If this young Roman fails to come aboard on my terms, there will be no acceptable alternative for him."

Arcadia smiled nervously.

"What have I done to suggest that I am not wholly in agreement with you, Father?"

Atarix intently scrutinized his daughter's face.

"Nothing, I hope. Nevertheless, I offer a timely word of advice before you go see him: Bar your emotions at the gate; emotions may seem harmless, but they are emissaries of destruction."

Arcadia entered the dining area and found Marcellus staring across the room, deep in thought.

"Well, did you have a nice conversation with Father?"

Marcellus gazed Arcadia's way and raised an eyebrow.

"Conversation implies two parties involved in discussion. I recall only one."

"That's Father. Was he trying to influence you to stay in Prusa?"

"His tone held more the aura of an ultimatum."

"When Father feels strongly about something, he expresses himself that way. But, now that you have been here for several days and have sampled our amenities, have you reconsidered?"

"So now you're here to finish the sale. All right then, just what are these amenities?"

"Certainly you could not have failed to notice the impressive sight of our own Mount Olympus. On a clear day, the view from the top is stunning."

"I can imagine. What else?"

"Have you availed yourself of our natural hot springs?"

"Too busy," Marcellus responded tersely, then added, "Natural, eh?"

"I can see that you're already becoming more interested," Arcadia said playfully. "Might I add that we are only a short trip from the alluring and balmy waters of the Great Sea?"

"Short?" Marcellus questioned sharply.

"Well, a shorter trip than one from Diakropolis."

"I'll allow that. Anything else?"

"There is always me…" Arcadia responded, her voice trailing off.

"Come again?"

Arcadia frowned at him, her nostrils flaring.

"Me!" she said emphatically. "I live here, remember?"

"Trust me, I need no reminder."

Arcadia folded her arms in disgust.

"That's an odd statement, considering how you've been avoiding me."

"Me? Avoiding you?" Marcellus responded incredulously. "I haven't been able to get past your muscle-bound boyfriend Hercules even to have a short conversation with you."

"Apollos is simply a childhood friend, nothing more."

"That's not what your father implied. He called Apollos your prospective suitor."

"It was Father's idea to have Apollos around," Arcadia replied, lowering her head and voice apologetically. "He wanted to make you jealous."

"Well it worked!" Arcadia looked up hopefully at Marcellus. "Look," he continued, "my world's a little rattled right now, and you're one of the influences shaking it around. I need to go home and sort out some things."

"Why can't you do that here?" Arcadia moved close.

"Why is it that no one wants to let me leave? I do have a daughter in Diakropolis."

"Father has coaches. Your daughter could be here with your things in a matter of days." Arcadia slipped her hand in his as Marcellus held his breath. "You know, the possibilities for us are limitless." She drew within inches of him. Her perfume filled the air he breathed. "Father is very discriminating in the men he allows to associate with me. You should take it as a high compliment that he has permitted you to be with me. He recognizes qualities of greatness in you, the same that have attracted me to you."

"And what are these qualities?"

"Determination."

"You mean I haven't pushed over as easily as he had hoped?"

"Oh, hush. Compassion, courage," Arcadia continued, her lips now at his ear. "These are essential attributes of the one to whom Father would entrust his riches."

"I trust that means you."

"Yes, and his wealth, too. Remember, I have no brothers. My dowry would be considerable."

Marcellus pondered Arcadia's words as the two stood in a loose embrace. Her head rested on his shoulder; her face gently brushed against his neck. She continued to hold his hand in both of hers. He fidgeted at the air with his other hand for a moment, but then brought it around her back and tightened the embrace.

"Stay with me," she whispered.

It was an awkward moment for Marcellus, one in which he easily could have abandoned his resolve and allowed the power of his senses to hold sway over him. An effortless, affirmative reply to her statement was on his tongue, awaiting its cue. Every rational objection to his return home had been answered. There seemed to be no other reasonable course of action but to accept all that was laid out for him: the position, the prestige, the woman and the riches that followed in her wake. At the same time, however, Marcellus knew that there was something lacking in the whole. Like a minor deficit in an accounting ledger—inconsequential on the one hand, but exasperatingly unsettling on the other—he knew that the outstanding balance of his uncertainties over the woman and her father must be settled first. Such could not take place in Prusa, within the pervasive circle of their power and influence. Nevertheless, the moment was too sublime to destroy with further argument.

"You are very convincing, Arcadia," Marcellus said. "A wiser man would have needed much less persuasion. But, I am a fool and must prevail upon you for more time. Give me tonight to decide. You'll have my answer tomorrow."

CHAPTER 20

———————— ▼ ————————

It felt good to be in the cold outside air, but the short trip to his quarters did not clear Marcellus' mind. He wished for something definitive to help him make the decision to go or to stay. As he walked toward the door, he made a mental tally of things for and against the move to Prusa, nodding and shaking his head as he went. An eavesdropper might have taken Marcellus for a mentally imbalanced sort, gesturing vigorously as he conversed with an imaginary companion. The magistrate was greeted by an attaché who handed him a letter.

"This came for you today by Imperial Post."

Marcellus hurried to his room, where he sat at a desk and broke the letter's seal. He had exchanged letters with Claudia and he hoped that this was her reply. The writing was difficult to make out, obviously from the hand of a hurried or careless writer.

"*His honor, Marcellus, noble Chief Magistrate and wise brother.*"

"Septimus," chuckled Marcellus.

"*I trust that you are faring well in your new jurisdiction of Prusa. I await instructions on when to send Claudia and your retinue, including Jason. Your luggage is being packed as I write. Worry not about the brigands in the environs outside Diakropolis. They have been dispatched without remorse. Your river project proceeds with haste. Your legacy will live on in Diakropolis for generations. Send a post when your schedule permits. P.S. The tremor spared our fair city. Your devoted brother and beneficiary of your prodigious leadership, Septimus.*"

Marcellus scratched his head. He was familiar enough with his brother's mind to recognize this to be the thoughts of another. Marcellus pondered who might be the source of the presumption that he had accepted the position at Prusa.

Now, confused even more, he paced the room. *I need counsel. Clear-headed, plain-spoken counsel.* Marcellus thought for a minute as he paced, then he halted and smiled broadly. In an instant, he was out the door and striding toward an adjacent building, where the military officers displaced from the garrison were quartered.

"Can you direct me to the quarters of my captain?" asked Marcellus of the surprised guard at the entry.

"Yes, sir. Take this hall all the way down, turn right, third door on your left."

Marcellus moved quickly and, in a moment, was knocking on the door of his able guard.

"Enter," came the husky voice from within.

Marcellus opened the door and found the soldier securing a new strap on his sandal. The captain was dressed only in a nightshirt and sprang to attention at the sight of his superior.

"Magistrate, sir!" The captain saluted with the hand holding the thong, striking himself in the chin. Marcellus laughed.

"At ease, Captain, at ease."

The guard fumbled with the shoe, and then hastily pulled up a chair for Marcellus.

"You surprised me, sir. Had I known you were coming…"

"Say no more, Captain. You couldn't possibly have anticipated my visit." The magistrate looked around the Spartan quarters.

"It's not much, I know, but I rather prefer things simple," commented the captain.

"And that's exactly why I'm here," replied the magistrate.

"To see my room?"

"No," Marcellus chuckled, "to talk plain and simple. Let me explain. As you know, there has been a great push to see me installed as the chief magistrate of Prusa."

"That's an understatement."

"I am torn in my decision. On the one hand, there is little question that Prusa occupies a greater position among the cities of the province. Added to that fact is the governor's desire that I should accept the appointment. On the other hand, I feel a strong commitment to the city of Diakropolis, a sentiment that seems to arouse a great deal of opposition."

"In the words of an uneducated soldier, your arm is being twisted to stay here."

"Yes, that sums things up well."

"What do you want from me?"

"Advice."

"From me? You are the wise one here, sir."

"I'm not so sure anymore. I know you have a great practical sense about you and, frankly, I know of no one else with whom I can talk."

The captain rubbed his stubbled chin.

"My intuition tells me to stay out of this one. The stakes are too high. But, I'll go ahead and step into it—only for you.

The soldier flipped the sandal over to the corner to join its mate and he looked intently at the magistrate. He was a veteran soldier with an impressive résumé of campaigns to his credit. For the last several years, he had been assigned to Diakropolis and to other cities in the region, where he protected and escorted the likes of Marcellus.

"I don't envy you, sir. You want plain and simple? That's my life. An order comes from above, that's my task. You, however, have all these people pulling and prodding you, pumping you with information on one side, siphoning it off the other and, still, you don't know what these people want. Somewhere in all of that, you have to decide what *you* want to do."

"And how do I do that?"

"You have to read the signs. Gathering dark clouds on the horizon mean rain. Where vultures gather, there is death."

"You are the last person I'd expect to speak in proverbs, Captain."

"We military types are philosophers, too. Let me give it to you plain. This game is rigged."

"Rigged?

"Yes. There's something going on that you're not supposed to learn."

"Well, what is this mystery?" said Marcellus, leaning forward in his chair with eagerness.

"I have no idea, but I've seen this many times. You're fortunate; they're giving you a way out."

"What a minute. Who are they?"

"Your buddy, Siros, and this Atarix fellow."

"They have no power over me." Marcellus stiffened indignantly.

"You just haven't been around long enough. They have every power over you—your kind, that is. What's bothering them is that they don't have power over *you*, specifically. They're accustomed to seeing things go their way, and most of the politicians are game enough to play along. Those who don't—well, they just disappear."

"Not everyone has aspirations for great visibility in the empire," countered Marcellus.

"I don't mean disappear from public view. I mean disappear. Take your predecessor here in Prusa, for example."

"Are you suggesting that his death was not accidental?"

The soldier laughed.

"Not judging from the barracks talk. He crossed Atarix sometime before his tragic accident."

"So they—meaning Atarix and Siros, I presume—are trying to involve me in some illicit activity here in Prusa?"

"Not here in Prusa. They are trying to get you *out* of Diakropolis."

"Why Diakropolis? I'm told that Prusa is where things happen."

"I've been in Diakropolis for several years now. Its image as a sleepy little town of small importance has been carefully crafted and protected. Talk among the soldiers—granted, we're not all princes—is that serious money changes hands under the tables of our fair city, as well as the cities of Bithynia."

"That could not happen without the complicity of the officials."

"Siros has owned every public official since I've been around. I'm sure that the same holds true for Atarix."

Marcellus stared pensively at the flickering flame of the lamp above the captain's head.

"Everyone, except me."

"And you'd better pony up or watch your backside."

The magistrate fixed his gaze on the soldier and smirked.

"You don't think they'd attempt some sort of...assassination, do you? The governor would be livid."

"No, the governor would grieve and orate and proclaim a statue be built in your honor, or some such memorial."

The captain leaned forward and spoke in a serious, hushed tone.

"He'd never know. That's the twisted genius of this circle. You may be a gifted administrator, but you need an education in the ways of the political jungle. It's eat or be eaten. Linus knows. I'm surprised he hasn't lectured you on survival."

"Maybe he has, but I just didn't listen."

"You have two choices. Play according to their rules, or stick to your principles and fight back."

Marcellus rose to his feet and circled the room.

"Is Linus involved?"

"You know him better than I do," replied the captain, watching the magistrate pace. "I suspect that the governor is just trying to appease the moneyed class, while looking good in the eyes of the emperor."

The young judge made a few more circuits around the room, and then stopped.

"What do you think I should do?"

"You may not want to ask me," said the captain, with a grave chuckle. "I'm a fighter by nature. All this bullying and arm-twisting gets my dander up."

"I knew there was something about you that I liked," said Marcellus.

"Yes, but when I think of the money I could've made..." The captain shook his head. "Look at me. Over fifty years old and still playing soldier."

"You're not playing, Captain, and neither am I. Let's go home. When can we set out? Two days?"

The captain studied Marcellus and judged him sincere in his decision.

"It's not as easy as that, sir. Don't look for a send-off party. You'll have to string them along while we prepare, then leave under cover of darkness."

Marcellus grimaced.

"I've strung them along for several days now. I think Atarix made his final pitch tonight. He'll be looking for an answer in the morning."

The captain sat in deep thought for a while. The magistrate studied the sturdy features of the veteran soldier as he slumped forward in his chair, elbows on thighs, fingers together, lips pursed, humming softly as he thought. In the leathery skin of the captain's complexion, worn with years of conflict, Marcellus saw character that was lacking in the flushed, pouting faces of the wealthy. Finally, the captain spoke.

"Does anyone else know the contents of that letter?"

"No, I just received it this evening. The letter was sealed."

"Good, then we have our excuse." The captain motioned Marcellus to return to his seat and pulled his chair close. "Here's my plan. As far as anyone knows, that letter came from your distraught daughter who needs you home immediately."

"I see. Can we leave sometime tomorrow?"

"If you're serious about returning, then we must leave tonight. We've traveled light so far. Anything we leave behind can be replaced."

"What about provisions? They'll know that we are leaving."

"Surprise is everything. We'll take a few things that we can scavenge from our rooms and try to pick up the rest on the way. If that fails, I know how to survive on the land."

"Will it be just the two of us? What about the other men who rode with us?"

"I can trust one, no, two. They will come with us. The others can return later."

"When do we start?" asked Marcellus, his pulse quickening.

"I'll meet you at the stables in an hour. I've made friends with the stable master and I should be able to procure some horses. There's a little moon tonight. We should be able to put some miles in before sunrise."

Marcellus grasped the captain's hand and hurried off to prepare. Outside his quarters, the magistrate passed the guards as nonchalantly as possible, and then quickly moved to his room, where he packed a few articles of clothing and gathered what food was available. He was nearly out of the building again when he realized that he had left his books and documents, prizes for which he gladly would have sacrificed food and clothing. His leather bag stuffed, Marcellus quietly stole down the hall and passed through a little-used door that opened from the garden onto a small path running alongside the building. The guards never noticed the magistrate's departure. Within minutes, Marcellus was at the stables where the captain and his two chosen soldiers already were assembled. The only eyes that witnessed the departure of the four into the dark city streets were those of the stable master, now richer for his confidence.

The company moved silently through the back streets of Prusa with only the rhythmic clip-clop of the horses breaking the hush of the night.

"We have little food," whispered the captain, as he pulled close to Marcellus. "With any luck, we'll be able to properly supply ourselves at the way station."

"I have a few things, but they won't go far," said the magistrate.

The men continued on, following in single file behind the captain's lead. They went relatively unnoticed, drawing only a stare from an occasional insomniac or late-night carouser on the way home from his binge. Presently, the magistrate goaded his horse to come alongside the captain and his mount.

"I have an idea where we can supply ourselves quite well. Turn down this street."

The captain was puzzled at the order, but complied. He studied the buildings as they passed, trying to discern where the magistrate was leading them but, in the deep darkness, the streets all looked the same. Marcellus brought the group to a halt outside a door and he quickly dismounted.

It took several minutes of persistent and gradually intensifying knocks before the door finally was answered. A bleary-eyed servant poked his head through the opening and widely blinked several times.

"Tell your master that the chief magistrate of Prusa has immediate need of his services."

The minutes that passed found Marcellus and the captain engaged in a tense but quiet argument over the wisdom of the detour. The dispute came to an abrupt and victorless end when Hermas appeared in the doorway.

"Sir, what brings you to my house at this hour?" asked the nervous man.

Marcellus took Hermas by the arm and led him into the courtyard.

"I helped you once, Hermas. Now I am in need. I need food and water for four men—enough for several days journey—and I need it quickly."

"But, why…?" began Hermas.

"No time for explanations. Just do it—please."

By now, a few other servants were awake and watching the scene with intense curiosity. Hermas promptly put them to work gathering the necessities as he began filling skins with water. Marcellus ferried the skins to the soldiers outside. It took only minutes for the team to be well outfitted for the journey back to Diakropolis, and Marcellus thanked Hermas as the pair walked to the doorway.

"I am indebted to you for this," said Marcellus. "I will not forget it."

"What you did for me and my friends goes far beyond this meager act, Your Honor."

"Time will tell." Marcellus clasped Hermas' shoulder. "We must be off."

"Sir," Hermas said abruptly, stopping Marcellus in his exit. "Are you in danger?"

Marcellus paused to choose his words.

"I must leave for home quickly—a personal matter."

"Beware of the way stations. They are very dangerous for a man of your ambitions."

Marcellus sensed that Hermas understood something about his circumstances, and he shifted uneasily.

"Sir," continued Hermas, "at the seventh mile marker, there is a cluster of wild olive trees to the right of the road. If you pass through this grove, you will pick up a trail that winds through the hills until you reach a village. It is a small village, but you will know it by the narrow ravine you must pass through before you arrive. There you will find others like me. They are of the brotherhood of my faith and they will help you at the mention of my name."

Marcellus thanked Hermas for his assistance and turned to leave.

"Magistrate." Marcellus turned to face Hermas. "I will stand with you."

Marcellus looked intently at Hermas, who stood at the doorway holding a torch aloft. Hermas' face was lined with concern, but courage lit his eyes. The magistrate smiled and touched a finger to his own lips.

"I was not here tonight, Hermas. Do you understand?"

The host paused, then nodded and withdrew into the courtyard, returning the street to darkness.

The company made no more stops on their secret passage out of Prusa, save for an obligatory halt at the entrance to the city. The foursome emerged from a side street onto the main road near the ornate structure that marked the official city limit. The guards were startled out of a game of dice and made an amusing sight as they fumbled around to gather the appropriate attire and weaponry. The captain felt it better to trust their fortune to the greed of the guards than to risk an uncertain alternate route out of the city. His hunch was correct, and soon the group was on their way without detainment.

"That was easy," said Marcellus to the captain as they rode off.

"Ha, those fellows will be at Atarix' door within the hour, looking to double their take."

The somber truth of the captain's words spurred the company to a gallop. The pale moonlight on the landscape gave enough light to move along at a brisk clip, and they took full advantage. After several minutes, however, the road cut into a series of rifts and sharp curves, and passage became slower. The men moved along steadily for two hours, the captain periodically calling a halt to carefully survey the path. Marcellus was relieved to be on his way home and, with each rise in the road, he felt the seduction of Prusa and its aristocratic conspirators slipping. Even so, he felt a pang of desire for Arcadia, and he thought of her forbidding charm. Marcellus wondered if Arcadia were to come to Diakropolis, would he hold a similar allure for her.

The company's progress now was reduced to a slow walk. The moon, which had played cat-and-mouse with them through the broken clouds, now disappeared for what promised to be the last time, as a heavy bank of clouds moved in. Compounding the limited visibility was a thin but pervasive blanket of fog that filled the shallow valley through which ran the road. The captain led the team on foot, holding the reins of his horse with one hand, while probing the ground with searching eyes.

"Now I know where we are," called the captain after several minutes had passed. "We are two miles from the station—here's the marker. The road is relatively straight for the next mile, then a large bend and another straightway. We'll be there before daybreak."

"Good job, Captain," praised Marcellus. "The fewer observers, the better."

"Here, take this," said the soldier.

"What is it?" asked the magistrate.

"A rope. I'm not that good. Take a hitch around a strap and pass the rope back."

The captain hoisted himself onto his horse and moved the group, now loosely joined, forward into the thick, dark mist. They moved steadily in the gloom, faster than normal considering the conditions, led by the confidence of the veteran soldier. The fog grew denser and dampened the cadence of the hoof beats, as well as the skin and clothing of the men. There was a surreal loneliness and monotony to the scene, and Marcellus struggled to stay awake.

Suddenly, the silence was broken by a cry from the end of the line. Marcellus felt himself pulled backward and he heard a heavy thud.

"What is it?" barked the captain.

A nervous voice came from the last man in the company.

"I'm down, sir. I think my horse has pulled up lame!"

The company gathered around the fallen comrade, whose leg was pinned under the torso of the horse.

"Here, let's get the beast up," said the captain, and the three men pulled the animal to its feet, freeing the soldier.

"I'm all right," assured the man. "Better check the horse."

The captain inspected the steed as best he could in the blackness, relying mostly on tactile sensation as he ran his hands along the animal's extremities. A nervous whinny and sudden shifting of the horse indicated that the right front foreleg was injured.

"I think he stepped in a pothole," complained the captain. "Curse me for taking the pace too brisk."

"Don't scold yourself so severely," Marcellus said firmly. "You can't control the elements."

"This will set us back, sir."

"So it will. I'm sure that this will be just the first of many challenges."

"Just leave me, sir," said the injured horse's rider. "I'll fend for myself and make it to the station in due time."

"I will not approve of that, soldier. Too many dangers. We go together."

"Your Honor," intoned the captain. "Do you really want to jeopardize your, er, return in this way?"

"We go together!" Marcellus replied emphatically, ceasing the debate. "Captain, may I speak with you a moment?" The two men stepped away from the others.

"Back at Prusa, Hermas—the owner of the house where we stopped—gave me directions for an alternate route through the hills."

"Why should we chance that?"

"He suggested that we might be in danger at the stations ahead."

"All travelers are. Our swords will settle any disputes."

"I sensed that he knew of my predicament, though. There could be treachery ahead."

"I'd rather take my chances on an imperial road than the back country. Where does this route lead?"

"It takes off a mile back. We passed it without my knowing it—I must have been lost in thought. It takes us to a village that Hermas says is friendly."

"Whose friends?" the captain inquired pointedly.

Marcellus hesitated.

"His friends, I guess."

"Christians?"

"Yes, Christians."

"A word of advice, sir. Before you get in any deeper with these people—keep your distance. The stories I've heard would curl the hair on your back. Trust me, any treachery up the road will pale to their antics. Now, we had better move on—conditions are worsening."

The final miles to the way station were slow and arduous. Visibility worsened as the final hours of the night rolled by, and the company's pace was terribly limited by the injured animal. The magistrate remained determined to see the injured soldier to safety and he resisted the protests of the other men to allow the soldier to break off from the company. Finally, the group passed beyond the large bend noted by the captain and began the final mile toward the station.

The depth of the blackness lightened noticeably as the men drew within a quarter mile of the station. Their hoped-for predawn arrival now was impossible, and the captain conferred with Marcellus over their plan.

"I think we can safely part company now, Captain. I suggest that we take to the hills above the station and, hopefully, regroup on the other side with a fresh horse."

"Let's hope they're sympathetic at the station."

"If not, then we're down to three."

Marcellus sent the injured soldier hobbling on toward the station, with instructions to try to procure a horse without divulging the nature of his business. The magistrate did not witness the brief conference the captain held with the soldier before separating. The other three men climbed into the hills that rose sharply above the road. As they inclined, the thick morning mist that filled the trough of the roadbed began to thin, and the early light of dawn greeted them. Marcellus and the captain both were glad for the recovery of sight, but they were concerned that their movement no longer was hidden from view.

It did not take long to gain the rise above the way station, which still lay hidden in the mist below. The men found a small clearing and stopped for a long-anticipated break. Marcellus flopped to the ground and brushed his limp, wet hair back.

"I wonder if Atarix and Siros ever travel this comfortably?" he joked.

The young soldier accompanying the magistrate and the captain took a long drink of water from the skin.

"Steady, soldier," warned Marcellus. "Have concern for the future." The soldier, a young man barely out of his teens, smiled sheepishly and returned the skin to its place.

The captain partially reclined against a large rock, though he kept vigil toward the bend in the road, still shrouded in mist to the south.

"Water, Captain?" asked Marcellus.

"Thank you," replied the captain, not turning away from his post.

"What are you looking at?"

"I can see the bend in the road from here—a mile off—that is, if the fog lifts."

"You're expecting company?"

"Maybe. I expect to see some traffic. Whether it concerns us or not will be the question."

"How long should we stay here?"

"I'd give it fifteen minutes or so. If we don't meet up with our companion on the road north of the station, we have to assume that he was unsuccessful. We've lost valuable time, thanks to my carelessness."

"Captain!" rebuked Marcellus.

The two men continued in their respective positions for several minutes more, when Marcellus sidled up next to the captain.

"There's something I didn't ask, though I wanted to do so. My brother—is he tied into all of this?"

The captain thought for a moment. Marcellus assumed that the captain was choosing his words, rather than genuinely thinking over the question.

"The deputy is not a careful man," the captain replied tersely.

"Go on," prodded Marcellus.

"From his first day in Diakropolis, your brother fell in with—or should I say, sought out—the company of Siros. He controls the games and most of the taverns, which, as you know, are two of Septimus' foremost loves. It was rumored that your brother had a sizable gambling debt, which made him beholden to Siros."

"So you think it's a good bet—pardon the term—that Septimus is part of this?"

"To be truthful, sir, I doubt that your brother's aware of what he's gotten into. They probably are just playing him."

"I hope so. I truly hope so. I can see that these people are not to be trifled with…" The magistrate paused as he noted the captain's body tense, and saw him peering intently toward the distant road.

"Captain, what's the matter?"

"There, in that break in the mist." Marcellus tried to line his sight with that of the captain.

"What? I don't see anything."

"It has disappeared into the fog, but I'll swear I saw flashes."

"That could be most anything—a reflection of the sun on water, you know."

"No. I've seen that sight hundreds of times. It can only be metal—helmets, swords."

Marcellus grew anxious.

"Maneuvers out of Prusa?"

"No, I checked with the stable master before we left. We're being pursued."

The captain spoke in a grave, but resolute voice. He did not upbraid himself verbally, but Marcellus sensed the captain's regret over the delay for which he felt responsible.

"We'd better move out," said the captain.

The company quickly assembled their gear, although the other soldier had to be roused out of sleep. The way down was more difficult, but they negotiated the irregular terrain without incident. They regained the road a quarter mile beyond and out of sight of the station. Here, the men waited momentarily for the fourth in their party.

"Are you certain that this man is trustworthy?" asked Marcellus, leaning close to the ear of the captain.

"He'll come through."

The station, located ten miles out of Prusa, was not a welcome place for a stranger. Such stopovers dotted the road system of the empire, offering rest and refreshment for weary travelers, as well as an opportunity to hire fresh horses. A garrison of soldiers provided a measure of security, although crime, usually at the hands of the hosts, abounded. This particular station incorporated a small, floppy tavern, the inadequacy of whose food was outdone only by its vile patrons.

The soldier left his lame horse in the care of a disfigured stable boy, and then entered the tavern in search of its proprietor. The inside of the small building usually was unkempt, but it was more so now, due to structural damage from the recent tremor. The garrison was empty, owing to the need for extra soldiers in the earthquake-torn city, or else the traveling soldier would have taken his chances with his own kind. He was directed to a small hearth, where a wizened man hunched over several charred loaves of bread.

"I need to hire a fresh horse—mine is lame."

The scraggly man turned and gave a wall-eyed inspection of the young soldier.

"What have we here? A lone legionary returning from the spoils of war, eh?" A derisive chorus of guffaws erupted from the smattering of hung over, early-morning patrons.

"Shut up, cretin, or I'll run you through and take a horse," the soldier shot back, placing his hand on his sword's hilt.

"You'll get nowhere with that talk, young Caesar. Just cool your heels for a moment and let me fetch you some food."

The soldier turned up his nose.

"No, thanks. I'm in a hurry. Now, about the horse."

"In a hurry, are you? Running? As you can see, there is none of your kind here."

Activity in the room ceased.

"My business is none of yours."

"My horses are none of yours, then," the innkeeper spat back.

The soldier reached for his sword, but held as he heard the shuffling of feet under the tables of the patrons. It was clear whose side they would take should a scuffle break out.

"Okay. I am on a military mission to Diakropolis. It is urgent that I get on the road, immediately!"

"Now who goes to Dia…What did you call it?"

"Diakropolis. It's northeast of here. I am in the company of its chief magistrate."

"Ah, a dignitary in my establishment!" The innkeeper strutted around to the approving cheers of the motley audience. "And where is His Highness?"

"He has gone ahead. He's probably miles down the road, by now. I'll not be able to catch him if you don't hurry up."

"If he's gone ahead, then you weren't important anyway," taunted the old man.

"Listen, you crusty old oaf," snarled the soldier in the face of the man, quietly enough to fall out of earshot of the curious assembly. "If you don't find me a horse now, we'll see to it that your lovely little restaurant is ground into powder. We'll finish off what that quake should have done."

The innkeeper sneered at the soldier, then spat into his hands and began kneading more dough.

"You Roman soldiers are so full of yourselves. Can't take a little ribbing. Sit yourself down; I'll see to your horse."

"Boy!" The disfigured stable boy limped into the room. "Take our guest some bread and water, then find him a mount. Be quick about it; I've got some letters for the post before it comes."

The soldier took a small table in the corner near one of the few small windows. The sight of the bread and the hygiene of the cook quickly quenched any appetite that he had. The soldier impatiently drummed on the table, anxious to get on the road.

Minutes later, he smiled as he heard advancing hoof beats. The soldier rose to leave, expecting the boy to enter, but, instead, he saw a company of cloaked horsemen dismounting outside. As they retracted their hoods, he recognized a couple of soldiers from the Prusa garrison among them. One remained hooded, his face hidden in shadow. The soldier quickly returned to his seat and nervously scanned the room. There was a door visible behind and to the side of the hearth. It led to a small room, which appeared to be some sort of office. It was unclear whether there was any other exit from the building. Escape would be fruitless anyway, the soldier reasoned. He would be no match for a company on horseback. He stole another look out the window. To his relief, the party had not shown any movement toward the tavern, but he doubted that this would hold true. The soldier calmly rose and approached the innkeeper.

"Have you parchment and ink?" he asked politely, hoping not to arouse the man's ire. "I need to post a letter."

"What need would we have of those things out here?" came the snide reply.

"As a mail stop, I assume that you have the essentials for correspondence."

"And if I do, what entitles you to use the Imperial Post?"

"This does," answered the soldier, presenting a folded document.

The innkeeper opened the double-folded parchment and squinted at the writing. Whether he comprehended what he read was of no matter; after several seconds the innkeeper flipped the document back to the soldier and hobbled to the back room, muttering as he went. The soldier returned the valuable passport, a last minute idea of the captain, to a safe place inside his tunic. The innkeeper returned with a reed pen, an inkwell and a piece of parchment.

"I'm putting this on your tab," grunted the innkeeper, and returned to his baking.

Trying to avoid the stares of the patrons, the soldier returned to his table and hastily wrote a short message. He then carefully folded the document and sealed it with wax from a nearby candle.

"Would you place this with the other outgoing letters?" the soldier asked the host, who grew increasingly irritated at being distracted, yet again.

"Put it on the table there and quit bothering me!" growled the innkeeper.

The soldier suppressed a strong urge to dispatch the unsavory man right on the spot. He returned to the corner table where he contemplated his next move. That move was unnecessary, as three of the horsemen entered the tavern and surveyed the room. The soldier pulled over his hood but it was too late to go unrecognized.

"Hello, mate," smiled one of the men, as the trio sauntered over to the table. "You're in that detachment from Diakropolis, aren't you?"

"Yes," said the soldier, clearing his throat. He recognized the soldier who questioned him as one of the men from the garrison at Prusa.

"We didn't know that you would be bugging out so soon. Are you headed home?"

"Yes, I am," came the forced reply.

"I see that you're traveling alone," said one of the other men. "That's a strange thing for a soldier to do."

"I'm just following orders."

"Oh? And what might those orders be?"

"They are not to be shared."

"You're not going to get very far on that lame horse of yours, my friend," chuckled the first man.

The soldier remained silent.

The third man now stepped forward. The figure remained hooded, but the soldier saw that his face was tanned and smooth-skinned, with more delicate features than the others.

"I think it would be wise to share those orders, soldier." The voice was that of a woman. The frightened man swallowed hard.

"They come from a high-ranking source. I cannot disobey."

The hooded one exchanged glances with the two other men, nodded, and then left. The remaining two soldiers firmly grasped the soldier under the arms and escorted him out of the tavern.

"I'm shifting his bill your way!" the innkeeper called after them. "Cursed soldiers!" He spat again into his palms and vigorously rubbed them.

The lame stable boy entered from the back room and clumsily announced that a fresh horse was ready for the soldier. The innkeeper clapped the boy on the side of the head.

"He won't be needing it, you imbecile! Now clean his table, get the mail ready, and burn this letter! I'm sick and tired of trouble—and it's only morning!"

The simple stable boy confusedly scratched his head and followed his orders as best he could remember. Tucking the soldier's letter into his belt, he brushed the crumbs from the table, stuffed the bread in his tattered cloak, and downed the untouched water. He then took a leather pouch and placed in it the various letters that had accumulated over the past day. He hung the bag on a hook outside the door, where it would be picked up later that morning. The stable boy smiled to himself, satisfied with his work. He began to return to the stable when he realized that he still had the letter that the innkeeper had given to him in his belt. He stared at it for a moment, trying to recall what the innkeeper had said to do with it. Unable to come to a conclusion, the stable boy shrugged his shoulders and placed the letter in the pouch.

CHAPTER 21

▼

"We can't wait any longer," said the captain. "The lad is on his own."

"I hate to leave him alone at the station," responded Marcellus. "He could be in danger, if things are as you suggest."

"That situation won't change if we delay. He'll do the right thing."

The captain's urgency held sway and the party rapidly moved out. The mists had begun to disperse, revealing a pleasant, cool morning. The horses seemed vigorous, considering their lack of appropriate rest, and the company made good time. The men had another twenty miles or so to go before reaching Nicea. With good weather and fortune, they would arrive before dark. They kept their brisk pace as long as possible, until the horses showed signs of fatigue. Marcellus had equestrian experience as a younger man, and he knew that it was unwise to push the beasts too hard.

"Captain, it would be wise to take a break. The horses are tired."

"I'm uneasy about stopping, not knowing how much distance there is between us and our pursuers."

"Another mishap with a horse and we'll quickly find out."

"All right, we'll pull into those trees ahead. I'll see if I can get a view from that knob."

The respite lasted only a few minutes, however, as the captain came bounding down from his position, cursing and puffing.

"Curse it if they're not a quarter mile behind and closing fast."

"You'd think that they would have given their horses a rest at the station."

"In all likelihood, they left their horses and hired fresh ones. This is going to be a tight race, sir."

"Then let's make the best of it. On to Nicea!"

The company broke out of the trees and into a prolonged gallop, their mounts straining forward, as foam glistened around their determined muzzles. They drove on but, after a short while, the pace slackened. Presently, the captain called a halt near a blind of bushes.

"What now, Captain?" asked Marcellus.

"I'm shedding this armor. The extra weight is only hindering us. Soldier, you do the same," the captain called to the third in the party.

"Is that wise? What if we skirmish?"

"Are you wearing armor?"

"Well, no."

The captain ripped off his mail and helmet and hid it with the other soldier's behind the dense clump of foliage. The captain smiled as he leapt onto his horse's back, now looking more like a common traveler than an experienced warrior.

"Could be the difference. Who knows?"

They were off again, moving rapidly along the cobbled pavement as it snaked between the hills on either side. Marcellus found the flight invigorating, but also a bit nerve-racking, as he contemplated the business of the approaching company. The captain appeared relatively unruffled, evidence that he had been through worse circumstances. The frequent curves kept the company out of eyesight of their pursuers, but the men pressed on as if the posse was on their heels.

Periodically, they would reach a rise where the vista opened up somewhat and Marcellus caught a glimpse of the land through which they sped. Away to the west, he saw the fertile, hilly land, gradually flattening as it approached the sea. To the east, the folded hills rose to meet the sparsely-populated, desolate Anatolian plateau. Perhaps one day he would be able to explore this ancient land, so new to the Romans, but so deeply carved by the hands of time and civilization. Slowly, each mile marker passed, attesting to the company's progress. The men were only a mile from the next station.

"Is it safe to stop ahead?" asked Marcellus. "We're now closer to Nicea than to Prusa."

"It could be friendly. I'm not against a watering stop, but we had best go before our friends behind us arrive. Confrontation would be unwise."

Marcellus agreed and it was decided that they would stop near the station for reconnaissance before proceeding. They pulled off the road into a secluded spot a short distance ahead. The men let out a collective groan as they dismounted. The horses stamped and snorted from the draining ride.

"We have been fortunate that there has yet to be traffic on the road—at least, coming our way." Marcellus recalled the few carts they had whisked past, whose startled drivers certainly would be interrogated as to any suspicious travelers about the area.

"I noted that as well," replied the captain. "Strange, but welcome. I'll be back in a moment."

Marcellus rubbed his steed and gave quiet encouragement in its ear.

"Horses are like men," the magistrate said to the other soldier, who chewed on a piece of dried meat. "They perform better if you explain their mission."

"Yes, sir," replied the soldier, smiling.

The captain bounded into their camp, his face taut with frustration and anger.

"What gives?" Marcellus asked anxiously.

"We are hemmed in," the soldier pronounced bluntly, as he drove his rugged fist into the palm of his other hand.

"How so?" Marcellus drew close.

"It seems that we have a welcome party awaiting our arrival at the station. I assume that their intentions are not friendly."

"How can you know? Who is it?"

"Unless these aged eyes are failing me, our friend Nikris awaits us."

"Nikris? Who is he?"

The captain laughed and winked at the other soldier.

"You'd know him on sight, sir. Nikris, together with that little Syrian, Dura, are the inseparable appendages of Siros."

"What in Trajan's name is he doing here?" asked the magistrate, incredulously.

"I'd wager that it's on your account."

Marcellus bit his lip and shook his head.

"What are we going to do now?" he wondered out loud, slumping to a seated position.

"I'm not sure but, by my estimation, we have about five minutes to figure out our next move."

Marcellus remained motionless for a moment, and then quickly rose to his feet.

"Okay, here are our options: One—we turn to face our pursuers. Not wise. Two—we go forward to the station and hope for allies." Marcellus paused for the captain's response.

"Knowing what I do about these places, I suggest that we stay away from the station."

"Our choices are simple now. We can stay here in hiding and hope they pass."

"A joke if they have any tracker worth his salt."

"Or," continued the magistrate, "we take to the hills and try to evade them all."

"That's all that we can do," replied the captain. "Which direction?"

"West takes us toward the sea. Easier terrain, but more open. We may be seen. East gives us an edge for hiding, but we may have to release the horses."

"Your choice, sir."

"I choose east, toward the river. If I remember the map, we'll intersect the road to Nicea from Dorylaeum. Our pursuers can't be watching that, too, but, if they are, we'll cut a line straight to Diakropolis if we must."

The river lay some twenty miles to the east on its course north to the Black Sea. A major imperial artery roughly followed the river, heading southeast from Nicea into the interior of the region. The path the trio would take was uncharted, but the converging ranks of presumably hostile parties left them little choice.

The men led the horses up a short embankment that bordered the road, and then dipped down into a shallow depressed area before embarking on a much steeper climb. The break in the slope was fortuitous, blocking their view from the main road. The captain's assumption that the Prusa party was only minutes behind was correct and, before long, approaching hoof beats were audible as they climbed.

"Take the horses ahead and occupy their mouths with that grass," said the captain quietly. "Whatever you do, don't let them neigh."

Marcellus and the young soldier did as the captain recommended, while the veteran soldier crouched to spy their pursuers. A tense moment passed without event, as the party down below moved past without stopping. A relieved captain rejoined the other men.

"That'll buy us a few minutes," he said.

"You think they missed our tracks?"

"I suspect they're anxious to join the other party at the station. Once they see that Nikris is empty-handed, our pursuers will be back, and much more careful."

The three men continued on, winding their way through tight passages, around toppled boulders, and across rifts in the rocky ground, some of which were fresh from the earthquake. The horses struggled and protested at times but, with much effort, the party eventually reached more level ground and the going became easier. Small, patchy forests coupled with frequent rises and dips in the terrain kept the men from seeing too far ahead, but they kept moving toward the sun.

"These lands are true frontier," stated the captain as the company moved along, now on horseback. "We might happen upon a village or we may see no one. Keep your sword ready, though. Wild animals are a certainty."

They moved cautiously after this, wary of every sound emanating from hidden places. They spoke little, keeping mostly to their own thoughts. Finally, content that they had put safe distance between them and their pursuers, the men broke for lunch.

Hermas had outfitted them well with provisions. Salted meat, bread, and cheese had the men groaning with delight. The three were exhausted; none had slept for well over a day. Each man agreed to each take short naps, leaving one to watch and listen. The captain agreed to the first watch. Marcellus yawned and laid his head on his horse blanket.

"What are the villagers like in the frontier?" he asked drowsily.

"They're a good sort, for the most part," replied the soldier. "A world apart, though. Strange gods, strange foods. Best to keep away if we come upon a village. They're a bit wary of the military and of Roman officials."

Marcellus needed no further explanation, understanding the historical oppression and exploitation of the rural folk at the hands of those in authority. Such practices left a wall of animosity between the city dwellers and the villagers, which often spilled over into violence.

"Shouldn't have much difficulty convincing them that we're neither," replied Marcellus, as he pulled his soiled cloak high around his face and drifted off to sleep.

It seemed like only seconds had passed before the magistrate was aroused for his watch by the young soldier. The captain was asleep, making deep sonorous sounds through his open mouth. Marcellus rubbed his eyes and slowly rotated his head from side-to-side, grimacing as he reached each limit.

Marcellus situated himself comfortably next to a rock, but repositioned himself when he began to nod off. Finally, he decided that he would need to stand to stay awake. There was little activity to occupy his attention, except for some birds and an occasional small animal. He went to his pack for something to read, when the snap of a branch in an adjacent copse of trees startled him. He stood motionless, waiting for some additional sound that would identify the source, but none came. Marcellus returned to his post and crouched. His heart raced as he pored over the small forest, straining to see any sign of life. A gentle breeze disturbed the branches of the evergreens. His pulse slowed.

Another snap from a different location ignited the magistrate's nerves. His head jerked quickly in the direction of the sound but, again, there were no visual clues. His heartbeat pounded in his head so loudly, that he was sure the sound was audible outside his body. Slowly and carefully, he withdrew his sword from its sheath. The nearly inaudible passage of the sharpened metal on the leather scabbard was enough to awaken the captain, who raised one eyelid but made no sound. The soldier instantaneously sensed the tension of the scene and needed no prompting to arm himself. Marcellus directed the tip of his sword toward the other soldier to gently prod him awake, but the captain waved him off, knowing that the man's inexperience might cause him to call out.

Suddenly, men of enormous size and fearsome appearance accosted the company on all sides. Before they could make any resistance, the three men immediately were hooded and bound. Marcellus fought his captors vigorously and instinctively, not knowing what to do if he managed to get free, until a heavy blow to his head plunged him into unconsciousness.

As he came to, it took several moments for Marcellus to gain some semblance of orientation. The image before him swam violently, and he was gripped by a pulsating pain on the right side of his head. He struggled to comprehend the sight before his eyes, while simultaneously piecing together the events that had led to it. *Road…climb…sound in the forest.* The sequence gradually fell into place until the memory of the abduction caused Marcellus to stiffen.

Alert now, Marcellus forced his eyes to focus on the bizarre scene before him. It was a camp of some sort, presumably within a forest. He was not certain of the setting for evening was advancing, draping everything beyond the light in darkness. The light emanated from a large fire some twenty feet in front of him. Its erratic flame washed the clearing in variable light and shadow, causing forms and faces to flash and fade. Marcellus recognized the faces as those of his captors. They were mostly men, all with fair hair and long mustaches that obscured their mouths. The neck of each was encircled with an elaborate torque, while their wrists were ringed with a variety of bracelets that jangled with their animated gestures and sent shafts of reflected light dancing off the dark forest backdrop.

Marcellus became aware of his immediate environment. He was tightly bound to a tree. Also bound to his right and left, respectively, were the captain and the younger soldier. The abductors sat in an open circle before him around the fire, with the three captives positioned in the opening in full view. The young soldier to Marcellus' left sat upright, his eyes glazed over in a fixed stare. The captain's head hung limply, his face swollen and bruised. It was evident that he had put up resistance during the ambush.

The magistrate studied the assembly. They were loud and rowdy, obviously full of spirits and dangerously raucous. One lavishly decorated warrior opposite him seemed especially to delight in the aggressive antics of the others, although none confronted him. This man, Marcellus presumed, was the chief. Behind him stood a row of menacing warriors, their hair thickened and bleached with lime. Each held a long shield and spear, and appeared to police the bacchanalian fete, thrusting a spear shaft into the side of a marauder who became too unruly or threatened the well-being of the chieftain. There were other ancillaries among the group: servers who saw that each cup was brimming with liquor poured from silver jars, and a curious man near the chieftain who seemed to make commentary on the proceedings, but in a tongue unknown to Marcellus.

The smell of roasted game filled the smoky air, causing Marcellus' stomach to burn with hunger. The young soldier remained catatonic, but now the captain began to moan and stir. Marcellus watched the officer as he came to his senses and assessed his circumstance. Before long, their eyes met with the grim realization that their predicament had grown far worse.

The festivities continued as dusk settled. The renegades grew more drunk and bellicose. Mock battles were enacted and blood flowed, unintentional but, real, just the same. Combatants had to be forcibly separated on numerous occasions by the spearmen to prevent the infliction of mortal wounds. As the regaling became louder, Marcellus and the captain had opportunity to converse.

"I feared wild animals, but never this," said the captain out of the corner of his mouth.

"What is this?" asked the magistrate.

"Oh, I forgot, you are a newcomer to this region. We appear to be guests of a band of marauding Gauls."

"I thought such fêtes disappeared with the conquest," responded Marcellus.

"So they say. Obviously not, though. I have heard of these brigands who adhere to the old ways and wreak havoc on the frontier, plundering villages and terrorizing the defenseless."

"Such as we encountered on the way to Nicomedia?"

"My hunch is that those men mostly were mercenaries dressed up like this sort. This is the genuine article."

"That man in the center. Is he the chief?"

"Yes. The odd fellow nearby, the one making pronouncements, is his bard."

"What is he saying? I don't understand the language."

"It's Celtic, no doubt. I've only heard a few words myself, but it has that ring to it. The bard's job is to praise the chief and to recount his exploits, so I assume that's what he's doing now."

Marcellus shook his head in disbelief at their situation and remembered the warning of Hermas. How much worse off would they be had he taken the route suggested by the leather worker?

"Captain, about these horrible tales of Christians, do you have any firsthand experience, or are they merely tavern legends?"

The Gauls now were so absorbed in their activities that the two men could talk freely, without threat of reprimand.

"I'll admit that I've steered clear of them, so I can't say from personal experience. There was one situation, though—I'll never forget it. I was a neophyte infantryman, assigned to the Syrian legion. The commander was a man named Lucius. He was known for two things: reckless courage and an intense animosity toward the Christians. I don't know how he came by the latter, but his hatred for them was well-known. Lucius would sell anyone out to the executioner if he found out the man was of the religion. Even brought his superior to trial. We were sent to besiege Jerusalem, you know, to put down the Jews. We weren't more than a few weeks into the siege when Lucius disappeared."

"Disappeared? Was he killed?"

"No one knows. His body was never found and no foul play was determined upon investigation. The word in the ranks was that Lucius was spirited away by the god of the Christians to be tortured for his deeds—you know, some sort of witchcraft. The more reasonable explanation was that the Christians had dogged Lucius' steps until they found an opportune time to snatch him—just like us here. That would explain no body being found. He probably was eaten."

"Really, you don't expect me to believe that the Christians are cannibals?"

"Have you ever read any of their writings or heard about their rituals?"

"Well, no."

"Bizarre stuff, that is. I hear that they perform ritual murders."

"I've heard no such thing," Marcellus said emphatically.

"Of course you haven't. Their adherents live under the threat of torture if they reveal anything."

"None of this squares with what I saw in Hermas and his household. I saw only compassion and selflessness."

"Well, I guess we're even. You have one experience and so do I. I'm just telling you what I've heard. But this I know: It's a growing problem, and if we ever get out of here, you are going to have your hands full with it."

Marcellus' countenance abruptly changed.

"Shh, they're coming our way."

Sure enough, the chieftain had arisen from his place and now was walking toward the captives. His bodyguard followed, as well as the bard, who kept up his incessant drone of exaltation for the leader. The remainder of the marauders watched with eagerness.

Marcellus tensed as he watched the vile figure swagger across the circle. The chieftain stopped first before the young soldier, now revived somewhat, but still mute. Grabbing a shock of the soldier's hair, the Gaul jerked back the head of the dazed man to study his features, and then abruptly released his grip. The young guard's head dropped with a jerk.

Next, the chieftain came to Marcellus. The magistrate thrust his jaw upward defiantly and returned the villain's gaze. The chieftain stared back indignantly, his bloodshot eyes standing out in stark contrast to the pale, lime-streaked face. The two men continued their silent confrontation for over a minute, with neither looking away. Finally, much to Marcellus' relief, the Gaul conceded and moved on to the captain. A deep growl came from the throat of the chieftain as he eyed the captain, and recalled the wounds inflicted by the valiant soldier to several of the renegades in a struggle that Marcellus never had the satisfaction to witness. The Gaul concluded his inspection of the captain with a sharp slap across his face.

The chieftain held out a hand to the bard, who placed in it a garland, crudely constructed from a weedy vine. The rogue leader set the leafy crown on Marcellus' head, grunted with satisfaction, and then strode back to his place amid roars of approval from the band of Gauls.

"What was that about?" asked Marcellus of the captain.

The soldier laughed grimly.

"I made a mess of his little party when we made camp. There'll be some sore heads among his baboons tonight."

Marcellus looked up toward the garland on his head.

"Was that some sort of ritual?"

"I've heard of such things as this—but I thought they were of the past, too," the captain replied somberly. His tone made Marcellus anxious.

"What things? Why is this wreath on my head?"

"You may not want to know."

"Come, you can tell me. How can things get any worse?"

The veteran grimaced, and then spoke.

"I believe they've chosen you as their sacrifice."

PART III

▼

CAPTURE AND RELEASE

CHAPTER 22

▼

In the days following the earthquake, Philip worked long and hard. He went about his tasks with aplomb, the clear-headed vigor that accompanies difficult labor when purpose and need are plainly evident. He had vaulted from unwelcome farmhand to essential provider and caregiver. When not looking after Pellas and Cecilia, Philip tended the farm, with its myriad of chores and responsibilities. He understood now the tremendous exhaustion experienced by Pellas in his struggle against the elements and Cecilia's infirmity.

The farmer's leg was seriously injured by the crush of the tree trunk, but he was otherwise unscathed. The entire limb was badly bruised, and a long gash on his calf was especially worrisome. Philip watched anxiously as the swelling increased with each passing day. Pellas said little to the young man as he dutifully cleaned and dressed the leg daily. Philip did his best to offer words of encouragement, but even his untrained eye could see that the condition of the leg was deteriorating. His pleas for Pellas to go to town for expert care were resisted with a scowl and an order to position the leg more comfortably.

Cecilia, on the other hand, was a delight to serve, and Philip did so with unbridled enthusiasm. Each morning after Philip fed the animals, he and Cecilia would share breakfast in her room and chatter away about all manner of subjects. The time sped and Philip would usually look outside and gasp at the lateness of the hour, knowing that a day's worth of work would have to be compressed into half that time.

He then would settle Cecilia in a chair next to Pellas, from which she could feed and talk with her father while Philip was away. Cecilia often would read for long stretches, mostly from her father's favorite war histories, while Pellas lay still with eyes closed. Philip would return at lunch and at the close of the day to check on both of them. After supper, the young couple would return to their conversation, often talking into the early hours of morning. The subject often turned to Pellas' condition, and the worsening injury cast a pall on what otherwise would have been unmitigated joy.

On the third evening after the earthquake, Philip trudged in from the fields and joined Cecilia at her father's side.

"How is he?" asked the weary farmhand.

"He's been sleeping all afternoon. The leg looks worse."

Cecilia pulled back the blanket to reveal the swollen, discolored extremity. Philip whistled quietly and forced a smile.

"Philip, I'm worried for him."

The young man reached for Cecilia's hand and tightly clutched it.

"You must speak to him—help him to realize that he must go to town. He might lose the leg, and then where will we be?" Cecilia broke down into sobs.

Philip put his arm around her shoulder. Although growing stronger, she was still frail, and it seemed to Philip as though he could gather her entire body within one arm.

"There, Cecilia. It will be all right. You and I, we trust in God, don't we?"

The young woman continued to cry inconsolably. Philip decided that she had had enough for one day, and he situated Cecilia in her bed.

"The leg looks very bad, doesn't it?" she asked.

"I'm no doctor, but I fear the worst if your father doesn't get treatment soon."

"Please speak to him," she said softly.

"I have tried to talk with him, Cecilia. He just won't listen to me."

"Try again—please?" Her request was so pure in sincerity that Philip's eyes welled up with tears.

"What more can I say to him? I tell you, he has turned a deaf ear to me."

"Philip, I know that he has been cruel to you and, even now, he shows no gratitude to you for saving his life, but he's the only family I have."

Philip sighed. He knew that he should have pity on the farmer but, since the accident, Philip had felt his desire to serve the cold, callous man become increasingly difficult. Were it not for Cecilia, Philip would find it easy to completely detach himself from the plight of the farmer. After all, wasn't Pellas drinking the bitter wine of his rejection of God and his insensitivity toward others of the faith?

"All right, I will try again," Philip replied halfheartedly.

"Thank you, thank you," said Cecilia, "and I will pray with all my heart that he listens."

"Don't get your hopes up," Philip said as he left the room.

Philip busied himself about the main room, straightening up after dinner while keeping an eye on Pellas, who lay motionless on the cot against the wall. His chores done, Philip sighed and pulled a chair next to the injured farmer.

"You'll be happy to know that I finished fixing the stable today," he said awkwardly. Philip concentrated on Pellas' face, but could see no evidence that he was awake. "It's not so bad anymore. Why, I wouldn't mind sleeping out there now." Philip laughed nervously.

The young man sat back in his chair and tightly crossed his arms. He knew that this conversation would go the same way as had the previous ones and wondered why he was wasting his breath.

"Oh, did I tell you? The house is in excellent condition. Not a single crack. It's a tribute to the quality of your construction."

There was no response from the farmer except the monotonous cycle of his open-mouthed breathing. Philip tapped his foot and whistled through tightly-drawn lips. It was time to lay it on the line for the farmer. Philip scooted his chair closer and leaned in toward Pellas.

"Pellas," he said quietly, "I don't know if you are awake but, if you are, I am going to say this for the last time. You will lose your leg and possibly your life if we don't get you to the city soon. That would not be good for Cecilia." Philip noted a slight change in the pattern of respirations and he saw a flutter of comprehension in his Pellas' lashes.

"Let me take you to the city tomorrow."

The farmer's lips separated slightly to reveal the tip of his tongue. He moistened his lips slightly and spoke in a tone that would have been inaudible, had Philip not been so close.

"No," came the terse reply. Philip shifted in his chair, his facial muscles tensed.

"Then let me see if someone will come to the farm to help." He waited several moments for Pellas to form a reply.

"No," the farmer said for a second time. Philip's nostrils flared.

"You're a fool, Pellas," he said, taking care not to let Cecilia hear. "In that room there lies your own flesh and blood, alive only by a miracle. Even now, she pleads with God to save your life, not knowing that your obstinacy bars the way for her prayers to be answered. And why? What purpose do you serve wasting away in stubborn silence, except to feed your insatiable arrogance with your last breaths? Is your pride worth leaving your daughter all alone in this world? You, who guarded her so obsessively, now abandon her to the wolves?" Philip placed his lips next to the farmer's ear.

"Of all the evils you have shown to me, or to the Master, this exceeds them by far. Your renunciation of God is now complete."

Philip abruptly rose and shoved his chair aside. He quickly strode to the door and headed out into the darkness, snatching his cloak from a hook on the wall as he left. Collapsing cross-legged outside the stable, the young man sulked with chin propped on one hand, and the other swatting at the ground with a leather strap. He felt miserable. Philip never had spoken such harsh words, however true, and the sour taste lingered in his mouth.

Good job, Philip. Now you can claim partial responsibility for his demise, pushing him over the edge like that.

But he had it coming. I can't let him waste away without letting him know his folly.

But you could have been gentle with the truth. Do you really think that kind of talk is going to convince a man like Pellas?

What about me, though? Am I a slave to this man? I'm here out of kindness only. I put my life on the line for his. I have no obligation here; I could walk at any time.

Then walk. What keeps you here? If the situation isn't to your liking, move on.

I can't do that—Cecilia has no one to care for her.

Then wait a few more days and Pellas will be gone. Then you are free to take Cecilia back to the Master and you can be off.

Well, I really don't want that. I've grown fond of her, and I could put up with the old man's stubbornness—he's mostly just bark, no bite.

Philip's face was a study of expression throughout the silent debate. His face contorted into a succession of frowns, smirks, and resignations, which mirrored the thoughts that raged in his mind. He looked up at the sky and watched the faintly moonlit clouds chase each other toward some remote destination. A host of stars revealed themselves in the breaks like a myriad of shining eyes watching him from heaven.

"God, what is your purpose for me here? I came to learn of Your love and give out a portion to others. I have seen that love in the eyes of Cecilia—so trusting and patient—but in Pellas, the opposite. And now, his resentment of You consumes him, even as death spreads from his leg into his body."

Philip stretched out on the cold, moist ground and pulled his hood over his head to conceal all but his mouth. His mind was exhausted and now joined his body in complete fatigue. How long he slept was unclear, although the moon had moved on, producing only a faint light behind the much thicker clouds. Philip's cloak was wet with dew and the cold deeply permeated him. It only took a moment before the scene at Pellas' bedside and the words spoken entered his consciousness again. Somehow, though, the brief sleep had restored a sense of hope for the situation. It was as if God had brought everything within Philip to a standstill for a purpose.

Philip groaned as he drew himself back to a sitting position. He could see the flickering lamplight dancing in the cracks of the shutters of the house before him. Then words entered his mind, clear and comprehensible—the words of One who truly knew love: *If anyone says, "I love God," yet hates his brother, he is a liar.*

Philip knew those words well. Written and taught by the man who referred to himself as the disciple whom Jesus loved, Philip had heard such authoritative words passed on at the church at Ephesus where John himself had served. *It is not your place to pronounce judgment on Pellas, for only God is judge of a man's thoughts and intentions. If you claim to love Me, you will love him as well. He is in the grip of fear and only My love is strong enough to save him from its grasp. Now go and be My hands, eyes, and ears. Speak My words, not your feelings. Accomplish My purpose.*

Philip was now sitting upright. A shudder passed through him from head to toe and, for a moment, he could not move. Then one of the goats bleated loudly, startling Philip to his feet and sending him toward the house. He quietly entered and hung his damp cloak by the door. Philip again pulled close to the farmer.

"Pellas." The farmer's eyes opened widely, and then settled half-closed. "I want to ask your forgiveness for my cruel words earlier. I guess I got full of myself." Philip cleared his throat. "I've done some thinking and praying. God helped me to realize that I have a lot to learn about showing the love of Jesus to others. I guess I thought of you as a project and, when the project looked like it was going to fail, I grew tired of it. Well, you may be a project, but you are not mine. God is taking you through the valley of death and, if He so wishes, you will emerge safely on the other side. I will go with you as far as I can, and I pledge that Cecilia will be cared for with the same devotion that you have shown, but I ask you—no, I beg you, come back to Jesus and choose life."

Philip grasped the clammy hand of the farmer, whose glassy stare remained fixed toward the ceiling. As Philip held Pellas' hand, toughened by years of labor, he perceived a faint force. As Philip watched, the knobby fingers slowly began to curl around his. They held their grasp for several seconds then released. Philip looked at Pellas' face. His eyes now were closed, but his facial muscles seemed subtly relaxed. A steady rhythm of breathing indicated that Pellas had fallen asleep.

Philip quietly rose from the bedside and knocked on Cecilia's door. She called him into her room, and Philip slumped into a chair next to her bed.

"Everything's going to be all right," she said.

Philip was surprised at Cecilia's words. This was exactly what he had come to say to her.

"But you were so scared earlier this evening?"

"There is no fear in love. God reminded me of this."

Philip brushed her hair with his fingers and smiled.

"He's had to do a lot of reminding tonight. I'm too tired to talk now. I think that tomorrow we'll see a big change. After chores and breakfast, I'm going to town to find a physician who I can coax back here. That is, of course, unless your father consents to go to town."

"God is working, Philip."

"I know. Good night, Cecilia."

That same evening, Siros was holding court with his own principals in his villa. The merchant sat in a chair surrounded by the usual ring of subordinates: Titus, Dura and Nikris. The ever-wary Gaul stood while the others busied themselves with finger foods and nodded mechanically with the inflections of Siros' voice.

"I will be direct," said the merchant. "I am not happy with your collective performance and my patience is razor thin."

"But Father," protested Titus, collecting a piece of cheese that escaped his mouth as he spoke. "What more can we do? These things are out of our control."

"Everything should be under your control," seethed Siros. "If it is too difficult a task for you, I can easily find others who are willing to try."

"Sire," began Dura, somewhat timidly, "earthquakes are an unpredictable force. Surely, you can't expect us to control them."

"I am not an imbecile, Dura. I do not expect you to predict earthquakes; however, since they occur with regularity, I would expect a smoother recovery. We have shipments to make, and I am concerned that we have insufficient manpower to meet those obligations. Since you are so casual with my delicacies—save me some of that caviar, since I went to the pains of bringing it in from the coast today—I assume that you already have begun to make reparations." Siros stared at each man in turn, with one eyebrow lifted in obvious annoyance.

"Well then, does anyone here have knowledge of what deficiencies there are to correct? A tally? An educated guess, perhaps?"

The trio looked at each other, and then Titus spoke.

"I guess I'll go first." He leaned forward in his chair and struck a more authoritative pose. "The mine weathered the quake with mixed success. We lost the entrance to one shaft, but it should be reopened in a couple of weeks. Rubble already is being cleared. The main shaft had damage to the water wheel, but it is still functional. Overall, things weren't that bad. We should be back to full operation within the month."

"That is, if we can find workers, sire," added Dura.

"How many are we down?"

"Five workers are unaccounted for, presumed buried in the collapse of the shaft entrance," continued the Syrian. "Another two dozen or so were injured. Some or all of these workers may be unable to return to mine duty."

"We can ill afford the loss of that many workers. Reassign the injured to the mint and double the workload of the others."

"We already have begun that process, sire." Dura's comment brought a wry smile to the face of Siros.

"We also lost five guards," said Nikris. "They were on a hunting party and failed to return. Their bodies have not been recovered."

"Five for five," quipped Titus. "We're even."

The scowl that contorted Siros' face froze Titus in his chair. Were he not the man's own flesh and blood, Siros certainly would have permitted Nikris to practice his violent arts on Titus.

"One day, my son, this will no longer seem to be child's play. For now, try your best to keep your wits about you." Titus apologized profusely and lowered his head in embarrassment. "Tell me more about those lost workers," Siros continued, a hint of suspicion in his voice.

"We know for a fact that they were lost in the mine," Dura said with authority.

"For a fact?" repeated Siros.

"Well, we're reasonably certain," hedged the assistant.

"We don't make policy on 'reasonable certainties,' my dark-skinned friend."

"I understand, sire. We performed a thorough search of the premises. The five miners were assigned to the shaft that collapsed, thus, our assumption that the men died there. Of course, confirmation will be forthcoming as the area is cleared."

"Let me know immediately when you have recovered all five corpses."

"As you wish, sire."

"Now, Nikris. This hunting party—is this routine?"

"We permit small groups to leave periodically to provide fresh game. They also walk a wide perimeter, looking for anything suspicious."

"And they disappeared without a clue?"

"We suspect that they were buried by the quake, but I will not rest until I know for sure," responded the chief guard, having learned from the miscues of Dura and Titus.

"Very good, my friend." Siros turned to the seated pair. "You two would do well to learn the ways of our esteemed Gaul, here. Vigilance is the key. Vigilance," Siros muttered again under his breath, and then withdrew inside his twisted mind for several minutes.

He was silent during this time, except for an occasional grunt or a short squeal of a laugh, the only outward evidence of the machinations that proceeded in the merchant's head. His unblinking eyes stared straight ahead without fixing on any object that might pass across their field of gaze. Beads of sweat coalesced into streams, which ran down Siros' face to disappear within the neckline of his tunic.

Titus was accustomed to these periods of bizarre meditation, but Dura squirmed uneasily. Nikris, as usual, showed no change in his demeanor. The spells had grown more frequent over the past few months, and, at times, Siros would appear to be locked in an animated conversation with some invisible companion. Finally, his eyes focused and he addressed the group in a loud voice.

"It is cruel of me to expect you to comprehend things at my level. Let me instruct you according to fact. Fact one: We need more workers, and unless you gentlemen care to pitch in at the mine, you will diligently labor to supply them. There are a dozen hyenas circling my operation at any time, sniffing anxiously for some show of weakness, so that they might destroy my empire and ravage its spoils. You, Titus, above all, as my son and heir, should fanatically address each detail of our business to see that this does not happen. Beginning tomorrow, I want the region scoured for anyone suspected of being a Christian. Use a wide net. Now that Septimus is in control, we can proceed with alacrity. Fact two: Brother Marcellus is in Prusa and he should be finding the city to be agreeable."

"Should be, Father?" questioned Titus, not intending disrespect. "Are we not sure?"

"We will make certain that the novice magistrate does not leave his new position, my insolent son," Siros boomed. Titus cowered in his chair. "Dura, make sure that the shipment to Heraclaeia goes out as scheduled. They are the only threat with teeth at this time."

The Syrian bowed low and quietly slipped out of the room.

"Titus, pay a call on Septimus. Tell him that the hour has come for his first repayment. He should expect a full docket, shortly." Titus nodded and filled his mouth with food.

"Now, go!" boomed the father, the force of his command blasting the son out of the room, leaving the older man with his Gaul friend.

"Nikris, come here." The guard came and stood close. "You alone are impeccably competent and reliable. I rarely misread a man, but I will confess that this annoying chief magistrate of ours has me befuddled. I want you personally to take a detachment of guards and go to Prusa. I need firsthand knowledge that he is there to stay."

"I think my services are more useful to you here, Siros. Don't you trust Atarix to inform you?"

"I have another reason to send you, my friend. If Marcellus, ideologue that he is, should somehow be foolish enough to decline his new post and return to Diakropolis, I want you in Prusa to intercept him before he ever reaches our countryside. Do you understand?" The Gaul nodded.

"I will coordinate a plan to sift the villages for recruits and then leave at once for Prusa." Siros smiled at the fearsome warrior.

"As I said, impeccably competent."

Nikris left at once, leaving Siros to his contemplations. The leader skewered a piece of cheese with a silver dagger and slipped it off the weapon with his lips. He toyed daintily with the knife as he chewed, his half-closed eyes once again staring blankly across the room. Slowly, his breathing intensified and his nostrils flared with mounting agitation. His hand opened and closed around the dagger, pulsing like a heart. Then, with a violent roar, Siros surged violently and sent the blade hurtling across the room, where it came to rest in a gilded panel. He eyed the result with satisfaction.

"That, Marcellus, will be your fate should you cross me."

CHAPTER 23

▼

The sound froze Philip in his tracks. He was only a hundred yards down the lane from the farmhouse, on his way to Diakropolis to seek a physician willing to come tend to the ailing Pellas. The night had passed uneventfully. Rising early, Philip tended the animals, and then aroused Cecilia and moved her to her father's side. After all was set, Philip set out at a steady jog on the first leg of his journey to the city. He hoped to return in the early afternoon, so the trip would involve a good deal of running.

Suddenly, a distant bell rang out. At first, Philip did not comprehend the meaning of the clanging, but then he realized the source of the sound. It was the warning bell that Pellas had given Cecilia to summon him in time of distress. Now, the bell served the same purpose for the farmer. Philip had positioned the bell next to Pellas, within arm's reach of Cecilia, and he emphatically instructed her not to be shy about using the warning signal.

Philip wheeled and sprinted back to the house.

"Are you all right?" he blurted out as he burst into the room.

"It's Father," said the distraught girl, pointing to Pellas and covering her quivering mouth with her hand.

Philip quickly drew to the man's side. Pellas' breathing was rapid and shallow, and his body was trembling all over.

"Is he dying?" asked Cecilia, scarcely able to form the words.

"I don't know. He's on fire, though," Philip added, placing a hand on the forehead of the ailing farmer.

"Oh, Philip, do something!"

Philip paced and vigorously rubbed his neck as he agonized in thought. He sensed that a crucial point had been reached in Pellas' condition, and that time was running out. After several moments, Philip drew close to Cecilia and spoke gravely.

"I don't know what to do, Cecilia. I could go on to town and leave you here, but there's a risk that no one will be willing to come back with me. There's another choice to consider…" His voice trailed off.

"What is that, Philip?" Philip clasped both of the girl's hands.

"The leg will have to come off if your father is to live. I think he has gangrene. If not, he'll soon get it, and it will kill him."

"We know that already. That's why you're headed to Diakropolis."

"We may not have enough time for me to go and search for someone, then get back quickly enough to treat your father."

Cecilia recoiled in horror as the gruesome realization came to her that Philip might attempt to amputate the leg himself.

"Philip, you're not suggesting that you would…"

Philip got up and paced in agitation.

"I don't know, I just don't know. I can't bear to think of it now, but, if I got up my resolve, I just might."

Cecilia was speechless, her mind overwhelmed by her emotions. Philip glanced between the father and daughter, shaking his head at the tumultuous events that the pair had shared over the past several months.

"Philip," said the girl softly, "last night I felt the Lord speaking to me, telling me that everything was going to work out. You felt it, too, didn't you?"

"Yes, I did."

"Then go to the city. If Father doesn't make it, or if no one comes with you to help, then that is the Lord's will."

"If that's your wish, I will go without delay."

"It is. Pray for us."

Philip squeezed the girl's hand and was headed for the door when a raspy sound came from Pellas' mouth.

"What was that?" Philip asked.

"I don't know. The sound came from Father."

Philip returned to the farmer's side and looked at him intently. Pellas seemed to be struggling to say something. The pale, cracked lips separated, and then moved in silence.

"What is it, Pellas? Do you need something? Water? Hand me that cup, Cecilia."

A frown passed over the face of Pellas and he shook his head. He motioned Philip to come closer. As the young man leaned in, Pellas summoned all of his flagging strength and forced out a few words.

"Take me to the Master."

Philip stood in stunned silence.

"Philip, did he say what I think he said?" asked Cecilia, her hopes beginning to mount.

"I think so. Pellas, do you want to go to the Master?"

The trembling farmer nodded. At that, Philip sprung into action, scrambling around the room to gather needed articles, while sorting out details aloud for the journey.

"Cecilia, we leave at once. You are coming, too. I'm not leaving you here alone. Sorry, Pellas, we'll deal with that later. We'll need several blankets and some water. I'm not worried about food—the Master has plenty. Let's see, I'll need to put out extra feed for the animals; they'll do fine. Good thing I repaired that hitch on the cart. That would have been a real fix. Give me five minutes and we'll be on the road."

Philip flew out the door and furiously went through his mental list. It took longer than five minutes alone to coax the ox to accept the harness, and even longer to generate forward motion but, in the end, Philip's whip prevailed and he pulled up at the front of the house. He laid blankets over straw in the cart to make a comfortable place for his two passengers. First, he gathered Cecilia in his arms and gently laid her in the cart. Pellas, being much bigger and heavier, required a good deal of effort, and Philip inadvertently bumped the farmer's head on the side of the cart while trying to avoid any trauma to his leg. Philip covered them both with several blankets, including some threadbare ones that he had scavenged from the stable. It still was early in the morning, and a chill hung sharply in the air.

Once situated, Philip flew into the driver's seat and goaded the ox forward. He had become a somewhat skilled driver in his short tenure on the farm, a skill that was now paying dividends. They could ill afford any further delays, and Philip anxiously checked on Pellas many times during the painfully slow journey. The weather, although cold, was favorable, and the trio made good progress. It was nearing noon when they reached the city limits of Diakropolis.

They arrived at the entrance to the city and managed to pass through the soldiers stationed there without much delay. One of the guards demanded some sort of unofficial fee. The others, apparently feeling compassionate that day, overruled their fellow guard and permitted the group to pass. This relieved Philip, since he had failed to bring any money, and he had nothing of value to offer the soldiers. A short time later, Philip and his passengers pulled up to their destination.

Their arrival launched the Master's household into frenetic activity. Dacia and the other servants darted about in a frenzy, getting Pellas and Cecilia properly situated. The farmer was first priority, though, and Philip insisted that he could get Cecilia settled without assistance. Dacia ordered that Pellas be brought to a little-used room. There, he was placed on a long, narrow wooden table that was covered with a clean, white cloth, and had a small pillow at one end. Two smaller tables stood adjacent to the long table in the sparsely outfitted room. One of these had a basin on it, into which a servant poured water. Two high windows allowed a flood of light to enter the room, but a large portion of light came from dozens of lamps stationed throughout the room, which now were being methodically lit by another servant.

Upon seeing the pitiful condition of Pellas, Dacia forgave all the rudeness the man had shown toward her, and she scurried around to make him comfortable. Philip arrived outside the door and timidly entered upon Dacia's invitation.

"Where are we?" asked the young man. "I've never been in this room before."

"Count your blessings, Philip," said Dacia. "This is not the room to be in voluntarily."

"I don't understand. What goes on in here?"

"No time to explain that now. Just watch and do whatever you're told."

As soon as the fading patient was secure in the room, the Master appeared, walking slowly but erect, his white hair blending in to a clean, linen tunic. He approached the recumbent figure, now shaking uncontrollably from fever, and placed a hand on Pellas' forehead. The Master's eyes closed and he raised his head toward the ceiling. All activity ceased in the room as those in attendance bowed their heads.

"Our gracious God and Creator of all that is good, we humbly come before You, and we ask for Your infinite and perfect perception to be enabled through our feeble senses, and for Your healing skill to be practiced through our fallen hands. We offer before You our brother Pellas, who lies within the jaws of death. If it pleases You, allow us to draw him forth from that place, and to restore to him life and health, so that he may serve You with gladness and boldness. We entrust his body to Your safekeeping, knowing that in all things You are perfect and sovereign. Fill this room with Your presence and grant us success, we pray, but may it be wholly for Your glory. In the Name of our dear Savior, amen."

There was a chorus of "amen's" around the room, after which the buzz of activity immediately resumed. Philip stood motionless as he watched the puzzling scene before him.

"Philip."

The voice was the Master's and it startled the young man.

"Yes, Master."

"You will stand near me and do whatever I say. Come now, things will become plain as we go."

With reservation, Philip took his place next to the elderly man and stood at the side of Pellas, who was stretched out on the long table before him.

"Tell me everything that you know about the injury," said the Master.

"Well," Philip stammered, "we were working up at the stream when the earthquake hit. Some boulders dislodged higher up and uprooted several trees. One of the trunks pinned Pellas at the leg. I managed to get him dislodged and back to the house. He didn't want any medical attention, or else I wouldn't have let him get to this point. I'm sorry, sir."

"Philip," the old man said kindly, "you have acted heroically and with all compassion. No one is blaming you for his condition. The leg, it was badly crushed, then?"

"Not really. At first, I thought Pellas had made it through unscathed. Things gradually worsened. This morning he became delirious. What are you going to do?"

"I am going to try to save his life, and, hopefully, the leg."

"You? Shouldn't he go to a physician?"

"Not if we want him to live," smiled the Master, winking at Dacia. "There is no one in Diakropolis who can handle this injury."

"I didn't know that you had this skill, Master."

"I understand, Philip. You have not known me very long."

"It was the Master who saved Cecilia, you know," said Dacia.

"Let us concentrate on this patient, Dacia. Do you have my instruments ready?"

"They're ready for you, Master. I just got them out of the boiling water."

The housekeeper brought over a small strongbox and opened the lid. Inside was a large collection of tools that Philip immediately recognized to be surgical instruments. Philip intently watched as the elderly man calmly selected several items that he found to be suitable, and laid them out on the small table next to the bed.

"In my long life, I have learned many things, my son," said the Master, addressing Philip as he set out the instruments. "The key is to be alert and willing to learn in whatever situation you find yourself. This is one of the skills I have developed, although how I came by the skill is a story for another time."

The Master then nodded to Dacia, who placed a small vial into the mouth of Pellas, who feebly took its contents.

"What is she giving him?" asked Philip.

"Extract of opium poppies and henbane seeds. It will give Pellas comfort and allow him to tolerate my examination."

After waiting a few minutes, the Master exposed the wounded extremity and he began a careful inspection. He pored over every inch of the leg, pressing here and there, sometimes moving the leg into various positions. The elder made no comment during this procedure, and Philip managed to control his curiosity, which was about to burst.

"Did he bleed much with the injury?"

"No, other than a cut or two."

"Did you look at the cuts after the accident happened?"

"Yes, to clean the mud away. They didn't impress me."

"Did the swelling and discoloration begin over the entire leg?"

"Actually, Master, it seemed to start around his calf, then it progressed to the whole leg." Philip could not contain his curiosity any longer. "What are you thinking?"

The Master gently turned the diseased limb to the side.

"Go around to the other side, Philip. Do you see this small wound here?" He pointed to a raised two-inch laceration on the calf. "I believe that this is the source of the problem."

As the Master pressed around the wound, a foul-smelling green discharge poured from the unhealed laceration. Philip swallowed hard and covered his face with his arm.

"I have seen this type of injury numerous times before when a soldier had a dart fragment broken off deep in his tissue. Dacia, I will probe this wound. First, we'll need to turn our patient over. Give me a hand, Philip."

The two men turned Pellas' body to a prone position, affording much better exposure of the area of concern.

"Hand me the acetum," said the Master, who then proceeded to clean the area with the substance.

Next, he took a large forceps and inserted it into the wound. Pellas moaned lethargically but he did not thrash, indicating that the analgesic's effect was in force. Spreading the wound, the Master took a probe and carefully moved deeper into the muscle. More discharge and bleeding followed. The Master ordered Philip to keep the area wiped clean, a task the young man carried out with mixed emotions. Although fascinated with the procedure, the thought of probing into a human body made him shudder. Dacia watched Philip's eyes carefully, searching for any sign that the young man's stamina might give way.

Deeper and deeper the old surgeon probed, sometimes gazing intently into the wound, other times with eyes closed and head erect, as if he were diverting all concentration to his tactile sense. Periodically, the Master would hum briefly, suggesting that he found something interesting. He withdrew the probe, plunged a finger into the flesh, and worked it around. His humming became nearly continuous. Finally, he withdrew the bloody finger and wiped it on a towel.

"I am convinced now. He has a foreign object impaled deep into his muscle that is the source of his illness. If we can extract it, the swelling just might go down, making it possible to save the leg. However, the object is irregular in shape and it will not come out easily. We will need to cut it out. Philip, hand me that scalpel."

"Scalpel?"

"Yes, the small knife."

Philip complied with trembling hands, and he watched as the Master coolly incised the leg, extending the wound on either side. As he did so, the elder calmly described what he was doing and for what reason. Philip found the narration intriguing, but preferred the ignorance of silence.

"The body of this muscle, as you can plainly see," said the Master, separating the incision, "is comprised of two parts. The object managed to penetrate between the two, making our job somewhat easier. Ah, here is an artery dangerously close. Good thing the object missed it, or Pellas would have bled to death before you got him back to the house."

"Are you going to bleed him here?"

"That is something the ignorant physicians do. Scripture says that life is in the blood. It makes no sense draining a man of his life in order to save it. Dacia, the bleeding is getting profuse. Let's apply a tourniquet."

"What is a tourniquet?" asked Philip.

"It is a tight band applied to the extremity, closer to the torso. It will decrease the blood flow and help me to see more clearly. Also, you won't have to sponge away the blood as often."

Philip sighed audibly at that news and watched as the Master and his house-keeper, turned surgical assistant, applied the band. That done, the Master returned to his work on the wound.

"That is much better. Look here, Philip. You can see the end of the object. Come closer, don't be shy."

Philip inched closer to the site, took one look, then swooned and hit the floor with a single thud.

"He's out cold, Master," Dacia said, after a quick assessment of the ashen-faced young man.

"Leave the boy there. He'll be fine. I'll need you to do double duty, though."

The next hour was spent in the arduous task of locating and freeing the offending object. Philip revived after several minutes, but he was of little use as an assistant and spent the time slumped in a corner of the room. Dacia alternately helped the Master and attended to Pellas, who required additional narcotic to keep calm. The pair worked as a perfect unit, a regimented ballet of manual dexterity accompanied by few words. The Master never flagged, and Philip marveled at the elder's vigor. The fire that burned in the Master's eyes as he labored over the farmer attested to his passion for restoring physical, as well as spiritual, well-being.

Finally, the requests for forceps, extractors and ligatures ceased, and the Master studied his work for a minute or two.

"Tourniquet off," he ordered, apparently pleased with the result.

"You're finished?" Philip asked excitedly.

He scrambled to his feet, steadied himself, and then stood behind the Master, partially shielded from the surgical site.

"I believe so. Here is the culprit."

The Master held up a bloody, jagged shard of bark that had been deeply driven into Pellas' leg when the tree trunk had collapsed on him. The puncture wound was deceptively small and it had closed around the shard, causing the delay in diagnosis and Pellas' slide into delirium.

"Praise God!" exclaimed Philip. "So Pellas is going to be all right?"

"It's too early to tell, Philip," said the Master, who now showed signs of fatigue. "The next hours are critical. We must watch Pellas every minute."

"Dacia, arrange a schedule so that everyone takes a shift. If Pellas doesn't take a turn for the better by tomorrow morning, we'll have to amputate the leg. I'm taking a risk here, leaving it on. I've seen these things go both ways."

"You mean, keeping the leg or not?"

"No, death or life," returned the Master, gravely. "However, I have a strange peace about this case. Let's turn our patient over so that he'll be more comfortable."

Pellas moaned as he was placed on his back. His eyes opened slightly and he struggled to focus on the faces around him. Eventually, his eyes settled on the face of the Master.

"Pellas, my son. We are finished. Take courage, the Lord will heal you. Even now, His angels are ministering to you."

The farmer struggled to speak.

"My leg," he managed, slurring the words.

"It is still your leg," said the Master, with a smile. "Now rest. If you have pain, Dacia will help you."

The Master slowly moved away from the surgical table and washed his hands in a basin of water. Dacia joined him, while two servants collected the soiled cloths and surgical instruments.

"Have the dressing changed and the wound cleaned every hour, my dear. It is good for the discharge to leave his leg. If anything changes, alert me immediately. Philip here will be good for a shift."

"I'll do anything that you need me to do," the young man said enthusiastically, "except, I guess, help with surgery."

The Master smiled reassuringly.

"In time, one's constitution toughens with these things. I wish to visit Cecilia. Where is she, Dacia?"

"I put her in the same room where she stayed before, Master. Are you feeling well?"

The weary man had placed both hands on the table and he seemed to be bracing himself from falling. Dacia rushed to the Master's side and steadied him under his arms.

"I am fine, dear woman," he said, shrugging her off. "I think I had better go to my chamber now and let Philip speak to Cecilia about her father."

"Perhaps you should take some food and drink," said Dacia.

"This is not physical weakness, my dear. Something dark is happening. I can feel it. The enemy is at work, but I don't know where or in what setting."

"The enemy?" asked Philip.

"The devil—Satan," clarified Dacia.

"He's always at work somewhere," puzzled Philip.

"His work is near to us, somehow," said the Master. "I need to pray. Take me to my room, my son."

Evening approached and the activity within the Master's house settled. Cecilia was comforted with the news of the surgery, and she encouraged everyone with her conviction that her father was going to be restored to health. Philip requested the first shift attending to Pellas, and he sat anxiously in a chair next to the farmer, trying to get comfortable with the erratic behavior exhibited by the sedated man. Several times, Philip called Dacia into the room for what he perceived to be downturns in the man's vital signs, but, each time, she found him to be stable. The other servants quietly went about their business of preparing supper and making provisions for the new houseguests.

In the Master's chamber, however, a silent battle raged behind a closed door. There were no witnesses to the conflict, at least none within the household of the Master. After he assisted the elder to his chamber, Philip inquired of Dacia as to the meaning of the elder's cryptic words.

"No one knows what he sees or hears at these times, Philip," she related. "He is attuned to the spiritual world to a degree that we can't comprehend—I do know this from past experience. Somewhere, the forces of hell itself are besieging someone whose life is intertwined in some way with ours. It may be many years before we understand why the Master was called upon to intercede this very hour, but it is likewise a call for all of us to join with him in prayer."

As Philip sat next to Pellas, he recalled the words of Paul in his letter to the very church in which he was reared. *"Our battle is not against flesh and blood, but against the rulers of darkness in the spiritual realms."* What conflict now raged in those realms that would affect his life? Philip looked at the face of Pellas: his eyes were closed, his lips moving slightly in incoherent, silent speech. Certainly, here was more than mere physical conflict.

Philip prayed. At first, his thoughts were disjointed and jumped from item to item, including things embarrassingly trivial. However, as he focused on the grave situation present in that very room, and on the unknown conflict that bore upon the Master, Philip's prayers became more fervent and defined. His pulse quickened and he felt strangely united with the Master in his warfare. Truly, this was faith at work, and the exhilaration of the effort nearly overcame the young man. The eternal God was enjoining finite man in a mysterious and indomitable cooperative, not out of need on His part, but out of privilege as His child and heir. Philip felt that he had stepped through a portal into a world both intimidating and irresistible; he did not wish to retreat.

CHAPTER 24

▼

Philip awoke without a sense of time or place. At first, he thought he was in Pellas' stable, but soon he recalled the events of the previous day and the young man realized that he was in the Master's house. The light of day had not yet entered the room through the sole window high above his cot. He sprang to his feet and groped to find the door. He then passed into a darkened hallway and down a staircase to the peristyle area. Once there, he found his bearings and raced to the room where Pellas had been treated. He knocked vigorously on the closed door and was invited inside by Dacia.

"How is he?" Philip asked breathlessly.

"Steady. No worse, but no better."

"But, no worse," emphasized Philip. "Should I go tell the Master?"

"Oh, no. He's quite aware of the situation. He visited Pellas many times throughout the night."

"What time is it?"

"Not yet six o'clock, I'd presume," yawned Dacia.

"You look worn out, Dacia. Would you like me to stay with Pellas for awhile?"

"That's thoughtful of you, but it is my shift. Why don't you go and report the news to Cecilia? She wanted to be awakened early."

Philip looked at the sleeping patient and then went to Cecilia's room, where he found the young woman already awake, propped up and reading.

"Good morning, Cecilia. Did you sleep at all?"

"Good morning, Philip. Very little, I'll confess."

"It seems as though I was the only one, then. I'm rather embarrassed."

"After all you have done, you have no cause to be. You deserve the sleep."

"Thank you. I have news of your father."

Cecilia's eyes opened wide and her torso straightened.

"What? Tell me!"

"He passed the night without event and he is stable. Dacia says that he hasn't shown any improvement, though."

"That will come today, I just know it!"

"Between your optimism and that of the Master's, there's little room left for doubt."

"Where has the Master been hiding, by the way? I expected that he'd stop by for a visit."

Philip recalled to Cecilia the strange statements of the Master and his own wrestling in prayer the previous evening.

"You know, I began to pray last night and it seemed that my perception of things deepened, somehow. I don't know how to explain it, but everything became so intense, so sharp. My words and thoughts, my concentration...oh, I don't know. It was just different. I was exhausted afterward, just as if I had been in a real battle. That may be why I slept like a rock."

"Imagine what it would be like if we could see as God sees, what visions there would be!"

"I'm certain that this house would be ablaze with the light from legions of angels," mused Philip. "I'm not so sure about the rest of the city, though."

"The world exists in darkness, except where we shine the light of our Lord. It is that light that attracts people."

"Indeed, no one stares up at the night sky and looks at the blackness," affirmed Philip. "It's the light that fascinates us."

"I think you'll make a fine evangelist, Philip." The young man blushed.

"Oh, I don't know. I may spend my days as a farmhand."

Cecilia smiled and rested her head back on the pillow. The two were silent for a minute.

"Philip," she asked tentatively, "if something had happened to Father—say, you were unable to free him from under that tree—what would you have done?"

"What do you mean?"

"Would you have moved on—to another town or village?"

Philip suspected that Cecilia's question really was about what he would do with her.

"To be honest, before you fell out of your bed, I would have run from that farm as quickly as my legs would carry me."

"And after?"

"That's a different story."

Philip was keeping his answers terse, partly to be convinced of her intent with the questioning, and partly because he did not know how much of his feelings for the young woman he dared to expose.

"In what way?" she asked, looking up at the ceiling.

"Well…" he began, and then paused briefly. "When I discovered you there on the floor, so helpless, the purpose in God's leading me to the farm became clear. It was then that I resolved to serve you and your father until the Lord told me otherwise. You were as big a part of that calling as was your father."

Cecilia wrinkled her nose at Philip's reply. It was less than she had hoped to hear, but not completely disappointing. She assumed that her paralysis and disfigurement had aroused a sense of pity in Philip, but she hoped that a force stronger than sympathy might bind his devotion. She scolded herself for thinking lightly of God's grace in providing such committed help, and she remembered her state before Philip began to see to her well-being.

Philip carefully eyed Cecilia. He sensed that his reply was not completely satisfying to her, nor was it to him. He cleared his throat.

"Yes?" she responded eagerly.

"I…I was just clearing my throat," he stammered.

"Oh," she said quietly.

There was another minute of silence, but the pause this time was awkward.

"Cecilia, I'm not very good at 'what if?' games. There are a thousand things that could have happened, but didn't. I'm too blunt to circle around an issue until I eventually arrive at its substance. So, here goes. That day, when I crawled through your window and found you, it was as if I had found the other part of me—a part, I'll admit, I didn't know was missing until I saw how well it fit. Your father is very ill, and his recovery may be slow and incomplete. You need someone to care for you and I intend to be that one. I want to be that one." Philip's voice quieted to a near whisper.

"And I don't want to stop being that one—ever."

Cecilia's eyes opened wide and her lips quivered.

"Are you saying…?"

Philip took her hand and knelt by her bed. Their eyes met and he ran his fingers over her marred face. She turned away, but he gently moved Cecilia's face back toward his.

"These scars are permanent insignias that you belong to someone else. I find them beautiful, as much so as the loveliness that resides beneath them and flows forth with your every word and gesture. No, I don't shy away from your appearance, Cecilia. I am envious of it. Would that I might be found worthy to bear such marks of ownership. But even though you belong to that One above, it is my belief that He would delight in entrusting your care to me—not as a mere attendant or servant, but as your husband."

Tears streamed down Cecilia's face as she quietly sobbed with joy.

"I don't know what to say, Philip. What I am hearing is beyond words."

"I knew this time would come. I didn't know when, but it seems fit that it is now. When your father is stable, I intend to ask him for your hand."

Cecilia's brow furrowed with concern.

"What if he won't agree?"

"He will. That much I have on conviction."

The pair gazed at each other for some time, with Philip cradling Cecilia's face in his hand, and she gently moving her cheek along his palm. Then, slowly but emphatically, Philip drew close and kissed Cecilia.

The last light of day was fading when the Master finally emerged from his room. He entered the dining area where the others were gathered for the evening meal. Pellas' condition remained largely unchanged throughout the day and he continued to manifest fits of delirium interspersed among drugged sleep. When Dacia saw the Master, she rushed to his side to guide him to the table.

"Now, Dacia, I am not an invalid," said the Master, shaking off her assistance.

"But you look so weak, Master," she replied.

"Nothing that a bit of food won't correct. How is our patient?"

"He's in and out. There is less discharge but the swelling has stayed steady."

"That is good news. It may take another day or two before we see definite improvement. Now, how about supper?"

Dacia scurried off to the kitchen and the other servants followed, leaving only Philip and Cecilia with the Master.

"It is good to see you about, my child," said the Master to Cecilia, clasping her hand tightly. "Your friend is providing good company, I hope."

"Yes, indeed," she said excitedly.

The Master's gaze dwelt on the young woman for a moment in apparent knowledge of the bond that was developing between the two young people.

"Cecilia told me about the unusual circumstances of your meeting," the Master said to Philip. "I prayed that somehow the two of you would come together. I knew that Cecilia needed a kindred spirit to talk to for her well-being."

"Why didn't you tell me that she was still alive?"

"It was difficult not to. If I had done so, any hope of reconciliation with Pellas would have been lost; however, I was apprehensive that Cecilia could be neglected. When I saw the steady draw on our pantry, I presumed that the nourishment was finding its way to her." The Master turned again to Cecilia and said, "She looks marvelous don't you think, Philip?"

The young man did not reply, but simply smiled as he gazed at her.

A servant entered the room and set before the Master a hearty plate of food. He leaned close to the two young people and mused:

"I think Dacia is trying to do me in with all of this food—death by gluttony."

The trio laughed and the Master set about eating his dinner. He showed no sign of fatigue as he devoured the entire portion and washed it down with a large cup of water and a small bit of wine. Philip had much to talk about with the leader, but conversation was limited to questions answerable in short sentences. When the elder finished, he pushed back from the table and smiled with satisfaction.

"I feel quite refreshed. Now we can have a proper discussion. What was it you were asking?"

Philip eagerly scooted his chair close.

"I'm sorry about that scene in the room with Pellas."

"Nonsense. It happens to all who aren't accustomed to such sights."

"Your surgical skill, sir—it was amazing! Where did you learn such exploits?"

"One tends to pick up knowledge when one has lived as long as I have."

"Living in Ephesus, I've seen the work of some of the best physicians. Your skill surpasses them all. Certainly, this is not a casual knowledge, sir." The Master sighed.

"I suspect that someone as inquisitive as you, Philip, deserves a more detailed answer."

"Yes, I do!" Philip responded excitedly, and smiled at Cecilia.

The Master inhaled deeply and closed his eyes momentarily, as if to decide how to begin a revelation of great proportions.

"You may be aware that I had the privilege to spend time with the Apostle Paul some years back. It was through Paul that I became acquainted with a physician friend of his, a great man of faith by the name of Luke."

"Of course, Luke. I've heard of him."

"Well, Doctor Luke provided assistance to me during a time of great distress. During our time together, I was able to learn the skills of medicine and surgery. I already had some loose experience, but it was Luke's teaching that refined my abilities. After I came to Bithynia, I found that the area was quite underserved with qualified medical personnel, so I gained much experience in the heat of battle, so to speak."

Philip was quite impressed with this revelation and he repeated it in its entirety to Cecilia, who smiled sweetly even though she had just heard the same story. When Philip was through, he turned back to the Master.

"Just how did you come to Diakropolis?" Philip asked without pause. "I don't believe I have ever heard that tale."

"That's because I've never shared it, my son."

"But why? Certainly someone with personal ties to men such as Paul, John, and now, Luke, would have a phenomenal story."

"Whether it is phenomenal or not is for someone other than myself to judge. Yes, there have been significant twists and turns in the pilgrimage that ultimately have brought me to this place, and, in due time, they will be shared. However, this is not the time. Besides, the tale is long, and I have neither the inclination nor the stamina to go at it now. I need to check on this dear girl's father." The Master began to rise.

"One more thing, sir, if I may be so bold," said Philip, and the elderly man resumed his seat. "Last night, when you returned to your chamber, I felt compelled to join you in prayer. As I sat beside Pellas, I was convinced that I was doing battle with some unseen evil. I wasn't afraid, for I felt the strength of the Lord, and I knew that His might was far beyond that of the enemy."

"That is wisdom from God and it will carry you through much oppression. But what is your question?"

"Did the darkness have to do with Pellas? Is the enemy trying to take him?"

The Master thought for a moment.

"That may well be, Philip. I sense that there is something beyond this house that requires our intercession, but, certainly, our adversary has been pursuing this man and struggles yet to wrestle Pellas out of the grasp of the Lord."

"But how do we find out the answer to these questions?" inquired Philip, growing perplexed.

"My son, do not get entangled in the pursuit of things which God will reveal in the proper time. Such misplaced curiosity is fertile ground for deception. Do the task God lays on your heart—nothing more or less. This I *will* tell you—the burden to pray, and to do so fervently, has not been lifted from my heart. However, we will mark these days in our minds, should the Lord bring to light the nature of His call to pray. Now, I must go."

Philip shook his head once the Master had departed.

"What a cryptic fellow. What do you make of all this, Cecilia?"

"I know little more about the Master than do you, but I am certain that he must have reasons for not sharing his past. As to our present situation, I am content to pray and to wait."

"I'm afraid that will take some practice for me."

Just then, Dacia entered the room to clear the dishes.

Dacia," called Philip, "Come here, please."

"What is it, Philip?"

"Come close." The housekeeper drew near. "Now listen, I'll give you something nice if you'll clue me in as to how the Master came to Diakropolis and what he did before he got here." Dacia drew back in a huff.

"You couldn't scare up enough niceties to get a morsel out of me, young man. Now, mind your own business and put your faculties to better use—like helping me to clear the dishes."

Philip complied, his ego bruised a bit, and he began gathering bowls and cups, while Cecilia covered her mouth and giggled.

The next day found Pellas resting more quietly. The fever had shown signs of abating, although episodes of shaking chills appeared off and on throughout the day. For the first time, Dacia had documented a definite decrease in the swelling of the diseased limb, a fact that she announced with exuberance throughout the house. The Master was pleased to see the drainage had stopped on his morning inspection, but he remained concerned over the leg's color. Moreover, Pellas had yet to maintain consciousness for more than a minute or two, or to have any coherent conversation. Dacia managed to get him to take small amounts of water, but even this was difficult, and could only be accomplished during his brief spells of wakefulness. Nevertheless, the signs of improvement lightened the mood around the house and it was hoped that Pellas soon would come out of his moribund state.

The Master spent the majority of the day in his chamber and he ventured out only for a brief look at the farmer in the afternoon. Even the elder's meals were taken within the confines of the small room. Philip grew impatient and paced around the house, often getting in Dacia's way. As usual, he enjoyed time with Cecilia, but he became easily distracted and unable to concentrate on a subject for long. Philip did not voice his concerns, but deep within he harbored a fear that Pellas would not emerge from his obtunded state. The young man determined that it would be best to return to the farm the following day to tend to the animals rather than to face another day inside.

The following morning was another dreary early winter day, wet and cold. Philip set out early for the farm, laden with enough food for a small hunting party, courtesy of Dacia. He spent a few minutes alone with Cecilia and left her with a kiss and a promise to return that evening. The day progressed without event as far as Pellas was concerned. The Master remained in his room all day, not even emerging to check on the farmer.

It was late in the afternoon when the atmosphere of the house changed dramatically. Dacia was in the room with Pellas when the farmer let out a loud moan. She raced to his side and found that the ailing man was wide-awake, looking around the room.

"Who are you?" he asked, trying to focus on the woman.

"It's Dacia, the Master's housekeeper. You are in his house."

"How did I get here?"

"You were brought here by Philip."

"Ah, Philip. I knew that rascal eventually would drag me back here."

"Don't start in on him, Pellas," Dacia scolded. "You were halfway through death's door when you arrived. Besides, it was you who asked to come here."

Pellas thought for a moment, struggling to sort out the details that led to his predicament.

"Oh, yes, I guess I did," he said contritely, his countenance softening.

"Welcome back," Dacia said, smiling.

"Thank you," the farmer replied weakly. "Is Cecilia…?"

"She's here."

"What about the farm?" Pellas asked with a hint of anxiety.

"Don't worry yourself about that. You have an excellent helper who has seen to everything. Philip's due back this evening from checking on the farm."

Pellas settled himself back on the bed. The thought occurred to him that he should check his leg. He did not recall his brief conversation with the Master after the surgery was completed and was concerned that something drastic had been done. He judged by the aching that the limb still was attached, but then recalled that amputees routinely retain phantom pain after the loss of an extremity. As Dacia watched with interest, Pellas struggled unsuccessfully to position himself where he could glimpse his leg.

"What are you trying to do, Pellas? You need to stay still."

"I can't see it," he growled.

"See what, Pellas?"

"My leg."

"Well it's not a pretty sight, so I would say be thankful that you can't."

"You mean, it's still on?"

"Yes, of course."

"Well, praise the…" Pellas stopped short of completing his exclamation and closed his eyes.

"What's wrong, Pellas?"

At first, the farmer did not reply for some time. Dacia asked again, but she sensed that there was something disturbing the man, which he did not wish to share. Finally, Pellas spoke.

"He saved me, didn't he?"

"If you mean the Master, then yes, he did—although he'll be the first to credit the Lord."

"How long have I been here?"

"It's been three days now."

"How much of that time have you been watching me?"

Dacia blushed and turned away.

"I suppose half of the time."

Pellas shook his head and again closed his eyes.

"Might I tell the Master that you are awake?" Dacia inquired.

"As you wish," Pellas said with indifference, then adding sharply, "but I don't want to talk to him."

"It is his prerogative, as your surgeon and the owner of this house of healing, to do as he sees fit, but I will relay your wishes."

The Master was in his chamber, eyes closed and huddled in a chair before a brazier, when Dacia's knock came. At first he did not respond—whether he did not hear the knock or chose to ignore it was not clear to Dacia. After a second, louder knock, the Master called out.

"Who is it?"

"It's Dacia, Master. I have news."

"Can it wait?"

"I think you'll want to know this."

"Very well, come in."

The dimly lit room failed to reveal the exhaustion etched upon the aged man's face until Dacia came close.

"Master," she gasped, "Are you well?"

"I am fine, my dear, just troubled."

"You must take your rest. And look," Dacia added, seeing the untouched plate of food, "You haven't taken a bite of your meal. You can't handle this strain."

"The Lord will determine what I can and cannot handle. Sleep will come in its time. The Lord bested my fast by thirty-eight days, so ease your concern. What is it that you came to tell me?"

"My goodness! I nearly forgot! It's Pellas—he's awake and talking."

"I suppose that's worth a break. Let's go to see him," said the Master, smiling.

"He, er, requested not to see you."

"Did you expect otherwise?"

The Master entered Pellas' room and unhesitatingly went to the farmer's side.

"Three days in the belly of the whale, eh, Pellas?"

The farmer opened his eyes and looked at the Master, puzzled.

"I'll explain later. How do you feel, my son?"

Pellas struggled over whether or not to answer. He looked angrily at Dacia, who stood partially behind the Master.

"Come now, Pellas. The Lord has seen fit to spare your life, you can manage a few words with me."

"Weak. Groggy. Pain shooting down my leg."

"That's to be expected. Here, let's have a look at it."

Dacia helped Pellas turn to one side and the Master gently removed the bandages from the injured leg.

"Hand me that stylus, Dacia," he said, pointing to the slate on which she had recorded her observations of the farmer's condition.

The Master proceeded to test Pellas' sensation with pricks along the foot and ankle. Several times the patient grunted, growing more impatient with each progressive stimulus.

"What are you trying to do?" Pellas asked pointedly.

"It appears that a complete recovery is not out of the question, Pellas, although I shouldn't be surprised. We serve a gracious God, and He has chosen to demonstrate this through you. What do you say to that?"

"I don't see why God is so interested in making such a fuss over me," Pellas muttered. "Can I see my daughter?"

"I think that can be arranged. Something so pleasurable can only speed your recovery. Dacia, have Veritas bring Cecilia to her father but, first, permit me to have a few minutes alone with Pellas."

The Master studied the pale face of the farmer.

"Can I get you some water?"

"Yes, I would like that." Pellas ran his tongue over his cracked lips.

The Master cradled Pellas' head under an arm and brought a cup of water to his lips. Pellas drank it down and relaxed back on the bed.

"Thank you."

"Well, one must admit that the path which brought you back under this roof has, indeed, been strange," began the Master. "But that is the way of the Lord. We make our plans, He orders our steps." The elder briefly paused for a response, but continued when Pellas failed to reply.

"There are two ways in which you can look at the events of the past several months, or any difficult situation, for that matter. One way is to assume that the events have occurred haphazardly, out of anyone's control—a strange run of bad luck or poorly-made decisions. The second way, of course, is to view these events as having been carefully orchestrated by the hand of the Master Planner—ordered, overseen, and carried out to perfection."

"Yes, perfectly bad. When can I go home?"

"Not so fast. You have some healing to do. Besides, Philip is minding the farm."

"Philip," said the farmer, with a wry smile.

"Yes, he's learning much about the difficulties of farming. According to Cecilia, he's done admirably, what with caring for the two of you."

The Master carefully reapplied the bandage as he talked.

"By the way, Cecilia looks remarkably well. It's a blessing to have the two of you in my house again. I am hopeful that we will be able to spend some time together."

"I am grateful for your care," responded Pellas coldly, "and I will find a way to repay you once I am home. However, I am only here to care for my leg—I do not wish to have any relationship with you beyond that. Now, when Philip returns, I would like arrangements to be made for Cecilia and me to go home."

"Pellas," said the Master sternly, "you once left my house against my advice and it nearly cost your daughter her life. I will not permit the same mistake twice."

"And what binds me here?" The aged man gestured toward the bandaged leg.

"You may walk home, if you like, but I would suggest that you follow my plan of rehabilitation." Pellas scowled.

"Is this a house of healing—or a prison?"

The Master pulled a chair close to the bed and slowly sat down.

"It depends on your point of view. The bars you perceive are those of your own making. I had hoped that your attitude toward me had softened."

"Oh, it has," Pellas said glibly. "I despise you much less, now that I'm reasonably certain that you're not an agent of the magistrate."

"That's a start. Perhaps, in time, I can convince you that the rest of me is genuine, as well."

"That is not likely."

Suddenly, Pellas grimaced and let out a cry of pain.

"What is it now?" asked the Master, rising to his feet.

"The pain," said the farmer, through clenched teeth. "Shooting down my leg."

Pellas writhed for several moments more, and then sighed and relaxed as the pain subsided.

"That may continue for some time. I am hopeful that it will go away completely."

The Master returned to his seat.

"Pellas, how can I convince you that I—and the Lord, for that matter—bear no ill will toward you? My only desire is to see you firmly rooted in the truth and trusting in the One who loves you."

"I am tired of words," the farmer groaned. "All your lofty ideas did nothing to spare Phaedra from the jaws of the beast or Alexander from the sword. And Cecilia will never be whole."

"It is true that ours is a faith of words—but they are words of power, spoken from the very mouth of God. Ours also is a faith of mighty acts—not merely tales of the past, but of deeds done in your own life. Would you have preferred seeing Alexander waste away in the clutches of his vice? Or your being crushed by that tree? Or finding your daughter as a corpse? These are things accomplished in *your* life, and for *your* benefit, to show that God is strong and trustworthy." The Master shook his head in amazement. "And greater still was the miracle that He performed in the life of a proud, cynical farmer, who shed tears of release and joy as he found peace with that God within these very walls."

"I don't care to revisit that scene. Much has happened since then. If you want to show me God, give me something that I can see—or touch."

The Master sat quietly for a moment, and then reached for a bowl on the nearby table. He withdrew a small piece of wood from the bowl and placed the shard in Pellas' hand.

"What is this?"

"That nearly was your demise. I removed the bark from your leg—but it did not come easily. The shard had to be cut away from your tissue, which had closed around the wood. I could have removed the entire leg to get the shard, but that would have been unnecessary. In the same way, God has cut away those things in your life that have threatened to bring about the demise of your spirit. God is a perfect surgeon—He removes only what is necessary. His aim is not to cripple, but to give you full capability to love and to serve Him."

Pellas held up the shard of wood and ran his finger along its jagged edge.

"My wife and son are dead, my daughter is paralyzed, and my livelihood is threatened. And you say God is a perfect surgeon? How can such loss possibly endear Him to me?"

"I don't profess to fully understand why He does what He does, Pellas. God is in heaven and I am a mere man. I do know this: He is a jealous God—jealous for our devotion. He can't draw near to a proud man."

"Am I more proud than anyone else?"

"Not in God's eyes. But it is with *you* that He wants a relationship."

"So He brought all of this calamity on me to strip me of my pride?" Pellas smirked.

"It may well be the case," replied the Master. "Of course, God has the right to work in another's life, too. Alexander may have needed to come to terms with his own faith by laying down his life. You must look at your own loss and ask God whether what was taken from you possibly was a hindrance to living for Him."

"I really don't care to live for Him," responded Pellas impatiently. "I made my decision before the magistrate."

"Did you?" probed the Master. "Is that truly your desire? Think carefully about your response—beyond the pain of your loss, into eternity. God easily can restore what is lost on this earth if you return to Him with a whole heart."

"He can't restore Phaedra."

"Not here, no, but you will be reunited with her. If it is a wife that you need, God will supply her."

"He can't bring Alexander back."

The Master smiled knowingly.

"Alexander is in the presence of the Lord now, privileged to die for His name. But, consider this—God may be restoring your son to you in another way."

"How so?" Pellas asked, looking puzzled.

"The young man who, even now, tends to your farm."

"Philip?" the farmer asked incredulously.

"Yes, Philip."

"Come now," Pellas laughed. "He's just a flighty boy. He'll be gone when the weather turns."

"He has matured a decade in the span of these few weeks. His devotion to you and Cecilia is unquestionable—as is her devotion to him."

Pellas was speechless. He looked through the Master, slowly turning the piece of wood over in his fingers. Of all that the Master had said, these words sparked an emotion quite different from that which Pellas had harbored throughout the difficult past months. The emotion felt foreign at first, yet strangely embracing. Pellas soon recognized it as a feeling of hope.

Their conversation was interrupted by a knock at the door. The Master rose and answered it.

"Master, John is here," said Dacia. "Should I ask him to come back?"

"No, my dear. I think I am finished here. Tell John that I'll be along shortly. Is Cecilia ready?"

"Yes, sir. I was just waiting for you to finish here."

"Fine. Bring her now before Pellas gets too weary. I think our conversation was a bit tiring."

Dacia hurried off and the Master returned to the farmer's side.

"I'll leave you now, my son, but think about what we've discussed. Now, a pleasant treat awaits you—one that surely will speed your recovery and boost your spirits."

Pellas stared at the ceiling, now completely alone. His mind was full and he struggled to hold on to a thought for more than a fleeting moment. Eventually, a scene emerged in his mind. There he was, pinned beneath the fallen tree, cursing the stubbornness of one who refused to be driven away from his side. Why did the boy not leave him and go to the one more worthy of his attention? Cecilia deserved rescue, she of such indomitable faith and inner beauty. Let the miserable one die in the grip of his divinely ordained snare, cowering like the weak animal that he was.

Pellas realized that what he had seen that day as insensitivity on the part of Philip, actually was a selflessness and courage that Pellas had not seen since…*not since Alexander*, he thought. That same reckless abandon that his son had shown, first in the pursuit of pleasure, then in the things of God, rested in the character of the young man who had saved the farmer.

He thought of Philip's dogged persistence in serving, despite the hostility of his host, enduring the shame of sharing a bed with rodents and of being fed like cattle. Pellas recalled the young man shivering in the cold, awaiting the charity of a morsel of food, even though it was through the boy's thoughtfulness that the food even was to be found in Pellas' house. Pellas' pain became even more acute as he pictured Philip bristling at the inhumane notion that he should be bound, in case the young man should escape to Pellas' imagined co-conspirators. Finally, the scene returned once again to the face of Philip, crimson from strain as he summoned every ounce of energy to extricate Pellas from his lethal trap.

Philip...Cecilia...Alexander...Phaedra...the Master. Pellas felt small, a tiny sapling in a forest of towering giants, struggling to catch the tiniest shaft of sunlight. His throat tightened and burned. He clenched his teeth to fight back an upwelling of emotion, but his struggling was of no use. Mist turned to tears, followed by huge sobs of remorse, then humiliation, then, simply, just tears. The process of brokenness had begun.

CHAPTER 25

▼

The Master quietly entered his chamber and approached John from behind. John sat slouched in a chair, one arm dangling to the floor, the other draped across his chest, snoring loudly. He had on the Master's old military helmet that often captured John's interest when he visited, and could not have seen nor heard the Master enter even had he been awake.

"John, is that you?"

The young leader of Lykos never awoke, but snorted and shifted his weight in the chair and once again took up the raucous tune he had been piping.

The Master took a nearby walking stick and rapped lightly on the helmet.

The startled John hopped out of the chair, disoriented and groping wildly for some unseen support. Finally, he turned and looked at the elderly man through glazed eyes.

"Master?" he said somewhat hoarsely.

"The conqueror has returned," replied the Master, gathering John into a warm embrace. "It fits you well."

"Oh, that," replied John, blushing and peering up at the rim of the helmet. "I must have fallen asleep in it. How long has it been since you wore this? It weighs a ton."

"I'm certain that it would feel strange on my aged head."

"How you could fight in one of these is beyond me."

"Once you realize that your helmet is all that stands between you and certain death, wearing it becomes rather easy. It's all part of the discipline of warfare."

John wriggled his head out of the helmet with some difficulty and replaced it on the table.

"I had been looking for your return any day, John. Word already reached us of your success, but I want to hear the full story from Lykos himself."

"It appears as though we both have tales to tell. Dacia tells me Pellas is back under your roof."

"Indeed he is, although the Lord had to shake the earth to bring it to pass."

"He certainly made full use of that tremor," replied John.

"You may begin," said the elder, settling into his chair as if for a long narrative. "And don't leave out a single detail." Then, in response to a hint of concern that flashed across John's face, the Master added, "Fear not. I have instructed Dacia to prepare a double portion of food for you."

John beamed a satisfied smile and promptly took up the tale of the fortunes of the men of Lykos. The Master listened intently, making no comment other than nods, groans, and thoughtful hums as key details passed by. He especially was aroused with the part about the company's miraculous deliverance from certain calamity by the unexpected earthquake.

"It never will cease to amaze me how God uses such events to move things according to His plan," stated the Master, somberly, once the account had concluded. "The shedding of blood for our cause distresses me, as you well know." He paused, as if recalling some long-forgotten scene in his mind, and then added with a wry smile, "but I have no quarrel with God doing as He sees fit."

John gave a half-hearted affirmation.

"You seem less than exuberant about the whole affair, John. Is there more to the story?"

John sighed and ran his fingers through the deteriorating plume of the helmet. "No, that's the sum of it."

"Your countenance suggests the addition is not entirely correct."

"Am I such an open book that you can read my very thoughts?" John protested. "If I do have mixed emotions, it's because once again I have fundamentally failed as the leader of this operation. If you wish to see my face beaming with joy, you'll tell me you'll take over again as leader. I'll do anything you ask of me."

"This is the third time you have made such a request, but it is no longer in my power to grant your wish. You *are* the leader. Only you can abdicate that role, but from the sound of things, your followers will not allow that."

"Followers? They would take after Thomas in a heartbeat. That earthquake was God's answer to Thomas' plea. To my shame, when he suggested we call upon the Almighty for aid, I argued against it. Imagine the foolishness of that! Here was the only One with the capacity to change our predicament, and I protested taking the time to ask Him for help."

"We are not all of the same temperament, John. In time, you will learn to resort to prayer first and last. In fact, I believe you took a giant stride that very day."

"Wouldn't you rather have a leader who requires less training? After all, Thomas—."

"It is not for what you are that I selected you to succeed me, but what you can be—if you are faithful in the process of training. You may not always have Thomas with you, so it is invaluable to learn from his strengths while you can."

"Is this a premonition?" asked John warily, wondering whether the Master had some sense of the future.

"I am not a prophet, just prudent. We are the prey, you know. Thomas is less wary than you. The trusting bird often steps into the snare. But let us not think on such gloomy things when the power of God has been so wondrously displayed. Ah, here's Dacia now bearing some of her arts. You'll think more clearly on a full stomach."

John conceded and sat down to a satisfying presentation of food and drink. Within seconds, he had plunged into a side of roasted rabbit. After several minutes of unrelenting gnawing, John looked up at the Master inquisitively, his mouth full of tender meat and juices dribbling down his chin.

"Care for some?"

The Master chuckled and declined.

"No, thank you. I eat like a tortoise these days: infrequently and with great effort. Besides, you are the one who earned it. Chew on!"

The Master studied John's mannerisms as he ate; coarse and unrefined, there was little about the man that remained hidden. For that reason, his flaws were easily uncovered. There was an impatience that often turned into rash behavior; his speech could stand an extra measure of grace; he possessed a willfulness that sometimes impeded good judgment. Such volatility in temperament could bring calamity upon their mission should the right scenario present itself. Yet, courage and cunning were demanded if success was to be theirs, and those traits ran deep in John. Moreover, his loyalty to Thomas and the others was a quality that regularly warmed the Master's heart. For good or ill, the fate of those in the mint and mine appeared to lie in the hands of the impulsive man across the room.

"Have you given thought to the next move?" asked the Master once John's pace of eating slowed.

"We have a window of opportunity, providing that Siros hasn't the faintest idea what has transpired. The quake did a good job of burying our tracks, not to mention those of our pursuers." John grimaced. "Except for Argo's victim, that is. I tried to stop him."

"That guard did not die a second earlier than God had ordained, I assure you. Whether the deed was right or wrong is between the Lord and Argo."

"If we can create a large enough diversion, we could potentially empty the entire mine at once."

"You must remember their families, as well," cautioned the Master. "That will take quite a diversion."

"We'll have to see what Thomas conjures up this time," said John wryly. "A flood, maybe."

"Take care not to make light of how the Lord delivers His saints. Speaking of that, however, there is another reason I sent for you. My spirit has been troubled lately."

"Has Pellas been getting the best of you?"

"Pellas is Pellas. Actually, I am quite pleased that he is here. At least we can talk face-to-face. No, something else has been bothering me—something that carries great importance to our cause, I believe. I have been burdened to pray day and night. This room has been a veritable battleground."

John knew that the Master spoke of the spiritual realm, but nevertheless he stole a glance around the room.

"Then I will go and see if Targus can learn anything else that might be hiding up Siros' sleeve."

"There is no end to the evil that man can conjure, John. That is not where the true battle lies. This is where you are needed most. Together, here—you and I, on our knees—we can accomplish much. Like that old helmet, prayer is essential battle gear for the soldier of God. In due time, the object of my distress will be revealed; the result of our struggle in prayer will come to light."

The Master slowly descended to his knees and motioned John to do the same.

"Would that the armor of God came with cushions for the knees," the aged man said, a tired smile forming on his face. He inhaled deeply through his nose, his eyes shining brightly and his countenance raised in eager anticipation.

"When I was a young warrior," he continued wistfully, "I loved the smells of the battlefield. I would rise early, when the mists still hung heavily about the camp. Wrapped in a cloak, I would huddle around the dying firelight and search out the enemy with my mind's eye. What folly had he devised now to wrest himself from the control of the empire? What hopeless cause had he taken up that would soon be dashed against the unbreakable force of our might? I won the battle there, before arms were ever taken up. The rest was simply bringing to pass what had already been accomplished within. The fight is still won here, John," the Master said passionately, clutching his breast. "To be certain, our foe is far more practiced and clever than a ragged army of frontier barbarians nipping at Rome's heels, but infinitely more powerful is the Sovereign that we serve."

"I guess I am more a man of action," replied John apologetically.

"My son, you have yet to see prayer for what it truly is. Do not be deceived into thinking that swirling blades and daring escapes constitute the meat of God's campaign. As Solomon has written, the Lord will deliver the needy when he cries for help."

The Master sighed deeply and clasped his thin, bony hands together. His eyelids narrowed to slits as he stared straight ahead. John assumed the same pose but watched the Master out of the corner of his eye. He sensed that the old warrior was looking through the furnishings and walls of the room onto some invisible scene. The Master continued in a low, contemplative tone.

"In my dreams I have seen a face—that of a young man—his features illuminated erratically, as if by dancing firelight. There are others nearby. Swaying. Dancing, possibly. A festival of sorts. But the face I perceive is not one of happiness. I have struggled to identify him, but cannot." The elder paused, and then lifted up his voice in supplication. "But You know, O Lord. Reveal it to Your servant if it is Your will. Even so, I entreat You to deliver that one from his trial for Your glory."

John squirmed uncomfortably. He felt out of place, like an eavesdropper on an intimate conversation between two close friends. Questions swirled in his head. What was the Master seeing, and whose face was it? Thomas, perhaps? It would make sense that the Master was somehow attuned to Thomas' welfare. Soon, the possibility that his companion could be the subject of the Master's distress gripped John.

"Master."

The old man made no reply, but continued deep in prayer.

"Master, is it Thomas?" The Master stirred.

"What? What did you say?"

"Could the face belong to Thomas?"

"I should know his appearance, I would think. Why do you ask?"

"I left him—in Anakrakis."

The Master let out a low, very faint groan. "Tell me more."

"He wanted to seek out the brothers in Anakrakis. I wanted to come home. This time I didn't give in."

"Targus stopped here yesterday," the Master said somberly. "He warned that Siros is intensifying his efforts to apprehend our brothers and sisters."

"What's new about that?" responded John, trying to suppress a growing apprehension.

"He has set up a base of operation in Anakrakis. The chieftain there is looking to curry favor with Siros and is quite cooperative."

John's face tightened as he comprehended the implications of the Master's news. "Thomas is walking into a trap," he said ominously, "that is, if it has not already been sprung. I must go at once."

John abruptly rose to leave.

"Steady, John," cautioned the Master, struggling to his feet. "Thomas is resourceful."

"Yes, and by your own admission somewhat gullible. He'll seek out those of the faith, I know he will." John started for the door. "I'll need provisions—."

"You need patience, my son. Wait a day or two. If he doesn't return, then we can act. Many a great work was spoiled by rash action."

"Many a stalwart soul was lost by delay, too. If Thomas has been captured, I'll see Siros roasting on a spit!"

"John!" reprimanded the Master. "Fatigue has loosened your wits and your tongue. Stay here the night and let sleep soothe your fears. God has ordained the appropriate end for Siros."

"The quickest way out of this whole mess is with a well-placed sword."

"There are not enough swords to go around, my son. Do you forget the recklessness of Simon Peter in the garden? God has a plan, even in persecution, John. Remember, our citizenship is in heaven. There is gladness in suffering for the sake of Christ."

"That's fine to say when you're not the one suffering," John offered sourly. "I have no doubt but that your mystery face belongs to the true leader of Lykos. I will not sit idly by and leave him to the devices of his captors. Tell me that you don't share my apprehension."

"I'll admit to some concern, but we do not know—."

"Soon we will. Now, if you will not grant me provisions, I must leave to scavenge what I can."

"Take what you wish, John, but I urge a night's sleep on this matter."

"As if I could sleep. No, I am off this very night. Look for another man in that vision, Master. He will bear a sword!"

John swept out of the room and nearly bowled over Dacia, who had arrived to clear the dinner utensils.

"Come with me, Dacia!" he commanded, compelling the woman away from the Master's chambers. "Scour your pantry for something that will speed me to Anakrakis!"

The Master listened as their footsteps faded away and shook his head in lament. *Impulsive. Hot-tempered. Strong-willed. How like me. Protect him, Lord. And Thomas.* A chill came over the aged man. *Perhaps I have misjudged his potential.* He walked to a brazier and stoked the coals, which crackled and shimmered with new life. Peering intently at the glowing embers, his thoughts drifted back to the ethereal scene etched in his mind. *Who are you?* Out of the fresh flame, the Master perceived a pair of unblinking eyes, glazed with fatigue and disquiet—but no reply was forthcoming.

About the Author

Dr. William D. Reynolds is a practicing ophthalmologist in Tampa, Florida. He attended college and medical school at the University of South Florida, and completed his ophthalmology training at the University of Alabama Medical Center at Birmingham.

A musician and composer as well, he has written and arranged numerous works, including a cantata for chancel choir and two instrumental albums, *Images of Christmas* and *Images of Florida*. He has also served as Worship Pastor at Christ Community Church in Tampa, Florida. He resides in Tampa with his wife, Linda, an accomplished portrait artist, and their four children.

0-595-30908-9